The Eye of the Queen

The Eye of the Queen

PHILLIP MANN

GOLLANCZ
London

This edition published in Great Britain in 2001 by
Gollancz
An imprint of the Orion Publishing Group
Orion House, 5 Upper St Martin's Lane, London WC2H 9EA

A CIP catalogue record for this book is available
from the British Library

ISBN 0 57507 238 5

Printed in Great Britain by
The Guernsey Press Co. Ltd, Guernsey, C. I.

To my mother,
Audrey Mann

INTRODUCTION

by Dr Thomas Mnaba, Director of the Contact Linguistics Institute on Camellia

Marius Thorndyke is dead.

And immediately I must caution myself, for if we have learned one thing at the Contact Linguistics Institute it is that Earth is no yardstick whereby we can measure the known galaxy. When I say "dead" I mean simply dead in an earthly way. He does not breathe. His body is no more.

However, if the pages of his diary are to be believed, then it seems that something of Marius Thorndyke lives on in the rich psychosphere of Pe-Ellia, and that "something" will affect the future of our own world and our interstellar probings. More than this I cannot say. We must wait with patience until another Pe-Ellian ship comes to us.

Three months ago, on October 24th 2076, I received Thorndyke's battered travelling bag. It was delivered to me by two people I had never expected to see again: the Pe-Ellians Jet and Cook.

They arrived in the late evening. I was working in my library on Camellia, and as chance would have it, looked up from my work and out into the garden at just the moment their travelling pod appeared. It glowed against the dark trees like a giant ghostly pearl. I saw them step out quickly and their transport disappear with what I knew would be a soft plop—like the sound of a dead bird falling to earth. Once you have heard that sound you never forget it.

I was too surprised to move, and it was not until they had crossed the small lawn and were crouched outside the French windows tapping on the glass that I fully realised what had happened. I let them in as quickly as possible and Jet closed the curtains behind them.

"Secret visit. Hush hush," he said, and I remembered how he liked to dramatise things.

Both Pe-Ellians stood before me—or rather stooped, I should say, for my house on Camellia is not a contact station and is only built to Earth normal standards. Their eyes blinked upwards rapidly and they showed their open palms in the most basic and familiar of Pe-Ellian greetings. They filled the room with their musty, sweet smell.

We greeted each other warmly like old friends, which we are.

Cook's skin seemed a darker green than I remembered and I was aware of a sadness about him. Jet, on the other hand, seemed more vital than ever, and he slapped the backs of his hands together in a gesture which I knew indicated great excitement.

"My first time off Pe-Ellia," he said, "but not the last."

Cook spoke. "Sad tidings. Diver-Thorndyke took his last walk to the melting pot a short time ago. He was at peace at the last. Before walking he gave this bag to us and asked us to deliver it to you in person. This we have done." So saying, Cook hoisted the leather bag into the air and placed it firmly on my desk. "There is a letter inside."

With this duty discharged the two Pe-Ellians relaxed. They squatted down on their haunches with the palms of their hands resting on their knees. Both stared at me, waiting.

Clearly they expected me to open the bag.

This travelling bag had been an inseparable part of Thorndyke's luggage ever since I had known him. It had been presented to him on Orchid and was closed with a Callis Hasp. I was glad to see that the Hasp was not sealed. It opened easily.

Inside the bag was a letter addressed to me. I set this to one side for the moment. Next I carefully removed the CLI encoder, which I had carried with us when we departed for Pe-Ellia. Its control panel glowed brightly, showing that all circuits were functioning normally. Below the encoder was a box containing completed spools, each one numbered and dated in my own hand. Next came my drawings and botanical notes. All had been carefully arranged. Finally, at the bottom, were four grey volumes. Thorndyke's diaries. I lifted them out and noticed how stained and scuffed they were.

Everything had been returned to me. All the recorded and written evidence of our visit to Pe-Ellia, which Thorndyke had insisted remain with him when I departed, had been returned. He had kept his promise.

I turned to the letter. It was written in Thorndyke's own hand.

This letter is, in effect, Thorndyke's last will and testament, and the book you are now reading is an attempt to fulfil some of his final requests.

The text of the letter is as follows:

On Pe-Ellia
Beside the stream
Date Unsure

Dear Tomas,

First I ask forgiveness. I never wanted to hurt you, but when the final push came to shove I could see no alternative. I hope as you read the pages of my notebooks you will come to see more clearly what forces were working on me, and what drives were alive within me. If you cannot understand then I know you will at least accept.

Please regard these notebooks and the encoder material as definitive. I have read through everything and have deleted nothing. When I insisted that you left with me all our recorded evidence of Pe-Ellia I was merely protecting myself. I feared that too great a hullabaloo on Earth might affect me here. Remember Winter Wind and the solemn way he declared "Thought is alive"? Well, he was right of course . . . and life is so sympathetic. But there was no need for my rudeness. I could have managed things better.

The diaries I want you to publish. I want you to obtain the largest press you can. I want everyone on Earth to know what has happened to me, and to gain some idea of the consequences of our encounter with Pe-Ellia.

I hope you can read my writing. My hands are stiff and I have asked Harlequin to assist, but he has the fist of a child. Strange, isn't it, that they created a great civilisation without ever feeling they needed to create a written form for their language?

Publish everything I have written. Please add any editorial material you feel will help to make the story more understandable or more coherent. I have found it hard to concentrate on specifics and must ask you to make links for the reader. Remember my advice to Tina Bertram when she came back from Bindweed professing love for that creature she had been working with. I said: "Write about it. Scabs, scales, pain, juices and all."

Do the same for me. In other words don't spare me. Don't feel you have to be kind to your old teacher and friend. That would not do. Be yourself, Tomas—balanced and judicial.

God bless, Tomas. From an old-style atheist that must seem strange, but so help me that is what I feel. I want you to know how deeply our friendship has stayed with me to the very end. I like to think of you as head of the CLI and of how busy you will be dealing with all the new civilisations which will be clamouring for your attention now that the Pe-Ellian barriers are down.

I close. If my memory serves me well, the *Lantern Ballads* put it nicely.

> More I would tell you if Time gave me time,
> But Time holds me by the sleeve,
> Tarry I may not.

When you read these words I shall already be in the melting pot. Jet and Cook have said they will carry these things to you.

Harlequin sends love.

Winter Wind died twenty-one days ago.

Enough.

Marius Thorndyke

Thorndyke's request that I publish the diaries intact and without abridgement is clear; its implementation has proved somewhat more difficult.

The same night that I received the diaries I read through them. I confess that I was shocked and dismayed at their contents. When Thorndyke dismissed me after eighteen days on Pe-Ellia I assumed that he was suffering from mental shock and that he would eventually come to his right senses. After my return to Camellia and Earth I daily expected some communication from him either calling me back or signalling his return. Had I realised that he planned to 'meld' with the Pe-Ellian population I would have stayed on despite the consequences.

However, one cannot rewrite history. With the diaries before me I settled down to try and put them together into a narrative framework. In this work I was greatly helped by Jet and Cook, who stayed with me for four days. They were able to clarify details of Pe-Ellian life that I did not understand. At my request they dictated passages to me that I have incorporated into the manuscript.

What has emerged is not a comprehensive picture of Pe-Ellia. That must wait. The commentary I have added to the diaries is intended merely to support them and at times provide an alternative viewpoint. Thorndyke and I shared many experiences, such as the banquet, but our interpretations of those experiences differ widely.

The diaries themselves are printed exactly as written. It was Thorndyke's lifelong habit to write by hand whenever he was making personal notes. The legibility of his writing declines markedly in the final sections of his diary. There were, however, no words that could not be deciphered.

So, imagine these diaries as I received them. Four time-worn, stained, grey volumes. They are stiff-sided, as this makes them easier to use in the field. They are bound with rings to open flat and the pages are unlined. Each volume contains eighty pages.

THE THORNDYKE DIARIES

Marius Thorndyke was involved in the Pe-Ellian contact from the very beginning. He had been in retirement from the CLI for two years and was staying in his flat in Paris when the Pe-Ellian ship first approached Earth. As the foremost contact linguist on Earth he was informed immediately and arrangements were made for him to be flown by special courier to the Space Center in Washington.

I have chosen to begin this account with some notes he made that first day. These are not part of the diaries which were delivered to me from Pe-Ellia.

April 2nd 2076. God knows what is going on. The whole of Paris seems like one giant traffic jam. The word in the streets is that the world is being attacked, but I don't believe that. I have spoken with alien intelligences, and if one mighty enough to attack Earth had torn through our defences then we would all be on our backs like flies. Alternatively our patch of blue, brown and green would by now be glowing a dull red.

But something big has happened.

Communications have broken down. All the television is doing is playing the "Marseillaise", and that isn't helping anyone.

Time to go.

(13.15) The quiet in the plane is indescribable after the hubbub of Paris. I am the only passenger. It is calm here, too. I have just watched a videotape and the situation is clearer.

Something has landed in Utah.

How, no-one knows, but this something has managed to glide past all our warning stations and was not detected until it was actually seen by an engineer working at the Lagrange 5 Torus. Now that *is* incredible. Anyway, he got the fright of his life when he saw this big green balloon closing on him. He radioed Earth. Earth contacted the Moon and somebody pressed the button.

The figures are still coming in. The Garfield Whip is not a toy to play with in your own back yard. And who but a fool wouldn't realise that a species (whatever) that can evade our defences could also neutralise the Whip?

It all looks very bad. I know that Chicago has been hit, and Porte Verde on the dark side of the Moon stopped broadcasting in mid-sentence. There is also some trouble in Brazil, but I don't know what as yet.

We have established a link with Utah and signals are coming in, but the picture quality is terrible. All I can see is something green against dazzling white.

There, now the picture has collapsed entirely, and I must bite my fingers and wait.

(23.30) Utah. So there it is. Green and glossy as a ripe Granny Smith. The searchlights surrounding it make it almost look brittle.

It is one of the biggest artefacts I have ever seen. I am told it is 876 metres in diameter, and that it dilates and contracts fractionally from minute to minute.

But the size is nothing. What perplexes us is that it has not landed, but hovers a mere ten centimetres above the earth. Why should that be?

Tomas Mnaba will arrive tomorrow from Camellia and Ceto de Pendragolia is already on his way from Tiger Lily. Celia Buxton has even left her books at the British Museum to come and join us. Others are arriving by the hour, so we are assembling a pretty impressive team of experts from the CLI. We have a temporary HQ here.

However, we are all aware that the initiative is not with us and that we must await developments.

I have just come from a military briefing session. The soldiers are playing a tight game. Apparently the destruction of parts of the Earth and the Moon was not the work of those aliens, as we had assumed. It was a by-product of our own Garfield Whip. I have already sent word that I expect a top level debate on this question.

Now we sit and wait. We all hope that the green sphere contains life, for then contact can begin and that is after all our business. We all speculate that what is suspended out there has been sent to us by that child of our theories, Species X.

(07.15) Contact.

Something has just spoken English to us. A black speck appeared on the serene surface of the sphere and widened into a hole. A door opened like a small oval mouth. There was something moving there. We couldn't make it out and all our electronic instruments went dead. But we heard the voice loud and clear. Slightly metallic. Not unmusical.

"We come in peacefulness, not seeking cruelty or the ending of life. We would speak with him whom you càll Marius Thorndyke."

End of message.

Now all eyes are looking at me.

Commentary

The events of that day are, I am sure, still vivid in the memories of all of us. I was on Camellia when the news of the alien visitor came through. I enjoyed a bird's eye view, as it were, of events on Earth.

There are only three points I wish to add in clarification of Thorndyke's narrative. The first concerns the Garfield Whip.

At the time when Thorndyke wrote his account the Garfield Whip was still considered a top secret weapon. Up to the present moment it has never been officially admitted how fortunate Earth was to survive the triggering of the Whip.

The Whip is the military child of those same Garfield Equations, which enable us to slip from star system to star system. By means of gravity generators, vortices in space-time are created.

These can be directed against specific objects. However, these "eddies", Frankenstein-like, cannot be recalled once created. This twisting of the fabric of space is permanent.

On that fateful day when the Pe-Ellian ship slipped into Earth orbit the Whip was activated. As we later came to know the Pe-Ellian ship, by its very nature, could not have been damaged. The lash of the Whip was deflected. A small portion of the charge brushed the Moon. An even smaller fraction was absorbed by the Earth. The main charge left our solar system. Had the main charge hit the Earth then that would have been the end.

My second point concerns Thorndyke's relationship with the military advisers on the Space Council. The history of antagonism between the CLI and the military wing of the Space Council is still to be written. To a certain extent the basic cultural philosophy underlying the CLI was evolved to combat the military strategists. Thorndyke lived with the permanent fear that at any moment the work of the CLI would be pre-empted for purposes of military intelligence.

While no-one could claim that Thorndyke was a pacifist himself, he abhorred the development of weapon systems in space. Despite his arguments, the military strategists won concessions time upon time. Thorndyke came to see the CLI as an outpost of sanity. One of the reasons the CLI was established on Camellia was that it was far from Earth.

Over the years that I knew him I detected a growing pessimism in Thorndyke. He came to believe, and these diaries bear this out, that Earth did not have a future. He once confided to me that he considered the human brain a blighted organ. "Ill-balanced" was the term he used. He believed that the rational parts of our brain were dominated by our darker primitive instincts—instincts which may have had some justification in the fiercely competitive primordial slime, but which were totally inappropriate to the present.

The paradox for Thorndyke, and he was well aware of this, was that he was a highly "instinctive" man, and on occasion a most belligerent one.

Finally I wish to comment briefly on Species X. This was a code name used at the CLI to describe the powerful but invisible race, which theoretically at least seemed able to control the direction of our space exploration. In a later section Michiko Hakoshima describes the genesis of this concept.

The first full entry in Thorndyke's Pe-Ellian diary does not occur until April 23rd, a mere three days before our departure. Thorndyke hardly refers to the events which occurred during the intervening three weeks and undoubtedly he was too rushed to settle down and write more than the official memos and reports. Of the notes which he did make during this period most are fragmentary.

The events of those three weeks have considerable importance, since they helped shape Thorndyke's frame of mind as we approached the departure date. The following is a brief summary of the main events.

Jose Borges, Chairman of the Medical Division of the CLI and Director of the Forensic Institute in London, was present on April 3rd when the Pe-Ellian ship opened. He describes that event:

> We were all gathered some five hundred metres from the sphere. A protective cordon had been set up. We were housed in mobile units, which were flown in during the night. Luckily someone had brought along an ordinary optical telescope and this we used to try to detect some details of the ship. It had been found that all electronic means of surveillance were severely distorted and subject to inexplicable blackouts. Even the telescope was only marginally effective since the sphere seemed to go in and out of focus.
>
> The sun was already bright when the door opened. We could detect movement. It appeared to us that the alien was humanoid and of considerable height, but we could not distinguish any details. We certainly could not see the dappled skin markings and the "plates" which are such a feature of the Pe-Ellians' appearance.
>
> The voice was clear. When he heard the voice and his own name called, Thorndyke looked at us in astonishment. Then he shrugged as if to say, "Well, someone's got to go," and waved towards the alien ship.
>
> He walked through the protective cordon of ground troops. He was still wearing his dressing-gown.

The commanding officer, who had brought his men to full alert when the door first opened, now tried to stop Thorndyke. An argument ensued in which the two men gave the onlooking Pe-Ellian a first direct lesson in colloquial English.

Finally the officer seized Thorndyke by his lapels and Thorndyke retaliated by pushing him back. The officer tripped and landed sitting down. By the time he had scrambled to his feet Thorndyke was running towards the Pe-Ellian ship.

Owing to the interference it was not possible to make any recordings of that first contact between Earth and Pe-Ellia. Later Thorndyke made a personal report to the Space Council.

As I approached the green sphere I felt a heaviness in my legs, and a sensation not unlike pins and needles. My vision became blurred and eventually I had to stop as I could not see where I was putting my feet. I knew I was pretty close to the ship as its greenness seemed to envelop me. I did not want to blunder into it. Still less did I want to enter it inadvertently and get caught up in its substance. I could not see the Pe-Ellian. I called, "I am Marius Thorndyke. Do you wish to speak to me?"

There was no reply for several minutes, and then I heard a powerful voice from what seemed like just a few metres in front of me. It said, "Welcome, Marius Thorndyke. Meeting you is an honouring us. I am of Pe-Ellia. I am called Calm After the Storm. I invite you to come with me now to Pe-Ellia. There are those who would speak with you and we have fathoms to say."

I was about to reply when I felt a deep nausea welling up inside me and I had to stumble back. The feeling of sickness subsided as I retreated from the Pe-Ellian ship. My vision also improved, though the sun blinded me.

This report was delivered orally on the afternoon of the day of that first contact.

It was at this same Space Council meeting that Thorndyke demanded that the CLI be given complete authority concerning the Pe-Ellian contact. This authority was granted.

When I arrived on Earth from Camellia a full contact mission was in operation. Ceto de Pendragolia had set up some of his gadgetry. Lars Frendrum was busy formulating civilisation probabilities based on the meagre information we had managed to glean so far. "Polly" Perkins was at work in her mobile lab, trying by every trick of technology to clarify the photographs we had taken of the Pe-Ellian and his ship. I took charge of the linguistics section. At that time we had nothing to work on save the short exchanges I have already quoted. We could not tell whether those words were a recording or live speech. Jacob Mendelsohn, my assistant and a specialist in the physiology of sound production, put our dilemma succinctly when he said, "We don't even know whether the Pe-Ellians have mouths."

Ceto de Pendragolia was the most upset of all. His instruments were completely useless and kept giving contradictory readings.

"Marius," he said, "you must go back there. I'm sorry you feel sick and everything, but I feel sick too. You must tell them to turn off whatever they got going in there so that I can get a crack at them. Okay? Perhaps if they do that, you'll feel better too."

Thorndyke agreed. He conferred briefly with Jose Borges, the medical expert responsible for contact linguist training, and then set off for the Pe-Ellian sphere.

I quote from Thorndyke's second report to the Space Council:

> As I approached the Pe-Ellian craft I felt the nausea and numbness come on me as I had before, but this time I was prepared. I used some of the mental exercises prepared by the CLI medical staff to quell my stomach and maintain my mobility. They helped. I was aware when the door opened. I did not wait for a word from the Pe-Ellian but called, "I am sick. There is something you are broadcasting that makes me ill. Moreover we want to look at you, but we can't. All our instruments are blind. We believe you come in friendship. Can you help?"
>
> Then I gagged and began a dry retching. I am told by those who were observing that I fell to my knees. Vaguely I heard a cry from the Pe-Ellian ship. Then there was silence, and then from within the silence came a whispering that grew louder and louder until it was a roaring. I thought my eardrums would burst. I had the fleeting impression that time was reversed and that space adjusted itself about me. Colours shifted round the spectrum. The Pe-Ellian ship became a giant tomato and the

white ground turned to black ash beneath my knees. Everything dipped to monochrome and after a few seconds faded.

Silence. I realised that I had my eyes clenched shut and that my sickness had evaporated.

When I opened my eyes I could see.

There was my Pe-Ellian, looking hard as bottle glass and shiny as lacquer. He was crouched in the opening of the spaceship and staring at me. My first thought was of a giant piebald ant, for he had his arms reaching towards me.

Then he blinked and his eyes turned upwards and I was myself again.

At the same moment that Thorndyke's nausea cleared all Earth's instruments began to function normally. We enjoyed one minute of clear vision before the Pe-Ellian rose to his feet and the oval door in his ship closed.

After this events moved quickly.

With our technology freed from its restraints daily reports appeared on the world's television screens. The panic which had erupted in some parts of the world subsided. Clear evidence replaced hearsay.

It became standard practice for Thorndyke to have short meetings with the Pe-Ellians in the mornings. At the Pe-Ellians' insistence not one of these meetings was longer than five minutes and no-one except Thorndyke was allowed to come close to the Pe-Ellian ship. Though we could hear and see everything that was happening the lines of communication were unbearably thin.

The following transcript from Thorndyke's fifth conversation with Calm After the Storm illustrates the difficulty Thorndyke had in communicating with the Pe-Ellian and the technique he adopted for this contact. Every communication began with the Pe-Ellian repeating the same phrases.

CALM: Thanking you for this meeting is a pleasure. My name is Calm After the Storm. I invite you to come to my home world of Pe-Ellia. You may enter now.

THORNDYKE: Do you think the air on Earth is sweet?

(Thirty second pause)

CALM: Pal-at-table.

THORNDYKE: Good. Would I like the air on Pe-Ellia?

CALM: Pe-Ellia is a safe planet. No hurt will arise to you.

THORNDYKE: How long have you known about us?

(Sixty second pause)

Is it your race which has deflected our . . . er . . . Earth's ships?

CALM: Is. You may enter now and come to Pe-Ellia.

THORNDYKE: Why did you destroy one of our cities?

CALM: We destroy nothing. We deflect all.

THORNDYKE: Will you leave your. . . .

CALM: We come in peacefulness not seeking cruelty or the ending of life.

THORNDYKE: Who are you?

(Sixty-five second pause)

CALM: I am Calm After the Storm. You may enter now. . . .

THORNDYKE: Will you step outside and visit us?

CALM: I . . . We. . . .

(The hole in the side of the sphere closes)

Each day Thorndyke invited the Pe-Ellian to step outside and each day the offer was rejected.

On the ninth conversation Calm After the Storm was joined by a fellow Pe-Ellian whom he introduced to Thorndyke as Fire-Sticks. It was noted immediately that Fire-Sticks' English was far more fluent. In reply to the invitation to visit Earth he replied: "We may not. On Earth dangers wait. I mean not disease and bugs. Such is easy. Such is nothing. But other terrors stand in our face. Sorry pal."

Despite invitations from most of the major cities in the world the Pe-Ellians would not move from their ship.

Finally Thorndyke agreed to go with the Pe-Ellians, but he made two conditions: first that I should accompany him; and second that a delegation of Pe-Ellians meet formally with some of Earth's leaders. This was finally agreed. Thorndyke described the reception in his third diary entry.

During these meetings and conversations our work at the

temporary CLI headquarters continued unabated, though the sudden flow of information we had anticipated after the second meeting failed to materialise. We were able to record a few snatches of Pe-Ellian language which passed between Calm After the Storm and Fire-Sticks and we devoured these like hungry dogs. We analysed Pe-Ellian height and skin markings. We theorised about their apparent lack of exposed genitalia. We studied their voice graphs and deduced their skeletal structure as well as we could. But when all these findings were placed in the balance they amounted to very little. Each night we sat up with Thorndyke and tried to plan a strategy for the next day's encounter.

For Thorndyke the days became a round of meetings, Space Council discussions, press briefings and official communiqués. We were amazed at his stamina. He made only two brief excursions to Brazil and to Chicago.

Throughout all this activity Thorndyke appeared to maintain a relaxed disposition. He was patient and polite and answered questions with a restraint that surprised all of us.

Only Michiko Hakoshima, the mathematician, who had known him longer than most of us, detected the warning signs that Thorndyke was reaching the end of his tether. She spoke to several of us before a major Space Council debate on damages resulting from the injudicious use of the Garfield Whip and warned us to "take the pressure off the Iron Duke. He's only human."

That next day, in the middle of the debate, he suddenly stopped in mid-sentence and complained of a headache. We all knew what that meant and were ready. Janet Bodley took his place on the podium and the debate continued without a hitch.

Thorndyke's first Pe-Ellian diary entry begins at this point.

THORNDYKE'S DIARY: ENTRY 1

April 23rd 2076. Today, after all the rushing and debates and conferences and conversations of the last few weeks, I finally pleaded fatigue and fled from the Space Center in Washington to the quiet and privacy of my small apartment in Paris. And I am glad to close the old door behind me. Those who know me well smiled when I excused myself in front of the Space Council by saying I had a headache. I have hardly ever had a headache in my life, but this has long been a private euphemism to signal to those about me that I am angry, tired, liable to explode without provocation, and in desperate need of solitude. Ceto de Pendragolia and Janet Bodley have agreed to run interference for the next few days until our departure and I have no fears of being interrupted. They are well able to cope with all the government departments and Space Council officials, and besides it will do them no harm.

This is the first moment of peace I have had since the Pe-Ellians entered our proximate space and came to settle that mere ten centimetres above the white salt flats of Utah.

What a tale. What timing.

But I mourn the destruction of Chicago and the loss of millions of acres of Brazilian rain forests and the destruction of the beautiful Porte Verde on the dark side of the Moon.

I have seen it. I made it my business to see it. Brazil is as ugly a sight as I ever hope to see. It is as though someone had taken a giant spike and raked it time and again across the teeming jungle, leaving furrows thirty kilometres wide. Whip is an appropriate name.

Chicago has a strange attractiveness. Here the damage is very specific, with no residual contamination. The centre is a congealed lava puddle about two hundred metres wide, adorned with frozen wavelets and bubbles. Beyond this puddle the tall buildings are canted over in the direction of the maelstrom's turning. They are like stripped pine trees after a fire. In one area there must have been some strange local disturbance, for here the buildings are stumps of glass. One has been twisted into a helix of silica.

The Moon, I am told, still looks like the Moon.

But I left it all with a heavy heart. How long before we blow the lot up? And our contact quests? Sometimes the banner of our idealism looks like arrogance to me. Perhaps we ought just to shut up shop and stay home. Would that make the universe a sadder place? I doubt it.

Now I have time to think and the truth is finally dawning on me. It has finally happened. We have been contacted. In four days Tomas Mnaba and I will depart on what must be accounted one of the most important voyages of discovery since Columbus, or at least since the *Lotus Chariot* dived through Garfield's pocket and re-emerged somewhere near Proxima Centauri.

Life. Intelligence. We discovered it then, on that first real space leap, and now intelligence has come knocking on our door.

For years I have dreamed of just such a coming. When I founded the Contact Linguistics Institute it was with just such a hope in mind. I wanted us to be ready, so that when the great and inscrutable stood before us we would not be unprepared.

Why then am I not more elated? Have I become so inured to the day-to-day fighting that I have lost sight of the larger project? Whatever the cause there is no denying that I, the privileged one, beckoned by name by surely the most powerful race in our neck of the galaxy, am now detached.

Perhaps I am just tired. The last few weeks have been hectic.

I am amused to observe myself, pottering like an old woman, fiddling with inessentials, picking up papers and then losing them, being fastidious over trifles. Thank God my colleagues cannot see me now. They would lose faith in the Iron Duke.

I console myself with the thought that nothing is ever wasted and that even vacancy has a place in creation. And order *is* emerging.

Two years ago, when I retired from the CLI, I thought I was dying of Carson's disease. But I have weathered that with hardly a limp and now feel as well as can be expected. Nevertheless I face the fact that this journey may be my last and I may never have a chance to say goodbye to my friends on Orchid or to fish in the swamps of Banyon. One thing I will complete: the translation of the last section of the *Seliica*. It is already in my head.

This morning I completed proofreading the final draft of the *Tapista Peru* after sitting on the manuscript for five years. It is now with the printers. While sorting out my desk I came upon some old translations of the *Lantern Ballads* of Persimmon. They are not as bad as I remembered and deserve to see the light of day.

That work will take me all of tomorrow. It is not essential work except in the sense that it all helps round off a career. I have dim forebodings. I cannot be certain, of course, but I think it is unlikely that I shall return to Earth except in a vacuo-sack. But we shall see.

However, it is not the thought of death that is troubling me. We contact linguists live so aware of death that if it cannot be classed a friend, it is at least a close acquaintance. Certainly we have no illusions. Remember Darion Weismueller and Varia Peresvetsova? They arrived back from Banyon after one of the most brilliant contact quests of all time. They had mediated in a war. They came into the canteen at the CLI on Camellia after medical clearance and we were all gathered to welcome them. I can see their faces now. They were laughing like children. Darion said, "I'm glad you are all here," and Varia added, "That makes it perfect". Then he ordered a beer and she had a milkshake and they both died.

So simple.

So right.

There is not one of us who would not like to go the same way—a simple withdrawal from life. I doubt I will have that fortune. No, it is not fear of death or dying that perplexes me. I am disturbed by something in the very nature of this quest . . . and so help me I don't know what it is.

I shall leave this problem for the moment and make myself a coffee and then settle down to the *Seliica*. Tomorrow, after a sleep, I may see things more clearly.

I have just realised that I have started another diary, leaving the old one half-empty. Now that must mean something.

Commentary

While I worked with Thorndyke during those last few hectic weeks I was surprised at how tirelessly he worked and yet at the same time how abstracted he seemed. I realise now that he was in a state of shock and that his administrative finesse and speed of judgement were a kind of reflex action. I don't think he had fully absorbed what had happened. The rest of us were slightly giddy and excused ourselves for it. Here, finally, was the contact mission we had argued about, discussed and planned for well over a decade. Thorndyke made all the right noises, of course, but I noted that whenever a speculative discussion got underway he excused himself and returned to the pragmatic work of times, dates and meetings. Clearly, as his diary shows, when he returned to his Paris flat and "closed the old door" behind him, the momentous nature of what was happening dawned on him.

The *Lotus Chariot* was the first ship with a human crew to Gee-Jay out of our solar system. This occurred on May 1st 2036. Among those chosen to be crew members was a young man of twenty-one, who was already making a name for himself as an analogue-linguist: Marius Thorndyke.

Describing this event in his introduction to Volume One of the *Grammaria Galactica*, Thorndyke writes:

> We didn't wholly believe the Garfield Jump spirals would work. Despite the successful ventures with monkeys and mice it all still seemed like part of a fairy story. To reach the stars! We would laugh rather than admit it was true. But there we were, edging out into a wider orbit, poised for the correct orientation and glowing faintly. Mars was a cherry you could almost pick through the porthole. Space was beginning to distort round us. The stars grew tails. We hoped for a speedy death at best, or an eternity dissipated in limbo at worst. We lurched, just like a train stopping too quickly at a station, and when I looked out of the portal, no Mars, no Sun, but in their place the restructured star-plan of Proxima Centauri.
>
> During the month we were away we became accustomed to the Gee-Jay Jump. We moved about and we found life and photographed it for all to see. There was no question of contacting Earth, of course, until we returned.
>
> It was while looking down on that first planet, Garfield's Planet, that I began to plan the structure of what was later to be called the Contact Linguistics Institute.

Carson's disease is rarely fatal, though it is extremely painful. Thorndyke contracted the illness while on Banyon and spent three weeks with his legs in a refrigeration chamber. His recovery was total and I observed no lack of mobility during the time we were on Pe-Ellia.

Thorndyke's ability with languages was already legendary when I joined the CLI. He was fortunate in being equipped with what he jokingly referred to as his "parrot gift". He could reproduce sounds and intonations with uncanny accuracy. This facility enabled him to become an excellent translator. Temperamentally he was not suited to work as a contact linguist in the field. Orchid, for which he conceived a great love, was his first solo contact expedition. The *Seliica*, which is mentioned frequently in his diaries, is the great epic of the Archadians (Thorndyke's pet name for the dominant race on Orchid).

The *Tapista Peru* is a sequence of hunting songs from the planet Tiger Lily. It is due to be published shortly.

The *Lantern Ballads* of Persimmon are arguably the most "alien" work that Thorndyke translated. The ballads are the work of a race that possesses only rudimentary organs of sight. They retain contact with each other and navigate by a complicated series of calls. These calls are all variations on the theme "Where I have been and where I am going". The songs warn of danger and also carry news.

THORNDYKE'S DIARY: ENTRY 2

April 24th.

> Till climbing cease and we behold
> The humpbacked clouds like rough hewn steps,
> And at their end the setting sun.

These are the final lines of the *Seliica*. Appropriate?

Last night I couldn't sleep. Time is slipping away like water through my fingers. Finally, at half past four I took a sleeping pill. (Half of one actually—I am still dithering.) I achieved half sleep. I enjoyed half dreams. My mind has this strange recall facility, which I have commented on many times before. Events from the past ran through my mind like a film.

First there was dear Michiko, running through the avenues of the CLI on Camellia at two in the morning and shouting, "It all adds up." She had two sets of papers in her hands and when she reached my villa she pounded on the door until the neighbours came pouring out of their doors to see what the commotion was. I was last.

"It all adds up," she shouted and fainted.

Then Martin Routham was with us, waving his arms like a windmill and shouting, "Attaboy, Marius, you can do it. Attaboy."

I seemed to be running in some kind of race and behind me someone was gaining. I glanced over my shoulder and there was Calm After the Storm loping along, blue and white. And with him was the big black and red one who calls himself Fire-Sticks.

They were both grinning from ear to ear and I could see their black gums and the hard ridges of bone they use for teeth.

Grinning. Ha.

We were rounding the last bend and I was wondering if I had any go left in me when I woke up.

I was in a welter of covers and sweating.

I spent the rest of the time till dawn reading through the *Seliica*.

Tomorrow night we have a social in Washington. I don't want to go to it. The Pe-Ellians certainly don't want to go and have been dragged there only by blackmail. Tomas will not be there. Poor fellow. He has had to return to Camellia and will not be back on Earth until 02.00 GMT.

He has been driving himself too hard. I have told him to relax but I might as well talk to a door. He has a stubborn streak. After all, there is not much we can do. The Pe-Ellians call the shots, as my grandfather used to say.

They keep saying that all will be well and that we are "not to distress". In fact they have said it so often that I begin to wonder if all *will* be well. Maybe it is all a great big trap, as that astrologer in Amsterdam keeps predicting, and we will be whisked off to some diabolical furnace while Earth is held to ransom.

That, at least, will not happen—and I am not referring to the Pe-Ellians' intentions.

Both Tomas and I have signed terminal release papers. Even if the Pe-Ellians were to put us in a zoo and then practise slow vivisection, Earth would make no concessions.

Not that Earth could do much anyway.

We shall be alone.

The Space Council has asked for and received assurances that we shall be safe. When I asked Calm After the Storm when we would return he replied, "When what is necessary has been concluded." I draw small comfort from that.

It is interesting to be on the receiving end of a contact quest. Knowing that the Pe-Ellians are looking at us makes me look closely at myself. At times I feel a stranger. I suppose that is the price one pays for being a contact linguist.

I am not the Marius I was at that funeral on Orchid. Nor am I the Marius who once played music to autistic children to see if there was a different kind of language there.

Mutability. Faces peering at me from the past. And I am back to my dream again.

I am an old hand with dreams. How often have I pondered their logic.

While eating breakfast I made a mental list of five points concerning this Pe-Ellian contact.

First, the Pe-Ellians must have known us for a long time. Linguistic analysis gives a minimum period of a hundred and fifty (± fifty) Earth years. I think it could be longer.

Second, they came on cue. Earth was geared up for a scrap.

Third, they could have wiped us out, but they didn't, which means either that they are not belligerent or that they need us intact. (NB: Both hypotheses could be correct.)

Fourth, they seem to want something from us.

Fifth, they want me. Why me?

Of this last I have no inkling, other than the obvious idea that I am the one name still alive most closely identified with Earth's contact programme. But there is a pattern, and if there is a pattern there must be logic.

I am still puzzling over my last encounter with Fire-Sticks. I am trying to work out what constitutes a Pe-Ellian individual. We have deliberated enough about skin markings. The significance of these markings (if indeed they have significance) is a question which I doubt we can solve until such a time as we can observe them interacting on a social level. God knows, he and Calm After the Storm couldn't be more different in appearance. But they share the same reserve. I could be completely wrong, but I have a feeling that Fire-Sticks could be more . . . more what? Fun, I suppose. Perhaps it is just that he seems to make more effort to be like us. He certainly makes more of an effort with our language and gives the impression of being more *here*. That, of course, makes him more vulnerable. He is the crack in the ice-smooth surface.

When I tested him with "rich" English he just gawped and I could see his brain working. Then life retreated from him and he glazed over like the rest. I was left talking to the glove but not the hand. When I said, "The exhortation from the bigwigs of our planet is that you should cut loose and seek to comprehend our mores by association with us," he stood still and his hands made strange passes and he leaned towards me as though he would speak. For a moment I thought I had him and that we would hear "raw" Pe-Ellian, even if it was just a cry of frustration. But then the veil came down. Since that moment Fire-Sticks has been like the walking dead. Will things be different tomorrow night? I doubt it.

I *am* interested, but a rather academic interest finally. I enjoy the puzzle, but I have given up hoping for that shattering insight which would reveal the whole of creation and lay it at our feet. One can hope too much, until hope itself becomes a burden. When I was younger, then I was ready. There was a time when I would have leaped up to answer the Pe-Ellian calling. I would have run to them with open arms.

In the silence I find it easier to write and face myself. I am weary of Earth and the struggle. My only joy is now in translation.

That is not true. That is affectation. I still enjoy the fight. But I am disturbed.

Where are they, these Pe-Ellians?

I could take the crushing hammer blows of a monstrous alien intelligence. I could understand the barbarism of a superior technology. I could even stomach the sweetness of moral supermen waving their fingers at us. But they are none of these.

They are shy and cold. They act as though they are afraid of us. They won't visit, and when they do venture outside their cool green sphere they are silent and reserved, so that talking to them is about as rewarding as talking to dummies in a shop window.

This alone makes them unique. I have never yet met a race that didn't want to talk. Once the ditch of unfamiliarity and fear is crossed we enter the market place. The reserve of the Archadians was a living reserve in comparison with these dead fish.

That is it. That is one of the reasons I am disturbed.

I am disappointed. Well, well.

I have sent the *Seliica* off to the publishers. The *Lantern Ballads* still need more work. In their quaint songs we see the limits of translation. If they ever appear in book form there will be ten times as many footnotes as text. I have asked Celia Buxton to prepare the phonic text.

I shall spend the rest of the day packing. In this alone the Pe-Ellians have been specific. They say that everything will be provided and that we should take nothing more than absolute necessities. I wonder why. They can't be worried about the weight problem.

Needs and wants. I have been caught this way before. I shall take luxuries. Cigars, an old fashioned hot-water bottle that can still be bought in London, razor blades and plenty of pencils. I may even throw in a toilet roll or two. The rest I shall leave up to Tomas. He is the official recorder and can be relied on to specify all our technical impedimenta.

I am glad that he agreed to come. We work well as a team. His thoroughness is a comfort, a bit like a safety net. He will dot the "i"s, though I am still quicker off the mark in the cut and thrust of language. He is loyal above all and knows me well. I shall depend on him heavily. Equally, he knows me and trusts me. He knows I will always dig him out.

To it.

Commentary

Had I had the opportunity to read this diary entry before we departed I should have been extremely worried. Some of Thorndyke's later actions on Pe-Ellia become more comprehensible when one takes into account the state of mind indicated in this diary. I am not thinking of his references to death or to the mild state of depression evinced in such remarks as "One can hope too much. . . ." Such depression is common before leaving on a contact quest and Thorndyke would have been as aware of this as I am. I am referring to his obvious partisanship. One of the basic rules set out in the Contact Linguists' Handbook reads:

> Do not rush to judgement. An alien race is not there to justify your prejudices, and you must always, at least in the early stages of a mission, avoid the temptation to like or dislike.

Thorndyke wrote those words himself when he was preparing the Handbook. A contact linguist is a neutral observer, who attempts always to understand the larger picture. Yet here is Thorndyke likening the Pe-Ellians to "dead fish", and he is judging them before he even knows them. Had he followed standard practice he should have sat down with me, his partner in this undertaking, and discussed the problem. If the problem had proved insoluble, he should have refused to go. It is as simple as that. There is very little room in the CL code for private likes and dislikes. Alternatively he could have pleaded for more time.

This would have been a hard but not impossible decision. When he was head of the CLI Thorndyke made decisions like this every day of the week. I can only conclude that even at this early stage Thorndyke saw himself moving outside the normal boundaries of the Contact Linguists' Code.

There is another matter allied to this, and this Thorndyke and I did discuss. Thorndyke persistently refers to the Pe-Ellians as "he". On a popular level this is without great significance. It is, after all, an inherent tendency in the human mind to ascribe sex to inanimate objects like ships, mountains and the Moon. However, a contact linguist cannot afford such licence. The nature of gender is an immensely complex question, which goes far beyond the Earthly concepts of "he" and "she". Normal CLI practice is to use special terms when dealing with any species of indeterminate sex. The Pe-Ellians certainly fall within this category.

If he had followed normal practice Thorndyke should have used the form *ta* for the singular where we would use he or she, *ta-de* for the possessive, *tas* for the plural and *tas-den* for the plural possessive. Such terminology is used in all official CLI documents relating to the Pe-Ellians.

I discussed this question with Thorndyke after I had heard him using the "he" form at one of the Space Council debates. In a friendly manner he told me "not to try and teach your grandmother to suck eggs". He maintained that he knew what he was doing and didn't want to "blind the Space Council with science". I regarded this as an unacceptable reply and said so. As things turned out, I believe that Thorndyke did fall into the mistake of ascribing gender to the Pe-Ellians and that this complicated his dealings with the Pe-Ellian called Menopause-Harlequin. In the present document I have chosen for clarity to follow Thorndyke's practice, as exemplified in his diaries, of referring to all the Pe-Ellians as "he".

Michiko Hakoshima is presently living in retirement on Camellia. She kindly prepared the following statement for inclusion in this book. I asked her to explain the part she played in the discovery of Species X.

> I was one of the first mathematicians to enrol with the CLI, shortly after its creation in 2037. One of the first projects assigned to me was to work out the statistical probability of our encountering a race more technologically advanced than our own. This became an ongoing project. The rapidity of exploration after the Gee-Jay transformer became standard meant that new information and therefore new probabilities were

permanently being fed into my already overtaxed computers. Marius didn't push me for a quick answer.

Another part of my work concerned vector analysis and here I became interested in a very specific problem. The Garfield Equations are both subtle and precise. Correctly tuned the Gee-Jay will give a flawless performance. One kilometre or twenty parsecs of displacement require the same basic equation. However, at a very early stage, when we were just putting out feelers into the galaxy, strange variations began to occur. These had no mathematical explanation! I conferred with Marius and he said there must be some flaw in the basic working (Garfield's own mathematics!) and he had me check through every assumption and calculation. This tied up a whole CLI team and I don't think Marius was ever aware how close I was to resigning. But I didn't.

This work took years.

Meanwhile variations continued to occur. Sometimes they were trifling, a mere .0007 per second of arc, but others were significant, up to one whole degree, and that can mean plunging into the heart of a sun.

I told Marius that the Garfield Equations were as sound as a bell, but that the variations were becoming frightening. This time he listened. Our research was given a top secret classification. Funds, staff and computer time miraculously appeared. Within weeks I had a pattern and a fix. *Pockets of space were appearing into which we could not penetrate.* Any attempt to enter those areas was deflected. How, by whom or by what, we had no idea. An unmanned ship was aimed directly at one of these pockets. When it returned we analysed the photographic evidence of where it had been. It had been deflected forty-five degrees! The conclusion was unavoidable. Our exploration of space was being corralled.

I returned to my earlier line of research on the probability of our encountering a race more advanced than our own. The facts were staring at me. According to probability fourteen percent of the planets we had encountered should have been approaching or have already developed an electronic technology. Of these, twelve percent should have achieved space flight. As it was the highest technology we had encountered was on

Tiger Lily, where the Marmel race had invented the steam engine. *We should by now have met Species X.* The conclusion was obvious to all of us.

Marius's story of my running through the streets of the CLI is basically true. I was in bed when the final readings came through, and I suppose it was so important to me that I forgot to put on my dressing gown. Marius's house was very close to the main computer section where I lived. I ran there in my night-dress. It was summertime, I recall. I don't remember fainting. I am not the fainting type.

These two reports on deflection and technology were tabled simultaneously at the next Space Council meeting. A violent debate ensued, which was fully reported at Thorndyke's insistence in the CLI monthly bulletin for December 2069. The effects of this debate and the publicity accorded it were far-reaching. There was excitement that a great and mysterious race was waiting to meet us. At the same time there was fear. It was conceded that Species X could represent a danger to Earth and her interests. This was one of the main arguments used to justify the full-scale development of the Garfield Whip.

The late Dr Martin Routham was a close friend of Marius Thorndyke. At the CLI he was in charge of the technical support division, and was mainly responsible for the development of the lightweight bio-crystalline encoder. This instrument is now standard throughout the CLI and is the main means of recording in any contact quest. It was just such an encoder that Thorndyke returned to me after our visit to Pe-Ellia. It is capable of recording both audio and visual signals. It has a wide temperature tolerance and can withstand any amount of rough use in the field. Perhaps most important from a contact linguist's point of view is that the encoder is equipped with self-referencing circuits (bio-crystalline). These give the encoder the ability to absorb immense quantities of contradictory material before its logic circuits become overtaxed.

"Rich" English is the deliberate juxtaposing of formal constructions with slang constructions. The use of "rich" language provides a very accurate index of how well a given language is understood. In this instance Thorndyke was doing more than trying to discover how well the Pe-Ellian understood English. He was using "rich" English in order to confuse Fire-Sticks in the hope of gaining an advantage over him.

Thorndyke's third diary entry was written the night following the reception at the Space Center in Washington. It is written in the third person. This is common in CLI writing as it allows the writer to be detached. It is frequently used when the writer is contemplating painful personal experience.

THORNDYKE'S DIARY: ENTRY 3

April 25th. The special room in the Space Center set aside for extra-terrestrial visitors was decked out as tastefully as possible, considering that the designers had no knowledge of the tastes of their honoured guests, the Pe-Ellians. They had chosen to drape the walls with green bunting, and a large green Persian carpet was rolled out on to the hardwood floor. Apart from the decorations the room was a cunning artifice. The chandeliers which hung from all corners and the middle of the ceiling did more than shed light. They contained the microphones and cameras which covered the entire room. They also contained little pipes which could evacuate the room's atmosphere within seconds, or alter the gases present in the room should such be deemed necessary. The ceiling itself was more than a ceiling. It could be raised or lowered to provide a comfortable height for the guests. The Pe-Ellians being tall, it was now at two-thirds its maximum extension. The double panelled doors, which would not have disgraced an Englishman's castle, were an air lock. The inner door would not open until the outer one was firmly closed, and vice versa. There were other safety devices but these were well hidden. Gas masks in the cupboards, nosefilters, fire extinguishers, etc. There were no windows, though this was not apparent since heavy curtains cover most of the walls.

Marius Thorndyke did not like this room, though he was familiar with every square inch of it. He was a dealer in natural space, but being a realist he accepted that it is in rooms such as these that important ceremonial meetings are made.

He was standing by one of the long tables which ran down one wall of the room, and which were laden with delicacies from the world's kitchens. He remembered the only two previous times when this room was used to entertain extra-terrestrial guests. For the Surf-Waders from Thalassa, a sister world to Earth if ever there was one, the food had been mainly eels. Many years after them had come the Pointer people from the cold world of Neige. For them the temperature of the room had been lowered to just above the freezing point of water. Thorndyke shivered at the memory. But both contacts had gone off well. Both races had accepted the undeniably alien world of Earth with comparative equanimity. Now the room was to be used for a third time and the temperature and the humidity were high.

Apart from Thorndyke there were only eighteen persons in the room. The President of the Space Council was there, looking uncomfortable in the heat; Marie Cortes, who handled public relations and who would look elegant in any situation; Ceto and Janet, who would have joint responsibility for the CLI in Tomas's absence; the Vice-President of the United States, the President of Mexico, the President of the United States of Africa and the Chairman of the NUES. These latter were talking quietly in one corner and picking over the Chinese spare ribs. The Secretary-General of the UN and the UN Secretary for Wildlife Management were strolling back and forth on the carpet. Eight reporters were also present. They were the lucky ones who had drawn the shortest straws. They were having to double as waiters. That was all. The room looked deserted.

The Pe-Ellians had requested that no more than nineteen people be present. Thorndyke smiled at the thought of the infighting which must have gone on beneath the smooth diplomatic surface to determine who received the valuable invitations.

Music began. The official anthem of the Space Council rang out, indicating that the honoured guests had arrived. Everyone in the room turned to the dark panelled doors. Those who had been standing inside a white circle taped to the carpet hurriedly stepped outside.

A light above the doors glowed red, showing that the outer doors were open. After a few seconds it blinked out and a green light replaced it. The double doors swung open ceremoniously.

There were five Pe-Ellians. They were holding hands and one of their number seemed to be having trouble keeping his legs straight. To Thorndyke it looked like a severe attack of Space Jelly. Not one of them was less than eleven feet tall. They were dressed in short grey garments, which consisted of nothing more than a large square of fabric with a simple hole cut for the head. They reached only to the waist. The garments seemed to accentuate their nakedness. Their bald heads shone in the light.

Thorndyke marvelled at the uniformity of their markings and the deep lustrous colour which filled up the plates of their skin. No two were alike and yet they were all similar. Thorndyke recognised Calm After the Storm and was shocked to see that his skin looked pallid. He seemed to be having some trouble breathing. The leader, who was slightly taller than the rest and who had a generally more craggy appearance on account of the bony ridge above his eyes, seemed to be chanting a soft song as he led them to the circle of tapes. They formed up in the circle and then squatted. The yellow eyes of the leader looked directly into Thorndyke's eyes. They seemed to look through Thorndyke and beyond him.

The music ended and a hush descended on the hall. The President of the Space Council coughed to himself and stepped forward.

"On behalf of all the peoples of Earth I welcome you to our planet and offer you friendship." He stepped back.

Silence. The leader of the Pe-Ellians, without moving his head, spoke a few words of Pe-Ellian, and Calm After the Storm rose to his feet. He kept tight hold of the hands of his fellow Pe-Ellians. He spoke Pe-Ellian, apparently addressing each of his companions, for each one of them replied using, as far as Thorndyke could detect, the same words. Then Calm After the Storm breathed deeply and drew himself to attention. His voice came from stiff tense lips.

"We come in peace. *(Pause)* Not see-king cruelties or the en-ding life. We will *(Pause. Deep breath)* speak with him among you called Thorndyke. She is known to us. For ever and *(Pause. Deep breath)* ever. Amen."

Calm After the Storm's mouth closed and his head fell forward on to the grey cloth covering his chest. His body remained rigidly upright as though clamped in a vice.

This was the most painful speech Thorndyke had ever witnessed. He felt that every word had been bought at the price of blood. And he regretted that he had forced the Pe-Ellians to come to this meeting. He should have gone with them quietly, allowing them to dictate the terms entirely.

"Amen," said the President of Mexico. Haltingly all the other children of Earth echoed him.

The Pe-Ellian who had seemed to be suffering from Space Jelly when they came into the room, now began shaking convulsively. The leader toppled forward on to his knees; his arms strained back as he fought to hold his balance. His head jerked back in one stiff movement and he called aloud in Pe-Ellian. Then all the Pe-Ellians were howling in unison.

Thorndyke knew what was coming. He felt the tingling in the air. He began to run through the mind exercise Jose Borges had taught him before his second visit to the Pe-Ellians. It was of no avail. The nausea hit him like a body blow. He doubled up with his stomach in flames and saw the other humans fall. At the same moment the Pe-Ellians rose to their feet with a shout and the double doors cracked open. Still holding hands the Pe-Ellians reeled through the doors and were gone.

With their departure the sickness subsided.

Two hours later, in his room at the Space Center, Thorndyke thought over these things. He was caught between excitement and fear.

Species X.

Pe-Ellia.

I hope Ceto made a good recording. We shall need all the help we can get.

Amen.

Commentary

In some ways this breakdown in Pe-Ellian decorum was exactly what Thorndyke wanted. For a few moments when the Pe-Ellians lost control he was able to see beyond the icy calm that the Pe-Ellians had affected on every previous occasion. At the time neither he nor I had any clue as to what had caused this breakdown or what had caused the onset of the nausea. It was not until much later, when we were on Pe-Ellia, that we discovered that these were all byproducts of what the Pe-Ellians called Mantissa control. The giddiness demonstrated by the Pe-Ellians was not a result of transformational ataxia, popularly known as Space Jelly. This appears to be a uniquely human condition. In some humans (not all) the Gee-Jay transformation shocks the central nervous system in such a way that the brain becomes disoriented. When suffering from ataxia an attempt to clench one's fist may result in raising one's leg. Speech becomes slurred and incoherent. Usually these effects wear off after a few hours.

I asked Cook and Jet to explain this incident at the reception. Here is Cook's brief reply.

"Ah, you Earth men. If I concentrate now I can still feel the pain of Stone Heart Rising (the Pe-Ellian leader at the reception). It is still here as part of your life. Great damage was done that day. We of Pe-Ellia count more Balacas and now in the melting pot than you could guess. Did you not think it strange that you never again met Calm After the Storm? And you have never asked about the others. The cries reached to Pe-Ellia. The Mantissa reached out his hand you would say and saved the game. Honour to him, for he saved your bigwigs too and the mission went ahead as ordained."

Jet spoke up.

"Hush. Even here on Camellia it is not safe to mention such things, and no Mantissa is riding near."

More they would not say. At a later stage of the diaries Winter Wind explains what the experience of Earth was like to the Pe-Ellians who made that first encounter.

So we approached the date of departure. Thorndyke comments that I was driving myself too hard. That is not true. I was deeply concerned that we were leaving for Pe-Ellia in such an unprepared state and felt an obligation to bring all our information together. Lining up an encoder is not something that can be left to the last five minutes.

The following is an abstract I prepared at that time setting out our main information resources.

PRESENT ENCODER HOLDINGS

(1) Visual and audio recordings of all known contacts with the Pe-Ellians.
(2) Linguistic/cultural analyses of all the above data.
(3) Medico/physiological analyses of all known Pe-Ellians, conducted by the Forensic Institute in London.
(4) Selection of all Earth news coverage and commentary concerning the Pe-Ellian visit.
(5) Synopses of major articles published on the Pe-Ellians.
(6) Current notes and suggested catalogue procedure.

This may seem a reasonably complete list and as far as it goes it follows standard contact procedure. However, the problem which I felt acutely was that most of the so-called findings were actually based on conjecture and not on facts. Commentary can never replace hard analysis. A few examples may demonstrate this point. Here is the final paragraph of the report prepared by the CLI language team.

> The Pe-Ellian language appears to be a composite of gesture and voice. Gesture seems to provide an emotional modifier and is rarely, so far as we can judge, independent of the spoken language. A catalogue of five gestures and their projected vaiues is on file. The spoken language seems to be polytonal. There are, however, marked differences in pronunciation between different individuals. Whether these differences arise from dialect or are manifestations of individualised articulation we cannot say. It is noted that certain phrases which seem to serve a ritualistic function are always pronounced in the same way. A tentative Pe-Ellian–English glossary of phrases and speech units is on file.

We were not to know at that time that what we heard on Earth was a purely ceremonial tongue, which is not used for ordinary communication. It consists mainly of quotations.

The medical notes are largely descriptive, dealing with skin patterns, colours, breathing rhythms etc. The London Forensic Institute comments:

> Our attempt at long baseline scanning proved a failure. Some force negated all our attempts to probe from a distance beneath the Pe-Ellian skin. Our request to conduct a physical examination was refused or at least ignored. Infrared scanning revealed a pulse in the Pe-Ellian abdomen. This may indicate a womb. We consider the differences in height of the Pe-Ellians important and some observations indicate that height may determine rank.

One provocative comment offered by the LFI was that the Pe-Ellians were possibly descended from something similar to lizards. This conjecture proved correct.

Briefest of all was the physicists' report. Ever since the Pe-Ellian ship had passed unrecorded through Earth's defence warning stations the physicists and engineers had been taxing themselves to discover how it was powered and of what it was made. Every electronic scan and probe drew a blank. The final sentence of their report reads sadly.

> We conclude that Pe-Ellian technology is not only more advanced than our own, but that it is also based on different assumptions, the nature of which we cannot begin to understand.

On April 26th at 12.00 GMT our journey began. Our departure is the subject of Thorndyke's next diary entry.

Thorndyke's Diary: Entry 4

April 26th. What was it Armstrong said? "One small step for man. . . ." Felt a bit like that myself, stepping up into the sphere. Momentous events measured by the human and the ordinary. And that is how it should be. Eternity is definitely perceivable in a grain of sand, and one step carries me into worlds unknown.

I am still in awe of the size of this sphere. The Pentagon cubed . . . pale green, slightly luminous. Absolutely silent.

No, it is not the size. It is the fact that it has not landed that fills me with wonder. For three weeks it has hung here, shedding our gravity.

I have to face the fact that any civilisation that can keep a million tons of spaceship suspended a precise ten centimetres above the surface of the earth cannot be all bad.

As I approached the sphere I whistled. The effect of the curvature of the sides was uncanny. It sent the sound in every direction except back at me. Like whistling into a vacuum really . . . and when you think about it, that is just about what we are doing.

I was surprised that there was no-one to greet us. The door hole was, of course, very large, and we walked down a luminous green tunnel to get into the ship. I have my travelling bag and Tomas has the encoder and a suitcase. To look at us you might think we were going fishing.

No-one from Earth has been allowed to see us off. I half wondered if, after last night's debacle, the whole visit might be called off, but not a word. No Fire-Sticks or Calm After the Storm. When we approached the sphere the door opened. Someone must have been on duty. So I suppose it is all systems go, with or without a welcome.

They hold us at a distance, like biologists with forceps. Do they really fear us? Are we so dangerous? Ha, show me the power in two small men. Are we considered the representatives of a belligerent species, who can be expected to arrive with bombs strapped to their tummies?

COMMENTARY

Thorndyke wrote the above entry a few moments after we had climbed into the Pe-Ellian craft. He strode back and forth, his notebook in hand, tapping his teeth with a pencil. I also remember him pressing the point of the pencil against the "skin" of the ship when the door closed. He seemed excited and caged—an explosive mixture.

The following is a transcript of the recording I made that morning:

Temperature 23.5 degrees Celsius. Air heavy and slightly scented. Exact scent hard to define—tomato plants maybe. Overall pleasant.

It is now thirty minutes since we entered the ship and so far there has been no sign of movement. If we have taken off then certainly I felt nothing, and nor did Thorndyke. The door closed behind us thirty seconds after our entry. "Closed" is very much an Earth term. It would be more precise to say that the space through which we entered became opaque and joined seamlessly with the walls of this chamber. I remember once seeing the supercooling of a pool of water at the Helsinki Cryogenics lab. That was similar. One moment the water was clear and we could read the writing on the bottom of the tank, the next moment the whole surface was white as an eggshell. This change was accompanied by a roaring. The closing of the spaceship door was silent.

The chamber we are in is like a flat-bottomed bubble. Everything is the same pale pearly green colour. There are no windows. There is no light source evident, but everything seems slightly luminous and we can see well.

The diameter of our room is seven metres. The height is impossible to judge. The curvature of the walls distorts my judgement. It could be five metres or it could be twenty, though I think the room is a sphere.

Our voices are deadened.

Round the perimeter of our room runs a wide, low bench, and in the centre of the room is a table. The table seems to have grown like a mushroom out of the floor. The table and bench are made of the same green material as the walls. Thorndyke has likened them to skin and that has some accuracy, though to me they feel more like the laminated C-plex fabric used in spacesuits. The walls are warm to the touch. This could be the warmth of life.

Thorndyke has just suggested that the ship is a great big space whale and we are Jonahs. I consider this impossible on a literal level and Thorndyke has conceded that he was joking. However we are both aware that his image has a poetic truth. We have been swallowed and we are journeying, we know not where.

There is nothing more in the chamber to describe. Our suitcases look decidedly out of place amid this spartan elegance.

The room as set up would make an excellent laboratory for sense deprivation experiments.

(12.38) A window has appeared in the wall. We are both looking out, and are not surprised to discover that we are still on

Earth. The window breaks the monotony and makes our chamber less of a cell. The walls are getting brighter . . . their green is now vivid and we are lifting. I cannot feel movement but I can see Earth falling away like a plate . . . I can see the curvature . . . we seem to be ascending in a spiral . . . no feeling of acceleration, but I see our motion . . . anti-gravity or some such force must be holding us.

The sky is moving from deep blue to black. I can see the stars.

The air is electric. I—

The recording breaks off. To my eternal shame I forgot a lifetime's training and gaped like a child on his first visit to the zoo, completely forgetting to make any recording.

Thorndyke was equally dazed, and only set down his impression some time later. In his diary the following account appears directly after his description of our entry into the Pe-Ellian ship. The account was written the day after our arrival on Pe-Ellia, that is on April 27th.

Thorndyke's Diary: Entry 5

It is easy to be wise in retrospect, but in all fairness I did know something was happening. It was not so much a pricking of my thumbs, or a physical sensation, but rather an awareness that my brain, or better, my mind was being peeled open. I did not feel that this was either hostile or particularly intentional. It seemed like an accidental by-product of my brushing against some titanic force.

As a boy I remember once standing in York Cathedral at a time when the organ had just been switched on. Nothing changed, but I was aware that the air was suddenly charged. The charge had to go somewhere and was resolved when the first notes pealed out. Such experiences mark one for life. In the ship the resolution took the form of a brief visual excursion. In no more time than it takes for a camera shutter to open and close Tomas and I found ourselves standing (as it were) in space.

I was looking up and saw "through" the whole spaceship. It was like the open lattices of a honeycomb with a million cells, and in the centre was a figure.

Let me put it another way. I thought I was staring at a brilliantly polished silver ball and the image at the centre was distorted and massive, but it was not my face.

There was Jacob's ladder stretching upwards and there at the top was . . . God?

No, I can't say that. Again I must call upon images from my youth. I was present when Ericson conducted his ion analysis of the Turin shroud and we saw the strange figure there shine like silver fire. I remember as well the face of Christ in a Byzantine cupola, glowing in the reflected sunlight. The entity, whatever it was that I saw, was both infinitely large and infinitely distant. It was hazy and indistinct, as though seen through water. I had no sense of eyes, only of presence.

At the edges of the figure the solid lines of the cell walls spread out like a giant spider's web and within these walls I saw Pe-Ellians, hanging motionless.

Then the shutter closed.

I remained staring at the green ceiling. I felt, perhaps, like Garfield, who was throwing bread to the ducks and watching the ripples when he conceived of the shifting time centres and had his first understanding of the equations underlying all modern space travel. But where was my discovery? God knows I have lived at the limit of my brain for many years and know my achievements, but never have I felt this. I have had the euphoria, but not the substance. Mine was the reflected glory of some momentary creative impulse, which swept me up and made me fleetingly glow. I was the mote in the sunbeam.

Commentary

What Thorndyke saw I did not. I saw only the stars.

The figure that Thorndyke describes is undoubtedly that of a Mantissa. However, the fact that Thorndyke should choose religious images to convey his feelings tells us a great deal about him and his state of mind during that outward journey.

Looking back on the event I conclude that the experiences were real, but that what we saw was a reflection of our own minds. For all his denials and ardent atheism Thorndyke saw the image of a known God. I saw the orbiting stars. All this helps explain why I am writing now and why, as I said at the beginning, Marius Thorndyke is dead.

This journey was Thorndyke's journey and I was an accidental accomplice. I believe the Mantissa was tuned to Thorndyke's psyche. Had I been looking upwards or chanced to look up in time I am sure that all I should have seen was the stars.

As for myself, I found the experience terrifying. I have walked in space many times, as have all contact linguists, but always I have had the comforting assurance of a C-plex suit and power pack. This time I felt naked.

My legs failed me and as I fell to my knees the walls returned. I remember I turned to Thorndyke to see how he fared and saw that he was standing with arms spread upwards. He did not tell me then or at any time during our stay on Pe-Ellia just what he had seen. I assumed that his experience had closely paralleled my own.

I sat on the perimeter bench to recover and Thorndyke paced about. I felt drained. He obviously felt elated.

When I had calmed down, my first thought was for the encoder. I checked its cells and power and was relieved that nothing seemed damaged. I began trying to describe what I had seen.

This seemed to upset Thorndyke and he asked me to provide him with all the information I could about our mission. He kept saying, "What do they want? What are they after?"

Shortly after this we received our one and only visit from a Pe-Ellian during the time we were on board the ship.

His coming was advertised to us by a tingling in the air—exactly as had occurred before the walls disappeared. I braced myself.

The section of wall in front of me glowed somewhat brighter and I could see a figure moving behind it. This time I did not forget the encoder. The following is a transcript of this meeting:

MNABA: . . . Thorndyke can feel it too. He has straightened up and is looking at the ceiling. I have pointed at the section of wall which is glowing. It is lit brightly. I see something moving.

Thorndyke has just signalled to me to make sure I have the encoder on. No foolishness this time. Behind the wall is a figure—a Pe-Ellian by his height. Details are difficult. Like looking at someone with the sun behind them.

There is a light breeze and the tingling is almost unpleasant. I can feel my hair lifting. The wall is opening, dissolving. I am not sure if it . . . The section of bench has evaporated.

Ah, it is Fire-Sticks. He is in his puppet mode, seemingly supported. His eyes are closed. His breathing is paced. He is clearly under the influence of some potent drug or is in a trance.

FIRE-STICKS: Gentlemen, pray beseat yourselves. This meeting is not ceremonial, but for info. only.

(His voice is dry and uneven.)

THORNDYKE: We welcome you. We wondered when someone would turn up.

(Pause)

FIRE-STICKS: Turn up what?

THORNDYKE: Just a way of saying arrive, come to see us, you know, pay a visit.

FIRE-STICKS: Do you mean you were expecting me? Did you foreknow my coming here?

THORNDYKE: No, not at all. Don't complicate things. We're not seers. We just guessed that you were not the kind of people who would leave two guests sitting all alone twiddling their thumbs. Can you tell us what is going on?

MNABA: What happened a short while ago when the walls disappeared?

(Long pause)

FIRE-STICKS: I am instructed to inform you concerning arrangements for your arrival and stay on Pe-Ellia and to ascertain your present requirements. First we will arrive Pe-Ellia some forty Earth minutes from now. We have created an environment which will make you feel at domicile. Second, upon location you will be in charge of Professor Winter Wind, who will make all future arrangements. Third, you are comfortable now? Can I offer you any refreshments, sirs?

MNABA: Well, I'm not hungry or thirsty if that is what you—
THORNDYKE: I want to go to the lavatory.
FIRE-STICKS: Defecate?
THORNDYKE: Urinate.
FIRE-STICKS: You may do your business wherever you wish.
THORNDYKE: Here?
FIRE-STICKS: On the floor. It will be taken charge of.
THORNDYKE: Would you do that?

(Pause)

FIRE-STICKS: No, but if I were you, I would.

(Pause)

If there is nothing more I will return, wishing you bon voyage and a happy stay aboard the planet Pe-Ellia.

MNABA: That appears to be the end of the interview. He is stepping back and the wall has already closed. Its brilliance is fading. Thorndyke has his back to me.

THORNDYKE: All for the sake of science and brotherhood.

MNABA: Thorndyke is urinating on the floor of the cabin. He has finished and stepped back. The small puddle is spreading out and is not dividing into streams. The floor appears to be completely flat. The surface of the pool is shimmering as though a breeze is passing over it and now—it has just disappeared! Evaporated—but there is no heat. Absorbed? There is not a bead of moisture left. Thorndyke is on his knees checking.

THORNDYKE: There's sanitary engineering for you.

Those among the readers who are not familiar with contact practice will perhaps be surprised at Thorndyke's behaviour. They should not be. It is an axiom of contact philosophy that one learns a great deal about a civilisation from the way it treats its own physical and industrial waste products. It is an interesting experiment usually given to trainee contact linguists to evaluate the Earth's cultures from an analysis of their uses and disposal of waste.

When they visited me Jet and Cook referred to this incident aboard the outward bound ship. It appears that the Pe-Ellians were amused by Thorndyke's act. The Mantissa controller atomised the constituents of the urine and passed them through the skin of the spaceship and out into the vacuum of space. Although we did not know it at the time every aspect of our environment was controlled by the sphere's Mantissa. The disposal of urine, like the fabrication of fresh air for us to breathe, posed no problems at all.

For the rest of that short journey we discussed and analysed as best we could all the information we had about the Pe-Ellians. Thorndyke practised the few words of Pe-Ellian we had managed to record, in particular the greeting which they seemed to use most frequently.

Our arrival on Pe-Ellia occurred exactly as predicted by Fire-Sticks. Just as we had no feeling of movement on departure so we had no sense of arrival. No windows appeared, the walls did not evaporate, and there was no bump to tell us we had touched down. We felt the by-now familiar tingling in the air. This made me apprehensive.

Suddenly the air felt fresher and the light inside the chamber softened. Thorndyke touched me on the shoulder and I turned to discover that the door in the spaceship had opened. I had been facing the wrong wall.

The next entry in Thorndyke's diary concerns our arrival and first meeting with Professor Winter Wind. In this entry Thorndyke uses the present tense although he is actually recording events that occurred some hours (or even days) previously. The manipulation of tenses when recording data is part of a contact linguist's training. However, it is not widely known that Thorndyke was blessed with an almost photographic memory and that for him the past was always that much more immediate than for most of us.

Thorndyke's Diary: Entry 6

I feel a fool facing a green wall. Something is happening out there. Mnaba feels it too. He is looking round, a bit whey-faced, hoping to spot the first signs of change. I content myself with a microscopic analysis of that portion of the wall where I believe the door existed when we entered, but I have to admit that I could be wrong. The problem with circles is that they offer no relief to those who are within them—just a continual horizon, which is always trying to creep round behind you.

My patience is rewarded. The wall opens like an eye. There is green and blue beyond, and the warm smell of the earth after rainfall, the smell of heaps of fallen leaves on lingering warm autumn days.

We pick up our cases and descend from the coach.

It has not landed!

It hovers a convenient human step above the surface. Are they mocking us? Tomas has tested the air with his nose and now holds back to let me pass. Ah, the gratuities of age and authority. I am tempted to perform an antique prat-fall, proclaiming to the waiting denizens, "Here I am, warts and all. Don't expect some sillypophical statement concerning the august meeting of two great species. I am more savage than the scientist. And besides, that polite ten centimetres or so of step bothers me."

I step down. The ground feels soft. The earth is covered with a carpet of succulent, thick-leaved plants. Good for the plough. A man could cut a clean furrow here and the air makes my mouth water.

We are in a clearing in what looks to be a jungle. Above me curves the great spherical pod of the spaceship, and above that the sky. It hasn't a blemish—the spaceship, that is. Its pearly green is freshly polished. In the sky there are other spheres—our honour guard—strung out like berries of mistletoe. That's it.

Dangerous fruit.

I can see no break in the wall of the jungle. No roads. No transporters. Tomas has joined me and we scamper out from under the giant ship. We are anxious lest it depart too swiftly and sweep us up in its monstrous wake. I realise I have begun to sweat in this greenhouse air.

Far to our left something moves at the edge of the jungle. It is a Pe-Ellian. He is accompanied by two boy Pe-Ellians. I guess they are boys, they seem so slight.

He has stopped and is slowly raising his right hand with the palm open towards us. A learned gesture and a friendly one. "Look, no weapons." But the thought crosses my mind that perhaps the Pe-Ellians are ambidextrous.

I raise my right hand in reply. Mnaba waves and has the encoder switched to audio-visual. I estimate that the Pe-Ellians are some three hundred yards from us. They are bounding towards us. Despite his obvious size, every movement is harmonious and vigorous. I am minded of the flow and power of a galloping horse.

"Professor Winter Wind, I presume." Quickly I run through the few Pe-Ellian phrases I have been able to memorise. I shall experiment with a greeting.

They are suddenly close, and I am aware of the true size of these creatures. The "boy" Pe-Ellians are slightly taller than me, and I am just over six feet tall in my stockinged feet and holding my breath. But Professor Winter Wind—he is a giant mottled tree of a figure. I estimate him at almost eleven feet. We saw a few such as him on Earth.

The smaller ones have stopped and let Winter Wind advance. He is blinking his eyes in a gesture I know to be friendly, but which also has something of a challenge about it. Will I quickly get used to the way they close their eyes upwards? Of course I will. I have faced stranger things, and what is more, come to love them.

Now Winter Wind is close before us. I will let him speak first.

"Happy landings. I am Professor Winter Wind."

A pleasing animated voice in which the studied accent suggests breeding and culture. One thing I note, and this is of the utmost importance: Winter Wind is *here*. He is *present. He is actual.* And, oh, the relief that affords me. I am aware of a vital, complex personality, responsible to itself. I say this to draw contrast between this Pe-Ellian and those we have met to date, Calm After the Storm and his ilk, who seem to me as real as the dummies used by ventriloquists.

Tomas Mnaba and I bow courteously in response to this friendly greeting.

"Thank you. And may your next change bring symmetry," I reply, putting a lifetime's experience and training into catching the nuances and whistles of Pe-Ellian speech. This, as far as we know, is their most common and respectful greeting.

He stares at me and slowly it dawns on me that I have somehow gone wrong and put my foot in it. His eyes turn upwards to slits.

His massive head rolls. The smaller Pe-Ellians turn their backs on us. A complex interaction is taking place before our eyes. His gesture is new to me. The slitting of the eyes means surprise. Of that we are reasonably certain as we have seen it a few times on Earth. But this rolling of the head leaves me baffled. Let us hope it is benign.

Either my greeting is incomplete, which I don't think it is, or inappropriate, which is quite possible. We will find out. Thank God, Mnaba is getting it all down. I realise that I must do something to correct this situation.

In English I say, "My name is Marius Thorndyke, and this is my friend and close associate Tomas Mnaba. If in my greeting I have said anything that gives offence, then I am truly sorry, for no offence was intended." Spoken like a diplomat.

Winter Wind has stopped rolling his head. His eyes are closed and he brings his hands together in a short sharp clap.

"It is passed," I hear him murmur, and his eyes blink open. He seems very serious. There is something almost comic in his being so serious.

He replies, "And no offence taken. I appreciate your attempt to handle our tongue, as you call it, and your accent is commendable, but you must know that such a greeting is impossible between us. Those who run before they can walk will surely tumble. An observation that applies to both of us. I am new to this work, and you remind me that I must be cautious lest I impute Pe-Ellian motives to Earthly actions. Let us go."

He turns, almost spins, and sets off towards the jungle. We cannot choose but follow. The smaller Pe-Ellians have hoisted our cases and fallen into Indian file behind us.

His little speech and homily was rather strange if not a trifle priggish. How often people who learn a foreign language discover a level of vocabulary and style of address that suits their personality. Is this also true of Pe-Ellians? At all events it is obvious that we are dealing with a responsible member of the Pe-Ellian race. His seeming lack of humour is not particularly encouraging. But, as I have said before and will no doubt say again, we shall see what we shall see.

On that profound note, goodnight.

"And may your next change bring symmetry." This phrase refers to the central event in the Pe-Ellian life cycle, the sloughing of skin. Pe-Ellians never stop growing and consequently age and height tell the same story. Each successive phase in a Pe-Ellian life is determined by the skin that is revealed after a change, and it is the hope of every Pe-Ellian that his seventh change will bring "symmetry". We have no exact equivalent in English for the Pe-Ellian word *straan*, which I have translated as "symmetry". To this concept should be added "harmony" and something like "pregnancy". *Straan* to the Pe-Ellians is the outward and visible sign of inward and spiritual fulfilment.

We were unaware of the complexities of this word and it was only gradually (as these pages will reveal) that we came to understand something of the profound significance of *skin* and *markings* in the Pe-Ellian philosophy.

During our walk in the jungle Thorndyke asked Winter Wind why his greeting had been inappropriate. The following transcript of this brief conversation illustrates not only the significance that Pe-Ellians attach to this greeting, but also the kinds of problems we encountered in conversation with Pe-Ellians.

THORNDYKE: But what I still do not understand, and you have not made clear, is exactly where I went wrong. I mean, that phrase, that structure of words, seemed the most common greeting used among you. Like our "How do you do". Can you tell me why, when I used it, it was inappropriate?

(Winter Wind nods his head slowly. Earth and Pe-Ellia share this gesture of agreement.)

WINTER WIND: But I fear you will not understand until you have been with us for some little time.

THORNDYKE: I'm willing to take the risk. Try me.

(Winter Wind seems to withdraw slightly. He takes on something of the look of the Pe-Ellians we observed on Earth. His tones become slightly wooden.)

WINTER WIND: I will tell you what I can, but you must not ask too many questions. The time is not appropriate.

THORNDYKE: Agreed.

WINTER WIND: That greeting, which could also be called a prayer, can only exist between Pe-Ellians who share a common evolution. It is a greeting offered by one who has achieved final *straan* to one who is awaiting such a change. It is not a common greeting on our planet. I have received that greeting only twice in my life and that was on very special occasions, for my symmetry is not yet complete, and I have undergone six arduous changes.

THORNDYKE: Is it a statement giving strength and health?

WINTER WIND: Very much so.

THORNDYKE: Like when we say "God be with you"?

WINTER WIND: What is God?

(Pause)

THORNDYKE: But I still don't understand why we heard it so frequently.

WINTER WIND: Two reasons. First, the journey to Earth and its hinterland was arduous and required iron-clad unity. Secondly, most of the Pe-Ellians who went to Earth had achieved at least one symmetry. They are among the flower of our people. We trust it is the same with you. That is all. I can speak no more on this. The topic has its dangers.

Winter Wind refused to speak any more and pushed on through the jungle. Thorndyke did not try to press him with questions. In fact he did not speak either; he had been silenced by Winter Wind's statement, "We trust it is the same with you", which could only have meant that Thorndyke was classed as among the best of human beings. The Pe-Ellians had apparently made a moral judgement concerning Thorndyke. Thorndyke, who had spent much of his life resisting categories, and who enjoyed the reputation of being a maverick now found himself classified as among the "flower" of Earth's people. A fact, which, as Thorndyke commented to me later on, rather changed the rules of our being on Pe-Ellia.

In the diaries no account is given of our journey through the jungle from the spaceship to the "cottage" where we ultimately lived. The journey had its significance. The following brief description is taken from my encoded notes.

Entrance to the forest is via a small track which is barely wide enough for two people to walk side by side. The track is very well defined and would appear to be frequently used. There is no evidence of roads or rail systems. From the way the big Pe-Ellian is striding along I guess that legs are this species' main mode of transport. Just as their spaceships can hover with ease, so the physical life these creatures clearly enjoy indicates a post-technology simplicity. Perhaps their power source is something as simple to them as is the lever to us—perhaps.

I hope the Pe-Ellian slows a bit. Thorndyke is sweating and I, younger than him, am finding the going rather hard. One thing that is hindering both of us is the vegetation. On each side the plants grow up like walls. Basically there are two types of plants: tall slender trees, which soar up branchless and then open into wide palm-like leaves, and short stubby shrubs like umbrellas. These latter often hang across the path. The leaves of the tall trees are translucent and we are walking in a permanent pale green light. Occasionally the canopy is broken and hard white sunshine burns down. I am reminded of the tropics on Earth.

As he walks Winter Wind seems to take delight in pushing through the umbrella plants. He raises his arms and touches the large fleshy leaves with his fingertips. When he does this the leaves swing back and Thorndyke has to be careful not to get hit in the face. For Winter Wind these leaves are at a convenient height, but for us they are a confounded nuisance. I observe that the Pe-Ellians following us just allow the large leaves to hit them. At least it has not been raining.

We have been walking for twenty minutes. Many of the trees have much wider girths than the trees near the edge of the clearing. The path has widened somewhat, which makes our going easier.

We have come upon a small glade and there are creatures playing. Hush. They don't seem afraid of us. The effect is very beautiful. Here the sun falls uninterrupted, and where the rays of light strike it is as though the plants themselves are glowing.

There, they have gone. Without sound or warning they uptailed into the bushes.

Winter Wind is being very helpful. As we encounter a new bush or insect or tree or animal he pronounces the name very clearly in Pe-Ellian. I have them all down. He has just made a very interesting observation that their names will be of great value in our understanding of Pe-Ellian stories. He seems to talk to us rather as if we are favoured pupils and he our teacher. True, I suppose, but is that why we are here?

We have stopped again, and Winter Wind is demonstrating how to stroke the plants. He begins at the outer tips of the leaves and moves his hand inwards, slowly lowering his palm until his whole hand is doing the stroking. I have a go, standing almost on tip-toe. The feeling is pleasant. The leaves are resistant and the sensation is not unlike stroking a cat when it arches its back under your hand. As your hand reaches the centre of the leaf where it joins the main stem you feel a distinct tingling, as though small charges of electricity are being released.

Thorndyke strokes and then strokes backwards. He pulls away sharply, as though stung. Indeed, he has been stung, and his hand is covered with hundreds of tiny spots.

Thorndyke says it hurts like hell, but the Pe-Ellians cluster round, seemingly more interested than worried. Winter Wind has taken Thorndyke's hand and placed it firmly on the leaf. He rubs Thorndyke's hand firmly down to the centre of the plant. He repeats this several times, as though trying to get rid of a persistent stain. Thorndyke says the pain is gone, but Winter Wind still holds him.

There is a sight! The mottled, arched body of the Pe-Ellian towering over Thorndyke and holding him firmly like a conscientious mother with a three-year-old child, making him wash his hands at the sink. I think Thorndyke feels something of this. He is looking at me in embarrassment.

Now Thorndyke is free. The pain has apparently gone, but a rash remains. Winter Wind studies the hand closely, as though he were reading a fortune there, and then nods.

Very seriously he has stated that no harm has been done except to the plant. Thorndyke has replied with a cryptic remark about a rattlesnake and a mother-in-law . . . I have no idea about this.

We have gone on. There has been a light but definite change in our guide. He speaks less. He has stopped mentioning the names of Pe-Ellian life-forms, although we have just encountered some magnificent butterflies and a whole army of bright green ants.

Now Thorndyke has asked for a pause. He is obviously quite tired, as am I, but I think he wants to ask some questions. I have noticed him building up to this: slapping the back of his hand into his palm, humming, muttering.

Thorndyke is trying to discover why the greeting he spoke was incorrect. *(Text already quoted.)*

Both are silent. Professor Winter Wind is brooding, his eyes veiled and inward. There is something very frightening to me in this combination of humanoid shape, great size and patent intelligence. This creature's moods have a weight about them.

Thorndyke is simply angry in a way that I have seen many times. He wants to argue. But there is no arguing with Winter Wind. I predict that Thorndyke will spend time on his own today working things out and making notes in his grey notebooks.

We walk in silence. The heat is high and the air under the trees is oppressive. About ten minutes ago our path veered to the right and joined a lazy stream. The water in the stream seems clear, but I cannot see the river bed. I have seen the dart of a fish.

I can see a clearing ahead—benches, a table, and what looks like a house.

Although I did not foresee it at the time, Thorndyke clearly felt an instinctive antipathy towards Professor Winter Wind from the very first day of our arrival. One can only speculate on how different the outcome might have been had they hit it off from the very beginning.

The next entry in Thorndyke's diary concerns our arrival at the cottage and his first encounter with Menopause, who later became known as Harlequin. Chronologically this entry belongs here, but I am inclined to believe that Thorndyke wrote part of it much later, possibly even after I had left Pe-Ellia.

Thorndyke's Diary: Entry 7

Strange Encounters

What does one expect of a superior culture? It is a question easy to pose and one which contains a contradiction. The very concept of superiority when applied to culture leads directly to Fascism and all its attendant evils, one of which is the destruction of culture. So let us drop culture from the lists.

So what are we to make of these Pe-Ellians? Are they humanity's superior? And if so, then in what ways?

I have all my life fought against the idea of *superiority*. I have believed that every person has his or her talents and that nothing but damage ever came from the segregation of human beings into those who achieve, and therefore have, and those who fail to achieve, and therefore have not. For these views, which are common sense to the layman, I have been labelled a maverick, since I am one of the achievers.

In terms of technology can I call these Pe-Ellians superior? I fear me I must. They are not just "more advanced", which is to say bigger and faster. They employ principles we wot not of. We are horse and dray; they are magnetic transit. They are so seemingly negligent of their technology that I begin to suspect that it is not what we call technology at all, but something else, something completely different.

What then of their intellects?

They are bright, there's no denying that, but I am not consumed by a feeling of inadequacy before genius. Aristotle or Shakespeare could give them a run for their money. Their intelligence is manifest in their grasp of our language and I detect that they know several Earth tongues. It is also allied to something deeper which, for want of a better word, I must call spiritual.

Why am I made uncomfortable by that?

They teach me something of what the word spiritual means. They live here and elsewhere. (I do not mean that zombie state.) When I am with the Pe-Ellians I feel that their creative lives are elsewhere and that with me they are in a state of bated breath. They contain a secret, the nature of which I cannot guess. I have never known anything like this before. No, not even on beloved

Orchid, where I found more purity than I could comprehend.

At the same time the Pe-Ellians are inconsiderate and I shall enjoy telling them so. They walk us through jungle till we are draining sweat, they lecture us and they expect us to understand their mores without ever taking the trouble to explain them. Intelligent they may be, but I would fire them from the CLI for incompetence, not to mention hubris.

Then again, perhaps the fault lies with me. Perhaps I am getting too old for these quests.

Can a mind wear out like a pair of shoes?

Of course it can. History has hundreds of examples of men who were creative in their youth and died finally, champing their gums and destroying their finest achievements.

So to today. For the most part the journey through the jungle was a joy. I got a bit tired, but that is neither here nor there. Overall I felt younger. Gravity here is just perceptibly less than Earth—enough to put a spring in my step. I should have been content with learning the names of the birds and the bees. Instead I tried to delve beneath the surfaces and met with abstractions and confusion.

As much my fault as Winter Wind's I suppose, but it still depresses me. Anyway, we walked beside a river which sang and came eventually to a clearing. The first thing I saw was the cottage. They had half-buried it under the ground.

The upper storey and what I assume would be the roof were both visible, but even they had undergone a cubist transformation so that parallel was no longer parallel and facets grew out of corners. The gables of the roof soared at an angle more appropriate to a church and at the apex *fused* with the trees of the jungle. I observed also that the main supports at the corners were extensions of tree stumps. This shows biological engineering of a very high order.

The door to our cottage was reached down a ramp which angled steeply into the earth. Up in the angle of the roof was a facsimile of a mullioned window, which did not lead to an attic. By an optical illusion I do not understand, the window seemed to look out into the surrounding undergrowth. The purpose of a chimney had obviously completely defeated them. The chimney, which was a bent stove pipe, was stuck into a tree and set some thirty centimetres above the roof proper. The stonework changed texture as you walked towards it. In one corner the stone wall seemed to waver.

Extraordinary. I was reminded of a stage set. Nothing was real. Clearly, life was conducted underground and this whole contrivance was a concession to our presumed tastes.

"Do you like it?" asked Winter Wind.

I nodded, as I guessed he had had something to do with its creation.

"We tried to make it look familiar," he said, with what I am sure was a note of pride, "while at the same time giving you some idea of how we live and the way we see things."

"How long have you been studying our civilisation?" I asked.

"One change. Ah, but your living habits confuse me. I have concentrated mainly on your languages and some of your history. It seemed to me that you Earth people were very nostalgic, so I tried to provide a symbol of nostalgia. Should there be woodbine and clematis climbing round the door?"

Winter Wind must have obtained some copies of old Christmas cards. Whatever their means of gathering information, they are very good. Winter Wind says he has been studying us for one change. Well, I have no idea how long that is, but let us guess it is about two hundred years. That would take us back to the time of stagecoaches and before there were any aeroplanes. It is a world which we can no longer conceive. This cottage comes from such a world and the Pe-Ellians understand it no more than we do.

Incidentally, I touched their pseudo-stone. I was not surprised to discover that it felt like the skin of the spaceship.

While I was studying their cottage another Pe-Ellian arrived. He appeared suddenly out of the river, popping his head over the bank and calling out, "Cordial welcomings." He emerged from the river on to the bank in one movement and stood there dripping. It was a beautiful flow of movement and I was reminded of Winter Wind galloping towards us. This Pe-Ellian was almost as tall as Winter Wind but his skin tones were considerably darker.

He moved to the back of the clearing, where a low waterfall tumbled over bare rock. There was a ledge and he settled himself comfortably so that spray thrown up from the waterfall fell lightly on his skin.

"Welcome to Pe-Ellia," he said. "We have awaited your coming with great anticipation."

"This is Blackness of Midnight Carbon," said Winter Wind by way of introduction. "At least, that is as close as I can get to translating his name. He is an historian of our planet, and may possibly be one of your teachers."

"As a name it is a gobful. Call me Jet," said the Pe-Ellian and stretched, opening his mouth and baring his teeth rather as a cat does.

Both Tomas and I bowed.

The irritation I had felt with Winter Wind over our discussion on Pe-Ellian greetings was disappearing. With the arrival of this bright and breezy Pe-Ellian, life was becoming distinctly more interesting.

I was aware of movement above me.

Ah, fearfullest of all
Are the half-seen things.
Shadow people waiting.
Child dreads catching the man.

Winter Wind looked up.

"Let me introduce Menopause," he said. In retrospect his manner was that of a hostess forced to introduce an unbidden and unwelcome guest.

Menopause.

What can I say now? I am still reeling. I will try to do justice to him later. But briefly, what I saw was a Pe-Ellian shape. Long and thin, he was reclining along the contours of a tree branch. Indeed, so closely identified was he with the contours of the tree that he seemed part of it. But that is nothing. His body glowed and his eyes were marbles of yellow fire. He stared at me and winked slowly, as though he had completed taking a long exposure film. I say his body glowed. It seemed divided into slabs, plates, scales, and at the junction of each plate was a bright pulsing red line. It was from these junctures that the glow came.

What I was staring at struck me as more alien than anything I had ever encountered. Beside this thing Winter Wind was a humble village parson. If I had been struck by lightning I could not have had a greater awareness of raw direct power.

The spell was broken by the arrival of another Pe-Ellian. He came scurrying up the ramp leading from the cottage. He was wearing a long apron which trailed on the ground and was rubbing his hands in a way that reminded me of my mother when she was cooking and trying to get the flour off her hands. He seemed shorter than the other Pe-Ellians and was somewhat stouter.

"Heard your voices," he said. "Came as fast as I could. Everything's ready." Even his voice was fruity.

"And this," said Winter Wind, "is Cook. He'll try to find what foods you like and is in charge of everything to do with your physical wellbeing. You'll naturally be seeing a lot of him."

Cook shook hands and then astounded me by curtseying. Clearly he had studied Earth closely. No sooner had my hand closed on his than he pulled his hand away with a jerk. He took hold of my wrist and turned up my palm. He inspected the small sting marks, which had nearly faded and which I confess I had forgotten.

Words flowed between the Pe-Ellians and finally Cook wagged a finger at me.

"Naughty boy," he said. His voice was the voice of a scold, and his attitude reminiscent of a nine-foot nanny.

Satisfied, he let my hand drop. "Now anything you want, can do. Quickly too. No trouble." He laughed then, with his hands waggling by his ears and his head bobbing.

They all laughed, Menopause excepted, and I was reminded of puppets at a fair. Perhaps, as with us, laughter for the Pe-Ellians can be a way of overcoming nervousness.

In the middle of the clearing was a low round table surrounded by contoured benches and one chair. Taking hold of me by the hand again, the Pe-Ellian called Cook directed me to the chair and had me sit down.

"You must be tired, poor man. Take a rest. I wanted to send bearers but Winter Wind wouldn't hear of it. He said you'd enjoy the walk. Did you?"

I believe I nodded.

In truth I was tired. Am tired now. Old age inhibits me.

As soon as I sat down in the chair the Pe-Ellians, Winter Wind,

Cook and Jet, arranged themselves on the benches. I looked at their faces, which did not betray their minds, and suddenly wanted to be alone. I knew, though, that first I had to clear up the Tomas Mnaba problem. Poor Tomas. They had left him out of everything and treated him with no more respect than they had treated my shadow.

Tomas of course did not say a word. He is far too polite and far too conscientious to kick up a fuss. He took up a position behind my chair and I could hear the soft hum of the encoder as it devoured every word and tone.

I turned to Tomas and said, "They seem to think you're not here. We must disillusion them." Tomas shook his head, indicating that he did not want a fuss.

However, if I have learned anything in dealing with aliens, it is that the old maxim "Start as you mean to go on" is universally valid. I saw no reason, and still don't, why this quest should be treated as different in kind from any other.

I turned back to the Pe-Ellians, who were looking on in what I hoped was astonishment.

"You may have noticed that I am accompanied by a fellow from my home planet. Allow me to introduce him. Tomas Mnaba, *Professor* Mnaba. Apart from any assistance he may give me, Professor Mnaba is a scholar in his own right and should be accorded the same rights and privileges as myself. Among such privileges I should include a chair."

This little speech was met with silence and then a sudden outpouring of Pe-Ellian as they all tried to speak at once. Abruptly Cook turned and, hitching his voluminous apron up, he dashed down into the house. He re-emerged seconds later carrying a chair which was a reproduction of the padded swivel chairs we use at the CLI. He placed the chair between the benches used by Winter Wind and Jet and, saying something ceremonial in Pe-Ellian, invited Tomas to sit. Tomas was embarrassed. When he had sat down, Winter Wind made a snuffling noise in his nose, which must be the Pe-Ellian equivalent of us clearing our throats before we speak. Dropping the words distinctly, as a man might drop pebbles down a well, Winter Wind spoke.

"We deduce from your tone that you are displeased. We do not fully understand the reason. If we have been discourteous then we apologise. In our defence may we say that had we introduced him, then according to our mores, that would have dishonoured both him and you. You, Professor Thorndyke, because you are the senior. You, Professor Mnaba, because you are the junior. We believe that you were once Professor Thorndyke's student. If we had introduced you by name then it would have suggested that you were seeking to take Professor Thorndyke's mantle . . . and we all know that it is not yet time. Titles as such mean nothing to us. Respect for seniority means everything. No offence was intended and we offer the hospitality of Pe-Ellia to Professor Mnaba. We shall not make the same mistake again."

His answer surprised me rather. After Thomas and I had thanked him and made sure no feathers were ruffled I asked, "Why, if titles mean nothing, are you called Professor Winter Wind?"

"Because I am senior here and because we felt a title such as this would make you feel more at home. There is really no word in your language for what I am."

It was my turn to be silent. Jet stood up and clapped his hands. From the river we heard a splash and then a young (small) Pe-Ellian emerged like an otter on to the bank and joined us.

"This is one of my pupils," said Jet. "Allow me to introduce Keep Your Eyes Closed So That You Never Fear the Dark."

As he spoke the young Pe-Ellian's eyes opened wide and he murmured some syllables. He bowed his head, turned and walked to the bank. He was about to dive when Jet called him back.

"Where are you going?" asked Jet in English.

"Self death," replied the small Pe-Ellian and turned again.

Tomas followed this exchange closely. He spoke for the first time.

"Such elaborate proofs dishonour all of us."

"True," said Jet and spoke softly to his pupil, who was standing at attention. The young Pe-Ellian relaxed. "I have removed the admonition," said Jet and smiled.

Winter Wind snuffled. "We must proceed with caution."

Cook clapped his hands. "I suggest we drink before any milk is spilled," he said and on cue a young Pe-Ellian emerged from the cottage bearing glasses and a carafe of amber liquid.

I am no lover of wine and as it was poured the thought occurred to me that it looked like urine—the thought is not original. At the moment the thought was born, all the Pe-Ellians raised their heads and stared at me. Not one of them drank.

This needs thought.

COMMENTARY

The quotation Thorndyke uses to introduce Menopause is from a Woodbine collection of ballads and street songs called *Memories in the Orchard*. All the songs in this collection celebrate the changes that a Woodbinian goes through in life. Curiously, many races that we have contacted have the idea of life being arranged in stages. Most of the songs in this particular volume are concerned with puberty and young adulthood. This song, however, is an exception. It relates a series of adventures experienced by a Woodbinian youth during the course of his journey through the forest at night. It should be remembered that the Woodbinians of the Lethern race have only rudimentary organs of sight and depend mainly on a sense of touch. For them the world is filled with frightening shadow people.

As later stages of the diary make clear, Pe-Ellian ideas about death are quite different from the views prevailing on Earth. When Cook and Jet visited me I asked Jet to explain why he had chosen to speak the name of his student and thereby demand his suicide. Jet replied:

> You had it correct when you spoke of elaborate proofs. I wanted you to know how important name is to us, so I thought I would sacrifice Fear the Dark. I was surprised at your reaction but understood you. I know that young life means more to you than it does to us. By speaking that student's name I was elevating him to our company and that could not be. He had no choice really but to suicide or transform rogue.

Thorndyke's comment on the wine/urine association is important. This was for him the first clue that the Pe-Ellians might be telepathic. Of course, at that time I was completely ignorant of why the Pe-Ellians behaved so strangely.

Thorndyke drank the wine and then excused himself. He clearly wanted to be alone. Cook took us down into the cottage and introduced us to all the amenities there. Thorndyke describes this in considerable dètail in a later section. However at this point Thorndyke has inserted a brief introduction of the four main Pe-Ellians we had met to date. These descriptions are more in the nature of notes and one, that of Menopause, would appear to be the first draft of a poem. As far as I am aware this poem was never completed.

Thorndyke's Diary: Entry 8

Winter Wind

Five minutes ago he was standing in front of me.

For all that I am coming to feel that Winter Wind is self-centred and smug (and I am somewhat ashamed of myself for such feelings) I have nevertheless to admit that he is strangely beautiful.

He is the tallest Pe-Ellian we have met so far on Pe-Ellia. He has a characteristic stance I have noted. He leans forward with his head thrust out, with one hand placed behind him in the small of his back. In this position he towers over me. There is something of the predator in this stance. He holds himself rigidly stiff, with only his eyes and black lips moving. Abruptly he will break from this pose and move round the clearing with an easy flow of movement. I am aware of his weight and the muscle power which controls it. Once I came upon him staring down into the river. I was reminded of a statue of an American Indian. Like all the Pe-Ellians he has wide hips, which might make him ungainly were it not for his natural grace and vigour. But it is the skin marking that strikes one.

Winter Wind's skin patterns are the clearest. Imagine parchment. Creamy white, lightly flecked with eggshell brown. That is the basic colour of all his skin, and so far as I can tell it is uniform over the whole of his body with the exception of the soles of his feet, which are black. Of course I have not attempted any kind of detailed physical examination, but I have eyes. Now imagine that on this parchment I draw lines in slightly darker brown. The lines are horizontal and vertical, but not rigidly so. They follow the contours of the body. They define what I have earlier called the "plates" of his skin. Where the lines meet, uneven squares are formed. The whole pattern is harmonious without being stiffly regular.

Within the squares are markings. They could be the work of a master tattooist, but I am certain they are completely natural. They are black, a velvet blackness. They have the same balance and proportion as Chinese characters, which curiously they somewhat resemble. All the markings are similar, and all are variations on three curved strokes. No two "plates" are identical, and in this Winter Wind differs from the Pe-Ellians we encountered on Earth.

I asked Winter Wind if the designs on his skin meant anything like writing. He laughed at the idea, and said that they meant a great deal, but not in the same way as writing. The Pe-Ellians do not appear to have any form of writing, or if they do, I have seen no evidence of it. But I think I understand him. I am certain that what Winter Wind meant was that his skin has an aesthetic meaning. I am becoming more and more convinced that to these people there is a close connection between what we would call aesthetics (which they do not) and what we would call morality (which again they do not). At all events the skin patterns seem to be connected with health in its physical and spiritual aspects. When I look at my own yellow and calloused feet and scrawny legs I am half-convinced the Pe-Ellians are right.

The other night Mnaba was pursuing the Forensic Institute hypothesis that the Pe-Ellians are descended from reptiles. This may be true, though they are certainly warm blooded. As yet we know nothing about how they are born or about their reproductive system. We must both be on our guard against trite human assumptions about the Pe-Ellians based on our assumptions about reptiles. I mean this in both a moral and a physical sense.

But to return to Winter Wind. He is totally without hair, and does not understand its function. He seems to distrust it. Why? I speculate. Because it conceals all-important *skin*.

Winter Wind's baldness is assertive. His head shines in the sun. The beautiful skin markings stand out hard and sharp. Close to him, he seems to emanate energy, life and intelligence. When he stands or walks, the flow of his muscles is perceptible. When he sits he relaxes. I judge there is not an ounce of fat on him.

He is magnificent, I have to admit it, and dignified.

This dignity has I think been the cause of some tension between us. His manner is patrician, and that always makes my hackles rise. He seems disapproving. He makes me feel that I must be careful of my manners. He is parental.

Oh, I know I am going too far, and I know what Tomas would say to me, but so help me, that is what I feel. I have permanently to be on my guard lest I overstep some mark which I do not as yet comprehend. I do not feel the same way with Jet, or with that oddity among strangeness, Cook.

God alone knows what Winter Wind thinks about me. But I have already had one or two minor run-ins with him. These have had their value, for it is a truth that you learn more about a man when you watch him in passion than you do when he is sleeping. This is a universal law.

I have observed that Winter Wind's colour changes when he is getting emotional. It reacts as a totality, changing colour towards pink or brown. The effect is similar to that of a human baby, of which it is said that it laughs or cries with the whole of its body.

Jet

Jet, in an unguarded moment, once said to me that sometimes his skin hurts. When pressed for further details, he dived into the river (his favourite form of escape) and did not visit us again for several days.

But his chance remark tells us a lot. The lines forming the plates of his skin are black and close-pressed, like bars containing a prisoner. They lack the fluidity of Winter Wind, or the sloppy, slightly creased, slept-in-my-shirt look of Cook. Where the markings on Winter Wind are the filigree tracings of a master artist, Jet has stippled splodges, as if a child had held the paintbrush in his fist and jabbed down. At the same time there is symmetry in Jet, and I do not mean to suggest that he is in any way unkempt or ugly. There is a tension in him, a tension between the strength of the bars and the bluntness of the markings. In some ways he is more "virile". In contrast Winter Wind's fine workmanship is on the border of decadence.

I am already beginning to judge the Pe-Ellians in terms of their skin, and my judgements are both aesthetic and moral. I could be on the right track. I could be heading straight for the wilderness. Time will tell, as Jet keeps saying.

Beneath his bars Jet is bluish. When he has been swimming he seems to glow. He loves spray and loves nothing better than to sit beneath the waterfall with his arms raised while the water sluices down over his skin.

He lopes rather than walks, with his arms hanging down at the front, as though ready to dive at a moment's notice. I could imagine Jet wrestling. The muscles which support his giant head are more bunched than those of Winter Wind. This may reflect different living habits.

At the moment of writing I do not understand the relationship between Jet and Winter Wind. Undoubtedly Winter Wind is the senior, and Jet defers to him. But then Jet seems to lead an independent life. He gives an impression of being with us, not because he needs to be, but because he is interested in us. He was introduced to us as an historian, and I more or less accepted this was his function. Namely to record for whatever the Pe-Ellians regard as posterity the details of our meetings. Later, when things settle down, I will tackle him on this.

Cook

When I was on Banyon I had a mistress whom I called Nitro. There's a secret out of the bag. Ah, but those were good free-wheeling days, and there are many tales I could tell. Anyway, Nitro came to my camp one night and said she had been "accorded the honour by her people of becoming my companion". She said she wanted to learn as much as she could about Earth women, so that she could model herself on them and thereby carry out her tasks effectively. I lent her books and magazines, and was intrigued to watch her try red makeup on her yellow lips, to watch her comb her six foot mane of blue-black hair, so that it fell behind her instead of tumbling around her like a dress, to watch her struggle into a dress and contemplate the problem of how to fit a cloven hoof into a shoe.

Finally, and this is strange, she succeeded in being more *essentially* feminine than many Earth women I have known, and I was very happy with her.

I mention this now, not out of any desire to ramble on, enjoying my memories, but because I recognise something similar in Cook. Not that there is any question of sex here. I shudder at the thought. Cook is almost nine feet tall and about as sexual as a billiard ball. From his behaviour it would appear that Cook has taken the trouble to analyse in some measure the women of Earth. The source of his knowledge I do not know, but it is clear that he has no idea of what a woman really is. At least Nitro had an advantage here. She was female of her species, and as regards fundamental matters not at all different from other women I have known. Cook by comparison is a grotesque.

His voice seems pitched slightly higher than those of Winter Wind or Jet. This may be another accommodation.

He is pinkish. It does not seem to me a particularly healthy colour. The "plates" of his skin are large and uneven. He is the only Pe-Ellian I have ever seen scratch himself. Inside the "plates" is a design in deep green not unlike a flower with some of the petals missing. On his legs the designs have become blurred and the dark green becomes dominant. At a distance it looks as though he is wearing boots. The green is also spreading into his face so that he is slightly mottled. I shall watch him closely to see if I can detect any changes.

He is by far the most friendly of the Pe-Ellians. He actually seems to relish being with us and I have caught him listening in to us. He likes to try out new words and I have detected traces of my accent in his English. He laughs a lot in the strange Pe-Ellian manner though I am not always certain what he finds so funny.

He has let me touch him. I expected his skin to be smooth like a downy petal, but it is rough and dry. I asked if Jet and Winter Wind were the same and he said he didn't know. When I touched the markings he winced slightly. He has asked me to tell no-one about this. Perhaps Winter Wind will think he is trespassing on his preserve. I shall honour his trust.

Cook confounds our sense of gender. Why do I persist in thinking of him as "he"? It must be his size and baldness. The thought of a nine foot bald woman with no breasts is . . .

I have it. Something which has worried me from the very beginning. All the Pe-Ellians we have met so far—well, Jet and Winter Wind—have modelled themselves on men. Why I do not know. Perhaps they considered it more appropriate. Perhaps they are not even aware of it. If they did think about it, perhaps they thought it would make us more comfortable. I must be careful here. They are not *acting men*, but have *adopted maleness*. All except Cook.

I wonder if Tomas has noted this. I must confer with him.

COMMENTARY

Thorndyke's liaison with the Banyonian he calls Nitro was a secret well kept. I have checked through his writing on the Banyon culture, and have found only the following short reference.

> The mimetic ability of the Banyonese is truly incredible. They listen carefully and observe and then seek to recreate. This is done in a friendly manner, not as a parody, and the result is somewhere between Earth and Banyon, and as far as I am concerned wholly pleasing. The Banyonese are the first race we have encountered for whom it can be said that the alien intrusion holds no threats. They are natural born contact linguists with an ability to comprehend and adapt.

Thorndyke did not mention that he had touched Cook's skin. Concerning the matter of gender he did once ask me whether I thought the Pe-Ellians seemed more male than female. I replied that biological considerations apart they did seem to have adopted something of male manners, but that the degree of adaptation was minimal. The Pe-Ellians were then, and remain today, in my mind, the pre-eminent example of the neuter gender, being neither male nor female but the equal of either.

I raised this question with Jet while I was working through the diaries on Camellia. He replied:

Ah, sex as you call it. You of Earth think about it a lot. You do not just accept it. We of Pe-Ellia know much about love and ecstasy. We sing often of birth. Of touching and cool fingers we know all. We know submission and the surging of passion. To us you don't know half. You do not meld the way we do, nor do you enjoy sweet dreams.

We had to be careful with you, just as we had to be careful for ourselves.

All our knowledge of you came to us through a Mantissa. We all hunkered down with it for many years—absorbing, absorbing till we were brimfull. All our knowledge was filtered but balanced. If we seemed more male to you then that was an accident. Perhaps you of Earth are more male than female. Certainly I have never tried to be man-like. Nor did Winter Wind. That would have been pain. We are Pe-Ellia—nothing less.

Cook added:

I was the odd woman out. I did try. I had nothing to lose. I am sorry I did not try better.

In conclusion, it seems to me that the problem with gender was almost entirely in Thorndyke's mind. For reasons which will become clear later he was already moving beyond Earth. I have already commented on his unwillingness to follow standard CLI practice. He as much as any of us should have been aware of the dangers inherent in his attitude. Indeed he was aware, but chose to follow his own inclinations.

Thorndyke's Diary: Entry 8 *(continued)*

Menopause

Tiger, tiger, burning bright,
You taught me something, an inner secret when I first saw you,
There you were, lying along the branch, like brilliant foliage,
Nine feet of fire. They should call you tiger.
You know what you taught me?

What it is to be alien.
Beside you, Cook and Jet and Winter Wind are homely as old clothes.
You are so unutterably different, like a solid that casts no shadow.
Looking at you, I become alien to myself.
To feel the crenellations of my own skull.

To look out and in at the same time.
But you don't fit, do you know that? You don't belong,
You are an outsider among insiders. Your presence mocks this rational, intellectual, cool and decorous meeting of cultures.
You are a new leaf in autumn.

Later. Have asked Winter Wind about Menopause, and he apologised for him. Said it was the custom for those who were in menopause to be free to go where they want, do what they want. He said he hoped he hadn't frightened us. I also asked him why he is called Menopause and he said it was the nearest word in the English language meaning, popularly, a change of life. He seemed reluctant to talk about him. I changed the topic before he could say we needed to stay here longer before we could understand. I wonder if Winter Wind finds our naked curiosity alien. The Pe-Ellians were remarkably incurious about Earth. Perhaps they know us too well already.

Here is my speculation on Menopause for what it is worth. Menopause is undoubtedly going through some change. The Pe-Ellians divide their lives in terms of changes. I believe Menopause is about to change his skin.

I have the distinct impression that Menopause did not figure in Winter Wind's calculations and that Winter Wind would rather he went away.

Equally I feel that Menopause feels that there is something in all of this for him and may well stay with us. (What a lot of "feels" there are in that sentence and how little substance.)

Question. Shall I tell Tomas of my speculations? I think not. I have asked him about Menopause and he seems to believe he is a variant species. Perhaps he is playing the more patient game of waiting until Winter Wind is prepared to discuss. He seems less interested in Menopause than in Jet or Winter Wind. That I find incredible. Certainly Tomas did not feel that shock akin to recognition that I experienced in the clearing that first day.

Later. Can't sleep.

My imagination is going wild . . . jumbled thoughts of my childhood, half-formed ideas stuck in the silt of the past, wild speculations.

My head is a trunk of old clothes and someone is rummaging through it. Picking up the quaint old customs. Holding them up to the light. Looking at the holes and threadbare patches.

I feel as though I am bursting. Something is out there. Beyond the stream, beyond the clearing. Is Winter Wind standing with his eyes on fire?

Enough of speculation. I need sleep. But here is a question to sleep on.

Are our minds being bugged?

Goodnight.

COMMENTARY

As we shall see later, this idea that the privacy of the mind was being invaded became very important to Thorndyke and led to his first serious break with Winter Wind.

I now believe that what Thorndyke experienced that night was probably the attention of Menopause. Jet and Cook expressed horror when I mentioned this. I am not suggesting that Menopause was intentionally "rummaging". I see it as an accidental by-product of Menopause's interest in Thorndyke—an interest that Thorndyke has already chronicled.

In organising the diaries Thorndyke has been at pains to describe the stages of our actual entrance into Pe-Ellian life. The following entry has been inserted into the diaries to give a sense of continuity.

Thorndyke's Diary: Entry 9

The Cottage

I am an emotional man, and I have never sought to hide that fact. Sitting at the table, sipping the alien wine, hearing the alien jungle calls, looking at these alien faces, each with its own individuality and intensity, I felt more alone than ever before in my life.

This is not Earthsickness. I have never been afflicted with that. I am estranged from myself . . . and that is the loneliest state a man can know.

I glanced up into the tree and was relieved to see the one they call Menopause had gone. That was a relief. He is the strangest. I never heard him go.

So as I sat there I felt myself turn inwards. I heard their words, observed the careful, studied pronunciation, but their words were only a background against which I perceived myself. I warned myself to beware depression, which is like vacancy. Tomas Mnaba, I am sure, observed what was happening to me. (He knows me better than I do myself at times.) And he, good fellow, made the first move.

"I fear the journey has tired us more than we thought," he said.

The Pe-Ellians did not understand. They twittered to one another and Cook made gestures, which I interpreted to signify the concerned mode.

Tomas had been too polite. He had been lulled into a false sense of communication and had forgotten the third law of contactism: *don't beat around the bush.* Be blunt to avoid ambiguity. Say what you want to say.

I chimed in, "I want to rest for several hours."

I was glad to see that the Pe-Ellians seemed relieved.

"Rest for as long as you like," said Winter Wind. "Our schedule is so relaxed that it amounts to no schedule at all. Night will fall in three hours and then it will be dark for seven hours. If you require fodder then I am sure that Cook can—"

I waved him down.

"Mnaba may want food. I don't. This wine is sufficient. Thank you."

And that was that.

The young Pe-Ellian who had brought the wine came up out of the house and tried to take my arm as though I were some dependent old lady. My reaction, throwing off his arm, was rude, but so be it. We who live under the microscope have some rights.

Now as I sit back at my ease in my room I feel a lot better. Solitude has again worked its mysterious magic.

As is ever the case with the Con. Ling. quest, what another species provides for you tells a great deal about them and how they understand you. This cottage/burrow is a tribute to the intelligence and foresight of the Pe-Ellians. The roof, however, is a folly. At heart I feel they understand us and also wish to introduce us to their world. How strange that a house should be such an eloquent teacher. I was careful not to let them see I was pleased. I tried rather to give the impression that I take it all for granted.

After the wine tasting Cook took charge. He is a strange one. He hitched up his pinny like a girl in a ballroom gown and led us down into the hole.

"Like a grave," I thought, but the thought did not last long. I touched the walls of the tunnel and it throbbed with life. Immediately I thought of a unified technology. Perhaps some super-plastic which has a biochemical base.

The walls of the tunnel were green but not opaque. Beyond the walls I could see the roots of trees. I saw the lair of some Pe-Ellian animal, but what it looks like I do not know for it was not at home.

As we descended deeper and the light above faded, the walls began to glow. At least I think that was what happened. Light came from somewhere, but I could never see the light source. It was greenish in tint, but not at all melancholy. Behind one wall were something like ants. They teemed all over the surface, all busy, carrying bits of bark down to the swollen white sausage which I take to be the queen. And again I am struck by the basic similarity of all life forms, including these august Pe-Ellians. They obviously delight in seeing the process of nature, as indeed we do.

When we were about twelve feet underground Cook stopped us.

"We are now entering the house proper," he said. "We have based the design on the human hand, on its back and open in friendship. This entrance-way, you might say, is the little finger. You see?"

He offered his own hand, which is twice as large as mine.

"In this we are similar."

I must agree and disagree. It is true that our hands are similar in shape and function, but my hand is deeply lined and his is a multitude of facets. It opens and closes as mine does, but where my palm remains firm when I close my hand his becomes soft and yielding, with a loose pouch of skin in the middle.

Cook gives the overall impression that he wants to please, that he wants to discover harmony wherever he can. I must admit that I like the basic idea of his house plan and find him a pleasing guide. We moved down the thumb and the light grew stronger. As it grew stronger the walls became opaque. We were now walking a short flat stretch. Facing us was a membrane. Beyond it I could see a strange play of lights.

"This is your front door," said Cook. "It will open to your touch and it will always close immediately behind you. That's to keep the wee beasties out. Go ahead, touch it."

I did and the membrane spun open like an iris diaphragm.

We moved in. The flickering of light was now much brighter, but I could still not see what caused it.

"We are now entering the palm. This room is where we can hold meetings, have meals, have lessons. Do you like it?"

I know I didn't answer and I'm sure Mnaba was lost in awe as I was. As soon as we'd entered fully into the palm we could see the cause of that strange light. It was the ceiling.

The room was built under the river. The ceiling was the river bed. The rippling silver light was the sunlight streaming down through the water.

The effect on the room was extraordinary. The patterns of light fused together the ceiling and floor. We became shadows, ghosts rather, with radiant silver faces.

"Do you like it?" Cook asked again, and I detected what I believe was pride in his voice.

"It's brilliant," I said, aware of how inadequate was a comment like that. But Cook seemed satisfied.

"We thought you might like a sample of our—" he paused, seeming stumped for a word—"painting. I'll turn it down again, then we can see better. This is for contemplation only, not workaday business."

Cook crossed to one wall where there was a panel with small studs numbered one to ten. Stud number 5 was glowing a bright cherry-red.

"If you go any higher you get the sound of the river as well as the sight. You want?"

I shook my head. "I'll believe you."

Cook pressed button number 2 and immediately the ceiling dulled until all we could see were veins of light like flowing marble. The walls and ceiling became a more solid green. We could now see the room clearly.

It has six sides.

We had entered down the thumb and the passage is set in the middle of the wall. Four of the other walls have passages leading off them, corresponding I suppose to the remaining fingers. One wall is left and I tentatively designate this the wrist. In the centre of the palm is a large oval table around which are set tall upholstered chairs. The effect is archaic, almost the world of King Arthur.

Off to one side and looking quite out of place I saw my old armchair, which I believed safe and sound in my Paris flat. Cook saw me start when I recognised this.

"We took the liberty of copying this as exactly as we could. A few known belongings help to make even the most alien environment a bit more like home."

I was aware, as was Mnaba, that in saying this Cook was paraphrasing page 18, paragraph 5 of the Contact Linguists' Handbook. I am glad they have read it. It gives us something in common.

Next to my chair was a straight-backed cane and bamboo chair.

"We have done the same for Professor Mnaba."

The two chairs, side by side, struck me as a forceful statement. The difference between the chairs is the difference between us. My chair, full of indignant secret springs and spilled drinks, is a veritable half-deflated mangy bear of a chair. There is probably a fortune in spilled change in its lining. Tomas's chair is elegant. The bamboo is the colour of rubbed copper. Its lines are clean and firm. It is business-like, comfortable, springy and without ostentation except for the bright red beads worked into the arms which are in any case an abacus. Tomas's chair is a chair for all seasons.

"Have we done well?" asks Cook.

"Very well." And I meant it.

"Now I am mindful that you said you were tired, so I will not delay you longer. You may explore at your leisure. We have tried to incorporate much that is familiar and yet give you a few Pe-Ellian surprises which we hope will accord with your tastes."

He pointed round the room.

"That is the first finger. The master's finger, and it points to your private rooms, Professor Thorndyke."

Mnaba and I turned away. We did not want Cook to see our smiles. To criticise initiative is like pruning buds in springtime.

"The second finger is for Mr Mnaba—sorry, Professor Mnaba. And the third finger is mine. There is my kitchen, wash-house, abattoir and domicile. You can knock me up any time you like, night or day, no matter. Okay?"

We nodded.

"Over there, the what-you-call small finger is the pathway to the city. That is where the trains come. I'm afraid it is closed off for the moment as we haven't quite finished all the connections. Should be open in the next few weeks, though. Then you can travel where you wish. Now what is else?"

He glanced round the room, ticking off an inventory of items on his fingers.

"Ah, yes, these." He pointed to some blue disks which could be seen in all corners of the room glowing like little chips of sky.

"These are your caller switches. If you have any problems, anything, want something, just give us a ding-a-ling and we'll be there. You will find these all over. Alrighty, you recline or explore as you wish."

Mnaba and I both nodded.

He bowed stiffly. A Japanese gesture and in this situation a comic gesture. His long apron bunched up at his feet on the floor. This movement brought his face close to mine and this was the first time I smelled the distinctive odour of a Pe-Ellian. The smell is not unpleasant. Sweet, a bit like faded perfume, but with an underlying mustiness like mushrooms. If this smell became dominant it would be very unpleasant indeed.

We both bowed, feeling a bit foolish I might add, and Cook withdrew to the kitchen area.

When he had gone, Tomas moved over to the ceiling panel. He pressed number 7 and immediately the room was filled with the tinkle and roar of the stream and the ceiling boiled in sinuous silver ripples.

"Want to take a look at that," he said and climbed up on to the brightly polished table. (He removed his shoes first.) Standing on tiptoe Tomas could just touch the ceiling. He tapped with his knuckles but made no sound.

"Just like the walls," he called.

He rubbed the palm of his hand across the surface.

A shadow, a shape, a fish with long feathery gills came swimming down to inspect. Tomas snatched his hand away and then grinned at me ruefully. The fish bumped its nose against our ceiling. It stared at us for a full three seconds and then started to browse along the surface.

There was, of course, no doubt as to who was in the aquarium.

"I'm going to explore," I said to Tomas, who was still standing on the table looking rather foolish. He nodded.

Beyond the door leading from the palm to my quarters there is a short passage which rises sharply and curves to the right. These green walls are deceptive and I found I had to touch the walls to re-establish my orientation after I had passed through the door. I pressed on up the passage and could hear faintly the rush of the river as it tumbled over the waterfall. I rounded the curve and was faced with another circular door to which was attached a small plaque with my name on it.

I had an inkling of what might be in store for me beyond the door. On its placid surface ripple-marks were moving. The noise of the waterfall was louder too.

I touched the door and it spun open like a whirlpool.

I found myself in the middle of a waterfall. The river streamed across the ceiling in great surges and then tumbled in silver and blue down one wall. Through the curtain of water I could see the clearing. Jet and Winter Wind were still there. They appeared to be deep in conversation.

But the sound of the water was deafening.

As quickly as I could I found the control panel and pressed for silence and solidity.

I found myself back in my flat in Paris. I blinked and the possibility that I had been enjoying some exotic dream occurred to me. The waterfall vanished. My old Honeysuckle Call-cat carpet was under my feet. My desk was there. Tidied. A sure sign we were not in Paris.

I explored quickly and found that the Pe-Ellians had compressed my four-room apartment into a two-room flat. Gone was the kitchen (no great loss) and the pokey little north-facing glory hole which I euphemistically called a spare bedroom. Long ago I combined the comforts of a study, sitting room and bedroom.

I found that the bathroom was a fair replica but without the ever-present damp. The bed was different.

Later.

Have just got back from visiting Tomas and he is very content with his flat—to my eyes it looks more like a hospital room than a place for the healthy to return to sleep, but there we are. Variety remains what the poet called it. Tomas told me in tones of wonderment that his rooms are identical with his quarters at the CLI on Camellia.

I too am well pleased and if there is anything wrong it is the bed.

The bloody bed.

Commentary

I am informed by Cook that the following story is substantially true and that Thorndyke's bed was connected to a "Doctor" Mantissa. In Cook's own words, "We wanted to be sure that nothing ailed him in the night and to ensure he slept well."

As far as I was concerned, when I first read the story I regarded it as complete fabrication. I recall that Thorndyke did ask me to accompany him to his room and he asked me to sit on the bed. He asked if I considered it comfortable, to which I remember replying "yes". He did *not* ask me whether I could feel the bed moving. Without doubt he was merely waiting to observe my reactions.

Had I felt anything I would probably have reacted pretty much as Thorndyke did.

As it was we discussed encoder alignments and categories and I finally excused myself.

Thorndyke's Diary: Entry 10

Marius Thorndyke had never had trouble with beds.

This could be because he had never thought much about beds. Beds were to him quite simply the things you lay down on when you were tired and the things you got up from when you were rested. The splendours of canopy, carved posts, brass and interior springs had never impressed him.

All he required of beds was that they be of reasonable height, reasonably solid and of course, inert.

To all appearances the bed on Pe-Ellia seemed just that.

The first intimation of trouble to come occurred when he sat down on the bed to take his shoes off. It could have been a delusion brought about by tiredness but it seemed to him as he sat there that the bed moved slightly beneath his buttocks and then seemed to seize his bottom in a gentle and altogether too familiar embrace. He stood up quickly and stared in amazement as his bed straightened itself like a schoolmarm straightening her dress.

"No telling what kind of tricks a bed like this might get up to," thought Thorndyke and called Mnaba.

Tomas came quickly. He was dressed in striped pyjamas and had an old dressing gown draped over his shoulders. He was as always carrying the encoder.

"Take it easy, Tomas," said Thorndyke. "This isn't work. Just a little experiment. Please sit down on the bed."

Mnaba sat down.

He sat looking at Thorndyke, wondering what was going to happen next.

"Feel anything?" asked Thorndyke.

Mnaba looked at him.

"Where?" he asked.

"The bed."

Mnaba spread his hands along the cover, pressed up and down

very gently as though expecting a trap, and then shrugged.

"Nothing," he said. "It's a bit softer than mine and a different kind of fabric but that's—"

"Didn't you feel it move?"

"Move?"

"Ye gods and blind fishes. Move, yes, squirm about a bit, you know."

Mnaba shook his head and stood up.

"Well, it didn't do anything for me. You probably dozed off, or a touch of space jelly. Muscle contractions after space flight are a common occurrence. Some people even think they're walking on the ceiling or . . ."

"I know all about space contractions. Hell, I've had them often enough, and I know when I'm asleep and when I'm awake."

"Yes, Professor."

"Thank you, Tomas. You've been a great help."

"My pleasure," answered Mnaba. "If there's anything else I can do for you, just call."

So saying he picked up the encoder and made for the door. Thorndyke could not be sure but he thought he saw a slight smile on Mnaba's otherwise impassive face.

"Goodnight, Marius, and sweet dreams."

"Yes. And the same to you."

Mnaba pressed the door. It opened and he was gone.

Alone again Thorndyke wondered if he had been mistaken. He stared at the bed and the bed stared back at him impassively. It was perfectly smooth. The wrinkles where Mnaba had sat had completely disappeared.

"Oh, what the hell," thought Thorndyke, when in Rome—" and he started to strip off his trousers.

As he sat there in his underpants, peeling off his socks, there was no mistaking the gentle kneading that was going on under his bottom. Thorndyke concentrated on the job in hand. If this were some freak form of space contractions then he hoped it would go away if he concentrated on something else.

Worst of all were the moments after he'd peeled back the sheets and climbed into bed. As if it were a cue for action the bed received him and began a vigorous massage of his arms and legs.

Thorndyke lay there as tense as a man being shaved by a blind barber.

Finally he could stand it no longer. He ripped back the sheets and stood up. The bed made itself in what Thorndyke thought was dumb insolence.

"*Cook*," he yelled, and strode off in search of the kitchen.

Cook heard his call and came hurrying into the Palm Court.

"Is there something amiss?" he inquired.

Thorndyke beckoned with his finger and marched back to his bedroom. Once there he pointed at the bed. "It writhes," he said. "I prefer stillness."

Cook was thoughtful.

"I'm not sure what I can do about that for the moment," he said. "You see, in a way the bed is alive. . . ."

He waved his hands in frustration. "Language, language. Alas, I am not a linguist, only a do-gooder. The bed is—" he sought for a word and then smiled, "sentient. It perceives you and only you . . . to soothe you . . . we thought you would like it. I suggest you try talking to it."

"Talk to a bed?" Thorndyke's voice was deep and deadly sweet.

"Yes," said Cook, beaming and oblivious. "Try to tell it what you want. Think to it. Pray to it. It will try to understand . . . if it is not acceptable I will try to change things tomorrow. Perhaps if all else fails, you could sleep on the floor."

Thorndyke could think of nothing more to say. Obviously Cook had solved the problem to his own satisfaction, and after a few polite inquiries about the controls in the room and the waterfall window, he departed.

"Would you talk to it?" asked Thorndyke, as Cook stepped through the door.

"It wouldn't listen to me," said Cook and was gone.

Feeling somewhat ridiculous, Thorndyke regarded the bed and then slowly, and with a creaking of joints, got down on his knees. He put his ear to the bed and listened.

Nothing.

"Now listen, bed," he whispered, trying to project his thoughts out through an imaginary hole in the middle of his forehead, and resting his head lightly on the counterpane. "I don't want you to move, see?" The bed rippled slightly. "I want you to be still. Not disturb me."

A lump like a pillow tried to shape up under his head.

"Stop it," said Thorndyke and after a few moments the lump subsided like a tyre deflating.

"That's better," murmured Thorndyke. "I don't know how you work, but I hope you understand me. I want you to stay inert. Not a movement. Not a flicker. Now I'm going to climb back into bed and no funny business. All right?"

The bed didn't even tremble in reply.

Thorndyke took a deep breath and warily pulled back the covers. The bed yielded like a regular interior sprung mattress and that was all. It was superbly comfortable. Thorndyke felt himself relax slowly.

"What a day!" he thought. "What an extraordinary day. Was it only this morning I was still on Earth?"

He felt on the bedside table and found a pencil and the diary he had put ready, intending to make notes.

"Must get things in order," he thought. But the pencil rested idle in his hand.

He listened to his own breathing.

He felt silence about him. It seemed that within the silence he could hear echoes. The bed, though now inert, was alive. He had a sudden fear that if he slept the bed would close on him like a giant hand. That fear opened his eyes wide. Helplessness and futility led to laughter. And laughter eventually led to sleep.

I wonder if the bed can understand that?

Commentary

So ended our first day on Pe-Ellia.

Like Thorndyke I also wanted to put the day in order and review what had happened to us. In accomplishing this I was supported by a lifetime's habit, for I have always been a diligent note taker. Thorndyke had often commented on the fact that both he and I were "pen and pencil men". Where most people rely on recordings we still wield the pen. When I had finished my notes I played back some of the day's recordings and ran a cross-indices check. I knew that in a few days I would probably have to begin the arduous task of redefining the reference systems. The encoder is a fine instrument but it has its limitations. If as a contact linguist you have plenty of basic information then you can usually define the catalogue indices with reasonable accuracy from the very outset. This of course depends on a good and continuous flow of information over at least as many months as constitute a planetary cycle.

In our circumstances these conditions did not apply and I had therefore programmed the encoder to catalogue in accordance with Base-Plan alpha, the most comprehensive plan of all. As is outlined in the *Grammaria*, Base-Plan alpha is a catch-all programme. It is crude and cannot be relied on for fine discrimination. I could already see that this system would very quickly prove inadequate. For one thing, Base-Plan alpha depends on a carefully graded sequence of questions which relate together, for example, climate and archaeology. Base-Plan is a programme worked out for contact linguists who are in command of the flow of information. We were not. As Thorndyke put it: "It's the Pe-Ellians who cut the cake and we'll just have to content ourselves with what they want to give us and what we can find grubbing about under the table."

To redefine the encoder I would have to go back through all our major classifications, determine those that were redundant and deduce new bases. For example, in Base-Plan alpha, skin is simply classed under biology. Its other weightings are comparatively light. This would clearly need to be changed. I estimated that we probably had three to five days before the bio-crystalline cells began to play up in response to the inadequacy of Base-Plan. We were attempting to ram square pegs of information into round holes of logic.

I was skirting round this problem, mapping out approaches, when Cook entered my room. He said that he had come to check that all was well and that I was comfortable, and to tell me that tomorrow would be a day of rest. Interestingly, he said that Winter Wind and Jet had found the contact ordeal particularly trying and had decided that we needed more time to settle in. From his comments I was able to gather that in some strange way our state of mind (the phrase Cook used) had a powerful effect on the Pe-Ellians. I asked him then if he himself felt affected by us and he gave that strange hand-waggling-by-the-ears gesture which indicates laughter and said that he was made of far sterner stuff. Then he left, after asking me to pass on the message to Thorndyke.

I noted at the time that Cook seemed to be merry, intoxicated but not drunk. It seemed that there was an excess of life bubbling up inside him.

I decided to give Thorndyke the message and after locking the encoder set off for his rooms. As a concession to convenience his apartment and mine were joined by a short corridor which, if one thinks in terms of the Pe-Ellian plan, was a short connection between the first and second finger. As I approached his door I could hear snoring. I decided not to wake him but nevertheless looked in on him.

The sight of him lying back, mouth open, caught me by surprise. In sleep true age shows. The Thorndyke I was most familiar with was the vital, always slightly aggressive man with sharp, hard, blue eyes and nervous and impulsive movements.

What I saw on the bed was an old man with all the vigour drained from him. In repose his face had an expression of sadness. Lines which during the day showed animation now seemed burdened with care. I was disturbed by his shallow breathing. His hands and fingers resting on the coverlet moved with a gentle convulsiveness as though stroking feathers. An old man.

For the first time I faced the possibility that, despite Pe-Ellian assurances to the contrary, Thorndyke might not survive the trip. That thought created a hollowness inside me.

His own mortality was again preying on his mind as the next item in his journal indicates.

THORNDYKE'S DIARY: ENTRY 11

My ambition is. . . .

But before I go on, should I not pause and acknowledge that there is something faintly ridiculous about an old man talking about his ambitions? Time was. . . .

My ambition is to continue to have courage to spit into the wind without worrying unduly about the consequences. Which is to say that my ambition is to continue as I have done in the past. A profile of courage.

There. And why am I writing this? Because I am starting to laugh at this pretty conceit of courage. I begin to suspect that the whole of my life has been some kind of conceit. A profile conceived and offered to the world when I was a young man. Since that time I have played my part with verve and panache and have concerned myself hardly at all with the inner man. My life is a curve and it is now bending back on me; it is a mighty overhang, which, started by the smallest tremor, may come crashing down.

For years I have felt that a big bang was coming. When I retired I had visions of a graceful retirement spent amid friends and books and memories. The whole beautiful picture was to be lit by a gentle, but still warm, setting sun.

Of course it didn't happen. I became a hermit. I could have had friends about me; but friends ceased to matter. They could not tread that final path with me, and every visit and friendly call merely served to emphasise my final isolation.

"No man is an island," saith the poet, and oh, what a lie.

When I was a boy there was a song, a hymn I believe, which my mother used to sing to me. Some of the words are in my mind now. "Breathe through the heats of our desire thy coolness and thy balm. Let sense be dumb, let flesh retire, breathe through the earthquake, wind and fire." And so it goes on. Now I am not so far advanced in my dotage as to start chasing after a God I lost in my youth and never missed. That would be grievous indeed. But I do perceive that there is a virtue in humility which I have never understood. Coolness and balm. And now when I would like to be humble and simple I find a lifetime's activities and habits, all piled up and in the way. I have become so accustomed to spitting into the wind that I doubt if I can do anything else.

Which brings us to Pe-Ellia.

I am not particularly psychic myself but I feel that I am fated to be on Pe-Ellia.

I must be aware of the danger of romanticising. There is nothing heroic about nemesis, just as there is nothing beautiful about death. By rights we shouldn't even say a rose is beautiful or mountains or a sunset. Nature is.

They are.

That's all. Facts.

And to me, Pe-Ellia and Fate are linked and both are facts.

While on this theme let me mention another *fact*, and that is that I still don't know why we are here. Of course, on one level I'm here because they invited me and Pe-Ellians pay homage to the idea that old age and wisdom have some kind of connection. Then there is that complication introduced by Winter Wind when he talked about the "flower of our people". There is more to this than altruism or deference to old age. The Pe-Ellians have a purpose, or several, of that I'm sure. They *selected* me. If they'd wanted an enduring contact then they would have chosen a younger man. One of the young fellows from the Institute; someone with a crackling brain and a name to make. I could name half a dozen. But they wanted me.

I wish I'd stayed at home with my translations and "Roses and Bitterness".

There we have it. Yes, the great, magnificent *Seliica*. Let me tell the words. They will bring comfort.

Seliica Seliicta
Pen'hinnem ma rl Arcta
Rurara Rurecta
Penlin'na to so Marcta

Roses and bitterness,
Tributes to old age.
Sad is the journeyman
Moving to stiffness.
Mirror time. Dark time.
The face of the Youth
Is pale at the sight.

Now there's an epic, and what magnificent people. The Archadians. No wonder I love them, and swim back to them so often in my mind.

They believe that the sky is about to fall any minute and as a consequence are prepared always for any disaster. If they laugh they always say a short prayer afterwards—not that they seem to believe in prayers.

What can you make of a people who regard everything they have achieved as just a stage in a slow descent into meaninglessness? Entropy obsessed them but it did not seem to make them sad. Resigned rather. Having accepted the worst they had room for a wild humour which was anarchic and sacrilegious.

My, but they gave me a hard time. When was it? 2053. It is a story I have never told in its entirety.

There I was, thirty-eight, and sick of administration after fourteen years as head of the CLI. I was rarin' to go, as they used to say, and Orchid was my first solo. As usual I landed after the marines. The first thing that struck me was that these people, who had somehow managed to fail to domesticate the horse, did not fall down and worship Earth's magnificent technology. We have often been mistaken for gods; here we were taken as confirmation of fears long held. The Archadians gathered in small groups on the ash round the space ship's perimeter and stared at us silently.

I was taken to what they assured me was their best house—a rambling one-storey hut in which one of them had thoughtfully painted over all the old murals with a fresh coat of dark brown paint.

Well, I settled in and got to work. The language wasn't too hard and I was lucky that Steven Rollo who'd spent six months there in '49 had prepared such a full analysis. One of my first jobs was to gain the confidence of the locals. I contacted the regional headman, Badfar by name, and arranged a meeting.

The appointed time came and passed, and it was only when I went to the door to see if I could see him coming that I found him standing there. He had anointed himself with something like onion juice and began slapping the palm of one hand against the back of the other hand as soon as he saw me. (This gesture was the equivalent of what we might call pulling the forelock. Its meaning is literally "I will carry your burden for you.") Apparently it had never occurred to him to knock at the door to let me know that he had arrived.

With much hand slapping he entered my lodgings.

I suggested that he sit down, but he said he'd rather stand, thank you.

I offered him a drink, but he said he didn't drink, thank you.

This I knew was a downright lie as I had seen him reeling about the streets some three days earlier.

I began to feel, though I couldn't put a finger on it, that I was being made fun of. I decided to push ahead with business.

I asked if I could see some of their books and paintings, please.

No, very sorry, this wouldn't be possible, and besides they weren't worth seeing anyway, just a few moth-eaten old volumes and some daubings on a wall by an amateur.

Was there a library?

Yes, there used to be, but now it was used as a stable since the kind newcomers had shown how the horse could be made to pull a cart.

Did they have a museum?

There used to be, but now it was a cowshed.

"That's the way things are round here. Bad to worse. Shame you didn't come a few centuries ago, then we could have shown you a few of our odds and ends."

Not to be put off that easily I said I'd like to see their cows. This stopped him for a moment, and then he said the man who had the keys had gone away and couldn't be contacted.

Was there not a spare?

Sorry, but that had been lost years ago during the earthquake.

And so it went on.

On a later visit I again taxed him on the question of the museum and suggested that we could knock the door down. Badfar looked at me with a reproving stare and then lectured me for a full two hours on the value of wood and private property.

On another occasion, much to my shame, I offered Badfar gold if he would just let me look at one of the Archadian books for a couple of hours. Nothing doing. He was the headman and the headman had to be above reproach.

And so it went on.

But I knew all the time he was lying. There *was* a library *and* a museum or their equivalents and they were deliberately keeping me from them. I was repeatedly fobbed off with any excuse.

After several weeks of this treatment I was getting desperate. But I was also learning. I had learned, for instance, how to understand some of their unspoken language. I also overcame my shyness when a crowd of people would gather round me in the street and stare at me fixedly with their mouths hanging open like so many village idiots. This, of course, was a sign that they were concentrating. Badfar was best at this and perhaps this was why he was headman. One time I summoned him to my makeshift office and asked him directly what he would do if he were me and wanted to see the library. He stood open-mouthed, staring at me for a full three hours. I pretended to fall asleep so that I wouldn't have to keep looking at him. I knew that he wouldn't leave. Finally he cleared his throat, spat on the floor and said, "If I were you, I would stop asking questions. No good ever came of that."

That was the last straw.

I started to curse him. I let fly in fifteen tongues. I burned him as well as I could in his own dialect and was rewarded with a smile. Then I kicked him out.

I went to the window and shouted out into the street that I wanted Ditchwater and fast. This was their local rot-gut. The Ditch was the local name for the communal latrine.

A buxom young wench arrived at my door with a sack full of bottles of Ditchwater, courtesy of Mr Badfar. I spat on the floor when I heard his name, accepted the bottles and slammed the door.

That night I drank Ditchwater. It is the kind of drink which, if you get it past your taste buds, does cruel things to your stomach. Outside I could hear whispered conversations. Faces peered in at the window.

"Let them," I thought and drank on alone and stoic.

That I passed out is obvious. I woke up in bed, mother-naked and feeling as if I had been trampled on by a horse. Surprisingly my head was clear, and I had a brilliant idea. I wanted to get into the library, yes? All right, I'd show them.

I rummaged through my books and found an old Bible, one that had lots of illustrations. I threw on a cape and a pair of the voluminous bloomers that pass for dignified apparel on Orchid and set out for the house of Badfar the headman.

I was still pretty drunk and my legs carried me crabwise half the time. As luck would have it, Badfar's house was at the bottom of Stand Up Lane, next door to the city Ditch.

I mistook the door.

Even as I fell in I remembered to keep my mouth closed.

Badfar opened his door with a taper in his hand. I stood there soggy and slackmouthed, nodding at him and holding the Bible, which luckily I had never released. I must have smelled worse than him, for he motioned me to stay where I was and then went and fetched a bucket of sandalwater and threw it over me. Then he gave me dry bloomers and cape and motioned me inside.

We sat down at his table and he looked at me. Not questioning, you understand, just looking. Waiting for what would happen next.

I thumped the Bible down on the table and began leafing through the pages. Finally I found the picture I wanted. It was Christ on the cross and one of the most gruesome images I have ever seen.

He looked at it closely in the light of the taper. Slowly his eyes grew wide. He stared at the thin spreadeagled body. At the blood dribbling from the palms, so carefully painted by the artist. At the watery feminine eyes. At the crown of thorns, which the painter had drawn with such care that you could see the way the flesh puckered where the thorns bit deep.

Finally he looked up at me and frowned. He broke the vow of a lifetime and asked a question.

"What?"

"A god we worship," I answered.

He became excited then. The first time I'd ever seen anything except the sturdy, passive, stone-wall face he presented on all occasions when he visited me.

He went to the door and called outside.

"Come and see."

Next he went through to the back room and I heard two thumps as he kicked his wives out of bed.

People came crowding in from all quarters and soon the room was packed. From somewhere a couple of bottles of Ditchwater appeared and were handed round roughly from mouth to mouth.

They stared at the picture and touched it and talked to one another excitedly and laughed. That was the strangest thing of all. The way they laughed. You would have thought that poor picture of Christ was a cartoon cut from a paper.

Most of what they said I could not understand. They spoke a quick vulgar language, which no-one had thought to tell me about. But I understood the sense. They were pleased. They were flattered. They were honoured that I should show them something like this. They reasoned: anyone who can worship such an image of suffering, anyone who can spend so much time and energy painting all the ligaments of pain, must really understand what life is all about.

I didn't realise it at the time, but they assumed that I was somehow responsible for this picture.

Someone started singing. The song was in the language I knew and had a popular refrain in which everyone joined. This song I never got round to translating, but its theme was similar to the story of Jonah and the whale.

The party broke up. People drifted off home. Before I left I ripped the picture out of the Bible and pinned it up in Badfar's house.

The last I saw of him that night he was standing in front of the picture with his arm curled round one of his wives and was bawling out the refrain of the song.

Next morning a delegation arrived at my hut and they handed me a key. They'd found it, they said, after searching high and low. If I wanted to glance at some of their rubbish in the library, I'd be welcome.

I would. I did. I loved it.

And in that way I came to discover a pearl of peerless price. The *Seliica.*

Why have I written all this? Well, it remains a fact that for me just to have known these people of Orchid remains a source of strength. To write about them in this way (and I have never before divulged the exact details of my meetings with them) gives me strength and makes me less alone. I know that if I were on their planet now I could talk to them and they would listen. They would not smile, nor would they offer any help. They would walk with me.

But I am not with them. I am alone and my problems have no corporate solution.

Post scriptum. Shortly after writing the above I fell asleep. Indeed I have been asleep for hours.

Just as on Orchid I have woken with an idea of what I should do, must do, tomorrow.

For the moment I want to add a note concerning a dream that is still with me. The first part concerns Orchid and the second Pe-Ellia.

When it came time for me to leave Orchid I had already completed my translation of the first part of the *Seliica.* I wanted to give my friends a present, something they might appreciate. I translated into their common tongue parts of the *Rubaiyat* of Omar Khayyam. It was a great success, for although they did not have equivalents for all the words, they understood the idea and adapted words from the Old Persian into their language.

As I was packing my bags to leave a small delegation came out to my hut. They brought with them a present in a box. It was a book. The covers were beautifully worked and the craftsmanship was exquisite. Formerly I had been led to believe that this was another art that had died out centuries before.

Anyway, time was late and I did not have time to open the book, only to admire it as a work of art. This obviously pleased them. In retropect I should have been suspicious. The book was closed with a Callis Hasp. (A puzzle lock. Some of the puzzles have no solution and this is a source of Archadian humour.) At all events I put the book in my bags and hurried down to the perimeter where the military were cooling their heels waiting for me. I had already delayed the departure for over a month.

We were soon in space preparing to jump back to Camellia, where I had a meeting with the Space Council. I hurriedly unpacked the book and quickly solved the lock.

I opened the book. The pages were made of the finest cream archol paper *but there was not a word printed on them.* The book was a total blank. Here is where my Pe-Ellian dream begins.

In my dream I showed this book to Winter Wind and to Menopause. Winter Wind scrutinised it and seemed to read the blank pages. Menopause took the book and placed his hand on the opening sheet and then traced round it. He did not say a word.

Then he handed the book back to me. Then his mouth fell open in a way that was so characteristic of the Archadian gesture that I found myself laughing.

That vision of his finely etched face and the sharp high cheek bones with the slack, gaping mouth beneath was with me when I woke up. What the dream means, if indeed it means anything, I do not know.

Time will tell. But at least I feel clearer now. I am astride the stallion and although I do not know where this headlong journey is leading me, nevertheless I feel more secure.

Commentary

Our first full day on Pe-Ellia began late. I was woken by an insistent tapping sound coming from outside my window. I climbed out of bed and drew back the curtains and found myself staring into the face of a brilliantly-plumed yellow bird. I don't know who was more startled, the bird or me. At all events the bird jumped back, its quills rising in astonishment, and then it turned and ran with a humpy movement into the jungle.

My window faced directly on to the jungle and was a splendid vantage point from which to observe the natural comings and goings of jungle life. My room, the highest point in the house, was reached by climbing a sequence of shallow steps leading directly off from the Palm Court. From this room I had a clear view of how parts of the house were fused directly with the vegetation. A tree trunk grew out of the wall and was itself an extension of the wall. The bark and the wall were effectively the same material, though different in colour. Where the wall of the house joined the ground there was no seam. I was at a loss to explain this. It seemed that the house, which was obviously an artefact, was also a completely natural part of the tree. I could only conclude that the Pe-Ellians were masters of biological engineering and could command trees to bear this strange fruit.

My study of the construction of the house was interrupted by the arrival of Thorndyke, who said there were cornflakes and coffee waiting downstairs if I was feeling like breakfast. I was.

Over breakfast we discussed what had happend the previous day and I told Thorndyke of the message that Cook had given me the previous night. Thorndyke seemed delighted. He said he'd been poking about outside for a while and had wondered why he'd not met anyone. Just as we finished eating Cook arrived, entering down from the clearing.

"Sleep well, boys?" he asked. I said I'd slept like a top.

Cook threw up his eyes in horror at the idea. Thorndyke did not mention his bed.

"Okay, boys," said Cook, beginning to gather up the breakfast dishes. "Here's how we do things round here. Us Pe-Ellians normally only tuck in once a day. That's half an hour before the sun closes and then that meal can go on as long as there are things to talk about. During the day we hardly ever speak to one another, unless we're busting. For you, of course, an exception we make. You eat whenever you like. Just come to the cookhouse and holler 'Food'. When you get hungry I'll always be somewhere about. But if you can't find me just finger one of those."

He pointed at one of the panels.

"Someone'll arrive. For you we allow conversation any time."

"Thank you," said Thorndyke.

"But I better warn you boys, here on Pe-Ellia the granting of conversation is an honour. Okay? Course, with me you can talk anytime. I don't count for much. I don't know much and I'm on my way down anyway, so it doesn't matter much to me anyhow."

He said this quite matter of factly.

"The real hombres you gotta get into is Jet and Winter Wind."

"What are you reading at present?" asked Thorndyke suddenly.

Cook stopped, obviously surprised. His eyes closed to slits and then blinked several times. He raised his hands in front of his chest and the gesture had something insect-like about it. He said nothing for a few moments and then dropped his hands.

"There you go," he said. "If you'd spoken to Winter Wind like that he'd 'a clammed right up. Me, I'm different."

"Sorry, I'll remember that," murmured Thorndyke.

"What makes you think I'm reading anything?"

"Just a guess," said Thorndyke. "I reckoned that none of you Pe-Ellians would learn only spoken English."

Cook looked at him for a few more seconds.

"Well, you're right, anyway. I got a copy of *Incident at Stone Water Creek* by Tex Abalone. Do you know it? Is it a good book?"

"Are you enjoying it?" asked Thorndyke.

"Yes," (*with relish*) "but there is much I don't understand."

"Then it's probably a good book. I haven't read it myself, but perhaps Tomas has. He's a cowboy and Indian fan."

This, of course, was a complete fabrication and I was somewhat nonplussed when Cook turned to me with obvious delight and said, "Hey buddy, drop you faster'n you can draw breath." Two of his slim fingers were pointed straight at my throat.

Never having read one of that genre of books in my life I was at a loss as to how to respond. The only thing that came to mind was "Whoa Silver". It seemed to satisfy him.

Cook was happy. He scooped up the remaining dishes into his hands and departed for the kitchen. We could hear him singing. After a few moments he came back into the room. He was wearing his long apron again.

"One thing is strange though," he said. "Them cowboys, they talk kinder to their horses than to one another. So long." With that he left, heading up for the clearing.

"If I am not much mistaken," said Thorndyke, "friend Cook is going to be a source of great joy to us."

I nodded.

"Well, here's my programme for today," said Thorndyke, standing up. "I propose to be alone. There are lots of things I want to get straightened out. Only interrupt me if something exceptional happens. If Winter Wind drops by, tell him I'm busy observing silence." He winked and departed for his room.

I decided to spend the day exploring. I took the encoder with me and attempted some primary classification of the flora of the region.

One fact emerged very quickly. In the immediate vicinity of the house there was a relatively restricted range of plants. Within four square metres I counted only five varieties. Statistically this was far less than I had expected, given the obvious fertility of the soil and the dense growth we had seen on our journey to the house.

This first survey, which I conducted a few metres from the house, took all morning. I did not collect any plants but enjoyed myself making sketches—a private hobby—and taking photographs with the encoder.

Over lunch I asked Cook to give me the names of the plants in Pe-Ellian, which he did. Thorndyke did not appear for lunch and Cook never asked about him.

Lunch consisted of some very white cake, which Cook insisted on calling bread, and a crumbly greenish confection, which he described to me as cheese. All this was washed down with a cordial, which to my mouth had a taste not too far removed from peppermint. During the meal Cook was particularly anxious to discover whether the food was "Earthly". I said no, but that breakfast had been. This seemed to dash his high spirits a bit and he confided that the breakfast things had been brought from Earth along with other supplies (his cowboy book for example), but that this bread and cheese was his first attempt at synthesising our type of food. He promised to keep trying.

"Trouble is, see, Tomas, all the flavours you enjoy are inert," he said. I was not to know what he meant until some three days later when we had a Pe-Ellian meal.

During the afternoon I continued my survey and moved away from the house in a straight line. I decided to analyse another four-square-metre patch at twenty-five metres' distance. I also drew up a sketch map. Some twenty metres from the house I made a discovery: a narrow trench some four centimetres deep and thirty centimetres wide in which nothing grew. If you had taken a razor blade and cut the line of the earth you could not have made a cleaner break.

Plants grew right up to the edge of the shallow ditch and then stopped. One difference was immediately apparent. Beyond the ditch, beyond the perimeter, the variety of species was far greater. Within a space of less than one square metre I counted at least twenty-five. However, it was the trench that interested me most. I began to follow it.

This was quite difficult, for at times it passed through dense clumps of jungle where vines and creeper were woven together as though in a tapestry. I noticed that though nothing grew in the trench itself, nothing stopped the foliage traversing its boundary above. The average height at which the first leaves and creepers crossed the trench was about one metre. After following it for about ten minutes I came in sight of the house and realised that the ditch followed an arc. My distance from the house had remained constant.

Next I crossed the path that we had followed the previous day. The trench was clearly visible and I decided that being so interested in the house and clearing, both of which were now clearly visible, I had failed to observe this small depression. Beyond the path the ditch continued and disappeared into the foliage. I presume it continued across the river bed, although I could not see that.

I retraced my steps carefully and began to follow the other arc. This led me up a rocky hill. In fact it was less a hill and more a pile of boulders. I could not see how far these continued on account of the jungle canopy. *The trench cut through solid rock*. Its depth had increased here to almost ten centimetres.

I climbed up the rocks and again heard running water. I found myself high above the river looking down on the waterfall. I could see the roofs of the house clearly and pick out the place where Thorndyke's rooms would be.

I could see nothing which suggested the existence of his roof/window. Looking away from the house, the river flowed swiftly, emerging from a dark tunnel in the jungle. Across the bank on the other side I could just see where the trench continued.

My vantage point, perched on a rock above the river, gave me an overview. I was able to detect a slightly different shading to the colours. I noticed that the green of the vegetation inside the perimeter was slightly darker than that outside. The rocks were also of a deeper colour within the perimeter.

With everything safely recorded in the encoder I returned to the house. All was quiet.

The table was set.

"Dinner is served," announced Cook, resplendent in apron and white chef's hat.

"Howdy," I said, remembering the word from a film I had once seen.

"Howdy," he replied. "After my miserable achievements at lunchtime I have been practising. We have seven courses. Graded by colour and texture. I have read one of your cookbooks and it says colour and texture are important. Am I right, buddy?"

"Well, taste plays a part too," I answered somewhat guardedly, for I felt rather bad about how he had taken my comments at midday.

"Didn't say nuttin' about taste," he answered. "I just kinda figured that if you got the other two right then the taste'd just come along natural like a mare on heat following the stallion."

He paused and was clearly waiting to see what I thought of his choice of simile.

"That's a graphic way of putting it," I said.

"Bang bang," he replied, delighted. "Will Professor Thorndyke be joining us?"

"I don't know. If he doesn't come, don't worry. He often doesn't eat when he's working and he doesn't like to be disturbed."

"He is a thoughtful man," said Cook and curtseyed. He sat down on one of the large chairs facing me and watched me eat. It was a friendly scrutiny.

The meal, as regards taste, was a pleasant experience and Cook had obviously worked hard to discover the kinds of things that human beings liked. The colours ranged from dark green, a hard chewy kind of cake, to a brown soup. The meal was finished with black coffee which he confessed had been imported.

The only disturbing part of the meal was the arrival of Menopause. He entered when I was into my second course, a pale green omelette, and sat down next to me at the table. The "scar" lines on his body seemed more vivid than they had on the previous day.

I could not be certain, but he seemed antagonistic to me. After all these months and the events that have intervened, I am still convinced he was trying to make me feel unwelcome, though not in a deliberate way. He was responding to forces beyond his control. At that time I put his behaviour down to differences between alien and human. As a contact linguist I coped with it. Even so, I noted that in comparison with Cook or Winter Wind he was gross to the point of insult.

He sat down and "growled". It was a sound halfway between someone clearing their throat before spitting and a simple animal growl. He took pieces of food from my plate and tasted them and then put them back. He dabbled his fingers in the soup.

Cook, I was amazed to observe, seemed oblivious to all this, and continued chattering as if nothing was happening.

When he was not fiddling with the food Menopause stared at me, observing my every movement and at times imitating me.

Shortly before the meal was finished he stood up from the table and shouted a word I did not understand. I sounded like "ktsa" and upon hearing it Cook immediately stood up and went into the kitchen. He returned after a few moments with a bowl covered with a cloth and gave it to Menopause. Menopause then growled at him and at me, drawing back his lips from his black gums.

I admit he frightened me. In retrospect it seems obvious that even at this early date Menopause had made some sort of decision which excluded me, and therefore saw me as some kind of competitor for Thorndyke's attention. Certainly Menopause was trying to unsettle me and make me feel an outsider.

After he had gone I could hardly concentrate on the meal. I found I was grateful for the idle chatter of Cook, who acted as though Menopause had never been present. After the meal I went to Thorndyke's room, but he was busy writing. In my own room I went through my notes on the day's activities and pondered on the strange perimeter. I believe the air on Pe-Ellia must be soporific for humans, as I felt a great drowsiness. I was barely able to finish my notes before I climbed into bed and fell asleep.

I have provided these details of our first full day on Pe-Ellia since that day is nowhere mentioned in Thorndyke's writings. He may well have written the section in his diary describing the house and made the notes for the poem on Menopause during that day. His diary entries begin again on our second full day on Pe-Ellia.

Thorndyke's Diary: Entry 12

I woke with the dawn and the dawn made me feel clean. A pale salmon light was pouring in through the walls. I thought at first I was floating. My body felt as comfortable as water floating on water. I can hardly remember ever sleeping so well.

On my desk was a sheaf of papers so I judge yesterday was creative. It passed in a blur. There is something strange in the air here. It makes me want to get things off my chest, to discover things I wanted to say, but never knew I wanted to say. I think I will leave the regular recording to Tomas. . . .

Anyway, as I say, I woke with dawn. I watched the bed closely but it did not make a move.

They have gone to a lot of trouble to recreate my toilet. It is identical to the one in Paris. Even the thump as the cistern fills is the same.

Faeces.

I watched the flush do a thoroughly good job (that's not like Paris) and wondered just how they were getting rid of my waste products. Surely not just atomising them, or whatever it was they did on the spaceship. They probably sent them off to a forensic lab.

Talking of faeces reminds me of my old friend Jerome Wilkinson, who spent his whole working life in a lab that specialised in the analysis of extra-terrestial turds. He pursued his speciality with the creative curiosity of the true scientist.

One thing is certain. These Pe-Ellians don't just flush the whole mess out into the rivers and seas. We still do in some parts of the world and that no doubt strikes them as crude. We are bulls in china shops, no less. We have a bad pedigree to say the least. Our science is primitive and dangerous. Why do they bother with us? They could sanitise us.

Have decided to let my beard grow. The face that stared at me from the bathroom mirror this morning surprised me with its familiarity. I don't know why, but I had expected something different. Perhaps to look younger.

I had just finished ablutions when a surprising event occurred. I decided to look out in the clearing. The walls disappeared when I touched the button and there, standing under the waterfall, letting it cascade all over him, was Menopause. He was facing my room, but obviously could not see in here. A concession to privacy. I walked over to the wall and he was only an arm's length away from me.

He is definitely losing his skin. There are pouches under his arms where the skin is loose, and I could see the way the water pushed the skin about. He seemed to glow more brightly, as though the water were massaging his inner fires.

Out in the clearing something moved. I saw the tall figure of

Winter Wind emerge from the jungle and approach the bank.

With a speed that amazed me, considering that Menopause has always seemed to move slowly, he leaped up the rocks which formed the waterfall (and I suppose the outside of my room), and scampered half-swimming and half-crawling across the ceiling and out of sight. From his haste I judge that Menopause didn't want to be seen, or perhaps for these people ablutions are private.

Winter Wind certainly didn't seem to see anything, though of course that could be Pe-Ellian tact.

Tact.

I have determined to try an experiment. Outside the glade is warming up. The sun is touching the treetops and the sky has lost its pearly colour and is moving towards bluish-green. Professor Winter Wind looks very content. He's produced a jug of juice and is sitting on the side of the bank and, for all I know, humming to himself.

Being old before I am wise I will try a prank that would have delighted me in my youth. I shall wander out stark mother naked, quite calmly, early morning constitutional type of walk, and sit down beside him. Before I do, however, let me note that Winter Wind, for all talk of age, looks fine and lithe. He's hunched forward at present, gazing into the river with his gold-flecked eyes. A fish has just jumped and Winter Wind has rolled on to his back and is waggling his hands to his ears, obviously deeply amused. The absence of an anus is disturbing. His bottom is merely a sit-upon.

The mirror has almost undone me. I am all flab and pouch. My genitals look like an afterthought, my legs are yellow and veiny, feet calloused and horny, arms thin. Only my chest remains broad with still a hint of muscles. *Sic transit gloria mundi.*

Commentary

Marius Thorndyke was in vigorous health. He was not overweight and kept himself fit by playing tennis and swimming. It is interesting that he here makes no reference to his full head of hair, which he always wore long in the fashion of his middle years and which, skin markings and height apart, distinguished him from Winter Wind, who was of course completely bald.

Thorndyke's Diary: Entry 13

A digression on nudity.

The only naked thing I have seen for many years is my own face. In which case familiarity has bred not contempt, but tolerance. Thus the experience of wandering naked through this apartment and outside is completely new.

Nudity is a pile of crumpled clothes
Nudity is cold lino, fur between the toes
Nudity is one's own smell and strange breezes
Nudity is palpable as a naked thigh, contours, plains and passages
Nudity leaves much to be desired
Nudity is sitting down on a hairbrush
Nudity is to be vulnerable to drawing pins, sharp corners and eyes.

Commentary

The diary is disjointed at this point. Clearly the events described greatly disturbed Thorndyke. He adopts the objective style for the next entry.

Thorndyke's Diary: Entry 14

Before Thorndyke could lose his nerve he crossed to the door and headed down the passage to the front door. To be walking naked felt strange. Vulnerable. Slightly foolish. He was aware of small currents of air that played across his back and buttocks.

The Palm Court was in near darkness.

Without pausing Thorndyke pressed on outside. The iris door opened with a snap and the warm vegetable air engulfed him. It was like—

Thorndyke considered for a moment. It was like being dried with feathers.

Winter Wind was waiting for him. He was still sitting with his feet in the river, but had poured a glass of juice and held this out to Thorndyke as he emerged from the passage.

"Welcome sun come," said Winter Wind, speaking Pe-Ellian slowly and distinctly. He smiled.

"May it warm your skin," answered Thorndyke without a moment's hesitation. He knew this was a safe reply. Winter Wind had taught it to him on the trek through the jungle. The words were easy and rhythmical and would fit easily into a popular song if ever Thorndyke returned to Earth.

"Your accent is remarkable," stated Winter Wind, returning to English. "I look forward to teaching you Pe-Ellian."

"When shall we start?"

"No rush. Get weathered first."

Thorndyke took the glass that was offered to him and sat down on the bank.

"To clarity," said the giant Pe-Ellian, raising his glass.

"To friendship," smiled Thorndyke.

He could feel the Pe-Ellian relax. It was a calm harmony; a drifting with the morning and the sun, a linking with the easy rhythm of the wind in the trees.

Thorndyke dipped his feet in the river. The Pe-Ellian didn't seem to notice that he was not wearing any clothes. Thorndyke did not feel embarrassed.

"From the rising of the sun unto the going down of the same," he murmured to himself and let the surging water glance and butt against the balls of his feet as though he was standing on the river.

"You like doing that?" asked Winter Wind with interest. "It is one of our pastimes also. We have a special name for it. We call it 'Touching the Present'."

"What does that mean?" asked Thorndyke.

"You'll find out," answered Winter Wind, and stretched.

Thorndyke contemplated his feet and wondered about a society which built philosophy out of dipping one's toes in a stream. But what a horrifyingly static society this could be, he thought, in which every action is embalmed with meaning and tradition.

Thorndyke contemplated his feet. He realised it was years since he had looked at his feet. Really looked. They were bony and yellow, with thick toenails like chips of sea-shell and a white chalky substance gathered under the nail. Even in the bath he'd always washed his feet with the minimum of interest. And now there they were. Strangers. Smiling up at him from the tumbling water.

"Have a swim, why don't you?" said Winter Wind.

"Are there sharks?" asked Thorndyke.

Winter Wind sat up and looked serious.

"I thought sharks only lived in the sea."

"They do. They do. Just a figure of speech."

"There are no dangerous fish, if that's what you mean, at least not this far up the river. In any case this area is protected. But even if there were sharks they would be more afraid of you than you of them. That is the way on this planet."

Thorndyke digested this and then smiled.

"You've convinced me," he said. "Here goes nothing." He put his weight on his hands and leaned forwards until he overbalanced and fell with a splash into the river.

Down he went. The water sang in his ears. He was surprised that he didn't touch the bottom. Turning and looking up he saw the streaming silver surface. One pull of his arms and he drifted up to the surface and blew out air lustily. He saw that he had drifted downstream a few metres and was almost at the edge of the clearing, where the river disappeared into a tunnel in the jungle. He struck out for the side.

On the river bank was a tree which thrust its roots deep into the stream. Thorndyke seized one of the roots and felt it slimy but strong. He held on and let his body trail out and felt the gentle massage of the stream.

The sun, which had by now climbed higher into the sky, cast its beams deeper into the clearing and touched the oblique roofs of the cottage.

"Gonna be a scorching," called Winter Wind. "Come and drink some more, and I've got bread too. We can eat and have a talk."

"Okay," answered Thorndyke, and began pulling himself upstream using the roots and grasses beside the bank. He reached the place where he had tumbled in and Winter Wind reached down his strong mottled arm and helped him out.

Thorndyke flopped down out of the river. He remembered the graceful way Jet had lifted himself out. Winter Wind beamed down at him.

"Do you feel more comfortable without your second skin?"

Thorndyke blinked, at a loss for a moment.

"My second—oh, my clothes. No, no I feel fine. Splendid, in fact."

"When you wear clothes, is it to help you hide that?" The Pe-Ellian pointed at Thorndyke's genitals. "Or to keep it warm? It looks very exposed."

"Both, I suppose."

"Is it cold now?"

"A bit, but it is rather nice too. Clean feeling."

The Pe-Ellian studied Thorndyke's genitals and then looked at the smooth skin where his own body forked. Without any warning he reached out and took hold of Thorndyke's penis in his hand and held it firmly. He rolled it in his fingers.

"Not too cold." He let it go.

Thorndyke, who had clasped his hands involuntarily when the large Pe-Ellian took hold of him, relaxed consciously.

One, two, buckle my shoe,
Three, four, knock at the door,
Five, six, carrying sticks.

It is not the first time something like this has happened. I remember Tiger Lily, and the way the natives there conducted a physical examination. Fingering every orifice. Cooing at goose pimples, shredding dignity. After Tiger Lily I thought I would never be able to look myself in the face again . . . still less let another person touch me. But I overcame that.

Thorndyke relaxed.

He thought he detected a slight touch of humour in Winter Wind's steady gaze.

"That kind of thing . . . er, taking someone's . . . er, penis in hand . . . uninvited, as it were. Well, on our planet it's not done."

"Sorry," said Winter Wind.

The bastard *was* amused. God damn him.

"It's rude. I mean, I'm a bit old to care really, but I just ought to warn you."

Winter Wind stared at the water. His eyes were slits of concentration.

"Why did you come out here without any clothes on? You seemed to be inviting . . . interest. I thought I was complying."

It was Thorndyke's turn to stare at the water.

"I don't know," he answered finally. "I suppose you looked so comfortable, and I didn't think you'd mind or be embarrassed and I wanted to see what your reaction would be, and I thought it might be a gesture of friendliness on my behalf."

Winter Wind thought about this. He broke off and ate a piece of bread, chewing vigorously. Finally, with mouth still partly full, he said: "I don't mind, and naturally I'm not embarrassed, and I appreciate the gesture, but if you would be more comfortable in clothes, then please do not feel any constraint to act like us. That would be as futile as it is impossible."

"I'm quite comfortable as I am," answered Thorndyke, looking at his feet. "I was just letting you know that, in general, Earth people don't like other people messing about with them . . . not without an invitation, that is."

Winter Wind nodded. He took more bread and sipped some juice.

"When will I be invited?" he asked.

Thorndyke isolated his personal reactions and turned them to ash. He concentrated on the pure linguistic exchange and its significance.

"You will not be invited. You can never be."

"Ah, because I am not a man?"

"No."

"Because I am not a woman?"

"No."

"Because I am an alien?"

"Well, no."

"Ah, because it is secret, private?"

"Yes."

Winter Wind relaxed back.

"Then I respect that. But for us, you know, there is really no such thing as physical privacy. We have no sex, or what you would call sex. For us privacy is important, but it is privacy of the . . . self, of that which is inner, that which grows with you as you grow older and wiser, as you pass from change to change."

He paused and pulled his knees up to his chin.

"If I understand you correctly, for you privacy is physical as well as mental. It is tied up with your sex drives. When I touched your sex organ, I became involved with your privacy in the way that a loved or invited one might. You thought I was inviting you to . . . that I wanted you to. . . ."

Winter Wind became confused in his thought. He was trying to grapple with a problem, the nature of which he could not comprehend. He stared at Thorndyke and a pale flush began to suffuse through his skin. Incredulous, he asked: "Could you think that I wanted to love—I, who all that makes a man, lack, and woman too?"

Thorndyke sat still in acute stony embarrassment.

"I didn't think anything," he said gruffly. "I was caught by surprise, that's all."

Pause.

Suddenly Winter Wind rolled on his back and waved his hands beside his head. He uttered what could have been a prayer or an oath in the Pe-Ellian language and then somersaulted forwards and dived straight into the stream. When he broke surface he was laughing. This was the first time that Thorndyke had really seen Winter Wind laugh.

Winter Wind's whole body shook and the creamy parts of his skin turned pink. His mouth was open and a whinnying sound emerged. He beat the water with his hands, reminding Thorndyke of a seal begging for fish.

When his laughter subsided Winter Wind paddled in a circle and then pulled himself up on to the bank.

"That's better," he said. "We old ones should remember our dignity." Then he exploded into laughter again.

"Come, come," he said. "Let me not think you prudish. Even you must consider the spectacle of you making love to me as comic."

Thorndyke did not feel like laughing. He was disturbed by the alien laughter and felt relief when Cook emerged into the clearing carrying more bread and juice.

"Come and get it," called Cook.

"Come, eat," said Winter Wind expansively, "and while you are eating you must tell me more about your sex life."

I remember most clearly the events of that second morning on Pe-Ellia. I slept late and like Thorndyke woke up feeling very refreshed. After washing I went to see if Thorndyke was in his room as I was anxious to tell him about my discovery of the strange depression which ran round our house. He was not in his room. His wall, however, was translucent and I could make out some figures in the clearing. I could see that Thorndyke was naked!

"I've gone native," said Thorndyke as I emerged into the clearing. I could tell that he was deeply embarrassed. "Why don't you follow suit?"

Even this attempt at humour was strained. I declined but accepted a glass of the fruit juice. It tasted somewhere between mint and aniseed. Winter Wind watched us carefully. Finally he said: "Professor Thorndyke and I have had an interchanging of intimacies. He has given me much to think about. Let us spend the afternoon in rest. Perhaps this evening we can talk some more."

He stood up, said something in Pe-Ellian to Cook, and with a polite bow left us.

Cook began clearing the dishes.

"Banquet tonight, boys," he said.

Thorndyke told me what had happened with Winter Wind. He told me in true contact linguist manner – cool, sequential and purely factual. I was impressed with his gravity, but did not regard the event as highly significant. I too compared what had happened to Thorndyke with the physical examination on Tiger Lily and there can be few experiences more prolonged or embarrassing than that. Contact linguists became accustomed to having their bodies investigated and their sexual practices discussed in detail. I told Thorndyke that he was making a mountain out of a molehill and that the Pe-Ellians were showing themselves to be no different in kind from any other species we had investigated. I suggested that we could even take comfort from this fact, as it established a point of linkage between this Pe-Ellian contact and other contacts with which we were more familiar.

Thorndyke seemed mollified and we passed to other topics. I told him about my discovery of the perimeter ditch and neither of us could fathom what it might mean. We decided to wait a few days, until we had seen more of this planet, before bringing the matter up.

Our discussion was friendly and close. Gradually, though, I became aware that Thorndyke was only giving me part of his attention. I suggested that he might be more comfortable if he were to go in and get changed. He departed with obvious relief. I did not see him again until much later in the day.

I believe the following notes were written by him shortly after he had returned to his room. In any event, they certainly refer to the breach that occurred with Winter Wind during the late afternoon.

THORNDYKE'S DIARY: ENTRY 15

Coolness and balm!

The contact linguist's training helps, but it is not enough. I would like to break something. I devised the code, most of it anyway, but the truth is "Do as I say, not as I do".

The heart of my problem is very simple. Invasion of privacy. Last night I felt as though my brain were being pecked over. Today it has been my body.

Tomas is right. Tiger Lily was physically worse. I know that. But there the investigation was accompanied with oohs and aahs. Juices were greeted with nods and winks of recognition. I was not a thing on a plate. I was a living being, complex and warm. Even the fish knows passion in mating.

It is the clinical, the rubber gloves and forceps attitude that angers me.

No, I am wrong again. It is the laughter.

It is both.

Winter Wind knows passion only by proxy. "Please do not feel any constraint to act like us. That would be as futile as it is impossible." How true.

Was he mocking me? Was it my embarrassment that amused him? Does this seamless creature take pleasure in seeing us curling on the end of his tongs? I am going too far. But in my privacy I can afford to.

Privacy, that is the beginning and end of the matter. I am offended by him.

I too want to protect the privacy of my inner self. It is not because I am older and certainly not because I am wiser; it is a matter of dignity and Winter Wind should realise that.

I must find the answer to some questions. The frontal approach is best. No jiggery-pokery by innuendo. Straight out. This planet feels mentally alive to me. I think I am being tapped. I remember that incident when we first arrived, and there was wine and I thought of urine. Remember the bed.

Why we are here we do not know. Is it to be slowly milked of our emotions? Are we their pornography, to be read like a book?

Mottled sexless aliens reading cowboy books! What the hell do they think we are?

I have turned "on" my room, and I find the roar and lather of the waterfall match my mood. I observe that Winter Wind, Jet and the thing they call Menopause are taking their ease in the garden. Now is the time. Catch them when they are least expecting it. Accuse and let the truth come from their defence. I shall prepare my arguments.

COMMENTARY

Thorndyke came to me in the Palm Court while I was relaxing, watching the river life through the ceiling. He had the light of battle in his eye.

"They're up there in the clearing. Let's go and get some answers."

I was unaware of the cause of his anger or of his plans. I picked up the encoder and followed. We entered the clearing at something approaching a run, and must have appeared to bob up suddenly over the ramp.

The initial reaction of the Pe-Ellians was extraordinary. Menopause, who had been crouched by the table, uncoiled like a spring and leaped up into the tree where we had first seen him. He glowed a vivid red amidst the dark green leaves and spat at us as he leaped back and forth from branch to branch.

Jet, who had been lying back, sat up and then stood and stepped back a few paces. Winter Wind remained seated, though there was none of the languid relaxation I had observed in him on other occasions.

A transcript of the confrontation follows:

THORNDYKE: I'm glad to see—

WINTER WIND: Now is not fit—

THORNDYKE: —to see that you were expecting me. I have certain questions—

WINTER WIND: I repeat that the time is not fit. Tonight over food. Hair down with liberty to allude confident with confidence—

THORNDYKE: *Now!*

(Thorndyke said this with almost a shout. Before the echoes had died Winter Wind sang something in Pe-Ellian. We did not understand what he said at the time, though we later came to understand that he was calling for a Mantissa. As he sang Jet dropped to all fours and Menopause started jumping up and down in the tree. The two faced one another. Thorndyke, head pushed forwards, legs apart, hands loose. Winter Wind, suddenly more alien, eyes reduced to yellow slits, his hands raised limply before him like a praying mantis. His skin had turned ashen.)

THORNDYKE: Are we bugged?

(Winter Wind made no reply.)

Don't play the innocent. Are we overheard, listened in to, secretly watched? Minds explored? Thoughts read? Privacy invaded? If so, I demand that we be told, and that we be informed of why we are present. And further I—

(At this point Thorndyke's voice trailed away. He stood still, staring at Winter Wind, who for his part did not blink. Only his hands moved. They opened like claws and flexed as though powered by a giant pulse. Suddenly he stood up and rested both his hands on the table. He towered over Thorndyke, holding his head just a few inches away from Thorndyke's face. Winter Wind spoke, but it was not his voice that I heard. Normally Winter Wind's voice was evenly pitched and slightly nasal. This voice was soft and deep

and distant, and unsettling. Yet I saw Winter Wind's lips move, and there is no doubt that the sounds came from him, even though they were not of him.)

WINTER WIND: I will say this once and there's an end. Neither now, nor in the future, will your privacy ever be . . . tai koi rai. . . . Breached. Broken. Seduced. . . . You have no adequate word in your language for your own suggestion. Your minds run wild like mountain streams; they bleed without reason. We strain to ignore. We train ourselves to be ignorant, but it is not easy. I give you sober warning. . . . Save your thoughts for yourself. Do not accuse us. Do not think we are remotely like you. Remotely.

For what you have said I could command your self death. Perhaps later, over food, we may approach this question. *End.*

(Winter Wind straightened up and raised his hands high above his head. I thought for a moment he was going to strike Thorndyke. Then he relaxed, turned and walked out of the clearing. Jet, who had knelt silent during this speech, stood up wearily like an old man. He also was grey, as if with fatigue. He crossed to where Thorndyke stood like a statue and spoke in a gentle tone.)

JET: Perhaps we will meet again. My presence was more by way of courtesy, you understand. I regard that obligation as dissolved.

He turned, and with a short run dived into the river. I never saw his head emerge. I was about to cross to Thorndyke—who I thought must have been hypnotised, for he had not so much as blinked since Winter Wind started speaking—when I heard a rattling above me. Menopause dropped into the clearing. He turned to me and bared his fangs and then crossed to Thorndyke.

If he had wanted to hurt Thorndyke I doubt I could have stopped him, but I had the feeling that he meant Thorndyke no harm. He stopped in front of him, peered down into his eyes, and then started to lick his face. At the same time he crooned high and then falling notes, a kind of keening, but not a cruel sound. Slowly, I saw Thorndyke relax. He started to totter and Menopause caught him and lowered him into a chair.

Next he turned and looked at me. He seemed to be fighting with something in his mouth, his throat convulsed.

"Help him," he said, in a voice like tearing cloth. Then he jumped on to the table and up into the tree and was gone. I looked at my watch. Only two minutes had elapsed since we had entered the clearing.

Thorndyke was weak, but could walk. I helped him to his room, where he asked to be left alone. Strangely he seemed to be a bit merry. Weary, but content. He said things like, "That question got him a bit stirred up, didn't it?" and, "Mnaba, my boy, we're on the way. We're started." I left him lying on the bed. I hoped he would rest.

The following account was written shortly after the confrontation.

Thorndyke's Diary: Entry 16

I took it like a spike between the eyes. My anger was enough to carry me through. I knew my words . . . but then the Pe-Ellians upended me . . . like a man practising his anger in front of a mirror, who suddenly realises he is railing at himself, and feels chastened because the words he wanted to throw at others fit him. That's what they did to me.

How they did it remains a mystery, but one thing is proved beyond any shadow of sherlocking doubt . . . I spell it out. I spell it out. *They are mindreaders and for them the power of the mind is all-important* and *they are afraid of us*.

If they are tuned in now, then they'll know I know. And being bright etc. they'll know that I know they know etc. etc. etc.

Notwithstanding, I do not believe that they are tuned in. I believe Winter Wind was telling the truth when he said they were "straining to ignore" the "bleeding" of our minds. (Incidentally I must get Mnaba to run a check, if he can, on the kinds of material Winter Wind must have read.) I believe I touched him on the quick when I accused him of invading our privacy.

God knows I can hardly sit down, I'm so pepped up. For the first time I really feel, believe, know, we are in above our heads. For the first time we are dealing with a species for whom ethics is a way of life.

Think about that.

Can you imagine a species whose everyday existence *depends* on ethical decisions. Depends, mark you. I don't understand their system yet . . . but I have some hints . . . while I was in the trance I saw something of how they think. Each one of them is a universe. As I suspected, each one shows himself through his skin, and each skin shows the true creature. For them thought is a living tangible force.

I accuse Winter Wind of the crime of being a peeping Tom. The accusation is given power by means of my anger. I "bleed all over the place like a mountain stream", as Winter Wind states, and the thought stings him like acid. It defaces and defames him.

His protection . . . ? Here we come to it. What stopped me? I was getting going. Just warmed up and *wham* . . . I took it between the eyes. Let me try and set down what happened.

They were jumpy when we came into the clearing. They all knew something was happening—that was my first clue. I suspected I was trespassing over some kind of boundary. For any future contact linguist who may read this, may I state that if you want to know a culture you can either swim with it, or lash out against it. Both bring their own kind of result, and sometimes both techniques are necessary. But if you use the lash-out technique you run the risk of being mangled—or worse.

Anyway, I knew I was committed to the confrontation technique and that there was no alternative. I decided on an old trick: never let your opponent quite finish what he was going to say. Ride roughshod was the olden way of saying this.

All right, so I ride roughshod, and I can see that my rudeness is effective. I begin my accusations. Then suddenly things aren't going quite according to plan. I say a few things too quickly, too rushed. Winter Wind lets fly with some Pe-Ellian and *wham*!

I see the power coming. It comes from everywhere. It takes me in its grip with the same care a dog shows when carrying its master's newspaper. The grip is as complete as encasement in marble. It flows into me like a fluid and hardens to adamant. Despite this I never stop thinking, my thoughts become charged. Winter Wind was a blur of purple. He was supported by a web of purple light, which flowed into him from the cottage, from Jet, from the trees above. Above me was green and gold, flashing and sparkling like fireworks. Menopause.

I hear his words, but it is not Winter Wind who speaks. No, Winter Wind speaks, but someone else does the talking.

Who? Who knows? I suspect that Winter Wind's words are intended to chasten me, but that is not the effect, for I am enlivened. I feel thought around me like smoke. I can hardly move or speak, but yet I want to climb a mountain, sing, swim, debate and play the violin—all at once.

I begin to realise vaguely why they are afraid. Our minds don't operate in accordance with their rules. They have developed a social system based on regard for the privacy of others. We come in and are like bonfires in an ice-cave.

Something of my euphoria is wearing off. I realise a danger. I have hurt Winter Wind, who tried to be a friend. We may be sent away. Earth may be pegged within its territory or worse.

I wait. If I could change the last few hours, would I? No. But I would do things differently.

COMMENTARY

After this incident we both became somewhat depressed. Cook did not present us with our evening meal. Cold cuts imported from Earth were set out on the table in our absence.

"Have we been sent to Coventry?" asked Thorndyke.

"I fear we have," I replied.

We went to bed early. I did not want to discuss this matter with Thorndyke until time had given perspective.

This first clash between Thorndyke and Winter Wind was of fundamental importance.

The following two passages were written at my request by Jet and Cook when they visited me on Camellia. I first asked Jet to describe what happened that day from his point of view.

JET: I was grateful to Menopause. He was our lightning conductor. Unprepared and flustered, we none of us could sustain the Thorndyke thought until we had a Mantissa on tap. Menopause took it, tied the thought to the trees, to the river, directed it against himself, and forced the rest back down Thorndyke's neurological orifice. All this he did to protect us . . . which is strange. Menopause had many lights. Wisely it is said, "Judge not in menopause". But despite all this some damage was done.

Winter Wind, who is now back in the melting pot, sacrificed more than the rest of us for you. He was at risk and the first to receive the flush of anger. This damaged him, but he was also damaged by his own anger. That is not your fault. That day five eggs died.

When Winter Wind called I summoned the Mantissa who supported your cottage and laid my mind open. Through me the Mantissa supported Winter Wind.

My home is one of the foci of the forest. I returned there and invited all signals of Winter Wind to come to me. In a world such as ours the very flowers reflect the passing of a sensitive mind.

It was towards evening that Winter Wind's call came to me. He had wandered the whole afternoon. He had held the Mantissa power close, diminishing it only a little at a time. Now he faced the truth that he could not contain Thorndyke. He had believed that his own will was sufficient to contain the random thoughts, the destructive ideas, and the dreams that poured from that remarkable man.

I and others who had taken charge of the contact experiment had opposed Winter Wind long before you arrived, and we prevailed. We made sure there were always Mantissa points close at hand.

But proud Winter Wind, ever the gambler, wanted none of this. "Open contact" he called it. He wanted the richness that comes from your hopes, like the smell of apples in autumn. He believed that left alone your minds would naturally develop discipline under the benign massage of Pe-Ellia, and that the yearning for oneness which we all saw in Thorndyke would come to dominate his darker nature.

Alas for Winter Wind, my friend,
That was not the way the song was to be written.

As soon as I heard the call I left my rest and was moving. I can move very quickly when I have to. I carried a transporter and a gown. I found Winter Wind stretched out under a marn plant.

"Hush," I said, for I could see he was in a sad way. "You are broadcasting like a karitsa. I will take you home with me. You can bathe with me." He stilled then, and his mind grew calmer.

"Six changes and still so weak," he murmured.

I slipped the gown over his head and shoulders, leaving the arms clear. As the fabric settled over his skin he began to doze.

I charged the transporter with my own thought and slipped its coils round his wrists. They tightened, lifting. Soon he hung relaxed and suspended.

I led him home.

Home is a hole by the river.

My heart-room contains a Mantissa sump of clear silver water. I guided him there and lowered him in. A limp fish. The Mantissa took control.

When I had closed the door and sealed the outside I rejoined him but he was far away in sleep. The Mantissa said I should not disturb except to remove the five dead karitsas, which bobbed on the surface of the pool.

So there you are, Professor Mnaba, and I hope this is clear. I am sorry that you were dismissed from Pe-Ellia before you could visit me at my home. We would have had much to talk about.

Cook was not in the clearing when the clash between Winter Wind and Thorndyke took place. I asked him whether, despite his absence, he was aware of what was going on.

COOK: Aware.

I was aware well in advance, for as you know I was with you more than most.

Also I found you two complementaries highly sympathetic. So I saw something coming.

Like this. Like all things have form. Like ideas.

You people changed the world about you and I marvelled that you did not know. That day you went round the perimeter and Thorndyke kept a-room I watched the sky. There were specks on it but they were not birds. And the clouds drew apart as though pulled by threads. The sky became a clearer blue and I felt excitement because of this. Your searching caused this. Can I tell you that we Pe-Ellians do not feel what you call danger. We feel only excitement, and that is the closest we come to your emotion.

I felt great excitement then and still do in view of what Thorndyke's death means to Pe-Ellia.

I watched the sky and observed the fine track of your thought. I observed the light bend down to the earth and the way it changed the form of things observed. While Thorndyke wrote and you speculated the air became charged and could have killed a one too sensitive. The landscape became pock-marked with tiny whorls; time became knotty.

We all noticed it, I think, but me most of all because for me there is no hope. I represented no competition to Winter Wind, and would not have wished to. So, because I did not care for myself, I watched you openly and with great excitement.

I saw the way the air closed round you when you moved, and the way the walls roiled to your touch. Sometimes you were so sad you made me long to play music. . . .

So when Thorndyke came blazing out of the cottage I felt that I had seen part of it already and that I knew what was coming. Have you watched water when it comes to the boil? Just before the surface erupts it becomes calm for an instant. So it is with wild animals. Before the jaws open to take the prey there is a catch of breath and then a blur of movement. Before a storm there is, as you say, a calm. Between waves there is a lull when the spent wave is dying and while the young wave is bunching its muscle. Everything waits. . . .

That pause is very . . . important.

Then out you both came and the pause was ended.

Winter Wind betrayed,

By his own confidence,

By his blazing ambition for symmetry.

I felt his scream as he called for the Mantissa Loci. Sensed (almost you would say smelled) the death of his sensitive cells under the impact of anger. Knew when Jet opened his mind and when Menopause stepped in.

I was also aware of the calibration. You, friend Mnaba, were kept alive by Menopause. Did you know that?

Had but one tenth of the power summoned by Winter Wind been relayed to you then you would have become mindless as an empty shell. I mean that you would still have been beautiful, still capable of giving pleasure and instruction, still with form, but creatively dead. A finished work.

Menopause's calculations were a blur. He surprised me. I knew him before he began his last change and he never at that time suggested his potential. Thorndyke was stilled by a spiral of his own anger. Thorndyke stunned Thorndyke. That is very funny.

You, friend Mnaba, were by now introspective, so Menopause left you.

That is just as well. Though he saved you I doubt he would have been gentle with you.

With everything stopped and the clearing shut down the Mantissa Loci came through and spoke, manipulating Winter Wind's voice and body.

Those of us who were interested listened.

Menopause showed himself to be far more than just an onlooker. From here on we all knew that he was to be deeply involved with your song. Being in menopause he could see further into time than the rest of us. I think he did. May I tell it.

The death of Winter Wind.

Thorndyke's attempt to moult.

His loving with our queen.

His death with Menopause-Harlequin in tandem.

All these events are locked together and were already in process when Thorndyke challenged Winter Wind in the clearing.

And I, poor Cook, a might-have-been like Winter Wind and now a humble do-gooder, soon to make my own journey, I wish both our worlds well.

The day following the incident in the clearing we were again left completely alone. A young Pe-Ellian silently brought us food. It was a miserable time as far as I was concerned. I felt we were being judged. I felt also that Thorndyke had wilfully transgressed beyond the boundaries governing contact established by his own institute. I felt sympathy for Winter Wind, who had clearly been insulted, and wished that I could have spoken with him.

I realised that there was something excessive in Thorndyke's reactions to Pe-Ellia. While at that time I would not have used the word "unbalanced" I felt deep concern that he was becoming far too personally involved with events on Pe-Ellia and with the Pe-Ellians.

The relevant section of the Contact Linguists' Handbook is very clear on the perils of too close an identification with an alien culture. The contact linguist is encouraged to participate imaginatively with a culture, but at all times to retain a sense of selfhood. Failure to do so invariably results in a loss of objectivity and can constitute the first steps towards madness. There are cases on file in which trusted and highly respected operatives have suddenly gone rogue and attempted to manipulate the local population. The dangers to the local culture are obvious.

I felt that Thorndyke was steering a course perilously close to this threshold. He was starting to take sides.

During the late afternoon we were sitting together in the clearing and I broached this topic. During the whole day Thorndyke had alternated between a boyish and rather forced good humour and depression.

I asked him directly, "Have you conducted self analysis recently?" (Contact linguists in the field conduct standard self analyses at regular intervals.)

He looked at me strangely. "When am I not conducting a self analysis?"

I chose not to be drawn into this kind of dialogue. I pointed out that in my view Thorndyke was becoming too involved with Pe-Ellia and that he would be of greatest value to Earth and to himself if he drew back and exercised greater objectivity.

I have decided to quote his reply as recorded by me on that fine sunny afternoon by the river.

THORNDYKE: I know, Tomas, I know. But you see, I've spent all my life being objective, weighing and measuring, trying to treat my emotions as though they were quantities in an algebraic equation. Over the years it has become second nature to me. Feel an emotion in oneself: analyse. Observe an emotion in another: analyse. Only now do I come to see that an emotion may be sufficient unto itself—or rather, something to be ridden for the sake of the ride. Yes. A bit puerile, isn't it? But there we are. I feel that with one lifetime behind me I have now got a lot of living to do.

Have you ever wondered why old men with active minds often marry young maids? Well, it's not for the sex . . . well, not for most of them. No, it's an attempt to break with mental habits. Old age is little more than rigidity. The body, even the body in pain, is secondary to a mind that feels itself trapped in habit.

You'd think that we, trained contact linguists, would be the most open men on Earth. I mean, if travel broadens the mind, then we've seen it all. We've contemplated the unthinkable. We've had things done to us . . . we've all done things . . . you know what I mean. Well, amidst all this alien corn we have developed a code to help keep us sane. And please don't misunderstand me, Tomas, I believe the code is right. I believe and stand by the words we wrote in the Handbook. But what we did not adequately evaluate was the effect of prolonged control on the individual who practises that control. Control is a cancer that grows on the brain.

It is a matter of record that the best contact linguists are those who complete one assignment and then begin a new one the next day. Remember how we always tried to get the field men to take three months home leave living it up, and never understood why they resisted?

The strain of changing mental attitudes tells after a while. The contact linguists' code is so successful. And do you know why? Because it simplifies everything. It's like a drug. One can get hooked on objectivity. And that makes it hard to be both simple and sensuous.

In some ways I've been very lucky. I'm not a particularly good contact linguist. No, don't try and say anything. I know what I'm talking about and I've done a lot of thinking. My successes have been due to luck, a certain fortunate falling together of genes and guess work. The books have been mere library work—writing up notes, feeding facts into computers and finding the common denominators. That's not real work. A dextrous ape could have done as much.

The only thing I'll take any pride in is the translation work. And that is why I say I am lucky. The translations *are* good, but they are not enough.

Occasionally I've had a glimmer of joy—when I've crept for a few moments under the skin of another culture—and that has shown me how much I have missed. I've written about love while living in a walled garden.

When I was a lad, you know, I used to dream of the day that alien races would meet on some distant planet. I used to think of them as noble savages, as fungi, as rocks and even sometimes as being so alien that merely to contemplate them was to invite insanity. I thought of the battles too and the diseases and the . . . oh, a million things.

Finally it was literature that took all my love.

But literature is not life. It may satisfy the mind in any number of ways, but it is not life and any attempt to make it such is perversion.

I wanted—want—more. But by the time I came to realise this . . . I was getting old. Old. I could no longer run. Got dizzy when I rode a horse. Doubted my potency when I was with a woman. It's rather funny, really, but finally very sad.

When I retired from the CLI . . . well, I hoped that touring would give me some peace. Remember how I nipped from system to system? I loved the problems and freely admit that I found travelling easier than sitting still. But I kept wanting to go faster. I was running away from stillness. Sometimes I actually hoped that some half-ape would bop me on the skull and end it all.

Then Routham died. You took the chairmanship at the CLI. And I became something of a recluse, flitting between Orchid and Paris and Camellia. I buried myself in translations.

And then these damned Pe-Ellians show up. God bless them if they are listening in. What I had been hoping for all my life happened, but too late. Too late for me, I thought. I wanted to back off. I sensed that if I once became involved then a mass of pain would emerge.

The intellectual challenge hooked me. My vanity too. But I remain me. Unreconstituted. More plagued by doubts than ever before. I can't help it. I am sick of me.

Now you are right when you say that I am not acting with proper objectivity and due regard for reason. You are right when you imply that I could serve Earth better. But I'm not in this for Earth. I'm here for me.

I don't want *them* to be reduced to *our* terms.

I want them to reduce or expand or whatever *us* up to *their* sensibility.

Specifically I want them to kick me around. Re-form me.

You perhaps begin to understand why I get angry with Winter Wind. He's playing us at the contact linguist game and he's brilliant in some ways. But he wants a nice clean contact. The kind of thing we used to theorise about, and it won't work. It is about as healthy as sex without juices, if you'll pardon such a crude way of expressing it.

I can't prove everything I've said, Tomas. But that's what I feel. There's something here that I want. I know it intuitively. Something so grand . . . no, I won't call it destiny, such words only cloud the issue. I can't explain what happened yesterday. All I can say is that while I was out for the count I was more me than ever before. Strange, eh?

Understand?

No, course you can't. Not your fault either. Thorndyke imprecise. Mystical jargon. We lack a vocabulary for such things. I'll try to write a brief . . . in accordance with the Handbook.

You know, yesterday I felt happy. Delirious.

Today, well, I don't know. Today I am beset with doubts. The initiative is no longer with me.

Thorndyke stood looking at me and then his voice just trailed away. After a few moments he nodded towards the river, crossed to it and began taking his clothes off. He dived with a loud splash into the river and emerged upstream near the waterfall.

"I'm going exploring," he called, and began clambering up the slabs of rock that constituted the waterfall. I realised that he needed to be alone and I did not feel I would get any further with more questions. "Sufficient unto the day . . ." as Thorndyke would have quoted.

As I watched him climb I became suddenly aware of how artificial the waterfall was. The rocks were as carefully placed as in a Japanese garden. This led me to wonder whether the whole area in which we resided—house, trees, plants—indeed, everything within the perimeter I had discovered, was artefact. I looked at the grass at my feet and shuddered.

I sat in the clearing lost in thought for several minutes after Thorndyke left. I was brought back to myself by an electric tingling in the air and an immense throbbing. Nothing moved and yet it seemed as though all of nature about me was a giant drum skin on which fingers had lightly drummed. For a few moments I felt as I had in the space sphere just before the walls cleared. This time, though, nothing changed and after a few moments the throbbing died away gradually.

Life returned to normal: the river gurgled, the warm sun pushed the shadows further into the grove and birdsong returned. Only I was left with a racing pulse. Although I did not know it at the time, this convulsion in the air was caused by Thorndyke crossing the perimeter which divided our zone from the rest of Pe-Ellia.

I sat for a few moments collecting my thoughts. I remember I felt vaguely worried but did not know why.

I decided to move inside and work on my notes and classifications, for I have always found that such work calms me. I am fortunate that I can always lose myself in my work.

Some hours later Thorndyke came to me in my apartment and announced that he had had a refreshing ramble. He was munching a cheese and pickle sandwich, which made me realise I was feeling hungry.

"Has anyone called in?" he asked.

"Not that I know of," I answered. "I've been deep in all this, trying to get things organised."

"Well, there's sandwiches and ham and mustard and pickles and beer—German beer—on the table. Does that or does that not seem like a friendly gesture?"

"Friendly," I agreed.

"Bring your notes and whatnot and let's enjoy this pub dinner and then spend the evening in civilised discourse. We'll try and make more sense of this Pe-Ellian language."

That was just what we did. With the lights turned down in the Palm Court we could have been back on Camellia as in the old days, working on the *Grammaria*.

The next morning was overcast.

I was awoken by Cook, who said that as it was raining breakfast would not be served outside in the clearing but had been prepared in Professor Thorndyke's room. Fresh coffee was already awaiting me.

I felt that Cook was being especially friendly. This impression was confirmed by Thorndyke, who winked and gave me the thumbs-up sign when I entered his apartment.

The wall and ceiling were completely translucent but the sound was turned down. Rain on Pe-Ellia was like rain anywhere. It was a heavy downpour, such as one can find in England during August. The surface of the river was dimpled and the grass in the clearing had a pale glaze, showing that the water had not yet been absorbed. The overcast light brought out new colours and the absence of shadow gave the jungle a two-dimensional appearance. I announced my intention of going for a walk as soon as we had finished breakfast. Thorndyke said he would join me.

"Rain does not depress you?" asked Cook.

"No," we answered, surprised at his question. Our answer seemed to delight him.

"Good. Well, boys, before you move on out, I've got a mighty important announcement to make. But just for now, eat."

And eat we did. I have already mentioned the exhilarating effect of the Pe-Ellian air. It seemed to stimulate our appetites. I am normally a light eater and Thorndyke was no glutton. Nevertheless we were both able to pack away the food whenever it was presented. After breakfast Cook made his announcement.

"Banquet tonight. No holds barred. Welcoming banquet now that you've had time to get settled in and find your feet. Time to chew the rag. Okay. Might even be a few new faces."

"Will Professor Winter Wind be there?" asked Thorndyke.

"I hope so. If he can be persuaded he will come. Jet too."

"Good," said Thorndyke. "I would like to make amends for the clash between us."

Cook looked serious. He wrinkled the mottled skin above his nose and stared down at us without blinking. The effect was of intense concentration. Finally he spoke.

"I am sure there is no permanent damage done."

Thus ended our breakfast. Cook produced what he called sheaths and what we would call bicycle capes. He also explained to us that on Pe-Ellia the rain is considered a blessing and that all

Pe-Ellians try to experience the rain on their skins at least once each shower.

"So don't be surprised if you meet a few of them . . . frolicking . . . while you are out strolling."

Our walk in the rain was eventful. Thorndyke gives a full account.

THORNDYKE'S DIARY: ENTRY 17

Today I felt, as though for the first time, the cleansing effect of rain. I love the word "rinse". It captures the running of water, saturation and the clean feel of fresh linen. The morning was rinsed and so was I. Mnaba too I think, for in his own quiet way he was exulting. I could tell by the set of his shoulders and the way he strode, brushing against the ferns and hanging branches. I did likewise.

As I walk I feel under my feet the lift of the humus. The spongy fibres have expanded into springy cushions. Where we stop, the imprint holds for a few seconds and then is smoothed away. We follow a new path. It is a continuation of the path which brought us here. Tomas, who has been spending time on such things, can name many of the plants that we encounter. He is also working on a map of the area.

The first effect of the rain is that everything is lower, bowed down by the weight of the water. As we walk past and brush against the shrubs they release their water and spring up high again. I notice also that the rain on the leaves brings out different colours. I am reminded of the pebbles I used to collect as a boy when I roved by the seashore. Wet from the tide, the pebbles ranged through the spectrum. As they dried they lost their bright colours.

The same is true here. The rain has brought out the colours of the leaves and stems of the plants. The brushing tree, the one that stung me on the first day, has beautiful brown and green veins running through its leaves. They are so clear that as I stand underneath one of those plants I think I can hear the water gurgling up through the veins from the vegetable heart.

We saw few new species except for the mushrooms. You can actually watch them grow.

We came upon one which was about the size of a dining table. Its surface was pale green, with hundreds of thin dark lines spreading out from the centre and running to the outer edge. The underside was brown and feathery. As we watched, the edge of the mushroom turned down and curled under. I would not have been greatly surprised if a gnome had come trotting round the corner and offered us a guided tour.

Shortly after seeing this mature mushroom we came upon a young one as it was emerging from the ground. At first it was no larger than a dill pickle stood on end. The taller it grew, the fatter it became, until it was like a bloated marrow. The crown of the mushroom parted from the base with an audible pop, and it began to grow out laterally.

Tomas has a passion for mushrooms and I could see what he was thinking as the flawless creamy surface spread out in front of us.

"Perhaps at the banquet tonight," I said.

"Let's hope," he replied.

It was shortly after watching the mushroom that we came upon our first Pe-Ellian. He was standing in a small clearing and had obviously been dancing. The middle of the clearing had been churned to mud. He was standing up to his ankles in the mud and making slow passing movements with his hands. The rain, which had never let up, sluiced down over his bald head and body. I was reminded of a statue in a park.

As part of his slow steady movement he bent down and scooped up some mud and plastered it over his body, rubbing it into his markings with slow circular movements. He was oblivious of us as we stood and stared at him. Then I noticed other movement around him and saw that lying in the mud were other Pe-Ellians.

"Care to join them?" I asked.

Once, as a boy, I remember coming upon a mud pool in an old quarry. The mud was pure brown and deep and I was strangely tempted to eat it. I didn't, for though it looked like the finest chocolate, I knew it was mud. Instead I touched it and slowly pressed my hands down into it, pressing down, deeper and deeper, until my nose touched its surface. The strange thing was that the mud was still warm even at arm's depth. Feeling the mud grip my arms and push up between my fingers I wanted to bathe in it, lie in it.

As I watched the sliding, slithering bodies in the mud, I had a strong desire to join them. We moved on.

We saw many other Pe-Ellians and all seemed in some kind of trance. Most were massaging themselves. Before long we came to a large clearing which was similar in size to the one in which we had landed.

Judging from the height of the trees I estimate that the width of that clearing was about a mile. In the middle were hundreds of Pe-Ellians. They were running in the rain and turning somersaults. Some, we noticed, were deliberately tearing up sods with their hands and then trampling these to mud. The smell of the earth was very strong here: a smell of green leaves and running water. A smell that unites Earth and Pe-Ellia.

It was while we were watching the Pe-Ellians in the clearing that we both noticed a lightening of the air.

"Rain's lifting," said Tomas. Even as he spoke a milky sun began to appear through the clouds.

The figures in the clearing stopped their antics and stood still and upright like so many sentries. It was my guess that they were catching the last of the rain to wash their bodies. The rain slowed to a heavy fret and then stopped completely. Immediately steam began to rise from the earth and we lost sight of the figures.

"Let's head back," I said to Tomas, as I did not relish the idea of a long walk through the steaming jungle in the full heat. We turned back down the path as the sun broke through the clouds. From all about us came a high keening sound. The noise grew and grew until both Tomas and I covered our ears.

Still the sound could be heard as it reached a climax. I felt a tingling. I'd felt it before. On the spaceship.

The whole earth leaped at the climax of the wailing and we found ourselves thrown to our knees. For a second the air about us seemed to die. Then with a sigh life returned. The plants, I believe, sighed. The trees, which had drooped like puppets on a wet string, now drew up to their proper height again with a scattering of water. Colours, which had been leached in that second of death, now flowed again. Tomas had a silly expression on his face.

"Is this what happens at the moment when yin becomes yang?" he asked and then blushed. But there may be some sense there. I have my own theories.

We walked home and the air grew warm about us. Shadows returned and dazzling patches of sun. When we reached the place where we had seen the Pe-Ellians crawling over one another we found nothing but a mud puddle and that was already hardening over and cracking.

The only Pe-Ellians we met during our return journey were three that were almost albino. They were running with long relaxed paces and we had to step off the path to let them pass. I had the impression that if we hadn't stepped out of their way, they would have bowled us over and continued without a backward glance. As they passed I could see their bodies were patterned with fine pinpricks of black. Also that they were very tall, even for Pe-Ellians.

When we got back to our own clearing we found Cook waiting for us. He was streaked with mud.

"Been waiting about for some time for you guys to get back a piece," he said. "Figgered I'd better ask you if you wanted to eat Earthstyle or Pe-Ellian tonight."

"When in Rome," I said and turned to Tomas.

He nodded.

"Guessed as much," said Cook. "Pe-Ellian it is . . . which means you don't get no lunch. We always clean out the body before a banquet. Gives you plenty of nooks and crannies for packing in goodies."

Our faces must have dropped. Either that or he was pulling our legs, for he said, "Okay, lads, coffee's down below and waiting. I'm off to get things moving. Standing here won't empty the bath tub." With that he walked to the river bank and without removing his apron dived clumsily into the water.

Commentary

After this brief conversation Thorndyke and I moved indoors and enjoyed our coffee. Thorndyke excused himself and went to his room and I decided to complete some sketches I had begun. I moved outside into the clearing and set up my equipment on the table.

I had been working for about two hours when Jet arrived. He seemed in high spirits and willing to talk, so I asked him about the ceremonies in the rain and the three albino Pe-Ellians we had met and the strange way the air had seemed to die about us. The following is an edited transcript of his remarks to me.

JET: No ceremony. Not like wedding if that's what you mean. No religion. Just fun and games. We frolic. See, the days that the rains come down are the days that we can get together and drop our silence. The rain is a blanket which covers us all and makes us as one. It cools the skin and reaches deep inside and cools the fires. Ah, we are a strange people. So cautious and careful. Always walking the thin line. Our life is a relentless quest to discover who we are and where we fit in the universe. Not all life has a place in the universe you know. Some of it is Balacas before it gets going. If there is too much Balacas then all life becomes tainted.

We don't have much time for what you call relaxation. But when the rains come . . . then we relax. The rain on our skin is as wonderful as eating ripe fruit, or as having an idea or being held by a Mantissa. We don't have what you would call sex, but I think that to us the rain pouring down, trickling over our veins, evaporating from our domed heads, making the soil into mud, is like making love for you.

When the rains come we dance. We can't help it. We throw ourselves open. If there are other Pe-Ellians nearby they all join in. There is no danger of rupture, as the rain makes the skin supple and deadens the receptors in the brain. No transmissions can be sent or received. We slide in and out of the mud like karitsas new hatched. We slide over one another like soapy hands. Ah, so free. Perhaps at the next rain you will join us?

MNABA: What is Balacas?

JET: Balacas is futile life. Life that never was meant to come to fruition. Life that has no place in the great scheme. Life that can never lead anywhere. Life that is better budded. Not that Balacas is an evil state . . . it is just a wrongness. Too much Balacas and true life can become thin, for Balacas takes up too much space . . .

Balacas can transmit just like true life. . . . There have been cases, even of Pe-Ellians, who were Balacas pretending they were true life. They never succeed. Come the third menopause truth will out. We see their skins and it's pop into the melting pot with them.

That can be very sad, of course. Life can be cruel. I have known Pe-Ellians who have been true and who at one change suddenly became Balacas. Cook, for instance, is Balacas, but benign. He will go back to enter the mother yolk, but not for some time yet. He still has much to teach, and his students who came to him before Balacas are loyal to him.

I am past my sixth change and as you can see every window in my skin has its eye. A bit muzzy yet, but then so am I. I have not yet chosen my vocation. . . .

MNABA: Has Winter Wind chosen his vocation?

JET: Ah, yes, Winter Wind. Well, he hopes so, and we all hope for him. As you can see his skin is in fine fettle, no lacunae, no empty parentheses. Barring accidents he should have a painless last change and then he will be riding. He wants to become a Mantissa of the Crossroads. A Contact Mantissa. God knows we need them, but what an ordeal. He has been working towards this since his auspicious second . . . he is boneless meat, all lean and sweet . . . you are privileged to know him. And he is lucky that you are as you are and that you came when you did.

MNABA: You are speaking in riddles.

JET: Sorry. But it is not good for me to talk about him. Better that you ask him yourself.

MNABA: What is a Mantissa?

JET: You will accuse me of talking in riddles again. Later we will see a Mantissa. That will be your best answer.

MNABA: I saw three Pe-Ellians running. They looked white. All window and no eye. What were they?

JET: Ah, you saw *them*. And there were only three? You are sure there weren't five? Sorry, stupid question. If there had been five you would have seen five. That means that two have faded from the race. Now let me see, they began running when they failed their third change and they are now in their fifth. They should have passed away but a Mantissa chose to save them. They provide it with a kind of energy . . . I don't especially know what.

They will run till they drop, but the last one may return to life. I didn't know they were near here. They may have been attracted by you. You are powerful generators, you know.

MNABA: They nearly bowled us over.

JET: Yes. It is well to step out of their path. We shun them when we know they are coming. There is a story that I have heard that they run before misfortune. Even to speak of them is not good. I will say no more.

MNABA: Just one more thing. Something wonderful. When the rain stopped and the sun came out, it was as if nature breathed out and then in again. What was it?

JET: Ah, you felt that, did you? See, you are not as insensitive as you would believe. I think you know the answer. No? Ah, well, you felt life. You felt the breathing of our planet. It is life all over. The air, the water, the insects, oh, more than I can say. Let me tell you, when the rain stops we all clear our minds, vacancy. Then when the sun comes we draw back in Pe-Ellia through our jaws and skin. Our world renews us. I am glad you felt that. It is very precious to us. And now I must leave and prepare myself for this evening. Prepare yourself. Today you breathed Pe-Ellia. This evening you will taste it.

Jet stood up. He seemed suddenly in a hurry. He crossed to the river bank and without a word or a backward glance threw himself into the stream. Despite his size he made scarcely a splash.

This conversation left me wiser than before, but with more questions than answers. I was particularly pleased by the frankness and ease of the conversation. Although the time was short I felt it had been well used. I felt closer to Jet than to any of the Pe-Ellians we had met. I guessed that he had enjoyed his time in the rain.

That evening, the evening of our fifth day on the planet, the banquet took place.

THORNDYKE'S DIARY: ENTRY 18

This night we had a welcoming banquet. At least that is what the Pe-Ellians called it. As far as I am concerned it was a reconciliation banquet, intended to bring me and Winter Wind together again. It worked. I expect our days to be calmer and smoother hereafter. Now, as I write, I feel excited. Writing will calm me.

Preparations began about half an hour before the sun left the clearing. Cook arrived looking clean and refreshed. He entered the Palm Court down the passageway, which has up to now always been closed. This is the one that leads to some kind of metro. I immediately asked Cook if we would be able to use the transport system and he told me that as soon as it was "conditioned" we would be free to come and go as we pleased. I did not press him on what he meant, but decided to wait and see. In his arms Cook was carrying branches that were heavy with a fruit like peaches. I asked him if I could have one of the pieces of fruit as I was ravenous and the fruit looked so succulent.

Cook went through the head-waggling ritual which indicated amused surprise and muttered something in Pe-Ellian, but I couldn't catch his words. In English he said: "These are no fruits, but energised lights. The energy in these would surprise you if you bit into them. Probably death would ensue, for we note that humans have low resistance."

Chided and warned in this sweet manner I had no choice but to accept.

"Watch," said Cook. He put three of his fingers to his lips. Then he touched his wet fingers to a point on his forehead some two inches above his nose, closed his eyes and thought or meditated visibly for three or four seconds. Coming out of his brief trance he lightly touched each of the fruits with the tips of his fingers. As he touched them a swirling, smoky red light started to burn in each fruit. This light brightened until it settled to a steady pink glow. Soon every globe was glowing.

I found the glow comfortable and said so. I also asked what the energy source was, and how Cook had managed this piece of magic.

"Thought," said Cook. "Just like everything else. All I did was trigger what was already there. Just like you striking a match, only these'll keep burning a couple of days at least. They're pretty fresh."

He paused and looked around the room. I followed his glance and only then noticed that the light from the fruit made the walls rippled and veiny. They reflected the light, but several shades darker, and this made them look alive and wet . . . like the inside of a mouth.

"Bonny," said Cook in appreciation. "But standing here won't butter the baby. I must away to my pots and pans."

As he turned to leave I noticed that the pink light made the markings on his skin show clearly, as though his skin had become more transparent.

I relaxed in the glow of the Palm Court and enjoyed a leisurely cigar. From the kitchen came the sound of a stringed instrument. I listened enchanted and if I thought about it at all I just assumed this was music to cook by.

Tomas arrived. He told me how ruddy and healthy I looked and described an interesting conversation he'd had with Jet. He also cautioned me in his careful, polite way not to get into any scraps this evening. He has a theory that on Pe-Ellia emotion has great power that can be projected into the ether of this world, thereby causing pain. Certainly this idea is borne out by Winter Wind's reactions and speech. I agreed to hold my peace.

Tomas seemed content with this answer. He then went into the kitchen where he found Cook playing a musical instrument to a fish! Cook immediately stopped playing. He became very serious and insisted that Tomas leave immediately. He saw me looking and explained that any extraneous presence could upset the balance of the cooking. Tomas shrugged his shoulders at this. I shrugged my mental shoulders and continued puffing on my cigar. I have met many temperamental cooks in my time. The door to the kitchen closed firmly and no sounds emerged.

I suggested that Tomas go and tune his encoders for maximum cross-referencing, as I was sure there would be a wealth of material that night.

"Well bethought," he said and went off whistling.

Tomas whistling! I definitely began to believe that those glowing pink globes were not only calming but also slightly intoxicating.

The float-harp is the instrument Cook was playing. I had heard him play several times and had always assumed that the instrument was purely for pleasure. However I doubt if on Pe-Ellia anything is ever "purely" for something. As we found out later this evening the float-harp has other uses.

Jet arrived with a flapping of costume. He was wearing a black velvet poncho, which was so long it trailed on the ground. He said good evening and settled himself comfortably on one of the benches placed near the table. He adjusted his clothing so that every part of him was covered except for his arms and legs and head. Such was the effect of the black poncho that his head seemed to float above his body and his arms were two pink snakes.

"There's a good smell," he said. I confess I could smell nothing, but I nodded.

Next to arrive was Winter Wind. I was glad to see that he seemed unchanged. He was accompanied by two other very tall Pe-Ellians. Their names were translated to us as Unbroached Ancient Treasure Tomb and Laughing Gas. We immediately shortened these to Tom and Gus, which seemed to please them. Winter Wind told us that these two Pe-Ellians had passed the seventh and achieved harmony, and were keen to meet us informally since they had both been aboard the Pe-Ellian ship which had gone to Earth. I cannot recollect seeing them, but then, there were many more Pe-Ellians on that ship than we knew about. They said they were Mantissa Handmaidens. I immediately asked Winter Wind what a Mantissa was. Everyone laughed and I received four different answers.

Jet: "Doctor."

Winter Wind: "Teacher."

Tom: "Mechanic."

Gus: "Administrator."

All spoke at once. Clearly this needs to be sorted out, and Winter Wind has agreed to answer questions tomorrow.

"Tonight," he said, "should be more tangential. Touching the peach rather than seizing the whole of the fruit in one's hand."

Now where did he learn language like that?

We all settled down. The two Pe-Ellians threw off their cloaks and revealed skins of a dazzling greyish pink. That doesn't sound very healthy, I know, but they gave an impression of abundant health. Their skin markings, I noted, were completely symmetrical, as though each plate had been pressed from the same mould. Gus had a design like a feather or a fern. Tom's design was like overlapping stars.

Winter Wind raised his arms and spoke some rolling Pe-Ellian syllables. I have heard such language before. Usually it is an antique form. Something hallowed. It sounded as though he were saying grace, and as though in response, I swear the glow-globes shone more brightly. Alternatively, Winter Wind may have been merely saying, "Let the feast commence."

On cue Cook came bustling in and placed a large tureen in the centre of the table. "Soup," he announced, rather as a magician might say "Sapristi", and with a flourish removed the lid. The soup was pale yellow.

Floating in the tureen was what I at first assumed to be a large and rather lumpy dill pickle. However, when Cook ladled out the soup I observed that before each scoop he always pressed the "vegetable" and when he did this, small feathery webbed hands lifted from its side. Just before he served me I saw the creature's screwed-up little face, rather like a vole.

I was prepared for savoury or even a game flavour. I was not prepared for the sweetness which hit me with all the force of condensed milk.

Mentally I prayed that the Pe-Ellians would not turn out to be one of those races for whom sugar is salt and savoury means bitter as bile. Up to the present there had been no indications that this was the case.

Gus asked me how I liked the soup and I replied that I liked it well (which was true), but that my tastes inclined more to the savoury. He smiled and nodded at that. For some reason they all seemed pleased with my answer. Tomas said that he didn't think the soup was too sweet, which surprised me as I know that Tomas does not have a sweet tooth. I can say now that this was the first time during the evening that I was aware that our two personalities were being differentiated by the banquet.

We finished the soup, leaving the little dead animal in the bottom of the basin. I had prepared myself in case this was one of those meals in which protocol demands that the guests eat the "choice" delicacy. I thanked my lucky stars that I have both the digestion of a shark and the ability to turn my imagination on and off at will. I was reminded of the Banquet of Gums on Tiger Lily. (The Gums are the only thing one does *not* eat.) That banquet was the most nauseous of all and anyone who could endure the stench and still keep their jaws moving could face anything.

The little animal had served its purpose. Cook came in and prodded the animal and pronounced that there was still some goodness in it if anyone would like more. I declined but Jet and Tom had seconds. They ate with relish.

I asked what this dish was called and was told "primer". And why not? It primes the palate. It is the introduction to the meal and is essentially simple. The animal, I discovered, is called a quuaam and its sweetness is induced by a special diet. In their natural state quuaams are aquatic and I was told that many of them lived in the river, which flowed just over our heads, but that these would not be sweet and should not be eaten.

Winter Wind was very convivial and relaxed. He told me that on Pe-Ellia banquets always follow the same general pattern. The "primer" is always followed by a pause in the eating while the stomach "girds its loins" and beer is drunk.

Beer. Well, the Pe-Ellians have many skills, but among these beer brewing cannot be included. The lukewarm, headless, brackish liquid they called beer had an oily, recycled taste, which has nothing in common with the living drink we know as beer. I thought they had mistranslated and mentioned this, but no, they insisted it was brewed with yeast and gave me a very creditable account of how it was made. So beer we must call it. I was surprised to observe that Tomas, who is in the main a teetotaller, had a sip and then asked for more. In retrospect I can see this as another point of divergence between us. I have looked for a metaphor to describe what was beginning to happen this evening. The best I can find is that we are being "peeled" apart. Tomas is being "peeled" away from me. I am not sure that this is intentional.

I am coming to know these Pe-Ellians and to see the kinds of tracks along which their minds run. To the Pe-Ellians, enjoying a banquet is dependent on achieving a certain frame of mind. All the little ceremonies are aimed at guaranteeing this frame of mind. Their beer is, I am sure, highly potent, though not necessarily alcoholic. The glow-balls hypnotise in some strange way. The mind is deadened. No unruly shock can arrive to disturb the atmosphere. I stake a million that these Pe-Ellians, so austere, so pure, abstracted and cerebral, are also great sensualists and among the senses I would single out the sense of touch as the most potent. How do they get their thrills?

Well today we saw that they love a mud bath. Perhaps they also like scratching each other's backs.

Thoughts such as these were in my mind as I watched Winter Wind drain his mug of beer, wipe his hand across his mouth in a wholly Earthlike gesture and complete the sequence with a mighty belch. I decided at that moment to keep my mind as clear as possible. To enjoy to the full the tastes of the banquet, but to keep my faculties unclouded.

"We are relaxed at table," said Winter Wind, turning to me.

"You can do almost anything. Let your hair out," said Jet, downing the last of the soup.

"Food is a barrier, which prohibits offence," continued Winter Wind and smiled.

More beer was served and I was intrigued to see Tomas take a full glass and then enter into an animated discussion with Gus on the local flora. Good old Tomas. As I write the banquet has only been over a few hours and I am still buoyed up. I have just come back from seeing how he is. I found him sprawled in bed, fully clothed and snoring. I took his shoes off. I was tempted to photograph him for the encoder . . . but I am not that malicious. However, I shall take a scientific delight in discovering the state of his head in the morning. He has drunk not wisely but too well, and has had a very good time.

After the beer, Cook came in carrying a long plate on which was the fish that liked music. It was shaped into a circle with its tail thrust between its jaws and the teeth pressed through the tail. In appearance the fish was very like a very large rock cod of the type found in North Atlantic waters. Although it was cooked the skin retained a deep, almost glossy, blue-black colour.

Why had Cook played music to this fish? Why had Tomas not been allowed to continue watching the playing? I asked these two questions.

The immediate response was silence, accompanied by gestures and facial expressions which I classified as amazement and amusement. But no-one spoke.

"Let me guess," I said. "On Earth we have an ancient idea that harmony and health are reflections of one another. You play music to a fish just as we play music to chickens . . . it makes them feel good." I realised that I was quickly getting out of my depth.

"Perhaps music improves the flavour," I concluded, lamely I admit.

The Pe-Ellians nodded and looked at one another to see who was prepared to speak. Finally Jet took up the challenge. He smoothed his garment on his chest with one broad hand and began speaking slowly, choosing his words with great care.

"Yes, well, you're on the right highroad, but you have started at the wrong place. True that the Do-ev-ve can be a musical instrument and that Cook was once a master . . . I did not know you knew this . . . but in this instance the Do-ev-ve, what you called a float-harp, was being used as a . . . a . . . I am at a loss for translation."

"Bulldozer," offered Gus.

"No . . . no."

"Tranquilliser." This from Tom.

"Stun gun," offered Winter Wind.

All the Pe-Ellians seemed perplexed. Obviously none of them were satisfied with their selected translations.

"Alas, the pity of it is that you do not have a word for what the float-harp is . . . does. We use it as a way of bringing about the suicide of the flesh we wish to eat. For you see we cannot kill directly. We never kill . . . except sometimes by accident . . . intentionally. That is very important. We encourage an animal to reach its own particular perfection." Jet beamed. "Fulfilment, you would call it. We accelerate the process through the adept use of the float-harp. Every animal, indeed all life, has its own individual melody. But play this melody to a creature, and lo, it will flourish before your eyes. The building blocks of its body will all dance the same tune. Then, when melody and life are one, the flesh reaches perfection and it is then that we stop playing. We allow the surd notes of the great universe to come surging in. Waves from the farthest reaches of space. Galaxy-wide peaks and troughs. Think of that, eh?

"The small private melody is swept out of the body and joins the outward flow of time and thought. There is no decay or pain. Only simple death as old as time and . . . for us, the sweetness of what remains."

Jet finished speaking and smiled his cat-smile, revealing his black gums. I understand the general meaning of his words for the concepts are not unknown, but I did not understand what he meant by "the surd notes of the great universe".

He was still smiling as though in a kind of reverie when I asked him if the surd notes were connected with what we call entropy.

"No," he said. "That is your pessimism. It is almost the opposite of the surd. You see loss. You consider stillness the end of all movement. We see it differently. For us, stillness is an affirmation that life has moved on. We see everything as waiting and wanting to join the great flow of thought which envelops, surrounds, infuses and informs our universe. Only the pure may join this movement."

He looked at me quizzically. "The fish is happy and at the moment of its greatest happiness its life force is released into the expanding universe."

I nodded. As casually as possible I asked, "Could you kill me with the float-harp?"

"Of course," answered Jet without so much as a pause. "The float-harp is universal, but I wouldn't use a float-harp to kill you."

"What would you use?"

Silence. I cursed myself for my lack of tact.

"I would not kill you," he said finally, very softly. "But such things are best not spoken of, even at a banquet."

There I let the matter stand. Tomorrow I may ask Winter Wind for more information. Then again I may not. If I have learned one thing from all my years messing about with other cultures it is that you don't try to learn too much too quickly. Always one finds there are assumptions about life which are not articulated as a formal philosophy. I do not believe the Pe-Ellians have a philosophy as we know it. Nor do I believe they have a concept of rationality. Logical questioning can only achieve so much.

Anyway, back to the banquet.

When Jet finished speaking, Winter Wind took charge of the conversation.

"Come, come. Let's not insult the fish by tardiness," he said. He held a long thinbladed knife and cut cleanly into the side of the fish.

It smelled like fish!

Winter Wind divided it up into six portions. Cook did not eat with us, but hovered in the background clasping and unclasping his hands. Mnaba dissected his fish with all the care of the born naturalist. We both observed that the skeletal structure was similar to the fish's Earthly counterparts. With his examination complete, Tomas tucked in. I found the flesh somewhat too gelatinous for my taste, but did my best not to let this show. Accompanying the fish was a pink sauce, which I found exquisite, and ladled on to my plate liberally.

Halfway through the fish course I judged that the conversation had returned to normal and decided to return to the topic of the float-harp.

I waved to Cook, calling him over, and complimented him on the fish and sauce. This obviously pleased him.

"You clearly brought the fish to perfection. Tell me, is the float-harp difficult to play?"

Cook looked at Winter Wind and I am sure Winter Wind nodded. At all events Cook spoke.

"It is hard to play and the tuning is significant." This I believe, as the instrument has a hundred and twenty strings, many of which have to be tuned together.

"Are you a good player?"

"Not now." He looked at his hands. "Once, though, these could make feet tap."

"Ah, so the instrument is played for pleasure and is not used merely as a 'stun gun'?"

"The float-harp is always played for pleasure—but precautions must be taken. It is a powerful instrument that reaches beyond music."

"You play with a safety catch on?"

"Yeah. In any case a planxty should never be played using a tuning that relates to Pe-Ellians, or to humans for that matter. That is how I fell."

Cook looked round the room. I had the impression that he had perhaps said more than he should have, but everyone looked at him kindly.

"Can you tell me about that?" I asked, and this time I know that Winter Wind nodded.

Cook looked at me and pressed his large hands together.

Normally with Cook there is a sense of bubbling fun. Now he seemed sombre.

"It is not much and is easily told," he said. "Once, after the rain, on a day not unlike today, I went to the deep of the forest and played. It was not near here but in a part of our land where the days are warmer and the rains more frequent. I was a noted player, you understand, and when word passed that I was intending to play an audience gathered.

"On this day there were some twenty Pe-Ellians surrounding me and some small hind and several nests of birds. Birds are very susceptible to music. In those days, for it was long ago, I was an optimist. I allowed my tonal range to spread wider than I should have. Perhaps it was the rain and the smell of the earth on that particular day, but I played wildly, pressing the melodies well beyond the normal limits. I was young, you understand—and the mud—I had lathered myself well. I came to my senses when I saw the Pe-Ellians trying to run away. Several climbed trees after the fashion of the menopause though their skins were regular. Another ploughed his skin with his fingers. Some were on their knees. I stopped playing in confusion and the small deer fell in a tangle of legs.

"That day I was called before a Mantissa to explain."

"And?" I asked.

"Since that day I only play to cook. I became Cook. That is all. An end was begun."

While Cook was speaking I was aware that the others were all listening very seriously, very intently. Winter Wind and Gus were nodding as though they were remembering the scene.

Cook rubbed his hands on his apron and blinked with both eyes. Although I am reasonably sure this gesture means "No more words" or simply "I have finished what I wanted to say", its effect was profoundly pathetic. I felt I wanted to comfort Cook but lacked the words or the means.

"Karitsa calling," said Cook and departed in haste.

As soon as he had left Winter Wind leaned his huge head across to me and whispered, "He used to be a very fine—"

"The very finest," interrupted Jet.

"—float-harp player. He could have charmed the flowers so that they would have opened at midnight. I heard him when he was in his second, shortly before his . . . fall. Ah, he had a golden mandate. But that's the way with us." Winter Wind sighed.

Jet leaned over. "Cook rarely talks about it and we never mention it to him, you understand. His loss is great. His talent was unique."

I had the impression that Jet wanted to say more, but any further conversation was cut short by a scruffling noise which came from the main door leading to the clearing.

The membrane opened and there in the glow stood Menopause.

He shuffled into the room and the sight of him shocked me. Where his skin had lifted from his body it had lost its transparency and was almost opaque. Where it still adhered, the skin markings had lost all consistency and were little more than smear marks. The red lines which had previously defined his skin had all gone except for his face, where they seemed concentrated like so many red snakes in a jar. His mouth was a black gash which he opened and closed with a sucking sound rather like a grounded fish. His arms remained reasonably intact except for pouches of skin beneath the armpit. Of his legs, the feet seemed intact but for the rest you would have thought he had stepped from the Arabian Nights. His skin formed a kind of loose trousers.

As soon as he entered Gus and Tom leaped to their feet and moved across to help him. He waved them off with a growl. His eyes looked around the room and settled on me.

He winked first one eye and then the other.

That sounds ridiculous I know, but so help me that was what I saw. The effect was so comic that I almost gagged on my fork.

I looked across at Tomas. I could tell that he was disappointed to see Menopause. They have not hit it off.

Gus and Tom made a place between them at the table and Menopause settled himself in. His every move seemed painful.

But I had the impression that the pain was not physical. I know little of Menopause or menopause but I can judge that this change of skin is far more than a mere physical response to growing bigger . . . it has spiritual meanings I can only guess at. I observe with interest that all the assembled Pe-Ellians treat Menopause with great consideration.

Menopause settled himself. More beer was served. Tomas had another full tumbler.

The next course was called "strong flesh". I feared the worst.

"Because it makes you live a thousand years," explained Jet and that made me feel a bit easier.

"But you should be warned, this food contains some very potent herbs. It is very very savoury. Eat it with care."

The meat looked innocent. Rather like a large slab of veiny corned beef. When Cook cut it it seemed to have a very tight cellular structure. In the mouth it literally melted like marshmallow. The flavour shifted round from salty to bitter to aloes to bile.

"Hold it in your mouth as long as you can. Draw out as much goodness as you can, then swallow quickly," said Jet after I had taken a large mouthful.

I tried to. I held the dissolving particles in my mouth and the taste of the meat grew in bitterness. I tried to swallow but could only gag. The meat reduced to a clot in my mouth.

Cook came to my rescue.

"Aiyee," he said, "the dregs." And quickly picked up a napkin and had me spit into it. Winter Wind handed me a beer and I downed it at one swallow. The taste cleared slowly.

I opened my eyes and found that Menopause was on his feet. He was growling something and pointing at me.

"He is saying you have done well," translated Jet. "He says he expected no less."

"And he is right," added Tom. "Few can hold it in their mouths for so long. But we have some old ones who have trained themselves to chew the residue. Think on that."

"Why," I asked, surprised that my voice sounded normal.

"For strength," said Jet. "Everybody needs strength."

Menopause was still on his feet. He opened his mouth and pushed his tongue out. On the tip I could see the black grains that were all that were left of the meat.

"Menopause is very strong," said Jet.

Menopause kept his hands resting on the table as though he were afraid it would topple over. His eyes stayed on me and it was a strange gaze. Not unfriendly, not quite focused. It was the look of a child shortly after birth, when the eyes settle on a light or colour with interest. Finally he took the napkin and cleared the residue from his mouth.

"Do foods like this help you?" I asked Menopause and to my amazement he nodded as naturally as a person from Earth.

"Food is a great leavener," said Winter Wind. "That is how I think you would express it on Earth. In food there is freedom and safety. On Pe-Ellia we rely on food for more than just nutrition."

As he said this there came a call from the kitchen. "Karitsas."

Everyone stood up. Many times I have found myself enveloped in an alien ritual. On Tiger Lily I nearly lost my hands for not touching one of their holy relics. Later I almost had my throat slit for coughing during a solemn silence. This standing was like a national anthem.

So karitsas it was. Cook entered bearing a large brown bowl containing, as far as I could see, fried eggs. It was only when he placed the bowl on the table that I could see that the "fried eggs" were alive, and gently flapping their way round the bowl like so many overgrown amoebas.

"More health food?" I asked.

"And the best," replied Winter Wind.

Menopause sat down and leaned back in his chair with his mouth open.

"He wants feeding," said Winter Wind and motioned to Cook. Cook touched one of the creatures and it immediately rolled up into a ball. He scooped it up and dropped it into Menopause's gaping mouth. Menopause gargled for a few moments and then relaxed. His body just seemed to collapse, cave in. He lolled there, indecent as a drunkard, and snored. At least that is the word that Jet used to describe the rasping, gulping sounds that came from him.

"Don't worry, it won't have the same effect on you," said Tom, who must have seen my reaction.

Each of the Pe-Ellians leaned forward and selected a karitsa. They ate them with the same joy some people feel crushing a sweet grape against the roof of the mouth.

"I'll try one," said Mnaba.

As though in response one of the karitsas worked its way up the side of the bowl. It rested on the edge, its wafer-thin body rippling as it tried to get a purchase on the air, and then toppled off and landed on the table.

"It likes you," murmured Cook, as the karitsa righted itself with a flip and began to work across the table. Tomas's eyes bulged.

"Touch it on its crown," said Jet. "Gently, don't break the membrane." Thomas reached out and touched the orange "yolk". He was slow in reacting and the karitsa closed its moist body round his finger.

"Quickly to your mouth," called Winter Wind and Tomas dropped the karitsa into his mouth and pulled it off his finger with his lips.

His cheeks writhed. He closed his eyes and I could see the contact linguist training as he took charge of his throat and swallowed.

His eyes burst open. His body tensed and then arched. He clamped his elbows to his sides and threw his head back. His mouth opened and I expected a scream, but all he said was, "Ga Ga." After this he relaxed and a silly smile spread up over his face. He drew his knees up to his chest and curled up in his chair. If he had been a cat I would have expected him to purr. All he said was, "Goooooo."

All eyes were on me. Winter Wind was smiling.

I pointed at one of the karitsas which had climbed up the side of the bowl and said that I'd have that one.

"Catch it then," said Jet. "That's part of the pleasure."

The karitsa waved at me vaguely as I reached out. I dabbed at its dome and it immediately balled up and fell back into the bowl.

"Quick," warned Cook. "Scoop it out before the rest go for it."

I plunged my hand into the warm liquid and two other karitsas closed about my fingers. I lifted out my balled-up karitsa and before I could think dropped it into my mouth.

It flapped—and then it relaxed, exploding into the most beautiful taste I have ever known, though I cannot describe it. I swallowed by reflex and the taste filled the whole of my mind. I felt the karitsa flow through my veins and skin. It touched my toes and flowed up again towards my heart. I thought I would die and the thought was beautiful.

I relaxed. Or rather I should say the relaxing was done to me, for I had no more control than does a puppet when someone cuts all its strings.

My eyes opened. The world swam back into focus. I opened my mouth and said, "Ba Ba."

The world was bright and everything glowed with an inner light. The bowl in the centre glowed brightest of all. I could still see the karitsas, but now they looked as if they were made of quicksilver.

Mnaba glowed too. And all the Pe-Ellians. Only round my hand was there darkness where the karitsas which had clung to my fingers died.

Cook was there peeling off the dead karitsas, which had congealed. Everyone was looking at me. Mnaba too.

"What was that?" I murmured.

"Karitsa," they all answered.

I felt high and recognised the symptoms as such. God knows I've had enough practice with alien drugs but there is a difference.

The walls seemed larger. They were full of moving veins. They lifted me and I swam with them. My senses were detached from my body and bobbed round the room like a ping pong ball in a whirlpool.

I studied the karitsas and heard a sound of sleigh bells. I knew I was hearing their thoughts and enjoyed the sensation before I was whisked away.

I swung over towards Tomas and slipped into his mind like an oyster. He did not seem to notice.

Something in me recoiled from such intimacy and a protective fog gathered over him and me. At that moment he yawned.

I slipped through the fog and slid up to the ceiling. I could see myself. I could see Tomas. I could not see the Pe-Ellians.

No, that's wrong. I could see where they *were* but I could not see *them*. What I saw were barriers. Like cliffs of black granite. Impenetrable. Save for Menopause. His face was a shroud.

It was like a bundle of clothes that accidentally resembles a face, but without life. I looked at it for a long time before I felt myself sliding down some greasy rollercoaster and ended with a jump back in me. I too seemed to glow.

Now as I write, hours later, the glow is gone. But the memory, as they say, lingers on. I face the fact that the karitsa has in some way stimulated my telepathic power, or awakened a power that had long been dormant. I feel like a man who suddenly discovers that he has three hands—clumsy but with potential.

Returned to myself I was content just to slump and watch. For me the banquet had ended. I was glad the Pe-Ellians let me be.

Tomas was a transformed man. He was the heart and soul of the party. He spoke brilliantly. He analysed Earth and Pe-Ellia, he speculated on the similarity of their basic customs and compared their flora and fauna.

How long their conversation continued I do not know. Gradually, though, I began to feel a sense of alarm—a pricking of my thumbs and the hairs on the back of my neck curling.

My unease grew the longer I sat still. Finally I sat forward. Menopause moved at the same time as I did. I stared at him and as I stared at the shroud, which I have called his barrier, his face, his mental shield began to dissolve.

I looked into Menopause.

I looked into Menopause.

Mystical experiences are by their nature so personal that they cannot be communicated. We take on trust the great divines. You must just believe me when I say that I looked into Menopause and saw a face, a young face, an ageless face looking back at me and laughing, irreverent and joyful. The face was the face of my friends on Orchid. It was Tomas's face. It was all the faces I have ever seen rolled together. *It was my face.*

Perhaps it is true that wherever we look all we ever see or find is ourselves. As I looked at the face its laughter became quicksilver (like the karitsas) and I could feel it running all over me. The smile turned into clouds of blue and green flowers, which I could smell. The face turned to linen—to light—and was gone. It was replaced by darkness in which deep red fires burned.

I seemed to feel a wind blowing at me, urging me to enter that dark cave and plunge into those fires.

"*No*," roared a voice, which I knew as my own though I had not spoken.

The wind dropped. A greyness filled the dark cave of Menopause's face and this slowly reasserted itself as his "shroud". Everything was as it had been, but not quite. Previously his "shroud" had been as alien as the shields covering Winter Wind and the rest. Now it looked approachable. I felt as if all I had to do was reach out and whisk it away to reveal—

To reveal what? I do not know. Menopause's face? His face as it will be after the change? As it will be after death? I do not know and I am strangely lacking in curiosity. Time will tell. I wait. And I am moving.

I looked at the "shroud" for some minutes and then Menopause stood up. I re-entered the real world. Menopause stretched with his arms above his head and his hands like stars. And then was gone.

None of the others paid any attention to his leaving. They continued their conversation. I too stood up and bowed to the gracious hosts. They waved and nodded in farewell. Tomas smiled from ear to ear. I smiled too and came up here to my room. Here I have made my notes.

My window is on and outside the river foam falls like melting snow from a church roof. The party broke up, I judge, about half an hour after I left.

I went out into the clearing to say goodbye to everyone. Jet said he was going home by his favourite route and dived into the river. Tom and Gus said they would run. Winter Wind said he just wanted to "meander". So far as I can ascertain we parted the best of friends. I felt a sense of wellbeing and warmth towards everyone.

When I re-entered the Palm Court, Tomas had already gone off to his room and the table was cleared. I crossed to the kitchen intending to say goodnight and to thank Cook. I did not knock and Cook did not hear me coming.

He had his back to me as I popped my head round the door of the kitchen. He was holding his apron up with one hand and rubbing his side with long slow movements with the tips of his fingers.

After a few moments a line appeared down his side. It was a flap of skin like a pocket or a large but very thin mouth. He slipped his hand inside the flap (literally inside his body) and drew out an egg. The egg had a pearly white lustrous skin and was about the size of a goose egg. The slit in his side closed and his body became seamless as before. He held the egg up to the light, examining it, and then, satisfied, slit its leathery skin open with his thumb. Out popped a karitsa.

He held it in the palm of his hand and crooned to it softly. The karitsa rippled and then spontaneously rolled up into a ball. Cook popped it into his mouth.

He stood still for a few seconds and then his whole body shook. When relaxation came he crouched down on his haunches.

I withdrew. What this is all about I do not know. It raises more questions than I can answer. Will remember to ask tomorrow.

Tomas is abed. No doubt by now Jet has reached his watery home. Perhaps Winter Wind is out there in the jungle communing with the moon or the stars or whatever Pe-Ellians commune with. Menopause is no doubt scratching about. Or then again maybe he is resting up, getting ready to shed. How like a birth that must be. Wonder if I could be there when the skin comes off.

Tomorrow promises to be busy. Winter Wind has agreed to meet us for lunch and answer any questions. So till then.

Commentary

Many of the details in Thorndyke's account need clarification.

Float-harp: The float-harp is square and stands upright. Its height is about two metres and the Pe-Ellians play it while kneeling. It has a hundred and twenty hollow strings, which are tuned in groups of five. The strings contain coloured fluids. Its float characteristic comes from the pressure pads which are attached to each group of five strings. Each pressure pad has a ring on top so that it can be raised or depressed, thereby changing both the pitch and the quality of the sound produced. The instrument is played rapidly by plucking and strumming and to our ears its main characteristic is a wailing sound. However in the hands of a master like Cook its sound can vary from hard-plucked notes reminiscent of the xylophone to the sweep of a Hawaiian guitar. Pe-Ellian music does not have any formal rhythm as we understand it, but has what Cook once described as "emotional rhythm".

When Cook and Jet visited me on Camellia, I asked Cook to explain more about how the float-harp works. The following was his reply:

You know a lot about us, Tomas, how we live in sympathy. I was one of the most sensitive of my hatching. I was played to as karitsa. I was almost too sensitive to live. I could hear the babble of grass as I walked over it. While in my first I made the float-harp, as you call it, my own. I lived alone and played only to trees and grasses. A master heard me and invited me to study with him. I played him through his passing and learned the life scales.

At my second change I achieved symmetry, which is also called a Golden Mandate. That meant I only had to persist in the line I was following and I could become a Mantissa like my teacher.

All life has its rhythm, just as every atom has its unique history. I was one of those permitted by training, aptitude and fortune to perceive this rhythm. Really, you might say that life played upon me and the result of this was the sounds I produced from the float-harp. Through me "emotional rhythm" was manifest.

That is a rich experience—and dangerous, as I told you. I transgressed, got carried away, was wayward, and the result was death. The killing marked me. I was called before a Mantissa . . . he disfigured me. Removed my mandate. Set limits in my brain so that I could never again play within the Pe-Ellian scales. Made me Balacas. In other respects my skill remained, but I was like a singer who lacked certain notes. I changed trades—from Player to Cook.

I give rapture to fish. I'll soon be back in the melting pot.

Unbroached Ancient Treasure Tomb and Laughing Gas: We never met these two scholars again. At the banquet I asked them to explain their work and what they meant by "Mantissa Handmaidens". Unbroached Ancient Treasure Tomb was a historian who specialised in the very early history of Pe-Ellia. Before long it would be his duty to undertake investigation of an ancient tomb which he had discovered. To gain strength for this he was working as Handmaiden to a Singing Mantissa. He had taken the trip to Earth to toughen his mind with a "living primitive culture". He said to me, "We none of us knew how dangerous that would be."

Laughing Gas told me, with a laugh, that he was a "sandpainter and mudstirrer", by which I thought at first he meant that he was some kind of artist. He said that this was not so. He seemed to have no function other than to be wherever he was needed at the right time. "This," as he pointed out, "requires no mean skill. I have to keep in contact with all aspects of our society. I spend long hours alone testing the ether, wetting my finger to see which way the wind lies, trying to sense problems before they arise.

"I am called Laughing Gas because I am always in a good humour. Were it contrariwise I would be my own worst enemy and a cause of great discord."

I asked him about his trip to Earth and he told me that the experience had stretched him to the full. He'd had to be in ten places at once.

"As you can see I am now a Mantissa Handmaiden, which is to say someone is taking care of me for a change. I'm convalescing after Earth. I am pleased to say that I find Earth people congenial tablemates."

On a later occasion I asked Jet to give me an alternative translation of Laughing Gas's occupation. He thought for a minute and then said, "Policeman".

Karitsa: Thorndyke's report of his eating of the karitsa is certainly at variance with my experience. The unflattering portrait of my lolling back and saying "Ga Ga" I must accept, for during those few moments I was not conscious of myself.

To me the karitsa tasted not unlike mushrooms. It released its flavour in one rush and certainly, it was more than just food. I felt it speed through my body like a sudden attack of pins and needles that was ended as soon as it began; I felt totally enlivened by it. My companions' faces seemed more charged with life, but I had no sense of supernatural life, telepathy or anything vaguely occult. If Thorndyke entered my mind as he says, then I was certainly unaware of it.

At that time I remember glancing at Thorndyke, expecting him to offer some comments when we were talking about Laughing Gas's career and it seemed to me that he had dozed off comfortably in his seat. In other words I do not doubt the truth of what he thought he saw, though there is a far more rational, homely explanation—that he was dreaming.

With regard to his comments on my being "peeled away" from him, I feel that this movement was based within *him*. I do not believe it was stimulated by the Pe-Ellians. His observations are based more on movements which were taking place within him than on objective observations. I believe the subsequent events during our stay bear out the truth of this.

> "In working with an alien race your method of procedure and inquiry must largely be guided by that race's sense of structure."

This axiom from the Contact Linguists' Handbook proved to be as true for Pe-Ellia as it had been for Tiger Lily or Orchid.

On the sixth day of our visit we enjoyed what Winter Wind called The Day of Formal Explanation. The meeting was scheduled to take place after lunch. Thorndyke and I spent the morning preparing our questions. I combed the encoder files to make sure there were no areas of interest we had missed. I asked the encoder what questions it had to raise and it presented a list of a hundred and twenty-seven questions. I had my own questions based on my observations and naturally Thorndyke also had his. That morning we tried to bring some focus to our knowledge and establish our priorities. We realised that it would be impossible to obtain answers to even a tenth of our questions.

We decided to concentrate only on questions which related to Pe-Ellian dealings with Earth (with one exception—the question "What is a Mantissa?") We felt that if we could ascertain the Pe-Ellian attitude to Earth we would have a clearer knowledge of how to proceed. It was agreed that Thorndyke would ask the questions.

We took a light lunch of salad and fruit which we ate at the table by the river. As Cook was clearing up Winter Wind arrived.

Cook placed a small bowl of white cakes on the table and departed. Winter Wind took one cake, bit into it and said, "Let us begin."

He asked if we had many questions and then asked to have them read to him as a list. He was surprised that we had so few questions and that they seemed so restricted.

"Come, come," he said. "Surely you want to know about our

sex life? And what about our agriculture and our cities? And what about our basic science and do we suffer from indigestion?"

We confessed that yes, these things were of great interest but that in the interests of precision we had tried to organise our questions along certain lines.

"Ah, you want me to answer in compartments then?" asked Winter Wind. "I doubt I can do that. If I were to attempt it I would end up with oversimplification and you would end up making assumptions. Apart from that, consider. I am speaking an alien tongue and am therefore already constrained by what your language can handle. Better let me talk my own way. I get the general idea of what you want to know."

Thorndyke started to argue with him. Winter Wind finally silenced him by saying that he had heard about Space Council debates and had never yet understood why Earth people wrangled so much about procedure.

Thorndyke's account of this important meeting follows. He has condensed Winter Wind's remarks and changed their sequence. Nevertheless, the words he uses are almost entirely Winter Wind's own.

Thorndyke's Diary: Entry 19

Winter Wind is a wily old bird. I give him that. Whether he came here already knowing what he was going to say I do not know, but certainly he outflanked us. I can still hear him saying, "Holists. We Pe-Ellians are holists." As though he had invented the concept. No matter. What he said has been of great interest and has plugged a few gaps in our knowledge.

So picture him. Long, lean, glossy and tattooed. Hairless and stretched out on a bench in the sunshine like some latter-day Roman. He blinks his yellow eyes and speaks.

"Thought is a living thing. I believe you have a similar understanding for I note that you pay great attention to prayer and will power. Both indicate a reliance on thought. But what you do not appear to see and what I therefore must ask you to accept is that what you think profoundly affects your physical life and the physical life of all other persons. What you think becomes you and equally affects say that blade of grass. On Pe-Ellia the atmosphere is charged with thought in the way that a battery is charged with energy. Earth is the same. Earth and Pe-Ellia are alike in that both have a biosphere and both have what I shall call a psychosphere.

"The psychosphere is the realm of thought. It transcends both physical and temporal barriers. We who are alive at present are the heirs of all pasts. This is as much true of Earth as it is of Pe-Ellia. Pe-Ellia is, of course, much older than Earth, but even so we inherit the sins of our fathers just as much as you do.

"Now, there is this difference between Earth and Pe-Ellia. We on Pe-Ellia are as acutely aware of thought as you are of heat or gravity for example. You, however, who possess a staggering mental potential seem ignorant of your gift. You squander it in anger, pain and intrigue.

"You ask are we telepathic? Your question shows your ignorance. Of course we are telepathic—as you say—because all life is telepathic. To be alive is to take part in the vital process of thought. All life thinks and contributes to the expanding reservoir of thought. Not to be telepathic is to be dead. You, Marius Thorndyke, are terrifyingly telepathic as is Professor Mnaba. You are both terrifying because so ignorant of yourselves.

"How telepathic are we? The answer is totally. Therein lies a problem for us. We try to avoid the consequences of telepathy. You see, telepathy militates against individual development and for us that is the only kind of development. But imagine. Living within the mind of every other person. Or to put it another way, to have every other person living with your mind. To be bounden with a million and one taboos, inhibitions and consequences of imagined transgression. Better the closed mind free to roam and journey within itself than the levelled norm of equal knowledge. Besides, it would be unfair to the young to deprive them of the gathering joys of age. Telepathy is the last resource of the failing intellect.

"Occasionally we use this power in case of some disaster. In the past there have been times when our whole civilisation has been joined to confront some natural event, but since the growth of the Mantissa protectors such occasions have declined from infrequent to rare. Not once in my lifetime, and I am old, has there been a Pe-Ellian joining.

"The only time I ever open my telepathy is with the . . . er . . . queen or if I need the help of a Mantissa guardian." He tapped his fingers against his lips and thought.

"What else? Let me see. To contact a karitsa and get it ready for eating. That is about all. Between ourselves, never. That is the ultimate obscenity for us. To either parade your mind or seek to seduce another mind."

He looked at both of us and was obviously amused at something. "With you humans it is different, though. We cannot understand you. You welter in your thoughts. Sometimes you project specific thoughts. Sometimes you pour out emotion like a river sluicing over its banks. With your people we have to erect complicated barriers."

"Use your Mantissa?"

"Use our Mantissa," he nodded. "You see, we do not want to read your minds, and we are learning not to. We watch you, though. We are aware of the sympathy which passes between the two of you and the deep shared understanding, but we know that you do not communicate directly with your minds."

"We don't know how to," said Tomas.

"Ah," said Winter Wind and nodded.

"How long have you known of us?" I asked.

"We are an ancient race. Many centuries ago in your prehistory we heard the first mumblings of your minds. In a way those thoughts were not unlike the pleasing lisping of the karitsa. We studied them and one Outrigger Mantissa hung in your solar system for several thousand years trying to discover in which way you would evolve."

"Did the Mantissa land?"

"Land? We never land. You should know that. No, the Mantissa watched and watched and when the burden of watching became too great, it simplified its knowledge and a new Mantissa, a younger one, took over. Your Mantissa then went on a long holiday with a school of Angels and I know no more of him."

"Angels?"

"I think that is what you would call them. Space fish. They are a different order of being from you or I.

"The Mantissa's knowledge of you was very great. He forecast that you primates would obtain a manipulative advantage over other species. The younger Mantissa only stayed a few thousand years. He concluded that as a species you were fundamentally belligerent and given time would wipe yourselves out. The majority of species do, you know. At the same time, of course, we were keeping watch on many other emergent civilisations. You have visited a few of their planets now. Many lagged behind you on Earth. Some perished by their own hand. We watched in sadness. Others are beyond you and safe from you. We protect them.

"Anyway, to return to Earth. We soon became aware of the growing telepathic power of your race. In sheer vigour of output you rival us. Your planet shone like a psychic beacon for those who could see it. But it shone the colour of pain and agony. It shone with idealism also. It was an addled egg of feeling and we found we had to be careful to avoid unprotected contacts.

"Every two or three thousand years or so we would send an Outrigger to see what was happening to you. He would sip your planet's psychosphere and return.

"When you developed the power of the Sun on Earth we knew you were doomed. But somehow, somehow, you avoided that war and then you leaped into space. Your development of the Garfield Equations and the power they gave you to romp in the heavens forced us to take a closer interest. We decided to pen you until such a time as we could evaluate your next evolutionary change.

"You see, we need to keep most of the galaxy clear of your minds. Remember: thought is living and all powerful. Thought affects and infuses everything. Never forget that. Your ignorance of your power, your lack of discipline, your instinctive aggression, your vital passions and finally your bright inquisitive intellects made you wholly dangerous.

"We concluded that only an evolutionary change would make you safe. On this issue two points of view contended. One side held that the best change would be for your broadcasting power to be gelded. You lived happily in ignorance of your power. Perhaps this power was merely luggage from an evolutionary journey you never took. This side wanted to step in and actively interfere with your development. They concluded that you could be stripped of your power to transmit telepathically in a few generations.

"The other side believed that evolution always works in the direction of maximum good. It detected signs that you people, you Earth people yourselves, were close to your next evolutionary break, and that this would be the birth of telepathic self-knowledge. Many urged that we should contact you directly and study with you and help you and determine how well your race and ours could coexist.

"This point of view prevailed and we dispatched Outriggers with diplomatic personnel to all your known centres. And at the eleventh hour almost everything was lost. You turned your power against us. I nearly wept.

"The Outrigger deflected the Whip and it was an accident that some of its power fell on one of your cities. As you know, love of life is central to our being. Many wanted to tighten the envelope and restrict your movements to the main star systems you have contacted. It was at this time I spoke up. My ambition was well known and I had studied Earth. I argued that the fault was ours. Knowing your nature we should have made a more diplomatic approach instead of just arriving. Narrowly I won the day."

"What does Earth look like to you?"

"Tom and Gus were with the Outrigger. You should have asked them what it was like to descend to Earth. I cannot tell it as well as they, but this is how they described it to me.

"Before leaving for Earth the Outrigger Mantissa tuned itself to Earth. It was like hearing distant bells. Some were soft and mellow chimes, some were small and silvery, others were hard, brassy and alarmist. Tom told me he was frightened, for the bells were insistent. There was no tide in them, no ebb and flow. They rolled and roared on. He likened your planet to a loudspeaker which blares full volume, being insensitive to the ear pressed up against it. If you could listen to the mind of a Pe-Ellian you would hear the flow of water, the turning of worms in the soil, the murmuring of karitsas and the breathing of our queen. Occasionally there would be a roar of energy as a Mantissa spouted, but that would be all.

"Tom and Gus said they were happy when the Mantissa cut in and absorbed all of Earth's thought.

"Then they were there. The Mantissa allowed everyone in the Outrigger to sample Earth as they closed with it. Tom heard the shock as Earth recognised the alien ship. He felt the confusion and pain of Chicago. Gus received a visual pattern and described Earth as a giant rogue karitsa. Flapping wildly. A miasma of yellow and blue. He saw nerve forms. Bodies clenched together. Tumbling seas and sand storms and finally a vortex at the centre of which as a scream. Then the Mantissa cut in and again gave the Pe-Ellians time to adjust for the coming ordeal.

"A few Pe-Ellians suffered shock and were put into complete suspension. So, you see, being telepathic is not a bed of roses. At that time none of us really understood that you could not control your mental energy. I still find that hard to believe."

"Why?"

"For most races telepathy is a matter of survival. It grows with the nervous system and is comprehended as naturally as the use of the thumb, for example. You are the odd life out.

"This is all I wish to say about telepathy."

Winter Wind pulled his long legs up so that his head rested on his knees and his hands were clasped round his legs.

I ask, "How were you born?"

"From a karitsa. We all are. Here is a song we learn as little ones. I'll try to sing part of it.

In the beginning was the thought.
And the thought expanded and had no limits,
And the thought took settled form and became the universe,
Became our galaxy,
Became Pe-Ellia.
And the thought took life form and became the queen.
From the queen came karitsa,
And from karitsa came the Pe-Ellians.

"We are the first and therefore the oldest of all physically living things. The first and the oldest. We have an unbroken line from the tiny queen who could only wriggle to the present. We Pe-Ellians are one. A united race. Consolidated by centuries. Supported by traditions and Mantissa knowledge. Here is part of the story of my life.

I am Winter Wind in my sixth change,
I was Winter Wind in my fifth,

Before this I was Footprints in the Mud after my fourth change.
Before this I was Call Softly Lest You Wake the Sleepers,
And before this I had no name.
I was karitsa carried by Old Father Green Thumb,
And so on, and so on, and so on, back to earliest times when all names merge into the one name Ellia.

"I can tell you the names of all my ancestors if you want to hear them, but it would take many days to recite."

"Were the karitsas we ate last night the same kind you grew from?"

"Of course. We all contributed several. We all carry karitsas with us all the time. When the queen gives you eggs to bear it is a sign you are mature and stable. No-one can receive eggs before their fourth change. Look."

Winter Wind began to rub his side in the same way I observed Cook doing yesterday evening. His eyes became dreamy. After a few minutes a seam appeared in his side. Under his working fingers the seam opened to a flap and he was able to insert his hand. He withdrew three eggs.

He offered one to me, which I declined, and one to Tomas, who was too pop-eyed to answer. Winter Wind clearly took Tomas's amazement for a negative and slipped two of the eggs back inside his body. He rubbed the seam and it closed and secured.

With the same flip of the thumb I had noticed with Cook he slit open the leathery egg and out flopped a karitsa. He muttered something to the karitsa, which responded by rolling into a ball. This he ate in the normal manner. The empty shell he tossed into the river. In the clear light of day we could see the effect of the karitsa as it flowed through his body. His skin tone changed slightly to become more pinkish. His eyes brightened.

He spoke. "Afternoon tea, I believe you call it. Would you like some refreshment?"

I felt that my appetite had been completely taken away. Tomas looked green.

Winter Wind continued: "Karitsa is the greatest food for mind and body. Karitsa contains the accumulated experience of our race. To eat karitsa is to restate your identification with the whole of creation, not just with Pe-Ellia. You will come to like them in time. Though I think the expressions on your faces show astonishment not so much at the karitsa itself but at my eating it. Yes? There is a gulf we must bridge.

"You consider us self-eaters, but you see we value karitsa only for what it is, a distillation, not for what it might become, a Pe-Ellian. Moreover, we would not eat karitsa after it had interacted with the fluids of our bodies and had begun to develop into an embryo Pe-Ellian. However, it must be admitted we do not place high value on young life. Many Pe-Ellians are born and many die before their first change. Age is the true test of worth for us."

"Where do you get the eggs?"

"From the queen, naturally, when we sleep with her."

"How often do you sleep with her?"

"As often as necessary. She plants karitsas inside us. We carry them and eat them and occasionally feel the need to let one come to fullness. I have given birth to seven Pe-Ellians. Only one survived the first change and it is now serving as an apprentice with a Gardener on another planet. I wish it well.

"Naturally I would have liked one offspring to follow my calling as Contact Historian and one of them still might. I plan to give birth to some before long."

"Can we watch the birth?"

"Of course, but there is really nothing to see. I will get a bit fatter. I will spend more time swimming, and then one day out they will come slithering, complete with tail and webbed hands. The tail drops off in the first month and the webbed hands dry to more or less normal hands within the year. The eggs hatch inside me, you see. All very simple."

"What colour are they?"

"Depends. Some can be black, some white, some blue, some mottled. You see, skin colour is changeable with us. But they do not have a pattern. A pattern does not emerge until the first change.

"You notice these?" Winter Wind pointed at the marks inside the plates of the skin. "These are our fingerprints. They tell everything about us. Our health, our age, our purposes. The hope of us all is to reach symmetry, when every mark is the same and all the plates describe the same area.

"The first prints appear after the first change. They are smudgy, but give some indication of the innate direction of the person's life and character. Successive changes lead to greater clarification until the last change of all, the seventh, at which the skin should be perfect. Of course, one never really knows until the seventh what is going to happen. After any change the markings can be quite different—indicating that the line of one's destiny has altered. I did not begin as a Historian. I began as a Gardener, following in my incubator's footsteps. My third change was very painful. I came out of it and found that I had a new direction. Historian.

"There will be no more changes of career for me now. I am approaching my last change and it is almost unheard of for a Pe-Ellian to receive new directions after his last change. Of course, the last change is the most important, as that determines whether or not one has achieved symmetry."

"Do you hope to achieve symmetry?"

"Haven't I said so?"

"What chance have you got?"

"Every chance. At my sixth I almost achieved symmetry. That showed that I had merely to persist and all would be well. It was for this reason that I was entrusted with, and indeed requested, the opportunity to work with you. You, Professor Thorndyke, have a powerful mind. It strengthens me.

"If all goes well at the next change then I will request to become a Contact Mantissa. That is my ambition. There are few Contact Mantissae and as more and more civilisations come to maturity so the need for Contact Mantissae grows. However, if no Mantissa will consider me as a Handmaiden I can always die an honourable death and be buried without going back into the stewpot. I will travel first and then have someone play the float-harp to me."

"What happens if something goes wrong?"

"I hardly like to talk about it."

"Please."

There was a long pause. ". . . If I am disfigured. If I transgress in some way, just as Cook transgressed, then I will not achieve symmetry, and that will have been my last chance. I would be deeply hurt, for I have invested every moment to the ideal of Mantissahood. But I would have no choice but to go back in the melting pot and start again as something different. I would accept my doom and my friends would grieve for me."

"What is the melting pot? I've heard you talk about it and I've heard Cook—"

"Aye, yes. It is a literal translation. How shall I describe what happens? Our lives are cycles. The first cycle is the life of the karitsa. It is a selfless, sensuous time and lasts only from the time an egg is laid inside one of us until that egg is consumed or inspired. If it is consumed the life force of the karitsa enters the person who eats it. If it is not consumed fluids within us permeate the skin and interact with the karitsa to start a new Pe-Ellian. After four months of your time this cycle is complete and the young Pe-Ellian tears out of its shell inside us. It rests. When we sleep it emerges from us."

"What about the egg shell?"

"That is its first food. It eats the shell before it emerges. We keep the small fry with us for some weeks and then deliver them to the queen and she takes charge. All the young Pe-Ellians spend their first few years in the queen's crèche. Then they undergo their first change and their old skin is consumed by the queen.

"Markings appear on their skin. These are interpreted and the young Pe-Ellians join older masters. This first skin change celebrates the beginning of the major life cycle of a Pe-Ellian. In all we have seven changes. Each change is significant, but we call them all menopause. When a Pe-Ellian is in menopause he is sacred. He may do anything except injure life. It is a painful time. It is a time when we are susceptible to many influences, all of which can change the way we are when the skin finally comes off. You must have noticed the strange way Menopause behaves. As I said before, thought is living and can infect. In menopause we subject ourselves to the finest influences."

"Is Menopause a general name then?"

"Yes, anyone who is undergoing a change is called Menopause, for they are between states."

"How long does it last?"

"About thirty of your days. Maybe even fifty. It depends how radical the transformation is. If it is longer than thirty days then we know a major change is in the offing."

"How long has Menopause's change been going on?"

"It was, let me see, thirty days on the day you arrived, but we expect him to emerge any time now."

"Will he be greatly changed?"

"I doubt it. He was one of the main supporters of this contact mission. He was the first to read your work, the *Grammaria*, and was one of the main forces behind getting you, Professor Thorndyke, here. We worked together on this and then, without any warning, he turned menopause. He is younger than I, of course, and is just beginning his sixth. He was my student for the fourth and fifth, and is now a Contact Historian in his own right.

"The seventh change is the last and longest. I expect my seventh to begin some time next year or the year after. That completes another cycle. If after the last cycle one is still not perfect then one's body is consumed by the queen. We call it the melting pot for it is not only one's body that is recycled but one's mind and the totality of one's experience. Everything goes back to the queen, who is the ultimate spring of all knowledge."

"And if you are perfect?"

"Then you move on. You are free of being a Pe-Ellian in the simple biological sense. You become transcendent. You become neither dead nor alive. You may become a Mantissa or you may dedicate yourself to the greater space. Consider it this way. Pe-Ellia has its own psychosphere, which is entirely Pe-Ellian. But space, the whole of space, is also a psychosphere in its own right, and here dwell other entities. We are guardians of the greater space for this very small sector of the universe. There are other races beyond.

"When I become, if I become, an Outrigger Mantissa, a Contact Mantissa, I shall journey into the depths of space and meet them."

"How old are you, Winter Wind?"

"In your years—it is 1268 years since I emerged from Old Father Green Thumb. But time is not quite the same for us as it is for you."

"Now can you tell us, what is a Mantissa?"

"I'll try, but I've got a better idea. I'll arrange for you to visit one. I think you would like to see a Singing Mantissa. There is a very old one not too far from here. But to set your curiosity at rest. A Mantissa is a guardian. A storehouse of all our knowledge. A

Pe-Ellian who has gone beyond his seventh, and who has then chosen, having achieved symmetry, to continue in the half-land of Death/Life to help us, to organise, to plan and to record. Mantissae can do practically anything. After many, many thousand years of Mantissahood they depart. They give out their knowledge and depart for greater space."

"With the Angels?"

"Sometimes. Sometimes alone. But before they leave they make sure that all that they know is communicated to their Handmaidens. Later their Handmaidens settle down and become Mantissae in their own right.

"You began by asking me about telepathy. Let me tell you this. Mantissae manipulate thought energy and that is the source of their strength. A Mantissa is a link between the thought of Pe-Ellia and thought waves of greater space. It is both receiver and transmitter. You will understand when you see one.

"Now I begin to weary. I leave time for one last question. We will have many more opportunities to talk."

"Running round our cottage and this clearing is a little circular track, a small depression. What is it?"

"Ah, over there, near the xilia bush?"

"Yes."

"That marks off the building site. You see, your house is Mantissa managed. Within that perimeter everything is construction. When we knew you were coming we cleared the area and dug deep. We designed the Hand and the course of the river. Then we made a link-up and the Mantissa built everything for us and maintains everything. The walls, the boulders, the shrubs and trees are all Mantissa-made. They are artefacts. Adroit, imaginative control of the structure is all that is required. As with the spaceship, so with your house. Dream derived."

"But why? Why go to all that trouble? Are you protecting us or yourselves?"

"Both, naturally. But we all live in dwellings, burrows like this. We are all aligned with Mantissae. You will visit me at my house. Perhaps in two days."

Winter Wind stood up, stretched, bade us farewell and without a backward glance ran out of the clearing.

Thorndyke's Diary: Entry 20

Growingly I have the feeling that we are dealing with the wrong people. We should be talking to these blessed Mantissae, who seem to be involved with everything. They are the arbiters of this planet—of more than this planet.

I have also noticed that everything on Pe-Ellia seems to be transitional—a state between states. There are no definitive forms. Even death seems transitional. On Earth we say death is the only certainty. Here it appears as a stage in the merry-go-round of thought. Are we really such things as dreams are made of? Must watch Menopause. His time is near.

Commentary

The following morning Cook declared to be another day of rest. Thorndyke seemed happy with this and stated his intention to sit in the clearing and think. I chose to continue my biological observations and decided to follow the river as far as I could.

I told Cook this and he offered to pack me sandwiches.

The following entry describes Thorndyke's activities during that afternoon. I remember that I was aware of a strangeness in his manner. He seemed more preoccupied than usual. I judged that he wanted to be alone to mull over the previous day's conversation. I was not aware of any animosity towards me.

Thorndyke's Diary: Entry 21

Mnaba has heaved himself up the waterfall, over the river to the far bank, and is no doubt pushing through the xilia bushes and fan shrubs and the prickly weepers. Mnaba is both a boy scout and a scientist.

Of late he has irritated me more and more. Not that he has changed. He remains the same. It is that I have changed. Am changing.

But enough of that. I am about an experiment.

Thought. Thought is living, says Professor Winter Wind. So

here I am at the Great Divide where Mantissa artefact joins natural creation: at the small ditch discovered by Tomas during his last safari. I intend to see if my thought can have any visible effect.

I am at a place where the circular track joins the river in front of our house. It is a beautiful day. A day picked from boyhood. I feel hopeful and relaxed.

I stand astride the ditch and stare down at my old feet. What shall I think? I try the Lord's Prayer for starters, just to get me rolling along the right track. "Our Father, which art in Heaven. . . ."

No effect. This is reasonable and I try to stuff my disappointment into the background. I have always had an irrational faith in the sheer efficacy of that prayer. As though if one said it at the right time and place it would, Open Sesame-like, effect great marvels. What now to do?

My reasoning is as follows. If, as Winter Wind says, our house and the clearing are all spun from Mantissa thought, then that thought must be active now. Apart from any miracles of biological engineering and molecular jiggery-pokery any action which is now going on must be particularly acute along the perimeter where terra firma meets the Mantissa artefact. Think of the worms burrowing through from rich loam to Mantissa soil. Or the roots of bushes, for some bushes here are semi-sentient. So, along this border there must be a million and one little actions and reactions taking place. If the Mantissa can exist as it were on automatic pilot as far as the clearing is concerned, here at least on the perimeter he must always be awake and on guard.

I see an ant that resembles a cockroach. It approaches the ditch, feelers going up and down like railway signals, and stops. It sits on its back legs and its antennae go on to overtime. It explores every corner of its feeler space. Something is troubling it.

That something could be me.

The ant has backed off. It wanders in a semicircle and again approaches the trench. Again it stops. Again it feels about. If anything it is more frantic. Suddenly it turns and retreats, running in a fast, irregular, defensive pattern. I recognise those movements. I go back several years to a boy with a spade and an anthill and the ants boiling up like a black tide from the hole.

The ant is gone and nothing moves.

Some five yards away from me one of those squirrel-like creatures is approaching the river. He comes to the barrier and stops. I have this overwhelming impression that he is waiting at a ticket counter. Ah yes, he's got his ticket. "Pass brother." He hops over the trench and is into Mantissa land. So squirrels are okay, but no ants are allowed. Suits me; ants have always filled me with a certain loathing. I believe I can smell them. An astringent, mildly cat smell with a touch of formaldehyde for good measure.

Hold it.

Let's rethink that.

Mantissae are susceptible to thought, as are all creatures according to Winter Wind. So when I saw my cockroach ant perhaps I transmitted my reaction, and the Mantissa, careful for our wellbeing and happiness, closed the frontier. Exit ant.

Must ask Winter Wind about this.

Meanwhile I have brought a kitchen spoon with me. I dig into the dark true earth, which is moist and fibrous. I pull the spoon ploughingly towards me through the trench and meet undeniable resistance when I reach the lip of the ditch.

"What kind of mole is this?" says the Mantissa to himself. "Ah, no mole. Just mad Marius playing at farmers. Pass brother." And the spoon, released, springs towards me.

I dig into the Mantissa's brainchild. I quarry his thought. If this be thought then there be great matter in it. In texture it is not different from true soil. But where the wall of the ditch was breached I am rewarded by seeing the Mantissa at work. The crumbled soil evaporates and reconstitutes itself before my startled eyes. I have the distinct feeling that the Mantissa did this for me. . . . (Am I picking up some of this thought?) Perhaps he will show me other things.

I want to get closer. I have lain down in the trench, my arms underneath me, my forehead touching the soil. (I remember how I talked to the bed.)

"Now Mantissa, I want you to make something grow. Blue is my favourite colour. Grow me a blue flower, if you can. A flower I can pick and press between the pages of an almanac."

I concentrate bullets of thought in my head. Little silver spheres. Ballbearings of ideas. And I roll these out into the earth where they drop without trace. No ripples.

Nothing happens.

I imagine my mind is a lighthouse flashing clearly above the stormy waves. I close my eyes in concentration.

"Now Mantissa, do your stuff. A blue flower. I don't mind how big. And you can forget about the almanac." The thought bursts from my head.

Dare I open my eyes? What will I see? I am for a few moments confronted with an immense vacancy, as though I had destroyed the whole of creation, but had somehow contrived to leave myself hanging here in the void. "Oh God, our help in ages past." A panic akin to vertigo grows like a furry ball inside me and then subsides. I am again self-aware. I feel the soil pressed into my nostrils. I feel the damp of the earth strike through my elbows. I hear again, faintly, the stiff flexing of trees.

I lift my head. Open my eyes. Look about.

No blue flower.

And what did I expect? A miracle? Can Thorndyke summon up miracles like ordering groceries?

I am disappointed. True. But had a blue flower appeared I think I would have packed my bags to go. Thank God, God has tact.

I stand up. Brush off the clinging soil. Dust the particles from my knees (for I am wearing shorts) and stare at the earth.

There where I had lain, where my face was pressed into the soil, is a perfect negative mould of my face. It looks concavely up at me.

I am now part of Pe-Ellia. The lines and wrinkles of my face have been taken over by the soil. I have left my mark . . . but am also a marked man.

Commentary

When I returned from my hike up the stream I found Thorndyke was sitting in the clearing listening to the recording we had made of Winter Wind's conversation. He mentioned nothing about his actions during the day. That evening he asked Cook to provide him with a light meal in his room.

While I cannot say that his actions were strange in a pronounced way, I did note in my own diary that he seemed deeply preoccupied and was clearly mulling over some problem.

My day was spent pleasantly in an unsuccessful attempt to climb to the upper reaches of the river. Having crossed the river I found a track, which led out of our perimeter and ran along the bank. It was indistinguishable from the path we had followed the first day when we walked from the space sphere to the cottage. This track followed the convolutions of the river for about a mile. It ended abruptly at a stone step set in the bank. I guessed that the square flat rock served as a diving ledge. At this point the river opened out into a large pool. A waterfall cascaded down in several steps. On the far bank of the pool I could see a couple of large man-sized caves. These I speculated might be Pe-Ellian houses.

I decided to press on up the river, but found my way blocked by the rocky cliff face which formed the waterfall. It had all the appearance of being a rift fault. The walls were sheer and, except where vegetation had managed to establish a foothold, completely smooth. I theorised that the cliffs were somehow water-scoured. There was evidence of ripple markings. Remembering Winter Wind's words, however, I wondered whether one of their Mantissae might not have had a hand in it.

I worked along the base of the cliff for some time, but found no place where I could scramble up easily. I had not come prepared for such a rock climb. I must add that I did not feel this was a deliberate barrier to keep us enclosed. Properly equipped I could have climbed easily.

I returned to the waterfall and found a place where the noise of the tumbling water was muted by a stand of trees. There I settled down to eat the sandwiches Cook had prepared.

Thorndyke comments on the beauty of the day. I too was captivated by it. It was a day of freshness. Every colour seemed new minted, the very air seemed alive.

I don't know how long I slept.

I was woken by a splash close to me. I did not start awake, but rather rose to consciousness in the way a swimmer rises to the surface after a dive. The splash was repeated and I saw figures swimming in the pool. It seemed like a family. There were three reasonably tall Pe-Ellians whose skin patterns were a distinct yellowish orange. The plates of their skins were defined by strong black lines, giving them an overall tigerish appearance. With them were seven youngsters, not long hatched if I could judge from Winter Wind's description. The similarity between reptiles and the Pe-Ellian race is clearly evidenced in their children. These pups had tails, which they used in the way that alligators use their tails to swim. Their hands and feet were distinctly webbed. Their heads were recessed into the shoulders, making the upper part of their bodies somewhat stunted. In size I estimated they were a little over twelve inches from head to foot. The tail would add another six inches. The bodies of all the pups were mottled like walrus hide.

Whether they knew I was watching them I do not know. If they did they certainly didn't care. The taller Pe-Ellians launched themselves from the diving platform in easy lazy arcs. They entered the water with scarcely a ripple. The little ones hurled themselves crazily, twisting like otters and landing with much spray and squeaking. Occasionally one of the tall Pe-Ellians would seize one of the pups and throw it into the air. It would turn in the air, dappled by the sunshine, and then fall back, churning into the water.

I foresaw the accident. I was aware of the tree branches which hung out over the water. One young pup, distinguished by an almost coal-black face, obviously enjoyed being thrown in the air. He kept swimming up to the tallest Pe-Ellian and nudging him in the back, and the Pe-Ellian would oblige by heaving him up into the sky. His action in doing this was a swift underarm action as though he was throwing a rope up into the trees.

The play had moved away from the centre of the pool and out, closer to the edge.

As he was falling the pup struck a branch in the full of his back. I heard his back break. For a moment the body seemed to see-saw on the branch and then it toppled, heavy as a soaked glove, down to the water below. The Pe-Ellians swam over, dived and brought the body to the surface. They inspected it and the one who had thrown it into the air carried it to the bank and laid it out.

The game continued as though nothing had happened.

Young pups were still thrown, squeaking with delight, high into the air.

I stood up. I was shocked and amazed. Winter Wind had said that Pe-Ellians did not have much care for young life. Even so, his words had not prepared me for so casual an attitude.

My shock must have been transmitted, for the game stopped immediately. The three Pe-Ellians dived and emerged simultaneously a yard or so from the bank where I had slept. The effect was not unlike dolphins. They stared at me.

I nodded and mumbled a greeting in Pe-Ellian. Its equivalent in English is "Health to you".

They said not a word, but stared at me. Their three pairs of eyes never blinked.

Finally I could bear their scrutiny no longer. I moved away down the bank and came to where the pup lay. Its spine had clearly snapped and a thin trickle of water mingled with pale blood ran from its open mouth.

The Pe-Ellians kept pace with me, swimming down the stream.

I cannot say they were hostile. They just looked, and in simply looking with their large yellow flecked eyes they were more unsettling than any resentment or anger might have been.

Again remembering Winter Wind's words I tried to throw open my mind to receive impressions from them. Silence. But a living silence.

I decided to return home. I set out down the path and the three Pe-Ellians accompanied me until the path veered away from the river and plunged into the jungle.

That was the last I saw of them. When the paths rejoined the river several hundred yards later they were not waiting for me.

I reached the clearing in the early afternoon.

Later that evening, after Thorndyke had retired to his room, I asked Cook what he thought. He mused for a few moments, rubbing his upper lip with his two fingers, a gesture he had learned from Thorndyke.

"I think you parcelled them. Wrapped them up in your thought. I think you shot a powerful arrow, which pierced them. They would not be prepared. I can imagine. Oh boy. You and the old boy can whistle up a gale when you get aroused. They would be stunned. Yes. Your obedient servants, wrapped up in you."

Later Thorndyke emerged from his room. I found an opportunity to tell him what had happened. He listened attentively, but offered no explanation when I had finished. Obviously the matter preyed on his mind, for he wrote the following comments in his diary that evening.

Thorndyke's Diary: Entry 22

Tomas has had a day. Our experiences run parallel in that both of us have tried to communicate and receive.

I hope that Tomas has not inadvertently done damage. After that experience with Winter Wind it has several times occurred to me that we could kill a Pe-Ellian with a single spasm of hate.

Compared to us, Pe-Ellians are innocent. They have steadily distilled out unwholesome emotions (among which I suspect they include pity) and consequently have no resistance when they meet such emotions as anger or surprise in the raw.

The problem for me is to learn to receive, transmit and modulate. My experiences today have drawn me closer to Pe-Ellia. I want to talk with a Mantissa. I want to get under the *skin* of thought. I will experiment more tomorrow.

Commentary

Winter Wind joined us for breakfast and told us we were invited to his burrow for the evening meal. He said his house was typical and that he would try to invite a few acquaintances. He also told us not to expect a feast. We were to arrive in the late afternoon and Cook was to be our guide. The two Pe-Ellians departed together after Cook had announced that he would return in good time.

Shortly after they had left Thorndyke made a strange request of me. He referred to my adventure of the previous day and then asked me to go and see if the corpse of the baby Pe-Ellian was still by the river. I said that I was sure it wouldn't be, as in that heat any dead animal would decompose rapidly.

"In any case," I continued, "with this race's attitude to death, I imagine the corpse has already been put to good use, such as food for the queen."

Still Thorndyke persisted. I finally agreed since he was the senior member of the team. I realised that what he really wanted was to get me away from the house. I had no idea why. The following entry explains this mystery and shows that Thorndyke was aware of my feelings.

Thorndyke's Diary: Entry 23

Mnaba has gone, with bad grace admittedly. He doesn't understand and I can't explain, for if I were to explain I would prejudice the experiments. Our brains are powerful. We create more than ripples in the calm psychosphere of this planet.

Tomas, if ever you read this diary, please understand that our two minds interact and therefore muddy each other. I want to test the efficacy of my own brain. If I told you what I was doing, you could not help but think about it, and in thinking about it you might influence me, for better or ill. As it is, I have put you in a bad humour and that was not my intention. Go in peace. Bring me back a dead infant if it is still there. If not, calm yourself with the sun.

Now to work.

I am on the table in the Palm Court. I am on my back and the river bed is on full vision. (No sound.) It is swirling above me like the coils of a long, silver, iridescent snake.

The roof is an eye. I imagine it as a Mantissa eye. Vast and imperial, peering down into the depths of this dark room and finding *me* looking back. I want to communicate. I want to enter again that vertigo, that vacuum I felt yesterday. Rather I want to touch it, for as Winter Wind stated on our first day, "If we try to run before we can walk we shall surely stumble." I am the doubting Thomas, of course. Still looking for a sign.

I am not impressed with the Veronica trick of yesterday. That kind of photography is a kind of evasion. I know that the Mantissa is aware of me: I want to be aware of him.

I settle myself.

Relaxed, I let the light enter me. I am no longer a brain-gun firing thoughts. I am a light sponge and every pore is open. I imagine myself rising up to the roof, rising until my lips and nose are pressed firmly against the base of the stream.

The eye of the stream is not so large now. I have grown. I can encompass it. I can hold it. My mind is a bowl holding water.

I hardly dare breathe as I feel myself expand.

Somewhere beyond my eyes something has moved. I grow larger. I fill. I fill.

I rise like a bubble through the liquid of my mind and. . . .

I can see Mnaba with a thumb stick, pushing through the heavy plants.

Winter Wind on his knees with his hands in quicksilver. He straightens up suddenly.

A group running.

An ant the size of a horse and stinking of cats.

A corpse lying on a table with open eyes, staring, staring, staring. *Me*.

Abruptly the world spins on a pin and I am conscious of how hard the table is—and my eyes, how hot and dry.

Above me in the river I see a fish lazily work its way down to mouth the bottom. Not a fish. Too large for a fish. What then are those large fins? Surely it is some gigantic display fish with great red and gold and spotted fins and a tail like a feather.

Menopause comes clearly into view. The folds of his skin, so loose they are like an overcoat, undulate about him. He is holding his breath and his cheeks are puffed.

Somehow he attaches himself to the bottom and squats down on all fours. He looks through the base of the stream and nods to me.

I wave back.

He can apparently see me. I raise my hand in a gesture of recognition.

Tomorrow thunders a voice in my head, and I am rigid with shock.

My mental eardrums must be bloody, for I can feel a throbbing.

Menopause is gone now. The river is merely a river. I am lying here wondering what to do. Wondering if I can move. I am too confused, but I know I must set down what I have felt, and speedily.

My journey was fruitless. Of the little body there was no sign, or of any other Pe-Ellians for that matter.

When I returned Thorndyke was in his room resting. I reported to him that I had found nothing and he thanked me profusely (too profusely I remember) for all my trouble. He stated that he wanted to get his energy together for the evening's festivities. He made no mention of the experiments he was conducting.

For my part I was quite happy to put my feet up for a few hours.

Cook woke me. While I had slept my clothes had been laundered and ironed. I dressed quickly and went to the clearing where Thorndyke was waiting.

The rays of the sun were throwing long shadows across the clearing and the smell of evening was in the air.

Cook joined us. He paused on the bank of the river and breathed deeply. He held his breath for a few moments and then breathed out.

"We walk this-a-way," he said and strode out of the clearing, following the path we had used to approach it on the day of our arrival.

After five minutes he turned right on to a small track, which I had not observed when we arrived. According to my calculations this track should have brought us back close to the river although we did not catch sight of it.

After a while the path began to slope up gently. We emerged above the jungle and found facing us a rock cliff. Masses of red flowers, glowing in the final rays of the sun, climbed up the cliff. At its foot was a cave, the entrance to which was a perfect circle. The small path led directly to this cave.

Cook pressed on and we followed. It took us longer to reach the cave than I expected. I was fooled somewhat by the perspective, and when we entered the cave it was like entering one of the old railway tunnels on Earth.

Inside, the tunnel curved downwards in a spiral, like the inside of a sea shell. The walls were of the glossy, semi-transparent material familiar to us from our cottage. As we descended deeper into the earth the walls began to glow.

At the foot of the spiral we emerged into a large oval room. On the floor was a brilliant flame-red carpet, which turned out to be a kind of lichen.

Winter Wind was waiting for us. He spread his arms wide in a universal gesture of greeting and told us we were welcome to his "humble" home.

"Feel free to look about," he offered.

Round three-quarters of the perimeter of the oval room there ran a small stream. It entered through a crevice and tumbled in a waterfall. The river left via a hole. The water poured away without a sound.

A table, long low benches and a small cupboard were all the furnishings. Despite its simplicity the room struck me as eminently comfortable.

"No good for rheumatism," was Thorndyke's comment, but I could tell he was impressed.

Three short passages led off the main room and we had to step into the stream to reach them. The first room contained a large flat wooden platform.

"My bed," confided Winter Wind. "It is very old."

I rapped the bed's surface with my knuckles and was rewarded with a deep boom. The floor and half the wall was covered with a mustard coloured lichen, which glowed wherever we trod.

The second room was a kitchen, which seemed little different from our own. The third room was a mystery. We had no equivalent. It was roughly the same size as the other rooms, but was completely lacking in furniture. It was covered with a grainy, fibrous, faintly luminous fur, which in addition to being springy gave off a delicate perfume. Sound was deadened in this room. In the centre of the floor was a pool of silver. Its surface moved slightly as though there was something swimming just under the gleaming surface. The purpose of this room baffled me. Thorndyke gives a full explanation of its function in the following section of his diary.

When we had completed our inspection we assembled back in the main room, where Cook, ever the practical one, was busy setting out food and drink.

"This will be a simple meal between friends," he said.

Winter Wind, who had accompanied us silently round the house, now spoke up.

"I had intended to ask some other friends over, but they said they couldn't come." It was only then that I noticed that his manner seemed strange, nervous, or as though he were unwell.

At this point the Thorndyke diary takes up the narrative.

Thorndyke's Diary: Entry 24

The Visit to Winter Wind's House

Winter Wind knows what I have been up to. I could tell by his manner. He was jumpy. I caught him looking at me strangely, furtively. Cook also seemed a bit distant. They both had that slightly glazed look about the eyes—that ready-to-leap-behind-a-Mantissa look that we saw in its extreme form on our way to this planet. And I don't blame them.

Not that I have accomplished anything yet, but I have widened the circle of my acquaintance on this planet in a psychic sense and have met with casual interest. The man who sits on the park bench may show such interest in the dog which brings him the stick to throw.

For better or for worse a great deal of my mental energy, raw as it may be, is flowing round this place. And there is more to come.

I think Winter Wind thinks he is losing his grip slightly. This was his project and now it is taking an unpredictable turn. The monster has shown intentions of independence and is getting up from the couch and breaking the shackles. No, that's too extreme. But he certainly wonders what is happening and he's not alone.

This evening I tried to talk to him and draw out some more answers to questions. I asked when we could begin a proper study of the language. He said he didn't know. I asked how long we would be staying there. Again he said he didn't know, but that there was no danger. He hinted that wheels were turning within wheels and that the decision was not with him. I asked about "Angels", and he said that this was his silly translation and that they were nothing like what we called angels. Space fish, he said, was far more accurate, and that for me begs almost as many questions.

Tomas took all this down and I will have him sift my gleanings. The only success I can report is the solution of the sanitation questions.

Pe-Ellians have no anus, just as they have no independent reproductive organs. Yet they eat and drink and this implies a certain percentage of waste matter. So I asked myself how they got rid of it.

I had a theory. Deep inside their womb-larder I thought they could have something that processed waste products and that they would be able to dispose of them in the same way they fish out a karitsa. I half wondered whether some of their waste products might not enter the karitsa as a nutrient. I am reminded of the planet Tiger Lily, where a small sub-species called Tethys considers it the height of good manners and decorum to offer faeces as a birthday gift. As I say, I had my theories.

How far from the truth!

In some ways I am coming to see the Pe-Ellians as so simple and yet, because they are alien, they appear complicated. The Pe-Ellians have two important organs: their brains and their skins. They excrete through their skins. Whereas we strain in the small room, they immerse themselves in a "resting" bath, which draws their waste from them.

Winter Wind showed me his "toilet" and was surprised I didn't know, hadn't realised, its function. The blue, glowing grass, which covers everything, has a perfume that acts like a tranquilliser.

Every day the Pe-Ellian, if he is healthy, slips into his pool of . . . (I'll come to that in a moment) . . . and goes into a trance. If a Pe-Ellian is unwell then he can rest there for hours. The pool interacts with the skin (the main organ of sense) and removes whatever is causing the problem.

"And what is this silvery liquid, this quicksilver in your pool, Professor Winter Wind?"

"Liquid thought."

Liquid thought. He said this as simply as I might say liquid oxygen. My face betrayed my amazement.

"All right. Does planet-blood make more sense?" I didn't think so. I offered Mantissa juice or psychic purée and the conversation was on the point of breaking down when Winter Wind said, "You know you mustn't expect Pe-Ellia to be like Earth . . . it works in quite a different way."

Apparently this sump of . . . is connected via a "vein" to the local agricultural Mantissa. Winter Wind would not allow me to call the connection a pipe. It had to be "vein" for, as he insisted, it was alive. Apparently the whole planet is covered with a network of Mantissa sewer veins.

I asked Winter Wind if they had to be careful when they were building a new house, but he didn't bother to answer.

Tomas dipped his finger into the silver bath. It had the consistency of a thick paint or glue, but did not adhere to the skin in the slightest. There was not a drop of moisture, nor a bead of silver on Tomas's finger. But the skin was pink and fresh as a baby's.

For the most part the meal was dull. Winter Wind seemed to be glad when it was time for us to get going. The journey home through the night was uneventful.

I had a dream. Something about Menopause, but I can't remember quite what. I also caught the bed up to its old tricks—trying to make me comfortable—and gave it a good telling off. We shall see what tomorrow brings.

Commentary

The next morning when I got up I found a note from Thorndyke on the breakfast table. "Gone fishing", it said. And that amounts to all I know of what Thorndyke did that day. No details are recorded in his diary.

I spent the day dissecting flowers and was happy to be alone. Late in the afternoon he entered the Palm Court. He had been tramping.

"Ah good, you got my note," he said. "Have there been any messages?" I answered no.

Thorndyke nodded to himself and set off to his room, saying he was tired.

His actions and his air of secrecy puzzled me. I was already somewhat apprehensive about the way Cook and Winter Wind had become withdrawn. Jet I had not seen at all. Speaking for myself I felt rather at a loss to understand what was happening. At the time I never formulated the thought clearly, but looking back I can say that I was aware that there were currents shaping our lives and that I could not control them. I have never been one for mystery and here was Thorndyke creating mystery after mystery and destroying, so far as I was concerned, the unity of the team.

The team is the closest unit in the contact linguist's experience. It must be based on trust and respect. A team member must be able to rely on his partner to guard for his sanity. The best teams are usually composed of people of different temperaments, which is why Thorndyke and I functioned so well together.

That evening I asked Thorndyke to explain his actions. I told him I was worried for his wellbeing and that I was considering asking for contact to be established with Earth.

Thorndyke considered my worries gravely.

"Tomas, we have known each other a long time. I am sorry I have been neglecting you, but I must ask you to be patient. There are some things I am afraid to talk about for fear that my mind bleeds them to all the waiting ears. Take that on trust. Things are moving to some kind of conclusion, though I am not sure exactly what."

He stood stock still for several seconds, staring at me. Abruptly he sighed, turned, and set off for his rooms. The last words I heard him mutter were, "Sorry Tomas," and I am not even sure he meant to say them out loud.

I was far from satisfied with this answer, but I felt I could do no more that night.

Next morning I was first up for breakfast and was surprised to find the incredible Menopause sitting in the Palm Court waiting for us. In the dim light he looked like a man wrapped in a sheet. His skin had turned white and opaque. Only his face retained something of the original features. It was obvious that his time was near.

He growled a greeting and I stood up. I could see then that only his hands, feet and head were still clothed tightly in skin. The rest of his skin hung off him in laps.

Without a word he went to Thorndyke's apartment, opened the door and went in.

Cook was nowhere about. I looked and called for him in the house and then went up into the clearing. No Cook.

I was about to turn back into the house when Winter Wind came striding out of the jungle. At first I thought he was bruised, as though he had been beaten. His face was livid and his upper arms and neck mottled and bluish. I had never seen him like this before. I was about to ask him what had happened when he spoke.

"I am looking for Thorndyke," he said.

"Menopause is with him," I said. "He went in about five minutes ago."

"Aiee. Aiee. This must not be allowed to happen," he cried and rushed down into the house. As he ran he called out some words in Pe-Ellian. I followed him.

The confrontation took place in the Palm Court.

Menopause was there. Beside him and holding his hand like a little boy was Marius Thorndyke. They were obviously on their way up to the clearing.

No words were spoken, but I could sense a battle of wills between Menopause and Winter Wind. Menopause, wild and outlandish, seemed to dominate. They stared at one another. Winter Wind made a complex series of gestures, passing one hand over the other, but did not speak. Menopause appeared to have a nervous tic in his face. He screwed his face up tightly, and then released it suddenly so that his eyes seemed to leap out. His tongue went up and down in a quick sequence of moves, the like of which I had never seen before.

Abruptly Menopause tugged at Thorndyke's hand and led him round Winter Wind and up into the clearing. Winter Wind did not move.

As I looked at him he seemed to deflate. His energy, the inner tension, which gave him his vitality seemed to flow from him. Finally he sighed, drew himself up, and without a word to me walked up the ramp and out into the clearing. I followed him. Our cottage warren was suddenly very claustrophobic. I had a sudden fear of the walls evaporating.

In the clearing there was no sign of Thorndyke or Menopause.

I sat down on the bench by the stream and tried to think the situation through. I was now more than ever convinced that our visit had gone awry; at the same time I had no clear policy on what I should do.

In the event I spent most of the day down by the river. I worked with the encoder. I gave myself to my work. I continued my study of the flora of our clearing, paying particular attention to the way the trees and the house fused. I kept myself busy.

Cook brought the meals as usual.

He never asked about Thorndyke and I didn't ask about Winter Wind. It was a common truce, sealed by our mutual embarrassment.

During the afternoon Cook worked with me, explaining how the cottage was constructed, and how long it had taken. All this material is available and will be included in a later volume.

Thorndyke returned to the clearing as the sun was setting. He walked slowly and tiredly. In his hands he was holding a large shallow box. Its lid was closed.

He handed me the box and then flopped down into one of the chairs. The box was surprisingly light.

"A present?" I asked and Thorndyke nodded.

"Yes, from Menopause," he replied. "It is his sloughed-off skin."

"Aiyee," cried Cook softly from the side of the clearing.

Thorndyke's Diary: Entry 25

A short time ago I took it out of its box and laid it on my bed. It is lying there now like a crinkly plastic cut-out. If I could seal the great tear in the side and inflate it, it would be Menopause as he was.

Menopause has honoured me in a way that very few Pe-Ellians honour each other. It is all so simple. We are become blood brothers. For richer, for poorer. In health and in sickness. Till death us *do join*. Note that. I was very careful to be sure I understood the ceremony, and whereas I am being facetious in drawing parallels with a marriage service (parallels which nevertheless do exist) there is no doubt that it is death that will be the great joiner. So where do I go from here? And what do I say?

There is no doubt that Menopause has taken me over. That

much was clear this morning when the ether crackled and two friends charred each other to gain ascendancy over this poor mortal. I was frightened then. Undoubtedly I was in some way hypnotised. I was enjoying a shower. He faced me and seized the baggy folds of his skin and shook them.

"Breaking," he said, and then took my hand and made me feel the skin. It was silk and rubber. It was still warm with life, but dying. When I touched the skin I felt an all but overwhelming and embarrassing desire to wrap myself up in it. Now is that any way for an old man to behave?

My reaction, felt but not expressed, but understood all the same, was all that Menopause needed. Before I could pick up my clothes or even a towel he had seized my arm firmly. I could feel a sinewy strength in the fingers, such that I could not have broken the grip, and hesitated to pull too hard against it lest it tighten. I thought of those mystical bands which tighten round the heads of transgressors.

In the Palm Court was Winter Wind. Menopause was not expecting that.

I heard him hiss. I felt a great lightness. All this had happened before. All was predestined. The lamb was on the chopping block, the knife honed, just as it always is.

That hiss carried me back to an earlier time when I faced death in a closed room. On Banyon. I had been told to keep my room firmly closed, since after nightfall predators roamed. I had slipped outside to see the three moons rise like pearls on a string and never thought of the door, which swung silently open behind me.

Later in bed I was woken by a heavy movement. A sliding. Then came a snickering sound. A hiss. I froze physically, metaphorically and mentally. I felt panic beat on me as though I was a drum.

Again movement. Something worming over the bed and down on to the floor, and then back up again. Come morning I was as exhausted as a marathon runner. In the pale light I could see a thanator, as we called them. A cross between a snake, a slug and a centipede. Its total length was a little over two metres. It was coiled at the foot of the bed.

Even the slime of these creatures is fatal.

Their pseudopodia have minute claws, which inject their

venom. On their backs is a heavy carapace, which they drag when they move. The carapace has thick tufty ginger hair and it is this that makes the snickering hissing sound.

This memory flooded back to me when I heard Menopause, and if the psychosphere of this planet is as reactive as Winter Wind maintains, then no doubt my reaction helped muddy it.

I thought Menopause was having a fit. His face contorted like a howling baby. This was even more disconcerting at close quarters, for his skin was already starting to come loose on some parts of his face. The effect was like a mouse running under a sheet.

I thought Winter Wind was going to spout horns or spit blood. His face had the concentration and single-minded stariness of a man I once saw holding on to a pipe suspended over a rocket exhaust vent. If he had fallen he would have tumbled and bumped down the pitted metal into the very heart of the rocket engine. When we got him to safety we found that he had ruptured the blood vessels all along his arms, so fierce had been his grip.

These two faced one another and was it my imagination that the room dilated briefly like the beat of a giant heart?

Then Menopause was shuffling outside, dragging me up the ramp into the clearing. We stumbled round the house and into the jungle.

Luckily we didn't travel far, as I felt exhaustion coming upon me. We stopped near three large conical boulders. In the centre of these was a hole, which I recognised as the entrance to a Pe-Ellian house. It seemed fresh, new. I say this because the walls of the tunnel leading underground were bright and silvery like a new snail trace or a densely woven spider's web.

We went underground. The door irised with a snap, and I felt both trapped and safe at the same time.

Menopause didn't pause. He was breathing in great gulps, like a man who has just swum a long race. He plunged his hand deep inside the folds of his skin and drew out two karitsas.

"Take eat," he growled. I was horrified to see that the skin over his face had now come entirely away and his eyes were pits, which were as white as a boiled egg.

He sliced the karitsa with his thumb and the creature flopped out. Before nausea could build in me I gulped the karitsa down.

Again the explosion. Again the feeling of me straining against the confines of my own skin and bones. How can a body contain such energy and yet remain whole? I sat down and let the karitsa engulf me.

Menopause relaxed visibly and his panting stopped.

"Soon be free of this," said a ghostly voice from somewhere and I realised that Menopause was speaking from within his skin. "You are here to help me."

He shuffled off down the corridor and entered a large circular room. I noticed the lichen glowing and saw the pool of silver. It was much larger than the pool at Winter Wind's house. Menopause squatted down at the edge of the pool and stirred the liquid with his fingers. Then he slid forward and thrust himself, face down, into the silver. His skin spread out and ballooned as though filled with gas. When he was completely free of the edge he rolled over.

His skin had stretched and was almost without shape. I could distinguish his hands like giant white rubber gloves. They flopped about devoid of gesture or meaning.

"Join me." Again the ghostly voice, this time quite faint.

I crossed to the pool, sat down on its edge (the lichen was warm) and dangled my feet in the silvery fluid. They disappeared as soon as they entered. I tried to see my toes, but saw only my distorted face looking back at me. The liquid was cooler than the air and pressed tightly about my ankles and shins. I edged deeper and hoped I would be able to stand up and breathe. Finally I let go of the edge and felt the lichened side of the pool slip up over my back. I did not sink, but bobbed up and down on the surface like a float.

The currents in the fluid massaged my back and arms as I lay on the surface: I know of no sensation to compare with this giant peristalsis.

Using my arms as paddles I made my way over to the grey dirigible.

Again memories from the past thrust into the present. (They say a drowning man sees his life pass before him.) And again I saw the rocks along the coast where I grew up. Me leaping from rock to rock, trusting to the small limpets with hard shells like miniature teeth to stop me from slipping. On the top of one large boulder I stop and look down into the tide-filled pool of cold water. It is deep and wide, with fringes of anemones and bladder wrack. But it is not those I see. There is a body, a large sea beast, lolling there. I am surprised when there are signs of motion and the body convulses, but I cannot tell head from tail. It has no shape, only bulk. As I watch, the sun emerges from behind some clouds and shines across the water.

That day I watched from dawn until the incoming tide forced me back to the headland. I watched the body bump round the side of the pool. I watched its weak efforts. I saw a vent in its side which wrinkled and closed like an empty eye socket. I stood helpless as the tide sluiced in, lifting the grey bulk higher until it finally carried it over the margin of the pool. By some quirk of the tide the body was swept out to sea. The last I saw, the water round the carcase was puckered as thousands of scavengers moved in for their feed.

Such memories are dangerous. They can impede action. I paddled over and prodded his side.

"How can I help?"

"Think of helping me." The voice was a whisper from a well.

The request was like when someone says "Think happy thoughts". What does one think? I thought of Menopause as I had first met him, lying in the tree, with his livid veins. I thought of Tomas's face when he told me about his discovery of the perimeters; a face alive and intelligent. I thought of my mother—

There was a sound, which was neither a popping nor a tearing, but somewhere between the two. A seam appeared in the grey skin. Through the seam pushed fingers. They were white and bloodless. The hands of a bled corpse emerged.

It rested and then the seam widened. Another hand joined the fist and together they forced the skin open. It tore easily now, raggedly, like damp paper. Two arms burst through.

I saw a giant white egg push through. Menopause's head. His face was closed like a corpse.

The body was half out. I seized him under the arms and pulled. His body slid out of the skin like a knife from its sheath. He floated, spreadeagled like a skinned frog. I manoeuvred him over to the side and managed to get his head and arms to rest on the blue moss. This held him.

Next I paddled back to where the skin lay flat on the surface and began drawing it to the side. The skin was changing. It was contracting and losing its whiteness. I brought it to the edge and drew it up on to the bank. It had become again the image of Menopause—as recognisable as a sketch in outline, a transparency.

Behind me there was a hiss. I turned to find Menopause propped back on his elbows and trying to draw himself clear of the silver fluid. I ran over to him and placed my hands under his shoulders and heaved him higher on the bank. Finally, after much tugging and heaving, I had him clear of the pool and high and dry. This left me panting. I thanked God I didn't have a weak heart. Menopause is, after all, some ten feet tall.

His colour was different. He had lost all that unearthly pallor and was now more waxen. I can't say I thought the change much of an improvement; it still looked very unhealthy, but at least it was different.

The face remained impassive. Strangely beautiful. Not complete, an artist's sketch only. It lacked highlights and shading. As I looked at him I became aware of subtle changes taking place. His skin was no longer of uniform colour. Markings were beginning to appear and the familiar plate effect to emerge. But the plates were all of different sizes, all irregular, a jigsaw of shards. The markings too were not what one would expect. Some were rough amateurish splodges, others were circles and whorls. I could see one shape which fitted its plate perfectly and which was a replica of one of Winter Wind's markings. Then there was the colour. Reds and blues round the feet merged to purples and greens at the waist and finally to yellow and black at the head.

All this happened in the space of no more than five minutes. I watched Menopause develop like a photographic print. As his markings grew firmer he seemed to breathe more easily. I waited for the final spark of life.

The Chinese talk of paintings in this way: when you consider the painting of an animal complete, but lacking in life, *then* paint in the eye, but not before or an unruly creature will enter the world.

This was Menopause. I awaited the opening of the eye.

As the minutes passed his form grew stronger. Pastel tints turned to full richness. Fine lines became bold. Shapes took on depth.

When the eyes opened I was caught by surprise. They were as black as coal or as black as staring into the force cubes of the Garfield Jump generator, where energy licks about a blackness that absorbs all light.

"Menopause," I said when his eyes opened.

"I am not Menopause," he said, and I was pleased to hear that his voice had lost all its hissing and rough quality and was comparatively musical. "Give me a name."

I looked at him. He was all colour and whirls, dots and dashes, paisley and patchwork.

"Harlequin," I said. "It is an old name with us. The name of a performer, of a dancer, of a mime, and he looks a mite like you."

"Honoured," he said, and sat up. "I need to stretch, to run, to get some fresh air through me. I need karitsa." He looked at his arms and legs in amazement and then he looked at me. "I knew you had some effect on me when I was embryo, but this—I have never seen anything so fluid. This lacks all definition and code. Wait till the Mantissa recorder sees this. What destiny will he name this?"

He stood up. I was astounded to see that he was some six inches taller than the lumpish figure that had entered the pool.

"Now there is a little ceremony. I expect you are more in your unknowing mind aware of what is happening than you can speak. We are close now. Harlequin and—I must give you a Pe-Ellian name. I will name you Tuwununi, meaning the one who dives with his eyes open. There. A noble man. Harlequin and Diver. Now the ceremony."

He picked up his sloughed-off skin and, beckoning me to follow, left the room and entered the main hall.

"We Pe-Ellians are a lonely, independent race. We allow few to approach us. We are bearers or makers, that is all. We hardly live for ourselves, yet occasionally we fuse—is that a word?—we meld. We seek to break from our singleness by an act of trust. One of our Mantissa Singers is composing an epic on the theme that one day all Pe-Ellians will meld and that day will be the end of time. Then we will vacate time and the present and spread through the universe as pure thought." He paused.

"It is an idea," he said. "I propose to you that we meld. That we let our thought flow more freely between us. For you that is easy.

Your mind spews thought. But your thought has no direction. It is hard. Abrasive as the skin of rocks. I am more subtle and delicate. I cannot transmit freely. For you I will try. I run a risk. You are strong and the wrong thought at the wrong time might disfigure me."

He stopped and looked down at his body and then gave the Pe-Ellian equivalent of laughter.

"Perhaps it has already happened. For you were here at my change. Perhaps I carry all disfigurement and so I am strong. Perhaps everything is prethought and we are all motes in a Mantissa experiment. Perhaps I will kill you. Perhaps your mind will buckle under alien pressure. So, what do think, shall we meld?"

My answer was a nod.

And is not this secretly what I wanted? How many men are so overburdened with self that they long to push all overboard and start out anew.

"What word do you have for melding?" he asked.

"Marriage."

He was horrified.

"No, no, no. Nothing like that. That requires impossible fulfilment. I am Pe-Ellian. I cannot bear your baby. Is there no other way of making a bond?"

His reaction was so violent it stunned me. What strange beings these asexual creatures are. They are bean pods. Why, then, am I embarrassed when one of them talks about subjects he cannot know about? My conditioning is greater than I thought, and I remain a son of Earth.

"We have a bond between men . . . we call it blood brotherhood. I cut my arm to make the blood flow, you cut yours, and we join the blood. It means that the two persons swear to honour and defend and trust one another. There is no sex involved."

He nodded.

"We will do it that way. I will entrust the remains of my fifth change to you. Greater trust I cannot show. You may give blood.

He took the skin, which was now supple and clear, and draped it over my shoulders. It trailed behind me like a cape.

"Do we have a knife?" I asked.

"No, but this." He held up his thumb with its sharp karitsaslicing nail. Before I could move he had flicked the tissues of my upper arm and blood flowed. He scooped some up in the palm of his hand and rubbed it over his mottled cranium. Then he sliced his own arm and I touched my fingers to his blood and then rubbed it into my own wound.

I had a moment of unreality. As on the spaceship coming here, as when I tried to contact the Mantissa, so now. For a few moments I was not me, and then I was me again, standing in a dim room underground, with blood on my hands.

Menopause-Harlequin (for so I still think of him) brought a wooden box. He folded the skin as one would a garment and placed it in the box.

"Damage this, and you damage me. Do with it as you will." His eyes glittered at some thought I could not guess. "Now I must rest. Thank you Diver. We will meet tomorrow. You can find your own way home, I think."

And so I did.

Commentary

Thorndyke sat in the clearing for a full hour. He would not allow me to open the box and see the skin, but promised to show me the next day. He was totally withdrawn into himself. Finally he sighed and stood up.

"There may be some unpleasantness tomorrow," he said. "Be on your guard. I'm going in now to sleep . . . but if Winter Wind calls wake me up." He left, bidding Cook a friendly goodnight.

When he had gone I spoke with Cook.

"Are you worried by what has happened?"

"Worried. Sorried. But I do not see clearly. There is a pattern but I see only the corner. There is a shape but I cannot rub it. When I lost hope, long ago, and was forbidden to play the float-harp for pleasure, I felt as I feel now. We Pe-Ellians are finely tuned strings. We vibrate to any atmosphere. Now there is something happening but I do not know what, but I foresee patchwork. The destruction of symmetry. Smearing. Aieee."

He would say no more.

His words made me very uneasy. I too had sensed the flow of alien passions. I felt like an animal before an earthquake.

That night I slept poorly. I kept dozing and waking, thinking I could hear voices. Once I got up and toured the house, but there was no-one.

Eventually I slept.

Next morning I was woken by Cook, who was slapping his hands together in nervousness.

"Mantissa visit. Winter Wind waiting. Jet waiting. Meno-no, not Menopause . . . now he is Harlequin, a name I do not know. Everyone waiting, sleepy bones."

I dressed hurriedly and joined the others in the Palm Court. Cook was serving breakfast.

"Late," he said. "Late, I'm sorry I'm late. Here's bread and fruit blood. . . ."

"Juice," said Jet. "Calm down, Cook."

I looked round the table and was amazed at the change in Menopause-Harlequin. He smiled and greeted me warmly by name. I must have stared at him.

"Do you like it?" he asked, standing up and turning round like a model so that I could see all the markings which swarmed around him. A mad tattooist could have done no better.

"This is all Diver's doing," he said, pointing at Thorndyke. "I am scored by him, but I can live with this. Alien thought has never shown itself like this before."

"And never will again, I hope," said Winter Wind softly.

"Amen," chimed in Jet.

This conversation left me guessing. In retrospect, of course, it is clear that this was another stage in the confrontation between Menopause-Harlequin and Winter Wind. A power struggle was taking place before my eyes, but all I was aware of was the strain of the atmosphere. Jet seemed intent on avoiding any outbreak of open hostility.

"Today you will encounter two Mantissae. A Traffic Controller and a Singing Mantissa. We have a long way to go so we'd better start. Perhaps Cook will assemble a picnic. . . ."

"Ah, eat on the hoof. Already done," said Cook. "We can leave as soon as napkins are removed."

We set off. The door through which we had never walked now

dilated open as Jet touched the switch. We faced a corridor which glowed. The air tingled.

"This was completed only yesterday," said Jet. "There were problems, but that is why it feels so strong."

Jet led the way. Thorndyke followed, accompanied by Menopause-Harlequin and Winter Wind. Cook lugging a satchel of food, and I with the encoder, brought up the rear.

The next entry in the Thorndyke diaries deals with this journey and our meeting with the Singing Mantissa. It was during this visit that Thorndyke almost died.

Thorndyke's Diary: Entry 26

We were a bit like children. Tomas kept fiddling with his encoder, checking to see that the spools were clear and the power high. Eventually I told him to leave it alone or he would break it. As for myself, I was excited and confused. I was in Aladdin's cave. Everything was suddenly new to me. The change in Menopause-Harlequin seemed also to have changed me. I could feel the gentle warmth of the alien mind waiting cautiously. I felt closer to him than I have ever felt to any human being. I also felt in advance that today would be momentous.

Jet was boisterous, all up and at 'em. Cook dithered and charmed.

Only Winter Wind, poor victim, was bleeding. I did not see it as clearly then as I do now. I knew that there was strain between him and Menopause-Harlequin, but I did not realise that the strain was the first movement in a fight that could be only to the death. Nor did I foresee that I would have a part in the killing of Winter Wind.

So be it. I am nearing my own end and face down the same dark passage that Winter Wind has already entered.

Dark corridors. Yes. We entered a dark corridor beyond the iris door which led, we were told, to the city. The air was charged and a light breeze ruffled my hair. We moved down the passage and the light kept pace with us. After about a hundred yards we came to a circular chamber. Facing us were three dark tunnels.

I have never completely overcome my fear of the dark or of

being underground. In my experience earthquakes do occur. For something to say I asked how we could summon a train.

"Already done," said Jet. "As soon as you open that door a stimmu is summoned. It is nothing like a train."

I noticed that the lefthand tunnel facing us had a glimmer of light. The light got steadily brighter and obviously the tunnel curved, for I could see no headlights but just a silvery glow.

A fresh breeze blew. I imagined some Pe-Ellian equivalent of the Minotaur bounding down the track, showering silver fire.

The reality, when it emerged, was almost as shocking. My first reaction was that it was a shark, or rather the skeleton of a shark. Its giant silver nose emerged from the tunnel and sniffed the air. Then slowly and silently the whole body emerged. The ribs and bones were white and glowing. Covering the bones were transparent scales, each like a mullioned window.

The movement was slow now. Wary. The giant creature, which almost filled the chamber, began to turn on its axis. I was reminded of the care builders take when they carry a long plank and have to negotiate twists and turns.

"Is it alive?" I asked.

"Only in the same way your house is," answered Winter Wind.

"Ah." I noticed that the vehicle hovered five centimetres above the ground. There were no rails. No overhead power lines.

"It looks like a fish," I said to Tomas, and he nodded.

"That," said Menopause-Harlequin, "is pure coincidence. It is the best form for focusing thought and emotion. Such things, I think, are new to you. The Traffic Mantissa's mind lives in these walls. They are an extension of him. The carriage interacts with the thought to create motion."

I think I nodded. By this stage I had certainly concluded that what the Pe-Ellians meant by thought was covered by everything we regarded as life force. They manipulate thought as dextrously as we build bridges.

Jet licked his finger and rubbed it down one of the ribs. As expected the side split open. Inside I could see benches, similar to the ones in the apartment. There was also a rope arrangement like a spider's web and a low "mushroom" table.

"In we get," said Cook and climbed in.

Mnaba was next. He touched the side of the carriage and pulled his hand away with a cry of surprise.

"Static electricity," I said, trying to be amusing.

I placed my hand, flat and firm, on one of the scales. I was expecting a charge, but what I felt came as even more of a surprise. The scale was like skin, human skin, alive and warm and throbbing, as though my hand was on a pulse.

We helped one another inside and as we climbed the carriage rolled slightly like a boat.

Winter Wind, Cook and Jet all settled on to the benches. Menopause-Harlequin sprang up into the spider's web of ropes and began doing exercises. He twined his body in and out of the strands.

"Sometimes a new skin itches," he explained.

Tomas and I settled into low chairs, which must have been specially prepared for us.

The door closed with a sound like a plucked string.

The body began to contract and bend as the vehicle nosed round the walls. It chose the middle opening and slid forward. The bones glowed as we plunged into darkness.

"Try to relax," Jet called at me. "Try not to grip the cushions. It all sets up tension. You are perfectly safe."

There was no way I could judge the speed. The walls were featureless as far as I could see and there were no lights. We could have been travelling through smoke. I judged, though, that we were moving very quickly. A gentle thrust of acceleration was always with us. Suddenly the vehicle began to rise and fall like a big dipper. It was a slow, rhythmic movement, which made me feel slightly sea-sick. The Pe-Ellians loved it.

"This is called travelling the ridges," called out Menopause-Harlequin. "It is very beautiful, like in the days we were karitsas and enjoyed an effortless glide between surface and air."

Our vehicle shot into a tight bend like a roller coaster and began to slow down.

"We change here," said Jet, as our carriage hurled into light. "You'll see a few more Pe-Ellians now."

The station staggered me with its size. It was a vast amphitheatre into which you could have put fifty colosseums, and we had just emerged on one of the tiers. There were other carriages similar to ours. Some were just accelerating, others were jockeying their way down to the bottom of the amphitheatre where there were low buildings and exit ramps. We began to work our way downwards as we slowly lost speed. Another carriage rushed towards us and then banked at the last minute and swooped above us. I remember ducking and Jet laughed.

The main part of the station, ground level as it were, was packed with Pe-Ellians. I became aware of how few Pe-Ellians we had seen. Here were skin patterns undreamed of and colours and different races of Pe-Ellians.

Yes, Tomas, your speculations were right. The Pe-Ellians with the distinct beaks and ridges are indeed a northern race.

I counted six Pe-Ellians in various stages of menopause.

I saw many who were as tall as Jet and Winter Wind, but few who were taller. I saw no-one who resembled Menopause-Harlequin. His distinction was brought home to us forcibly when we descended from the carriage. He became a centre of attraction. Many Pe-Ellians paused to look at him in their sage, split-eyed way. They gave us (Tomas and I) but a cursory glance and then moved on. Something else struck me as peculiar. The silence. No-one spoke. This was a station, but there were no loudspeakers. The carriages and trains came and went without a sound. Indeed, the only sounds were the susurration of the air as the carriage swept past and the gentle lapping sound of bare feet on wood.

We were standing outside our carriage when I heard a whistling sound and a pop such as some people can make by putting their finger in their mouth and flicking their cheek. High above, on the uppermost rim of the stadium/station, a carriage emerged from one of the tunnels. Its speed was incredible. It hurtled round the rim like the ball in roulette and disappeared into another tunnel.

I was the only one who paid attention, except for Jet, who nodded and said, "Ah, in a hurry."

In the centre of the stadium was a high pyramid.

"What's that?" Tomas asked and was told that it was the hangar for the Mantissa Traffic Controller.

"Can I look?" I asked.

"He has made it known that he does not want to see you or know you," said Winter Wind, and with that I had to be content.

"What do most of these Pe-Ellians think of us?" I asked as we threaded our way from the carriage and joined the mainstream of Pe-Ellians crossing the amphitheatre.

"Ah, that is hard to tell," replied Menopause-Harlequin. "Most are blinkered. They know about you of course, but you are not part of their affair. Would you expect a weightlifter on Earth to worry himself professionally about someone who made paper-weights?"

"I am not quite sure I see your meaning."

"Would an organist worry about the flies lodging in his mighty pipes?"

"Not very flattering."

"Is the letter writer concerned about the stamp collector?"

"Yes and no. At least he might be interested," I replied and Menopause-Harlequin winked.

"Ah, you are so much of Earth. So refreshing. We need you as much as you need us. We are self-contemplating, still-centred and timid. We need an abrasive to raze against us and roughen our sleek hides."

This speech caught my attention. This was the first indication that Menopause-Harlequin had a strategy as regards us creatures from Earth. Winter Wind, I knew, saw things differently. Later I shall write about these differences, for they are important to understand the hows and whys of this mission.

We stopped at a second carriage. To my eyes it looked identical with the first, but Jet assured me it was altogether more robust.

"This is an outland carrier. This can pioneer under mountains and under the sea. That is why we have taken it, for part of our journey must be under water. We will cross a sea to visit the island where the Mantissa sings."

We mounted, settled down, and the fish carriage lifted. It began working its way over to where the terraces which made up the walls of the amphitheatre rose from the flat floor. We began to lift and as we lifted we accelerated. We overtook and were overtaken. I marvelled at the way the carriages managed to avoid collisions.

Soon we were high up on the walls and moving fast like a daredevil rider.

"Oops, missed our exit," said Jet, as we shot below an opening.

I looked at the opening behind us and saw another "fish" emerge.

"Thank God," I said.

We barrelled all the way round the amphitheatre and approached our exit again. This time there was no mistake. We dived into the tunnel and again I had the impression we were travelling through brown smoke.

This stage of the journey was short. My eyes had only just become accustomed to the gloom when we leaped out into the sunlight and then into pale blue water. The Pe-Ellian Sea.

You never found out, Tomas, but Pe-Ellia is mainly islands.

The craft slowed now and we could see down to the sea bed and up to where the surface rippled and shone. Giant trees of coral grew up from the sea bed and wove in and out. Fish popped out of crannies and peered at us latterday Jonahs. We slipped under the diaphanous shape of a jellyfish and its tendrils slipped over us.

"Are we still in the control of the Station Mantissa?" I asked.

"Of course," answered Winter Wind. "We can only move because of him. He is trying to give you an interesting journey. Taking you slowly. Before long he'll get a move on."

Even as he spoke we started to rise towards the surface, accelerating. We broke the surface like a javelin. Spray leaped from us in a rainbow. The skin of the craft changed slowly to an opaque violet, cutting out all sight of the sea and sky.

"We'll be travelling fast now," said Menopause-Harlequin, easing himself deeper into the nest of ropes. "Suggest you rest your mind. Don't want to be sick."

I noticed that all the Pe-Ellians were *resting* with vacant expressions on their faces. I felt drowsy, as though I had taken a sleeping pill. Mnaba was nodding.

Whether I dreamed or not I do not know. I remember I had the impression that our craft was many miles long, that it had become a violet tube stretching from where we mounted to our destination and that we were drifting along this tube. This is, I believe, how the Traffic Controller sees things. He detects our past and future and links them. We slide simultaneously through time and space.

The colour of thought is violet.

We came alive as the fish scales drained of colour and became transparent again. In front of us was an island, which looked to me like a single volcanic cone. It had the symmetry of Fuji or Egmont. We were diving towards a cave mouth which opened just a few feet above the shoreline.

We plunged into the hole with a gradual slackening of speed.

"Soon be there," said Cook. There was no mistaking his excitement.

We came to a halt in a small chamber very similar to the one connected to our cottage. We climbed out and I was surprised to discover how stiff I was. When we were all out the vehicle lowered gently to the floor and settled. The ribs bent outwards, providing a broad base. It now looked like a broody hen with a fish skull for a head.

Jet led the way. We walked down a short corridor and stopped in front of a red door. The air was still and cold, like the air in a tomb. Our feet made no sound. We did not speak.

Jet touched a small panel set in the wall and it immediately flared.

Above us a section of the roof glowed and opened. I found myself looking up into a tangled web of ropes and lines. Intertwined among the strands of the web were many Pe-Ellians. They all stared down at us. One of them wormed himself loose, sliding his body nimbly between the lines and then dropped through the hole and stood before us. He was taller than Winter Wind.

The roof closed with a pop.

The Pe-Ellian spoke to us softly. Winter Wind translated: "Welcome. I am called Chord. You are expected. The Singer has just begun the first canticle of the Mantissaiad, *The Journey of Life*. You will go in now."

He touched the door and it swung silently open.

We stared into a vast chamber. It was dark in the way that cathedrals are dark after the sunshine. One shaft of light fell from the roof and illuminated the Mantissa.

What did I see? So much anticipation . . . so much waiting.

There was a body, crouched it seemed. Round it gossamer and gauze. A statue draped in mosquito netting perhaps. The light was not bright enough for us to get an impression of his size. He was a giant mantis. He was a monster peering out of the tatters of his cocoon.

The air was filled with whispers and with humming and with the rustle of wings as though birds were flying there.

Menopause-Harlequin placed his hand on my shoulder.

"Behold your first Mantissa," he said. "You are fortunate he has just begun the odyssey. Were he advanced in the song it would be too dangerous for you to come in here. The power of some Singers is beyond reckoning and he is one of the greatest. The further they move into the song, the more the power builds up. At the climax no living thing can exist in this space." We began to walk towards the Mantissa.

"How long does the song last?"

Winter Wind joined me on the other side and it was he who replied.

"The Mantissaiad will last about two of your years. Perhaps a bit more. It is the song of our life, you see, and at each repeat it grows a bit longer. No doubt you will be melted into the song at some point. Your coming will be sung about."

"Who listens to the songs?"

Silence.

"A hard question," said Winter Wind. "No-one listens to them, but everyone absorbs them. They are born like thought in Pe-Ellian minds. Every Pe-Ellian grows up with these songs. They are with us when we dream and when we are awake. They tell us how to know that we are Pe-Ellian and how we came to be. There are words, of course, and the Mantissa knows them and that is enough. They are broadcast into the psychosphere and fill up every nook and cranny with life and rhythm."

"Are there many songs?"

"Millions."

"Are there many Singers?"

"Not many. Perhaps two hundred on Pe-Ellia but many others are scattered throughout the galaxy. But you see, to sing is the basic art of Mantissahood. All Mantissae can sing; only a few elect to remain Singers. The Outrigger Mantissa who surveyed the Earth was a renowned Singer of birth songs for the queen. In fact, one of the reasons he departed from Earth's vicinity was that his songs were charging Earth's psychosphere too soon and might have had a disastrous effect on the developing life there."

"What about the Pe-Ellian, Chord, does he want to be a Mantissa?"

"He aspires. Many try. Few succeed. That is good. Many things in life change for the worse, but Mantissae must always change for the better. Otherwise we are doomed, and if Pe-Ellia fails a hundred thousand civilisations will fall with it." Menopause-Harlequin was speaking and there was no disguising the anxiety in his voice. I was aware that Winter Wind, pacing on the other side of me, was also not happy.

I will digress a moment to explain what was happening at this time. I did not come to understand until only a few days ago.

These two Pe-Ellians were already locked in a struggle to use me. Menopause-Harlequin wanted me destructive and passionate, a child of Earth. Winter Wind wanted a chastened me, a sanitised-through-Pe-Ellia me. Both were profoundly worried about the future of their race.

Winter Wind's grand strategy was to gain mana from contact with Tomas and me, to effect a perfect *straan*, move towards Mantissahood and use these powers to give greater direction to the wild thought-energy factory that is Earth. His intentions, I must say, were honourable. Christian almost, and finally unrealistic. He would have benefited from a spell with us at the CLI.

Menopause-Harlequin was a different kind of being. He felt himself in the grip of some force greater than himself. He felt that he was impelled towards a liaison with me . . . our blood-brother relationship which I have already described . . . but did not know where this was to lead. Menopause-Harlequin felt he was part of an ongoing song whose story was not yet told.

Even as I write this I am aware of how little I yet understand. I have translated some poems for you. I know I am declining. I know that Menopause-Harlequin will go with me. But the final synthesis still eludes me. Perhaps I will understand more in the next few days and will be able to write it out for you.

So, to return to that day in the Mantissa Cathedral.

While speaking we were walking towards the Mantissa. We had covered perhaps half the distance and I was becoming aware of just how big this creature was.

Tomas caught up with me.

"How does a creature of that size manage to support its own weight?" he asked.

No-one answered that question for at that moment the Mantissa stirred slightly and I saw a heavy, hooded eye close slowly and then open again. I could see him much more clearly now. He was indisputably Pe-Ellian, but of an earlier generation. The hands and feet were definite claws. He was sitting back on his haunches with his two hands clasped round his knees. His head was ridged as though his spine curved up higher and was revealed outside his skin. All this I noted as we walked towards him. But the size! Nothing I have seen since on Pe-Ellia has quite matched it.

He was completely swathed in a filmy gauze-like material that enveloped him. I was surprised to discover that it was brittle, like chicken skin that has been fried.

"What is this?" I asked Menopause-Harlequin.

"You should know. It is Mantissa skin. For countless centuries he has not moved. He has sat there continually growing, outgrowing skins, and then the skins crack and tumble and dry. Those skins are part of the Mantissa's history. They will stay there as long as he does. But you get some idea of how old he is. Most of the true Elder Mantissae have flown."

His lips were moving, whispering a form of Pe-Ellian which was perhaps a common tongue at the time that Earth's oceans were forming.

I looked up at the giant face, mottled and lined, at the eyes focused on another time and yet alive in the present, at the hands with the great ribbed claws, and I felt humbled. I felt ephemeral. I could feel his *karit*, the word the Pe-Ellians use for thought and for which we have no equivalent. It was a great tide sweeping through the green/blue depths of space.

I knew (do not ask me how, but I knew) that if I touched him I would share the song. It is part of my vanity that I am impulsive. I edged forward, pushing through the sloughed-off skin. Some of it fell to powder at my touch.

"Where are you going? Be careful," called Winter Wind, and that was my cue. I scampered as quickly as I could, breasting the skin and tearing through. Before the others had realised what I was doing I was there. I reached out and pressed myself as tightly as I could against the Mantissa's talon.

They tell me I collapsed with a cry. They say that for a second the song paused in its rhythm. I knew none of this.

I was swept up. My soul expanded inside me and flew out through my eyes, through my finger ends and through the pores of my skin. I was a bolt of pure energy lifted by a Mantissa song. Below me I could see Winter Wind and the others as bobbing puffballs of light. They were clustered round a pile of rags that glowed redly—me.

I had no control over my movements. I drifted upwards. I slid past the Mantissa's slowly moving lips and away. I merged with the song.

Now I am tired of writing. It has been a strenuous day and tomorrow promises to be even more demanding, for tomorrow I shall meet the queen. Nevertheless I promise to try and write down what happened to me in the song.

Commentary

When Thorndyke collapsed I was sure he was dead. I have seen men drop dead, as though all the muscles supporting them had suddenly been severed. That was how Thorndyke fell. He did scream. We rushed to help him, but Cook held me back, saying I would only be in the way and might be in danger. The Pe-Ellian who had accompanied us began a soft keening noise and slipped to the ground. I learned later that this was a self death because he felt he had allowed something to interrupt the song. I was told that for the space of several seconds the song had stopped.

Jet and Winter Wind began carrying Thorndyke away from the Mantissa and back towards the door through which we had entered. Menopause-Harlequin stood facing up to the Mantissa with his hands raised. I was not sure what he was doing. He could have been praying.

Cook and I followed the body. Cook actually asked me if I wanted to be carried, if I felt strong enough to walk. I declined his offer and insisted on seeing Thorndyke the moment we got outside the Mantissa's chamber.

I quickly discovered that he was alive and uninjured, but he appeared to be in a deep coma. We placed him aboard the carriage and Menopause-Harlequin pulled down some of the ropes and made them into a stretcher.

Thorndyke lay there as though in state, and the only sign of life was the slow steady in-and-out of his breath.

No-one spoke.

We came home in record time and without changing vehicles.

At the cottage Thorndyke was carried down to his room and placed carefully on his bed. A hurried conversation took place between the Pe-Ellians in which Winter Wind and Menopause-Harlequin seemed on the point of disagreement. I saw both of them take karitsas.

Winter Wind and Jet departed.

Cook was visibly upset and wandered in circles saying things like, "Oh, the poor man. Lost in a wide, wide sea," and offering to make me tea or anything else to soothe my nerves.

I was shocked by what had happened, naturally, but nevertheless in complete control. I wished that the Pe-Ellians would leave so that I could examine Thorndyke for myself. This, however, was impossible. Menopause-Harlequin, who seemed in a way I did not understand at the time to have become the senior partner, announced that he was moving in to take care of Thorndyke.

I protested, but he simply closed the door in my face and I found that I could not open it.

Cook witnessed this and spoke to me.

"Rest easy. Professor Thorndyke is in no danger with him in there. He will do everything he can to protect him. Try to relax."

Later I spoke to Menopause-Harlequin and he explained to me what had happened to Thorndyke. I quote his words exactly:

"He has been exorcised. His life has been drawn from him. He is travelling with the song . . . but he will return I think. He is strong. His mind is all weathered hickory and ivory. He will integrate. But I do not know when."

I had no choice but to wait.

Thorndyke slept for five days.

On the morning of the fifth day he awoke with a deep sigh and asked for food. Menopause-Harlequin, who was holding both his hands, nodded.

THORNDYKE'S DIARY: ENTRY 27

I woke up to the crazy patchwork face of Menopause-Harlequin and it was a face as familiar and normal as my own. I felt that the alien had been shredded away and that the only thing out of place in the room was poor Tomas Mnaba. His eyes were popping. He spoke to me and his voice sounded clotted and strained. I seemed to be looking at him through thick panes of glass, which refracted and removed him.

I woke up with a vivid memory of where I had been and what had happened to me. I will try to tell this. I will try not to dwell on the incredible, but will be as pragmatic as possible, always remembering that I have been where no human being has been before.

The point at which I entered the song and touched the Mantissa Singer was important. Let me clarify. A song was being sung. When I touched the Mantissa I joined him in the sense that I was consumed by him. My life so puny, his life so strong. I was swept away into his mind and since he was "living" the song I entered the song. Clear?

I fear not.

His song at that point, as well as I can render it, is like this.

It is an early time, a time when there were still battles. Did you know that the Pe-Ellians developed telepathy to put an end to warfare? It is so. Now they are striving to move beyond telepathy. This was a primitive time. Skin markings were tribal and a cause for battle. There were many varieties of Pe-Ellian then. Some were like salamanders, others were like the Mantissa himself, some were like modern Pe-Ellians, but much smaller. Warfare was common and this part of the song deals with a commander whose name was Lightning and who pauses the night before battle to drink wine. The poem at this point concerns the way the wine flows round the cup, the way the cup reflects the "bowl of the sky" and the way that when the wine is drunk everything is changed.

Notes towards a translation:

Part of the pleasure with wine is holding the cup.
See how I swirl it round and destroy the heavens

Resting within. Beads and stars. Tumbled together.
I drink in the stars.

My forefathers, friends and enemies invigorate me.
Tomorrow, who knows, I may be up there with them,
And another champion will drink me down.

That was the poem I joined. I was fortunate that it was a reflective stanza. Had it been a battle stanza I would not be here now.

I have said that I was squeezed out of myself. The Mantissa paused in his song and that gave my stunned life a short respite in which to recover. Then the irresistible tide of the song built up and burst through the silence.

I became the warrior Lightning, belly deep in the yielding mud. I felt the hardness of my plated skin and the lingering ache of old wounds.

Already a telepathic power was stirring inside my mind and I could hear, like the beating of giant wings, the breathing of the universe.

The mud trickled and bubbled around me. Night sounds came to my ears. Sounds of sleep. Sounds of sharpening like darts in the night. Before me was the wine cup held in my two claws. I saw the stars dance on its surface and spread and run as I swirled the cup.

The wine became a shallow vortex of light, which drew me out like spun thread and into the tumbling stars.

I drifted with the stars. I may have seen Earth.

The colours amazed me. The sky was no longer black but a deep blue. Threads of violet linked the suns and moons. I was a bright silver point of light passing green and red planets.

How long I wandered I do not know. Sometimes the wine would swill again and I would tumble with the planets and stars.

I met friends too. Old friends I had known on Earth. Faces from childhood. Faces I did not know. Alien faces.

Then I was Lightning again and I was drinking the wine. I drank my past. I drank life. As wine I travelled inside a long dead Pe-Ellian gut.

How strange to be both the drink and the drinker and yet more than both. This state was exciting to contemplate. I was aware of so many other things. Touch for one. The Pe-Ellian sensuousness comes out in their exquisite perception of surfaces. When I was the wine I felt the cool smoothness and the dimples of wear in the wine mug. The mud puckered the joints in my plated skin. All was sensation.

Subjectively I was away for what seemed just a few hours. Long enough for the Mantissaiad thoughts to spread. Then I knew I was about to wake up. I saw Menopause-Harlequin like a bud of flame; and the flame became the face. I woke feeling younger and wiser—and hungry.

I woke with the conviction that it was my destiny to be on Pe-Ellia at this particular time, and that I needed to be alone on Pe-Ellia. The presence of Tomas Mnaba on Pe-Ellia was intolerable. Through him all Earth pulled at me. I knew with certainty that I would have to dismiss him. I hoped he would take it well, but well or not, he must go. I also realised that Menopause-Harlequin and Diver-Thorndyke are one soul. We are joined by a bond stronger than blood. I am part of him because that is my mind written on his body. He became part of me at my birth I believe. Some resonance that reached across space. Some harmonic.

Does this idea seem strange to you who hold this book? It should not. The idea is old. Plato had a glimmering of it. In the early days of the world, you know, there was far less thought interference. Our psychosphere was far less clotted and it was easier for sympathetic resonances to occur. Nevertheless, such resonances do still occur and space is far more alive than the astronomers know, who see only vacuum. Even now on Earth there are many linked lives—lives which are incomplete because their other half is on some other planet and no doubt yearning. I am unusual only in that I am joined with my other half, or perhaps with one of my other quarters, for there is no evidence I know of that says life moves in pairs. However, I digress too far and must return.

I awoke with the conviction that only I should be on Pe-Ellia and this conviction precipitated the dismissal of my friend Tomas Mnaba.

Commentary

Thorndyke's awakening was a gentle glide from sleep to awareness to consciousness. It was accomplished by Menopause-Harlequin, who was leaning over him murmuring some words (I did not have the opportunity to record them) and stroking the backs of his hands. When they delivered the manuscripts to me on Camellia, Cook and Jet told me that Harlequin had travelled out from himself and tried to keep contact with Thorndyke. They were not specific about how this was done, but it appeared to have been some kind of mental projection.

Thorndyke's eyes opened and he stared at Menopause-Harlequin. He sighed deeply—making up for all the shallow breaths of sleep—and turned to me. His pupils were dilated. They had an alien cast. His expression made me shudder. It was a sedated smile such as one may find in the mentally ill. It was the blandness of certainty—and I have witnessed fanaticism before. I called out, but his only response was a nod.

No doubt he is correct when he says that through me Earth pulled at him. I would put it rather more strongly. I would say that I was a reminder, a symbol if you like, of the rational world, a world which Thorndyke in his sensuousness wished to avoid.

Thorndyke's Diary: Entry 28

I was about to speak to Tomas, but then my tummy rumbled and I asked for food instead. "Time enough," I thought.

The ever gracious, tragically flawed Cook brought me cornflakes (yes), a leafy Pe-Ellian delicacy and a karitsa. The karitsa was agitated and almost leaped out of the bowl in its desire to reach me.

I touched it. It sphered. I ate.

Ah, how quickly I had learned to appreciate them. It saturated my nervous system with fire and ice and left me giddy but strong. When I had eaten I stood up. I found I was wearing a smaller version of the cape that Jet had worn the night of the banquet. It was good to be standing. Good to feel the blood flowing and the rush of air through nose and mouth.

"Let us talk in private," I said to Tomas. "Let us talk in the clearing with our feet dangling in the river." I wanted that sensation. I wanted the real flow of cold, hard, buffeting water. I felt the dream retreating and knew that what I was going to say would be both cruel and painful.

We went outside. Tomas chose not to paddle.

I said, "I know that I have broken most of the rules of the Handbook. Now I am going to break another. I want you to leave Pe-Ellia. I want you to ask me no questions for the moment. I want you to travel back to Earth, but without the notes or the encoder. You are to tell Earth what has happened, by which I mean you can tell them anything you like, for I do not fully understand myself what is happening. I only know, my old friend, that Pe-Ellia and I have business together and that our two minds neutralise each other. I ask you to trust me in this, just as you have trusted me in the past."

Then I attempted to explain something of the unity of Pe-Ellian life and thought and about Menopause-Harlequin, but I made a mess of it and floundered.

Tomas's mouth opened, but he said nothing.

"Later," I continued, "I will send you the encoder, your notes, my notes and my diaries. That I promise. But I shall not return to Earth."

Silence.

Commentary

As Thorndyke says—silence. I could think of nothing to say at first. To leave was impossible for me. It would have involved my breaking the most solemn oath. The contact linguists' code is not just a book of rules and regulations, it is a moral statement, which binds one to certain kinds of actions and ways of thinking. Of course, different situations demand different reactions and one cannot plan for every eventuality. In my eyes the events of those past few days made my duty abundantly clear. It was to protect Thorndyke from Pe-Ellia and from himself. We have many examples of breakdown on record. I believed that Thorndyke, for all his abundant vitality and obvious quickness of mind, was in a state of breakdown. My perception was complicated by my mistrust of Menopause-Harlequin, my feeling that Winter Wind was ailing, that Jet would sit on the fence and just contemplate. Cook, I knew, could be of no help for he was as good as dead already.

I asked Thorndyke to quote from the Handbook the section on responsibility, which he did. (It is a requirement of our profession that certain parts of this book are known by heart.) The section reads: "The contact linguist's first responsibility is to his colleague. Don't become a mother, but don't lose your heart. The effectiveness of your work lies partly in the knowledge that you are never alone. With this certainty one can face uncertainty. If doubt becomes too great concentrate on one another. Talk about what it was like growing up. What was your first language? What food do you want when the long haul is over? Find common ground. Ground yourself in the everyday run-of-the-mill humanity which is the basis of our civilisation."

He finished quoting and looked at me.

"There is a difference between us. To you this remains a contact quest in the classic mode, complicated, I grant you, by the fact that we are facing an advanced, complex and powerful civilisation—the like of which we have never known before—but nevertheless susceptible to the contact linguist code.

"For me this has moved beyond the code. It has become personal. You are right, Tomas, I am falling into the big trap: identifying with the alien. And if I thought as you do I would act as you are doing. But Tomas, Tomas, use the evidence of your eyes. What can the contact linguist code make of a Mantissa? How can we cope with a species for whóm thought is a building material? Add to that I am not a neophyte, a Johnny-come-lately. I am one of the oldest in the game. I helped write the damned code. Now doesn't that make you pause just a little? Think, consider, I just may be right. Perhaps the only way we can have a true contact with these strange beasts is by 'melding', as they put it. How and for why I do not know, but that mottled, particoloured oddity called Menopause-Harlequin and I are linked and I have no choice but to see this through."

That was the basis of our argument. Two points of view which could not be reconciled and on which there could be no compromise. I asked for a conference with Winter Wind and was told he was already on his way.

There was a gurgling near us and Jet's bald and glossy head broke surface. He swam to the side and pulled himself out of the water. His eyes rolled and arms gyrated in a gesture we both recognised as one signifying delight and surprise.

"Knew you would make it through," he said. "Good job Harlequin was with you. He is adept. But it was a blankety silly thing to do anyway."

"I don't know why I did it," said Thorndyke. "I just had to and now I'm glad. I feel like a bar of metal that has just been magnetised."

"The Mantissa rather enjoyed it too. He communicated that he rather relished seeing the epic through your eyes. That is a great honour. And all has worked out for the best."

"Well nearly," Thorndyke looked at me. "Every honour has its price. This is no exception."

Jet sensed something. I saw him retreat behind his eyes. He detached himself from us without even moving. I am certain that he was ready to slip back into the water at a moment's notice.

"What kind of price?"

"I have asked Tomas Mnaba to leave. I want to stay on Pe-Ellia alone."

"Um." Pause. "And what does Professor Mnaba think?"

He spoke as though I wasn't there.

"He is deeply hurt," answered Thorndyke. "And more than a little angry."

"I can feel that. We must wait and see what Winter Wind has to say."

He stood up and without a word went down to the cottage. I had no doubt he intended to confer with Menopause-Harlequin.

We did not have long to wait for Winter Wind. We heard a call and then the patter of feet running down the path. Winter Wind burst into the clearing.

He greeted us and was obviously delighted that Thorndyke was back with the living, but at the same time I could tell he was aware all was not well. However, he cannot have foreseen just what danger and damage was about to occur. In his diary Thorndyke describes the events of the next few hours.

Thorndyke's Diary: Entry 29

The Spoiling of Winter Wind

Certainly thought is living and like all living things it can be healthy or sick. I find I have my full share of sickness and nowhere was this better demonstrated than in the confrontation with Winter Wind. He was the tragic hero, unbending, and unwittingly moving down the line of his fate.

Memory is painful too.

I suffer before the memory of Winter Wind. But if I could have my time over again I would do it again. So, milk lie thou spilt and bridges be crossed and burned.

His delight in my resurrection, as he called it, was a joy to see. He beamed. He made complicated gesture language. He wanted to call a karitsa party and yet he said, "What is wrong?"

I explained that I was telling Tomas to go.

"Why?" he asked.

"Because my last life's work is here. Here is more fulfilment than I ever expected. But with Tomas here my pleasure is alloyed. I have become sensitive since my time with the Mantissa Singer and I feel Mnaba's presence like fire feels water. Soehe must go."

"Impossible," said Winter Wind.

"Nothing is impossible, either on Earth or on Pe-Ellia. I am starting to learn that and I am not the same person I was."

"If he leaves, then you must leave also."

"Excuse the ill manners of the guest, but I shall not leave. I have my work here."

Winter Wind was visibly shaken.

"Excuse me, you are not the man I thought," he said. "You will both leave without delay."

Though his words were mild they angered me. A warning voice in my brain said to trap my thought, but I ignored that. The Mantissa's face thrust itself into my memory and I knew a choice lay with me.

Winter Wind turned to leave. "I have nothing more to say."

I held the image of Winter Wind and Menopause-Harlequin side by side. Winter Wind as he was when he came bounding along to meet us. Menopause-Harlequin aching as his skin split and half mad with fear at what was happening to him.

"Wait," I called and Winter Wind stopped like a trained horse.

I didn't know what I was going to say. I suddenly saw clearly that the choice was mine. If I really wanted to stay then I had to overcome Winter Wind. Tomas would leave when he saw he had no option. Jet would not intervene. Cook, poor Cook, would weep for the sadness of it all. And his tears would be a poet's tears, observing the emotion craftily and observing the observation honestly. Menopause-Harlequin could not intervene.

The choice was mine. I stared at the mottled back of Winter Wind (he had not turned but stood waiting) and an unbidden thought snaked from my mind . . . *Despoil. Spoil.*

My thought was like a whiplash. Winter Wind made a sound the like of which I hope never to hear again and sank slowly to his knees.

The battle was over and won. The brash and expansive had defeated the courtly and closeted.

I felt elated and sickened at the same time. I opened my mind to the Mantissa to see if he had any guidance, but there was nothing. I opened my mind wider, seeking anything, anyone. Silence. The echoing emptiness of total exclusion, my only company my own cruel thought. An entire civilisation had turned it back on me.

At the same time I hardly comprehended the magnitude of what I had done. Afterwards, weeks afterwards, when the psychosphere was again settling down and absorbing me, Menopause-Harlequin was able to explain.

Winter Wind is dying fast. Today I visited him. He didn't speak to me, naturally, but I knelt by him and offered what I could of love.

Commentary

This concludes all Thorndyke says about Winter Wind except for a few short references later. I will complete the story up to my departure. I saw Winter Wind fall. I heard the sound, which no living creature should ever have to make. I felt a sickness inside me.

Thorndyke left the clearing and went into our cottage. I hurried over to Winter Wind and asked if I could help. His voice came from another age, like a voice calling across cold grey water.

"You should get your things together. Departure soon."

Jet came up into the clearing. I expected him to help, but he didn't look at us. He darted across the clearing and dived into the stream.

"Can I help you?" I asked. Winter Wind was fumbling at his side and I guessed he was trying to get to a karitsa.

Cook emerged from the cottage and joined us. He knelt by Winter Wind and helped him. Winter Wind managed to consume a karitsa. I have seen people drink double whiskies the same way with the same effect.

When the karitsa was down and had worked its magic, Cook helped Winter Wind to stand.

"I will arrange transport back to Earth or wherever for you," he said, and I was pleased to note that his voice had more life in it. "Forgive me if I don't accompany you. I had hoped to have that pleasure, but now—"

His voice trailed away.

"I will at least see you off. Cook will give you the details." Cook nodded. "Now I need to rest."

I took this as my cue for departure. Saying I hoped he felt better, I hurried down into the house.

Obscurely I knew what had happened. Not the details, only the outline. Thorndyke, I knew, was to blame, and I felt deep sadness that a creature as noble as Winter Wind should have been hurt by Thorndyke. I knew he had changed allegiance and I felt he had made the greatest error of his life. In my opinion he had deserted both me and Winter Wind. I considered that he was verging on madness.

Having now read the contents of these diaries many times I am compelled to change that judgement. I now realise that Thorndyke was in the grip of a force greater than himself. Neither he, nor I, nor Winter Wind, nor Menopause-Harlequin were free agents. We were part of a process, which in the fullness of time will affect the future of Earth, Pe-Ellia and the civilised planets we have come to know.

Among my personal possessions on Pe-Ellia I had some active

biopaper. I went to Thorndyke's room and knocked on his door. He was alone and looked haggard. I said I was preparing to leave and that Winter Wind had agreed to provide transport, but that I wanted a formal release. On the paper Thorndyke wrote the following letter.

The Senior Adviser,
Contact Committee, Pe-Ellian Division,
UN Space Council.

Dear Sir,
Professor Mnaba is returning to Earth on my specific instructions. As senior member of this team I have concluded that only one member of this team should remain here. I take full responsibility for the decision. I am retaining all research materials and will forward them to Professor Mnaba at some future date. I have every confidence that Professor Mnaba will be able to give you concrete details concerning this decision. Finally, I should like to add that throughout the expedition Professor Mnaba has conducted himself with the same dedication, intelligence and dignity that have characterised his work in the past. This deviation from standard practice is solely at my insistence.

Marius Thorndyke

Having completed the letter he waited till the ink had dried and then turned it over. The reverse side was the bioactive side. On this he pressed the full palm of his hand. Next he made a small incision in the lobe of his ear and secured one or two drops of blood. These were dropped on to the paper, where they were quickly absorbed.

Thorndyke handed me the letter and I folded it carefully. He asked about Winter Wind and I again attempted to convince him that either I should stay on or he should go with me. I particularly argued this last case, pointing out the many cases of delusion we have dealt with and the proven soundness of the contact linguist code.

Thorndyke was adamant and refused to speak about the matter. He asked me to bring the encoder and all documents to his room. This I did. I then bade him goodnight and returned to my room.

Exhaustion allowed me to sleep.

In the middle of the night I was woken by Cook. He whispered that transport was ready and that I could leave now if I wished.

I did wish. I got dressed immediately, collected my belongings and left the house. I did not say goodbye to Thorndyke.

Cook accompanied me down the path, which was reasonably well lit by the stars. The night air was fresh and cool and I could have enjoyed the journey had it not been for the circumstances. Cook was silent the whole time.

We arrived at the large clearing much sooner than I expected. Winter Wind was there. He was standing by a small version, almost a one-man version, of the sphere that had brought us to Pe-Ellia. It rocked gently that five or so centimetres above the grass.

"Farewell," said Winter Wind. "I never expected things would turn out quite this way, but I'm glad that we at least had the opportunity to get acquainted."

I thanked him for all he had done, for his courtesy, for his forethought and for his honesty. I also apologised for what had happened. He stepped forward to shake hands and in the light from the sphere I saw his face and upper body. Gone were the fine markings and delicate scroll work. His face was mottled, and ugly red stains like bruises were showing through his face and arms. Some of the plates, which had once been so regular, were now turning to mean little squares or slab-like triangles.

He saw my expression.

"The poison works quickly," he said. "Soon it'll be the melting pot and . . . Cook is now my brother. We are both Balacas. He has said he will help me at the end. So farewell."

I cried. Cook, showing some of his old energy, bundled me aboard the ship. The door closed.

The last I saw of Pe-Ellia was those two faces set against the stars.

I felt the departure. The ship jolted and that was all. The interior was identical to the ship in which we had arrived, but no windows opened. A short time later (I was so upset by everything that had occurred that I even forgot to check the time) the ship bounced slightly and the door opened.

I stepped outside and found myself in the garden of my own house on Camellia. They had not returned me to Earth as I had expected, but to the CLI. It was night-time and not a soul was to be seen. Behind me there was a sudden loud gasp. I turned in time to see the sphere that had carried me dissolve, leaving me alone in the chill night air. I hurried to my door, palmed the lock and entered.

No-one was expecting me so no-one visited the house and I was able to stay there for three days undiscovered until I sent my message to the Space Council announcing my arrival.

The rest is history.

The following are the complete texts of the last parts of Thorndyke's diary.

The pages are undated and I have left them in their original order, which may or may not be chronological. All titles are Thorndyke's.

THORNDYKE'S DIARY: ENTRY 30

Tomas's departure and the mess of things I made with Winter Wind took their toll, and I almost gave up and asked to be sent home or out into space or into their quaint little melting pot or whatever. But then Harlequin announced that he was going to begin instruction in Pe-Ellian. He also told me that Winter Wind had contacted him and wanted me to know that he had accepted what had happened and bore me no malice. That lifted a stone off my heart. Winter Wind said that it was all a part of the order of things, a phrase which curiously resembled Harlequin's idea that we are locked into a grand design.

So, I have now begun what we should have done weeks ago—I have started to learn their language.

And what strange lessons. Harlequin says, "Pe-Ellian is a language of feeling", and that is what he has got me doing. Feeling things. I am having to invent my own language to find words to describe something like lying in a hammock made of fishnet or chewing wool.

Class begins in the morning. I sit blindfold for breakfast and that meal is a carefully-orchestrated sequence of rough and smooth, raucous and dulcet experiences. He asks me to imagine feeling a shape, so I swallow my fruit juice, which is tart as green tomatoes. I imagine and remember the face of a drill instructor who taught gym classes when I was in school. He was a surly man who, I swear, tried to break those schoolboys he considered effete. *Move. Jump. Move. Jump*—and the juice goes down.

I regret that I am not very good at these exercises but I find them stimulating and breakfast has certainly become a vastly more entertaining meal. I ask Harlequin for Pe-Ellian words and we try to analyse the tastes. Thus: "How long does the taste linger? What does the taste make you want next? What colour was the taste?" Impossible questions, but fun. In comparing our two physiologies, Pe-Ellian and human, I realise that we are coarse-grained. Did you know that Pe-Ellians have extra sense nodes located in the patterned parts of their skin? They do. For them surface and sensation are merely two sides of the same coin.

After breakfast comes what I call the Indian Rope Trick. Behind the Palm Court are some webs of fibre such as we saw in the roof when we visited the Mantissa. I climb into these and swing and sway and slide, and young Pe-Ellians come and demonstrate turns and twists. This is always enjoyable. Each of the fibres is different, has a different texture. Some are rough as hemp, others as slippery as vaseline. I am told that this is primary training and that a good exercise is one which plays the full range of one's sensations.

This exercise is always followed by resting. During this I lie on my back and look at the river flowing past or at a leaf in my hands and try to project myself into them. Usually this takes until lunchtime. I eat very little and retire, tired, to sleep.

In the afternoon we study Pe-Ellian words and gestures. The gestures are all based on reaction. For instance, if I prick my finger, I pull my hand back and cry out in pain. In Pe-Ellian that might be the gesture to accompany surprise that brings no pleasure. Of course, in Pe-Ellian it is all much more complicated, and even now I only "know" some twenty-five gestures.

My old parrot gift is still with me and I experience no difficulty in memorising the sounds.

There is no written form of Pe-Ellian. I have been having a go at translation. About a week ago Jet came in and said he knew a song I might like. I wrote it down, using extended phonetics and a notation I have created to express the gestures. Jet was very interested but could not see the point. To him the poem was still growing and he felt that giving it definitive form would kill it. I said it could still grow despite the writing. The poem is a child song from the Queen series. This is a large collection of experience songs which can be sung to karitsas and young Pe-Ellians. The one I have tried to translate begins, I believe, before birth and takes the hearer through the first experience of movement and freedom. Harlequin says he does not think this is a very good example of the Queen series, but I say "Why worry?" In any case, it is the only poem I have come across so far of which I know more than a quarter of the words. Here's what I have to offer.

Child Songs from the Queen Series

No life but
Spring coiled.
   Stuck. Dumb.
Tight. Bounden.
But thinking.

   Move on.
This is not to be touched.
This bark rough and stiff wire
Excoriates like the kitchen grater.
   Move on.
   Less danger here.
Though still the shrill of a finger nail scratching
Can set the teeth of the world on edge.

   Move on.
   Mingle and mix.
Slowly, slowly slidee easy.
Too quick grinds to halt.

Faster now with fin and tail.
Flick the spray.
Slide swim
Glide slip
Fly.

I intend to include some other translations later. Getting back into translation is like putting the right hand into the right glove at the right temperature at the right time. (There is one Pe-Ellian word for all that.)

At the sensation exercises I am a dullard, frankly; and in truth I find them somewhat embarrassing. Harlequin says I am making progress and perhaps he sees more than I do. For me it is a pleasant work-out.

But the literary arts. O, that is a perfect joy. If we had begun like this instead of in that tortured way, how different our lives would have been! But of course that could not be. Our mental strength was too dangerous and outlandish.

I still forget myself, and although I have learned to curb my power of projection somewhat I still make mistakes.

As I have settled in here more Pe-Ellians have dropped in to meet and look at me—zoo-like. I don't mind. I have a toe-hold on their language and am slipping into their way of life like an eel into soft sand.

Thorndyke's Diary: Entry 31

I Visit the Queen

"I've got a surprise for you, Diver."

I was hardly awake.

"Far too early for surprises," I thought.

"The queen has granted you an audience—you will be the first off-worlder ever to see her."

That brought me bolting from the world of dreams. I saw Jet standing in my room with his back to the tumbling waterfall. I'd left the wall on for company while I slept. I can best describe his voice as smug. Even the slightly metallic accent which characterises his otherwise excellent English could not stifle that hint of the self-satisfied.

"Have you been pulling rank, Jet? Using influence in high places?"

"The queen is a law unto her self. I doubt if I could influence her," he added stiffly. "But she is aware of your presence, has known of you since the landing and has been informed that you would like to see her. This morning she said that she is willing."

I shall be interested to see her. Very interested. The Pe-Ellian attitude to her is confusing. Or rather, the confusion seems to lie in what they mean by "queen". I've collected some comments on her over the weeks.

"To sleep with the queen is to return to the roots of Pe-Ellia." *(Harlequin)*

"She's as immobile as a mountain." *(Harlequin)*

"When I first slept with the queen I was terrified. She was so alien and her touch made me cringe. Gradually I came to like it." *(Cook)*

"We eat the fruits of her body, the karitsa." (*Jet*)

"You can't talk of love with reference to the queen. She is, just like a tree is. But without her there would be no Pe-Ellia. She's as essential to us as air and water." *(Harlequin)*

"No, she's definitely not a Mantissa—in fact I don't think she's native to Pe-Ellia. Maybe brought here in the distant far-off when." *(Jet)*

"Perhaps she's more like a king, really." *(Cook)*

I pointed out to Harlequin that the Pe-Ellians I had spoken to were somewhat inconsistent in their attitudes and seemed uncertain as to just what the queen was.

"Ah," he said with a wink, "you are into the heart of Pe-Ellia here. Consider, we seek individual perfection. That is complete harmony between one's body and the great movements of space. What we see of the queen tells you more about us than about the queen. She is a malleable symbol."

I was not to be put off by fancy words.

"But she must have a corporeal form. Can I see her?"

"She's thinking about it."

So, when Jet announced a visit to the queen I was out of bed in a flash and calling for details even as I brushed my teeth. (I have lost a lot of my weight, by the way, and feel better for it.) Jet would say no more except to offer me a warning.

"Harken, Diver. To protect the queen you will be hooded. It may hurt a bit but that can't be helped."

"Hooded? Then how the hell will I get to see . . . ?"

"Not physically. Mentally. I'm going to tie you to a Mantissa so that you can't do any harm. Have you seen Winter Wind?"

"No."

"I'll try to arrange that, too. But he's failing fast and may not want to see you. In his boots I wouldn't. Anyway, the Mantissa will hood you. One pop of bad thought and he'll suck your mind as clean as a whistle. You won't even be able to walk. You'll become a radish and we'll start rebuilding you."

I think I was flattered. I was obviously getting into the heart of Pe-Ellia, for they were paying me the compliment of taking me seriously. That is always good.

So I was to be hooded. Another experience. I knew that no-one would deliberately take risks with me. Besides, I worked out that the Pe-Ellians are adept at hooding. Were not the representatives from their ship hooded to protect them from us while they were on Earth?

Harlequin arrived with Cook. Both were beaming.

"Smashing," said Cook. "This will lead to celebration."

We travelled by silver fish.

Shortly after we left Jet announced a diversion. A visit to see Winter Wind. Harlequin seemed a bit disturbed by this but Cook remained impassive. God alone knows what thoughts were passing through his brain.

The carriage stopped in a small underground chamber with one door leading off it. We descended and passed through the door and out into a leafy glade above a small shallow pond. A small river joined the pond and there, in the creek mouth, was Winter Wind. I recognised him though he was greatly changed. He was the colour of elephant hide and had thin veins of black running up to his head from his knees. Below the knees, as though he were wearing boots, he was altogether black.

He didn't see us when we emerged and continued sorting pebbles, crouched on the shingle of the creek bed.

I felt pity.

He turned then and waved to us and moved away up the stream. I could not tell whether the wave was one of greeting or dismissal.

No-one spoke, but we all turned and headed back into the tunnel. Jet broke the silence and spoke in rapid Pe-Ellian to Cook. I understood. Clearly Jet is not so well-informed of my progress in their tongue. I held my peace.

What Jet had asked was simply how long it would be before Winter Wind passed on.

"Three weeks, but it could be four. He was strong, but he will be quiet," replied Cook and the conversation lapsed.

I felt as though I had already attended his funeral. There were no condolences, no criticism of me, just a calm acceptance that several centuries of growth had been reduced to a ruin by one sour burst of thought.

I could understand why they wanted to hood me.

We arrived at the queen and there was a great coming and going of Pe-Ellians. Jet led us through the station and into a small antechamber that on Earth might have been called a robing room. In the centre was a silver pool identical to the one Menopause had bathed in before he became Harlequin.

"Rest yourself in that," said Jet, pointing at the pool.

I floated and then my legs began to sink. Soon I was bobbing upright. I relaxed, and as suddenly as the shadow of an eagle covers its prey, a giant hand closed over my mind.

My first reaction was simple surprise. I suddenly had no independence of mind any more. The "I" of "me-ness" shrank into a tiny dot—shrivelled would be closer—and I was bereft of will. Yet I could still think. I was aware also of this new presence beside me. Not unfriendly. A slightly ironic, gently smiling presence. A something so vast that if it laughed stars would be knocked from their orbit. There was the soft soughing as though I were close to some giant bellows.

"What's that noise?" I asked, amazed that I could ask such a question and yet realising immediately that I had been allowed to ask. It had been vetted and passed as soon as formed.

"The wind is the sound of time." The voice was my voice, dried and pressed a bit but nonetheless mine. But I was not the speaker.

"Can you see past and present, then?" I asked.

"And more."

There were hands on me lifting me from the pool. Harlequin inspected me, looking into my eyes, rubbing my temples lightly, blowing into the palms of my hands.

"Go now and visit the queen. She is waiting," said the voice in my head. "Walk without fear. I am beside you."

I tried an experiment. I tried to think of Winter Wind, but the thought would not form. My mind was locked in a canyon. I could no more change it than a man can alter the direction of a train merely by changing his seat.

We walked out. I was led like a sightless person and was glad of the support. We entered a cavern with a large domed ceiling.

In Xanadu did Kubla Khan
A stately pleasure-dome decree:
Where Alph, the sacred river, ran
Through caverns measureless to man
Down to a sunless sea.

The Mantissa was turning the pages of my memory and inspecting our literature! I was once in a Chinese imperial tomb on Earth—Qing or Ming, I forget which—and I remember walking down this marbled passage into cold and damp darkness. Our progress reminded me of that. Except that the dampness here was not cold. It was not the damp of water filtering down through limestone and dripping down to stalagmites. It was somewhat fetid, not unpleasant, an odour of life, moist and mysterious.

We left the rock-walled chambers and entered an area that was obviously under the control of a Mantissa. The walls became the familiar skin. The lighting was also Mantissa lighting—indirect, having no apparent source, but effective for all that.

Shall I compare thee to a summer's day?

In the distance was a pallor. I felt my breath constrict as when one wades into cold water. For a few seconds my brain was squeezed and released. This may have been the cause of the breathlessness. I do not know.

"Lo, the queen," said Jet.

I saw a grey shape which completely blocked the end of the tunnel. I could see that the flesh(?) substance(?) continued into caverns of its own on either side.

I saw that the greyness was wrinkled and moving gently, a slow peristalsis.

Apart from the wrinkles, which ran laterally, the only other characteristic was the spots. Dark little speckles.

We moved on again. My perception of size and distance were all confused. I had thought we were only fifty yards or so from the queen. The truth was closer to four hundred. This confusion keeps happening to me on Pe-Ellia.

"There'll be no running forward and touching the queen," I thought and was greeted by a distant sighing laugh.

O rare.

The smell became stronger and there was a trace of fish in it. Seaweed. Kelp and bladderwrack. The definite smell of another world. Not unpleasant, but I wanted to sneeze. The sneeze was lifted from me.

Ah, I could now see more clearly, and the black dots took on form and gave them meaning. They were Pe-Ellians nestling like flies on the wrinkles of the queen's skin.

"Is that what you call sleeping with the queen?"

"Yes, they are hard asleep."

In the wrinkles were small feelers which probed about. They were a kind of pseudopodia, for I saw one withdraw completely into the body of the queen. We were close now. In front of us a Pe-Ellian touched the body of the queen and then began climbing up her. He climbed past other Pe-Ellians, carefully placing his feet in the wrinkles, which at this range were more like ridges. He reached a clear space and here sat for a few seconds looking down at us. He was a fine specimen with glossy green-blue markings.

Almost absent-mindedly he dampened the ends of his fingers and rubbed them on his side. His body opened and immediately one of the pseudopodia snaked out and inserted itself inside him.

My gaze was held. I have watched love rites on many planets. Always mysterious.

With the queen's extension safely inside him the Pe-Ellian lay down and appeared to sleep instantly.

"He is receiving karitsas."

"How long will he stay there?"

"One sleep. Maybe two."

"Does he dream?"

"Fine dreams."

The queen made a convulsive movement. The resemblance to a worm was unavoidable.

"Is she aware of me?"

"Very much aware."

"How?"

"The Mantissa who is hooding you is in contact with her. He is the queen's handmaiden."

They also serve who only stand and wait.

Harlequin placed his hand on my shoulder.

"Have you seen enough, my friend?"

I nodded and was feeling slightly nauseous. The effect of breathing in the fishy air, no doubt.

"I have many questions though," I said.

"Later."

"I'll leave you now," said Cook. "I will return tomorrow. I am in need of a deep sleep and some sweet dreams." He bowed politely and then began climbing swiftly up the grey walls of the queen. He was climbing to a high place just under the roof. We watched until he reached his niche and then waved goodbye.

We turned and I was led up the gradual slope towards the outer air. My body was tingling. Pins and needles. It was reacting against the Mantissa control. He had perhaps neglected to pay sufficient attention to the circulatory system. At all events, to be walking again made me feel better.

We were soon out of the Mantissa-controlled area and into the warm air of Pe-Ellia.

We made our way into the ante-chamber and I climbed into the quicksilver pool. Immediately a sweet drowsiness overcame me.

"The Mantissa will withdraw from you soon," said Jet. "It may be painful."

They held my hands outstretched. I dreamed I was suspended in a dark well. From the depths of the well a voice spoke.

"The queen has enjoyed your visit. Through me she has sampled all of you. I gave her of your literature too. *The Tempest* is our favourite, almost a Pe-Ellian work—life beyond the actual—and the *Seliica*, which is your favourite. Very fine. In return the queen has suggested I give you a gift. Now I shall withdraw. Try to relax."

Relax! Relax it said. Imagine for a few moments I lost control of all bodily functions. My heart stopped. My breathing stopped. My mind blinked. The roar of the bellows was like the glare of a furnace and when I could bear no more I was returned to myself. I felt "me" rush into all the chinks and crannies of my being. My veins and arteries welcomed me back. My spine shrugged in happiness. Only the palms of my hands burned and my forehead and a point in the middle of my back.

Harlequin and Jet hauled me out of the pool and stared at me in astonishment.

"You have been . . . anointed."

"Blessed."

"Touched."

"Knighted."

The burning was fading slowly. I looked at the palms of my hands and I was marked. In each palm was a simple figure. It was not particularly elegant, rather as though a child had drawn the lines, but it was firm and solid and harmonious. I knew that I had the same on my forehead and on my back.

"That is the queen's mark. She has welcomed you to Pe-Ellia. She has understood your desires and made you one of us."

We returned. I remember little of the journey except Pe-Ellian faces peering at me in interest and amazement.

By the time we reached the cottage my presence of mind was sufficiently restored to start asking questions.

"I'm bothered. If the queen is only that big, then how do all the Pe-Ellians manage to visit her regularly?"

"Only what big?" Jet speaking.

"Well, I presume we saw her middle, so to speak, and that the head and tail were in different quarters."

Jet and Harlequin both laughed.

"You saw but a millionth part of her," Harlequin said. "She is vaster than you can conceive. She winds about under valleys, through hills, beneath the oceans (and they are deep). I am told she warms herself on the fires at the heart of our planet and also contemplates the stars. She is wholly strange. She is continually grovelling—no—grubbing, boring, digging, moving on. The caves where she has been are vast."

"Where did she come from? Is there a king?"

"We are all kings. About her starting place there are many tales."

Jet is speaking. Imagine him coiled up, knees under chin. A high serious face above his sexless body. "One story I heard in the northern part of the planet was that she came to Pe-Ellia as a drop of water. A pearl. She was magic even then. She landed on the leaf of a Snu-su plant. There the sun touched her and warmed her after the chill of space. One of our ancestors, Red Tooth by name, smelled her out and tasted her. He drew life from her. But she, the queen, drew life from him. He slept and dreamed dreams of valour and when he awoke he found she had grown. He picked her up and carried her along on his back through the jungle to his home, which was a hole on the side of a cliff above a stream. That night he tasted her again and again. Again sweet dreams of valour and peace caught him. In the morning he found her burrowing. He called his friends. They came and marvelled and stayed to taste. The more they tasted the more she grew. The more she grew, the more there was to taste. In that way we grew together. The queen and Pe-Ellia. But we are not the same. We are two species who discovered ourselves.

"Perhaps the queen is unique. Perhaps there are many such throughout the galaxies. I don't know. Winter Wind would have liked that question. I'll see if I can dig up the information somewhere." Jet glanced at me. "Sorry, didn't mean to be rude."

He hunched himself even tighter. "Anyway, we Pe-Ellians and the queen are not of the same species. Let's put it like that. Now we depend on her and she depends on us. We wonder what will happen when Pe-Ellia runs out of burrowing land. What then?"

Silence.

We sat there in the silence. Night was falling on the world outside. Above us the river boiled a rare thin gold.

"Any regrets?" asked Harlequin.

I looked at the shapes branded on my hands and felt lingering warmth where the Mantissa had touched me.

"Too late for regrets now. Far too late."

Thorndyke's Diary: Entry 32

How I Burned a Hole in the Wall

I woke up feeling angry for no reason I could think of, except possibly my dizziness. I keep having dizzy spells. Well, "keep" is the wrong word. I've had two or three such spells and they last only a few minutes, but when they pass off I am left debilitated and cantankerous.

I asked Harlequin if people on Pe-Ellia ever became angry, and if they did, whether or not it was dangerous.

"It is a private emotion," he told me, adding that it was dangerous if let loose.

Then a strange expression came over his face.

"That's another of our weaknesses. We need to explode emotionally, but we don't. We don't. We look at the red rage of Earth and we are afraid."

Anyway, as I said, I was cantankerous. Nothing fitted. I believe I felt homesick a little. The river tumbling beyond my walls irritated me. Cook was late with the breakfast and I spilled the juice down my chest.

"*Falla*," I shouted and hurled the glass at the wall. It bounced naturally and then bounced on the floor. I was denied the pleasure of even a good smash. "*Tiy-conna*," I yelled, as though the wall had ears and was susceptible to insult.

A spot on the wall close to where the glass had struck darkened, rather like a paper which is scorched from behind. To my alarm—and, I must add, fascination—the darkness spread and grew blacker. With a pop, a hole appeared in the middle of the discoloured patch and the wall ripped open.

The hole was about a metre in diameter. No sooner had it opened than soil and insects and God knows what came tumbling into the room.

"Cook," I called. He came rushing in and ushered me outside.

"This'll take a while for fixing," he said. "Think nice thought."

I began to explode again and then saw the funny side and started to laugh. I went for a walk.

Two hours later, when I re-entered the cottage, Harlequin and Cook were working on the wall. It was closed again, but it had a bruised, mottled look. Their hands were pressed against it and I could see their minds were far away, no doubt communicating with whatever Mantissa controlled the dwelling.

"The wall has become healthy again," said Cook.

"People who live in glass houses shouldn't throw stones," was Harlequin's contribution. He was clearly upset. "Be careful. Next time it might be the ceiling."

I mention this small incident merely because it helped clear up one of those things that had puzzled me while Tomas was here. Namely, why it took so long for the stimmu system to be connected to our cottage. I have puzzled over this word a great deal. Stimmu is one of the Pe-Ellian movement-words, of which there are thousands. It could mean glide or trajectory, but also implies rolling like a ball down a well-used track. I have even heard stimmu used in connection with birth.

As we know, everything within Tomas's magic circle is Mantissa powered. One Mantissa controls all the houses round here, and there are quite a few, I discover. The stimmu is controlled by another Mantissa and he is apparently very sensitive and touchy. Every time he hooked the stimmu up to our house our thoughts would upset him and he had to break contact. His mind rejected us rather as a body can reject an alien organ. At one point it was thought that we would never get a connection at all. The solution finally adopted was for the house Mantissa to step up his "insulation" and build a short corridor. This worked and we were connected to the greater stimmu network.

After Tomas left the Mantissa gradually relaxed his controls. As I became more and more Pe-Ellian it seemed less necessary for me to be so severely quarantined—but then I erupted and burned a hole in the wall. The stimmu connection is severed, and although I haven't been told I am sure the House Mantissa is back on full guard and at battle readiness to quash any wayward anger.

The whole thing seems to me rather comic, but they take it very seriously. . . .

No matter. I tried another experiment when they had gone. I placed my hands on the wall where it had been damaged. It was again a glossy green . . . the colour of mid-Atlantic—and I thought what Cook calls a nice thought. (This is nothing more than sensual response.) I have found that if you want to broadcast pleasant, healing, soothing thought, then the best way is to do something pleasurable to yourself. I pressed the palms with the queen's mark firmly into the walls. I enjoy the pulse of energy and life I feel in the walls, and I let this feeling flow through me and out again like a tide.

The walls brightened!

I did the same at the stimmu junction and the discoloured parts faded away. The wall grew strong and seamless.

You see I am learning control.

THORNDYKE'S DIARY: ENTRY 33

Of course I am aware that the whole thing is silly. I am of Earth. My every move says *Earth.* I carry with me the weighty impediments of culture and history and so my attempts to break the barrier are doomed to failure. Still I persist and am not downhearted.

There is no single state of reality. It has taken my coming here to show me that this is not a philosophy of despair, but rather one of hope.

Reality I have always seen as that which does not change. My weakness has been my continued questing for certainty, and now I find there is no certainty, only movement and change.

This is not profound I know, but I was shocked when I realised that I could not return to Earth, because I have sloughed off Earth and am branded now by Pe-Ellian markings. Menopause-Harlequin and I are part of a single life force and we have both undergone transformation recently. I know we will move towards death together and that that will not be too long away.

It is all a game really, and games have rules. How can I make you understand that sometimes, like now, I feel a weight of predestination? That thought I find horrible. If one is predestined, then all are predestined and we and all philosophy are reduced to the mindless ticking of a clock.

Perhaps there is something a bit less than total predestination. A state in which some latitude is available for the private enterprise of the mind. Before coming here I felt free and empty. Now I feel trapped but fuller. The other morning was the moment when I first became fully aware of the limits of my prison. I was practising my thought exercises, lying on my back on the table, trying to meld with the river above. It has become so much easier now. There are mental keys and each man must discover his keys for himself. I have trigger thoughts which, like self-hypnosis, shoot me into a different kind of consciousness.

So, I was drifting up, intent on identifying myself with the river bed and seeing if I could feel the water flow over and past me like a stone. But I didn't stop.

I ascended without control to a point high above Pe-Ellia.

Pe-Ellia was a blue pearl beneath me. I had the sensation that I was being examined. And then I dropped back down to the river bed and stabilised. I was shaken by this.

Let me explain further. The land of thought is also the land of dreams. Normal logic will get you nowhere. The language is symbols. Travel is the control of symbols. Knowledge is the perception of symbols. It is a dream in which you can control the dream. There are so many traps. So many dragons.

Pe-Ellia, let me say, is relatively safe. The Pe-Ellians have schooled themselves and sanitised their thought patterns so much that there are clear lines to follow. There are always Mantissa lines close, weaving like strong sturdy rivers through the psychosphere. I have met strands of my own thought. The spoiling of Winter Wind, for example. I think it was intended that I should see it. I saw this leprous thing wrapped in silk. This bag of tadpoles squirming. This bristled claw flexing to strike. All are symbolic.

The thought was safely held. A drifting Mantissa, whom I have likened to a garbage collector, travels the psychosphere, using his mind like a vacuum cleaner to suck up rotten thought. My thoughts were penned as surely as an angler keeps his fish in a net in the river.

Always I have enjoyed the drifting. Riding a poem like you ride a horse. Then came this imperious plucking. Dangling there, I felt eyes on me.

Now, if there is somewhere an entity capable of that, what is left of free will? Am I not being corralled at this very moment, my words dictated and shaped for me?

As I have said, inadequately, I am shaken by this.

Meanwhile.

Overall I am more elated than downcast. The dizziness does not worry me. It is the price one pays for being lightheaded.

I woke up just now with the realisation that it is Earth's destiny to come to Pe-Ellia and I am the forerunner for Earth. I have discovered a function. I feel less lonely now. But I should love to talk with the men on Orchid. I'll let the *Seliica* have the last word.

> You can't pluck music from a slack string,
> The bow is lifeless unless taut,
> The curve of the diver is a tight curve,
> And battles won must be battles fought.

Something will happen soon. I can feel it coming.

I cannot say what, but there is movement about me. For some reason I have decided to pack up all my books and put my notes in order.

Jet has been strange of late. He knows more than he will let on. He no longer speaks freely in front of me and must know how well I am coming to understand Pe-Ellian.

Nothing happens by chance here. That encounter in the psychosphere has its meaning and I must wait.

I am learning patience.

Thorndyke's Diary: Entry 34

Pilgrimage to the North

For three days we have been tramping over this grey plain. The one called Rai is in the lead. Crest erect and swaying as he walks. He tears the earth with his great clawed feet. He leaves a wide wake. Some metres behind him walks Harlequin. He is reduced almost to human scale by this bulking northern giant. Harlequin is subdued and has been ever since we left the cottage. He feels the initiative is not with him, and he is right, but where then does that leave me? I am third. My poncho hangs off me and drags in the dust and is already black and crusted. But it keeps me warm at night and I am able to wrap myself up completely. I use the fabric as a filter to keep the dust out of my mouth and eyes. It is not dust really, more like ash.

Across the whole of this plain the plants are dying. They are like spiky and pronged cactus. They do not die down, they desiccate. You can see the line where life ends and dust begins. They hold their shape like burned-out sticks of incense. So slight is the breeze here that many plants retain their shape until they are brushed by Rai and collapse into mounds of silt.

I must remain on my guard. Although many plants have fallen, and of those that do remain none are taller than me, still I could be engulfed. Walking on the dust is difficult. It is rubbery and at the same time like felt.

Soon the rains will come and all the plants will fall and the plain will become a wide grey sea of mud. I hope we are far away when that happens.

Darkness is falling and the sky is like dirty milk. We have stopped and made camp. Rai has scratched a trench which is already filling with water. I have watched him carefully. Before making a mark on the ground he studies the position of the plants. He reads messages there and is never wrong. The water is good when it comes welling up, but we have to be quick. With the slightest wind the dust forms a crust on the water.

The Pe-Ellians do not speak to each other and I only observe and offer no opinion. Our camp is silent. After drinking they move apart, say three metres apart, and each defines his own sleeping circle. Harlequin uses his hand, stirring the deep dust. Rai scratches with his horned feet, walking backwards, kicking up a storm. He tears the earth into a dyke and then settles down within this, working his body down into the dust until only his head remains above the surface. He seems able to lock his body in this position. How, I do not know, but I have watched him lie there with just his head thrust up from the dust. I think he sleeps, but then it is hard to tell with Rai.

Harlequin does not like the dust any more than I do. I am glad to see that the abrasions on his skin have healed, but he is still hurting. After we have all drunk our fill he uses the last of the water as a balm for his skin. Rai looks at him stiffly and with cold eyes. I wish I could share an ounce of his thought. When he has done washing, Harlequin spreads his own poncho on the dust and lies still. But the dust obeys its own laws and in the morning he wakes, lapped in silt.

Between the two Pe-Ellians' nests (for that is surely what they are) I make my own niche. I shake my poncho and then wrap myself in it. I try to level the sand. Where Rai has torn up and eaten some of the stumps of vegetation there is usually a flattish area. If it is damp, so much the better. This dust has great dangers for me. Last night a breeze came up. I was half buried before I woke up and then when I tried to cry out my mouth filled with the dust. I felt panic take me when I realised I could not free my arms. Rai reared up like a horse coming from a river and he dragged me up out of the dust as though I were a rag half-buried by the tide.

Harlequin didn't even stir. There is something here that numbs him. I am more alone than ever before.

How long our journey will continue I do not know. I am not strong and am feeling the effort, but that is incidental. The silence is worst. After their first few exchanges Rai and Harlequin are now silent with one another. Neither speaks to me. But it is not words that matter. I feel that we are within a cone of deafness. Pe-Ellia, the living planet, a place of water and warmth, is nowhere to be found in this deadness, and there is no rest in sleep.

I lie awake, propped up. Above me and to my right is Rai. Like all Pe-Ellians he breathes mainly through his nose and when he is asleep the slow intake of breath is silent, but he breathes out with a sharp hiss. The contact linguist in me is not dead. His breathing pattern is a clear sign of adaptation to this world of dust. Poor Harlequin has not adapted. He lies stiff as a log, with his life withdrawn down into a small ball of warmth deep inside him. Occasionally he sneezes. So do I.

The night is luminous. I can see no stars, but I am aware of the haze which hangs above us. The ash of these plants glows faintly and I can hear its particles whisper to one another.

I open my mind to the night as I do at home by the stream. Here is no echoing Mantissa song or the tinkle of thoughts of the crèche. Silence only. Desert fog.

I have time to feel sorry for Harlequin. This journey is not of his making. He knows little more about it than I do. I am sure that if Jet had spoken out he could have told us a great deal. It was Jet who brought the invitation.

"You are invited," he said, "to the North. Few of us know that land. It is an honour and will not be the same."

He would have left it at that and dived into the river if I hadn't run after him and called out, "Why to the North?"

"It is old Pe-Ellia. There are some who would look at you. They are gracious but you should take warm things. It can be chilling." Then he did escape.

Those were his exact words and I did not take them literally. But how typical of Jet that he should try to say three things at the same time.

I was excited by the invitation. There have been several mentions of the North and all of them have indicated a strange land, still Pe-Ellia, but different. Cook, for instance, when I told him of Jet's message replied: "Ah, North. Cold, too cold for me, but a place of great beauty and strength I am told."

Another Pe-Ellian—one you do not know, Tomas, but who pops in to see me quite frequently—whom I call Cleave, said: "I was North in menopause. Look at this mantle. I owe them a lot and will return one day. There the air is different. Things clearer."

Harlequin was less keen. At first he thought I would travel alone, but then word must have reached him that he was expected to accompany me.

I am disquieted by the feeling of wheels in wheels and cogs turning.

What did I expect? I suppose I expected Pe-Ellian ceremony. I expected curiosity. I anticipated meeting new types of Pe-Ellians (I have seen many such) and that they would cluck over me and look down on me like wise old birds.

I did not expect this brazen scrutiny. This contempt for my smallness—no, no, contempt is too strong, but they make no concessions. Perhaps for them Pe-Ellia is the measure of all, and we humans are far down the scale of reckoning. I am made to feel puny and in comparison with these lumberers I am. But there is more, and I have not yet got it clear in my mind. Why have they fazed Harlequin? Stranger still, why am I not more curious? I have become strangely passive—strange to myself, that is. There was a time, and not long ago either, when I would have had a hundred and one questions. Now my life has become a pool of water on which strange ripples play. I am content to be moved.

I am beginning to talk in riddles. I am beginning to sound like Jet. Let me tell the facts.

We stood in the clearing to feel the sigh of evening. This is something you can do on Earth, Tomas, or on Camellia. There is a moment when the day ends and the night begins. The plants control this rhythm, but we all respond. If ever you feel sad for Pe-Ellia, stand beneath the trees as the sun sets. Watch the shadows. Breathe deeply.

Harlequin has taught me well and I can now touch an atmosphere with my mind. I think in terms of the tactile. The sigh of evening is just that—the day is emptied out of the lungs and the new air of night rushes in. But breathe at that moment and you will feel your whole body quicken.

I slept then, or slipped into the trance state I seem to enter so easily these days. I cannot recall any dreams.

Harlequin woke me when it was time to leave. He was wearing one of their ponchos and had a spare one for me. The stimmu was waiting for us and we climbed aboard without speaking. This was the first time that I really became aware that Harlequin was more than just preoccupied. He was wrapped up in himself. He immediately swung up into the web and hung there. I noticed that he was panting, but it was not with the exertion. It was the atmosphere. The Mantissa was all about us. I felt us move, was aware when we hit the ridges, and then sleep closed on me. Once I woke briefly when we passed near the queen. My palms burned and I slept again.

When next I awoke we were in a cavern and the stimmu had settled. White light was streaming in from the cave mouth. I was amazed to see that Harlequin was still asleep. He was spreadeagled in the web like a skin that has been set out for drying. I touched him and felt his muscles contract, binding him tightly. He came to himself and tried to smile, but there was something wrong. I was aware of it too. A pressure. I felt Harlequin's astonishment and then his uncertainty . . . like a blind man who enters his sitting room to find that the furniture has been rearranged.

We climbed down from the stimmu and immediately felt the chill on the air. Oh, it was not cold by Earth standards, but after the greenhouse world of the cottage the air seemed sharp and bracing. Harlequin's skin puckered. As soon as we were away from it, the stimmu rose from the ground and began its careful nosing round. It worked back into the tunnel and began a slow acceleration. We stood and listened to the rising organ note as it built up speed in the depths of Pe-Ellia. Suddenly the sound was gone. The silence was total.

The cavern seemed natural except for the circular stimmu opening. I noticed thick stumpy stalactites sticking down as though a giant hand were locked in the rock. The cave mouth was triangular. Two slabs of stone were canted over so that they rested on one another. Everything had a weight about it, and seemed older too. The air was still.

Outside we emerged halfway up the wall of a quarry. At least that was what I at first took it to be. A path led down to the quarry floor. There were piles of rough rock and no vegetation anywhere. It was a lunar landscape the like of which I had never expected to see on fertile Pe-Ellia. Everything was covered with a fine grey dust. On the path the dust was disturbed and I could see the unmistakable footprint of a giant lizard.

Harlequin was in distress. He opened his mouth to speak but the only sounds to emerge were faint mewing noises. I watched him fight. His intelligent eyes mirrored his pain and surprise.

He raised his hands above his face, palm outwards, and seemed to rub the surface of the air. He closed his hands, clenched them to fists and then opened them quickly like stars bursting.

No response. He moved in a circle, stamping one foot, and with his hands straining above him as though he were being lifted from the ground by the wrists. Still no response.

Harlequin is no weakling. Among Pe-Ellians he is counted as one of the strongest. Did he not bring me back from the Mantissa dream? Has he not absorbed me? Yet he was powerless now. He was calling for life. No Pe-Ellian moves without knowing the lie of the Mantissa lines.

He crouched down, hands on knees, head hanging. He spoke to me from a distance. "We will follow gravity. Take care. This is an unfilled place and I make no impression here. There are walls round us. You are stronger here. I have no part."

I led the way down the path and Harlequin followed. I was dismayed at this change in our roles, but something in me responded. I do not desert my friends. As we descended I realised that what we were entering was not a quarry but a crater. I did not trust the stillness in the air. I have smelled danger before and it has the same burned mustiness on Pe-Ellia as on Tiger Lily or Earth.

We reached the bottom. It was littered with rocks, many of which had rolled down from the steeply sloping walls.

I looked round the high ridge where the crater met the white sky. The dark socket which led to the maze of the stimmu looked miles away.

"Set up," I thought. "Sitting ducks."

That thought must have been the trigger.

From behind the walls of the crater I heard a roaring. There was a crashing of boulders being pushed about and spouts of dust rose. I did not know where to look.

Insensitive though I am, I felt a part of the slam which stunned Harlequin. Poor beast. I have sometimes jumped like that when a chasm has opened up in my mind just before sleep. It spun me round and I found myself staring up into the face of a giant hawk.

Hawk was my first thought—the beak, the sharp intelligent eyes, the hint of a crest rising. The head looked at me over the rim and then advanced.

Hawk is silly. Nothing like a hawk except in the single-mindedness of its gaze. It was Pe-Ellian, as were its colleagues, but I named them dragon. The plates on their skin were armour and their hands and feet were claws.

The leader vaulted over the rim of the crater and set its body sideways. Its feet were like sledges as it rode down the sides of the crater in a welter of stones and dust. The others all followed. Size. I have become accustomed to bigness on Pe-Ellia and my neck no longer hurts with the effort of always talking upwards. Even so these were giants. As they bounded down the crater walls I could tell they were twice as tall as Harlequin. At the bottom of the crater they fanned out, forming a circle round us. They advanced, stamping their feet, and the dust rose in billows. One had a stumpy tail which he beat back and forth. Another had spines which rose along his back and shoulders. All had large clawed feet and their hands were talons.

Their leader I knew. I had met him or one of his ancestors when I touched the Mantissa. Was that a preparation for this?

I knew him to be gentle and ferocious. I did not feel fear for myself, just detachment, but I tried to protect Harlequin. They would have trampled him. He was lying unconscious and I threw myself over him.

I heard them stop close to us and then shuffle near until they were over us. I could feel their breath and smell, a sweetish oily odour.

Diver-Thorndyke's eyes were closed when he felt the tug near his throat. They were lifting him gently. It felt as though a shovel had been pushed under his stomach. Hoops slid under his arms and tightened. His feet dragged for an instant.

When he opened his eyes he was staring straight into the face of the leader. Dragon.

As carefully as a child carrying a glass of milk, the leader carried him a few paces away from Harlequin and set him down. He saw the tail of one of the creatures brush Harlequin and send him crumpled into a pile of rocks.

How long their examination lasted he did not know. Time was suspended in terror. He was aware of eyes and the smell of oil. He was pushed and turned. The leader nudged Thorndyke's hands open and they all studied the marks of the queen. Then the leader lowered his head and poked out his hard black tongue. It thumped into Thorndyke's palm, and then up into his face. Thorndyke passed out.

Poor Harlequin. They were hard with him. He is recovering now, but he could have been killed. When I came to myself I tottered round until I found him, dust covered, as grey as the rocks, and rolled up like a foetus. Every muscle was tight and at first I thought he was locked in rigor mortis. The deadness in the air had been lifted and some of my senses returned. I could feel, or seemed to see, life hovering over him like a dark bird with beating wings.

Nearby was a trench of water scratched for us by one of the lizard Pe-Ellians. Their footprints were all over, but that was all that remained of them.

I took off my shirt, steeped it in the water and attempted to wash off some of the dust. This brought him round. He scrambled away from me, insect-like, but with his eyes still closed. I sang out words in Pe-Ellian, part of one of their rain-dancing songs, and held in my mind the image of the clearing and the pure tinkling stream with the leaping fish. I made the air about me beautiful.

I watched him relax with a shudder like a tired horse, and his eyes blinked open.

He was scratched and bloody but nothing was broken. I helped him to lie down in the water trench. He lay there and his only movement was a slow opening and closing of his mouth. While he was recovering I prepared some food.

He surprised me when he spoke. His voice was normal.

"A close shaving you would say."

Pe-Ellian vigour is amazing. Had I been tumbled and rolled in the same way it would have taken me days to recover. After little more than an hour Harlequin rose from the water. The movements were painful but confident. He washed out his poncho and then, while it was still dripping, pulled it over his head.

We settled down to eat as the light darkened and evening fell.

"Why were they so rough with you?" I asked.

"They consider me Balacas." He looked at his skin, which had regained some of its life and colour. The whirling patterns stood out clearly on his arms and legs. "And I am."

We said no more and I sat in sadness. Winter Wind dead. Harlequin transformed into useless life. How much more damage would I do this planet?

As the last light faded we heard a rattle of stones in front of us. Rai stepped into our camp.

Rai is different. In shape he is like the other olden ones, but in his detail he is entirely original. He is covered in scales—small diamonds which have the suppleness of chain mail. The scales form patterns like a snake, and the patterns themselves form larger patterns. But this is nothing. What distinguishes Rai is his crest.

When he squatted down in front of us I thought I could see a ridge of bone running across the top of his head and down his spine. I saw the ridge move. He leant towards us and breathed in as though he were smelling us, and the ridge lifted. It formed a great fan. Spines supported and held the skin taut. I could even see a small pulse beating at the base of each spine. That was all I saw, for immediately I felt myself relaxing and drooping down on to the ground. Both Harlequin and I slept.

I have studied this crest in the clear light of day. It is covered with fine Pe-Ellian markings. His *straan* is brilliant, and I have no doubt but that Rai's crest is the seat of his power.

When I awoke I was stiff. Harlequin was squatting with his hands on his knees. I could tell that he had become distant again. The day was already white and I had no way of telling what time it was. I could hear a scraping sound. Rai was repairing the water hole. As he tore with his feet his crest rose and fell. I remember watching birds on Earth stretch their wings in the same way.

I stood up and in Pe-Ellian asked Rai if he was at liberty to tell me his name. He stopped and answered me, but I could not understand a word. It was a new language, but with the Pe-Ellian feel to it. Harlequin understood and he translated for me.

"He says he is called Rai. That is what you may call him, but he has forbidden me to interpret that name for you."

"Can he understand me when I speak?"

"Can."

Rai spoke again, this time with agitation. He pawed the ground, sending a shower of dust and stone behind him. His crest rose to full height, stiff as a sail in full wind.

Harlequin nodded slowly. "We are to proceed. We have been given passage. We will be walked. Rai is our guide and keeper. This is a beginning. I may not more to speak."

Rai growled out something else but Harlequin remained silent.

We drank in silence, ate in silence, and when we had packed up our few belongings, Rai led us up the crater wall and out on to this grey plain. We have been walking for three days and the days have been as alike as blank sheets of paper.

Now is the morning of the fourth day and a change is taking place. Rai has told Harlequin to wait and he and I are pushing on alone. Wonder of wonders, the drab landscape is relieved by a hill.

It is a solitary cone. Perfectly symmetrical. If I were not on Pe-Ellia I would say it was a volcano. But I am on Pe-Ellia and I recognise the distinctive shape of a Mantissa hold. Within that cone, perhaps some distance underground, a Mantissa sits, his mind reaching out and touching the psychosphere of Pe-Ellia. I try to test the air with my own feeble mind but there is blankness. Rai looks at me and his crest rises with a shrug. *He* is aware.

He is agitated and is urging me on in words I do not know, though his meaning is clear enough. Here there are very few plants standing. Most have collapsed into molehills of dust. The landscape is a flat grey desert. Rai is striding forwards like a ship powering its way against a heavy sea. I hurry after him with my poncho over my mouth and my eyes streaming. I cannot keep this pace up for long. I can see no reason for our hurry but Rai drives on.

The sky is darker and we have paused. Rai has motioned me to keep well away. He has stamped out a circle and is now standing in the middle with his arms reaching up to the sky. His crest is beating up and down, sending up billows of dust. He is transmitting—I am aware of that—and mercifully I am protected. I can hear the rustle of his skin as his crest opens and closes like a fan.

Now I can see why the sky is darker. Something is over us. It is indistinct in the grey clouds but I can see tiny points of blackness. It is like the skin of a fish. A canopy. It reaches to every point of the horizon. It is descending and contracting. There is a pattern of cells and points of darkness. They are gathering about the Mantissa hill. I can see them moving, streaming now, to settle round the hill. Dark fog. Frog spawn. Acres and acres of frog spawn settling round the Mantissa hold.

Rai is moving again. He has stopped the frantic beating of his crest and is ploughing his way towards the hill. I follow. There is really no alternative.

We are close now. Rai has stopped and has pointed to me that I shall continue on alone. He wants me to enter the mist. I cannot see the hill; it is completely shrouded. The points of darkness are clearer now, but there is little I can say about them. They are simply that: dark shapes, circles, moving within a grey mist.

I walk on. Something is compelling me. Step by step I enter the mist and am surrounded by it. The whorls of darkness keep their distance, retreating in front of me and then closing behind. I look back and can just make out the tall shape of Rai, crest erect and watching me. The mist billows and he is lost to me.

I can tell that I am climbing. The ground feels hard under my feet. The black spheres press closer. There is one above me. It is as big as a tent and is closing.

I am not sure at what moment I heard the voices. As the blackness surrounded me I heard singing. Hundreds of voices calling my name. I held up my hand, but could not see it. The voices were close to me. I expected at any moment to see faces. Friendly faces, smiling faces. I felt no fear, only wonder. I felt as though there was a voice for every cell of my body. I thought I was hearing the float-harp tuned to my scale. The beautiful darkness supported, lifted and flowed round me.

Then they were leaving. The blackness lifted from me and I could see my feet and the grey hillside. Above me hung a black swarming cloud and as it retreated the voices faded.

I didn't want it to go. I felt as though part of myself was leaving me. Oh, Tomas, as the last of the mist lifted I was shaken as though I had just dropped a few inches. I was wholly myself again.

I was sitting on the very top of the hill on a smooth flat stone. Spreading out from me to the very edge of the horizon was the grey plain. I could see Rai. He was no bigger than an insect. He had not moved. Clean as a furrow stretching out behind him was the track we had made as we approached the hill.

Somehow, the landscape seemed no longer so strange. I felt more at home here. I felt as though I could sit on top of this hill for days or weeks without hunger or tiredness. This was my land and I was proud of it. I was part of it.

I felt a summons and knew it came from Rai. Its gentleness surprised me. I stood and waved and began to make my way down the hill.

The journey home was without event. It was silent as before, but now it was a living silence and not the dead, closed off, numb silence we had felt previously. We met up with Harlequin and I was glad to see that he had recovered some of his spirits. He told me that I had been away for three days.

Rai stayed with us until we reached the crater with the stimmu cave. He would not come down into the crater but stood on its rim with his crest raised in a kind of salute as we scrambled down. When I looked back from the cave mouth he had gone.

The stimmu was waiting for us.

I believe I fell asleep even as we climbed aboard.

I awoke in the familiar tunnel just off the Palm Court. Cook was there and helped me down.

Cook. Ah, Cook. Wise Cook. He squeezed my face between his hands. Then he turned to Harlequin and offered both his hands. Harlequin fell forward and Cook took his full weight. He licked his fingers and rubbed the moisture into Harlequin's temples. Then he clasped him to him like a mother greeting a prodigal son. I have never before or since seen one Pe-Ellian cuddle another. Cook murmured a gentle song and I heard the word Balacas pass between them.

I looked at my hands, where the queen's mark shone hard and bright. As far as Earth was concerned, I too was Balacas.

The three of us made our way down the short corridor into the Palm Court. It was night-time and the river streamed darkly above us. We sat at the table and shared karitsa from Cook's warm womb.

Three days have passed since I arrived home. I have spent the time putting my thoughts in order. I am finding it harder to write.

Yesterday Jet called here. He tried to be casual, but a race which depends so heavily on gestures can be read like a book. He was curious and wanted to know all our doings.

I made a pact with him. Would he level with me? I think he was slightly afraid of me. He remembers Winter Wind and I am changed. I am less transparent, I know. I can put up a screen. I am older too. Since sitting on that grey plain I am centuries older.

"Tell me Jet, what was it?"

I described the rough Pe-Ellians who had injured Harlequin. I spoke of Rai and the grey plain and the Mantissa hill and finally of the entity which had settled over the Mantissa hold and which I had entered.

He sat with his eyes closed as I spoke and then stood up and motioned for me to follow him. We moved out of the cottage to the river bank. He beckoned and we both dived into the river.

I knew we were going to Jet's home.

We paddled down the river until we came to a large hole in the bank. Its sides were paved with stone and a slab of rock formed the threshold. Jet placed his hands on this rock and pulled himself headfirst into the dark tunnel. I followed.

Jet's house is like any Pe-Ellian house that I have ever visited: roomy, spartan and yet with just enough warmth and softness to make it comfortable.

We slithered down an earth-ramp and into a central room. Jet did not pause and offered none of the normal phrases of greeting. Instead he hurried straight through to what I guessed would be his sump room. By the time I caught up with him he was already immersed in the quicksilver lake, with his arms resting out along the surface.

"Here we may talk," he said. "Forgive my prophylactic. I am at an unease. I am not as carefree as Winter Wind deceased. Now you may ask."

I squatted down by the side of the pool and dipped my feet in the Mantissa fluid. I was amused by Jet.

"I only wanted to ask a few questions," I said. "And I wanted to speak to you as a friend. I am no danger to you, even in sadness or anger."

He shrugged, meaning, "So be it and begin."

"Tell me what happened to me. Tell me in Pe-Ellian if you wish, but speak slowly. I will ask if I do not understand."

He stared at me and his hands glided back and forth over the surface of the liquid. I was aware that he was reaching out from himself with his mind. He was scared. He was trying to contact me, to see, if only for a fraction of a second, through my eyes.

I dropped my veil. I thought of Rai and the grey plain and the strange living cloud which had descended on the Mantissa hold. Jet stared, and then closed his eyes and slapped the liquid with his hands.

He dropped below the brilliant mirror surface. I could not see him. There were no bubbles. There was scarcely a ripple. It was as though he had been pulled from below.

Seconds passed. I began to feel unease and wondered if I should plunge into the pool myself. Suddenly he burst through the surface with a powerful pull of his arms and blew out lustily. The silver ran down his head and arms in thin, tight rivers.

He was wholly Jet again. "I can tell you what I know," he said. "Though you have seen more than I have. I have never even been off Pe-Ellia."

"Tell me about the North, Jet."

"The North is our home. It is the home of old Pe-Ellia. Once it was warm as here, now it is a place for pilgrimage only. There the air is different and only the strong survive. Those that you met are strong indeed. They are all past their seventh."

My surprise must have shown on my face.

"They have chosen to develop like the ancients. Once Pe-Ellia teemed with—" he paused and searched for the word—"dragons. Then the queen came and we grew towards peace. But too much peace can still the race. Do you know that?" He paused. "No, I do not mean war. Those Pe-Ellians are brilliant and ruthless. They keep alive our links with the past. They challenge us with the authority of old ideas. Would you call them classics? Those Pe-Ellians are a moment. They are a point of balance. Past and present and some guess of the future. They are as we were when we abandoned the claw for—what we are now. They are as we were before the coming of the queen, and that is so long ago that I can scarcely think of it. You see, we were wise—no, intelligent—no, wise—even then; we were waiting, and then the queen grew. Do you understand?"

I did understand. "And Rai?"

"Rai is a messenger. He hears me even as I speak now." Jet raised his hands above his head. "I can feel him. He is lifting his crest in greeting. He is far away and alone. The rains have come and are pouring down his fin. He is belly-deep in mud."

"And the cloud with the hundreds of black eyes?"

"Ah, that was not Pe-Ellian. That visits Pe-Ellia. I think Winter Wind once spoke of it. We have a word for them. They are space swimmers. They were, are, and ever will be. They were born with the galaxy—perhaps before the galaxy. They are life in the purest form we know, and that is why we call them Angels. Occasionally one visits us and talks with one of our oldest Mantissae. They take an interest in us, for we are guardians of space, as you know. Why it wanted to see you I do not know. But what I do know is that nothing happens by accident. Something is moving. I can feel the ripples, but I cannot read it." He smiled the strange Pe-Ellian smile. "And I am called a Historian and I can't even read the present. Am I speaking in riddles again? I do not mean to."

He slapped the liquid again. "I can feel another question rising in you. Stop now. I have no more to give. I am not used to such hurry. Rest now. More later. Harlequin is worried. Pass."

Again he dropped from my sight like a stone, and the silver surface was still as a mirror.

I took my cue and left.

Thorndyke's Diary: Entry 35

I Am Given Eggs

The queen came to me in a dream. Her face was like a pekinese dog, but she was queen enough.

"I offer you eggs," she said.

"I accept," I replied, and woke up.

Exercises were strenuous this morning. All involved falling. Falling into nets, falling into the river, falling into a bed of leaves. We have just been joined by a group of youngsters and they frolic about us and generally enjoy themselves.

After exercises I was drinking juice when Harlequin came up to me and announced: "The queen has taken to you like a narcotic—and she wants more. She offers you eggs."

"What does that mean?"

"We shall find out. We should go now. It is not good to keep the queen waiting."

One of the beautiful things about being on Pe-Ellia is that decision and action fall naturally together.

"Okay," I said, modifying this with a gesture that added the pleasure component.

"Let's go."

Thorndyke's Diary: Entry 36

Many, many days later. I have lost track of time.

What I am about to try and write will call up all hidden resources of contact linguist training. I shall write in the third person mode. It will be easier.

Tomas, I am writing this for you. I no longer have any yen towards self-expression. Shortly I shall wind up affairs. I know that you always like to put the full stop where it belongs, and in this I am your pupil.

I am old now. At last truly old. With most of the vanity of the old age stripped off. I am hunched over my pain at my desk and I have turned out all rivers and waterfalls so that I can simulate night-time. I have my desk light on. I do not know the time, nor do I care. Cook arrives with tucker, as he now calls it. I eat and there's an end to the matter. Harlequin is with me. We have divided the pain equally, like two old pirates with stolen gold. It has taken its toll on him, by God. He sits crouched over opposite me like an old grandma. I shall ask Cook for a rocking chair.

I am called Menopause-Thorndyke now and if you met me on the street you wouldn't recognise me, though you would stare, you would stare.

I keep wishing it was Christmas. The main joy is always in the wishing and waiting, isn't it? As a species we're not very good at climaxes. That is why we love tragedy. It gives us something to look up to. Imagination aspires beyond our weakness. When the climax arrives in life we are so often wanting . . . I am rambling, Tomas.

Here is my account.

Thorndyke is sitting on a stone-cold stone bench. About him are carvings from the ancestral part of this planet Pe-Ellia. Beside him, stiff and unmoving as a wooden Indian, is his closer-than-friend-or-brother Harlequin.

This morning they have received a call from the giant-pale-worm-queen of this planet, saying that she wants to sample Thorndyke once more and to integrate him further into the life of this planet, wants him to accept karitsa.

Being the man he is and being already set on the trajectory of this latter part of his life, Thorndyke accepts.

Harlequin, who is himself a hybrid since being contaminated-influenced by Thorndyke, expresses his concern.

"I see more pain than joy in this. I have forebodings. Can we not turn back now?"

Thorndyke shakes his head and hides his own feelings.

"This is the kind of break into an alien life I have always longed for. I have tried to go beyond literature; now I have been offered a chance to go beyond—well, what?—myself, Earth, life. And I accept."

Bold words, O Contact Maestro Thorndyke. Could you have seen the other bank, would you have said, "Go o'er?"

Silence falls between the comrades and they retreat into their own thoughts. Thorndyke looks at the carvings which swirl round the walls. They are large, and he feels like a fly perched on the side of a Chinese vase. They are ancient carvings, he notices. The Pe-Ellians still have saurian tails and the plates of their skin are armour.

"Of a middle period," thinks Thorndyke, remembering a dream when he touched a Singing Mantissa and stopped a poem. The figures appear to be dancing round what is undeniably a portion of their queen. A Mantissa hovers in one corner and the sculptor has placed red glass or jewels in his eyes. Thorndyke realises how little he has seen of Pe-Ellian sculpture. A contact linguist scholarly lump rises in his throat as he thinks of the beautiful books he could have written. How he would have loved peeling back the layers of culture, revealing the meanings, coining new words to express ideas that had no part in Earth's history, preparing the monographs, films, adding a new volume to the *Grammaria*, watching Tomas or one of the new young scholars gobble up variables in the language and the psychological variants. Ah, yes.

> And who was it once on a golden day
> Met me by chance? She lying on a bank,
> Me, scuffing my feet on a gravel path.
> Both dreamers. Both lost along the way.
> I remember the sun and the shadows
> And the surprise and brown hair tumbled,
> And eyes that met, the green crossing the grey.
> Looking back through my telescope I say
> "There was meeting. There was a might have been."

Professor Marius Thorndyke realises the dangers of that terra incognita, the "If-only-I-had-land".

There is an unmistakable call. It is a ringing of the air and Thorndyke stands up. The room he is in has a small door at one end and it is through this door that he must pass. He will be alone. Harlequin is slumped in sleep.

"Mantissa induced," thinks Thorndyke as he feels his legs begin to carry him towards the door.

He moves as though on wheels, dollying into the doorway. Through the door he can see the Mantissa waiting. He passes through the door and the ringing abruptly stops.

This Mantissa is brisk and business-like. He is not a Singer. There are no cast-off shards of skin. His domain is spotless. Clinical. Sans sentiment. He stares with interest. The only relief in the chamber is the silver pool. It glows like sunlit ice.

"First we will talk," comes a voice, not unlike Winter Wind's. "Please be at your ease."

Absurdly, two Handmaidens carry a very earth-type bed from the shadows and place it near the pool.

"Can I not stand or squat?" asks Thorndyke, but he lies down and the Mantissa speaks again.

"The queen instructs me you are to be adorned and given womb capacity. I am a manipulator of forms. I shall undertake the transformation. I have studied your body and the operation is complicated. You have the right to withdraw now. The operation is dangerous. Bluntly, you may not survive. If you do survive you will not be the *you* you are now. I apologise if this is not clear."

"Clear it is," says Thorndyke.

"Will you persist?"

"Will."

"There is no return. The avalanche is at your heels."

"No return."

"So be it."

The air sings loudly for a few moments.

"Please to be placed in the Moi-i-ira (the quicksilver pool)."

I was afraid, Tomas, I was afraid. This Mantissa was like no other I had encountered. His objectivity was chill. I discovered later that one of his functions is to oversee the melting pot.

I could not turn back, but I hated his words. "Adorned." What did that mean? Was not that some kind of torturer's language?

And what was I to make of "womb"? I know I rationalised that karitsa needed to be kept safe and that one could stretch a point and call a warm enclosure where karitsas feel safe a womb, but I never thought seriously that they would try to give me one.

The quicksilver pool was familiar to Thorndyke and he was well enough advanced in the sensation therapy to take delight in the pool's trembling massage.

Blackness came.

This was not like normal unconsciousness. The world about Thorndyke drained of colour. It became like an old black-and-white film of the twentieth century and the black came to dominate the grey until there was nothing to see.

Thorndyke realised that his optic nerve had been pre-empted.

He felt a probing about him. In his mind an image of fish hung on racks appeared. It evaporated as quickly as it had come, but left him with a deep sense of being hung up for inspection.

The pain came slowly. It was like a burning from within. It was not a pain you could point at clearly or touch or scratch. It was internal—it came from a place where there should be no pain.

Thorndyke was surprised. He had expected the anaesthetic of unconsciousness. Were they going to leave him like this? To suffer? Alone?

He tried to call Harlequin with his mind. The thought was stillborn. For the first time in his life Thorndyke saw dead thought. It was like a smear of honey. It evaporated.

The pain was a ball of spikes which spun inside him.

Contact linguist training helped. He objectified the feeling. He processed it on to a symbolic level.

He thought of a bonfire blazing inside him—and poured water on it.

He thought of a meat-mincer and dulled its blades on stones.

He thought of carrion birds—and buried them rump deep in sand.

But the pain assumed more shapes. The quicksilver lake became lava and Thorndyke called OM.

I did, Tomas. I used the get-out. I called up the OM. I could see no alternative.

Commentary

OM is a rather sinister acronym. It means *Over-ride Mortality*. The OM is a technique taught to all contact linguists. It can be used only if the individual feels he is being taken over by an alien species. This is a problem which we have faced many times at the Institute. Many alien life forms are parasitic. For some reason the human brain and metabolism is more easily invaded than almost any known organism. If a contact linguist feels he has lost control of a situation he can call up the OM. It is an individualised programme which guarantees death instantaneously. It is coded in the brain in such a way that it cannot be triggered accidentally and must be linked to genuine volition. After each mission the OM sequence is removed.

Thorndyke's Diary: Entry 36 (*continued*)

It failed me, Tomas. The OM failed me. I must have passed out with surprise. You know, Tomas, normally only a sense of despair can trigger OM. I felt despair. Never have I felt so cast down. Even as I passed out I seemed to hear a voice saying, "Pain is the price you pay for learning." My old schoolteacher, Miss Olves, used to say that when I was nine.

Thorndyke came out of unconsciousness aware that he was completely in Mantissa power. So strong was the influence on him that he never thought to look down at his body, but merely stepped up out of the Moi-i-ira and set off down to where the queen waited. In his nostrils was beauty. Thorndyke seemed to float like a soap bubble as he raced to the queen.

He left the Mantissa chamber, turned down a corridor and saw, a mere hundred yards away, a segment of the queen. Nestled into her wrinkles were many Pe-Ellians. Thorndyke knew which place was his, and moved towards it as confidently as he once found his place at the reference library. He reached the queen and stared up at her grey-white trembling bulk.

A memory of the time he faced the Singing Mantissa must have possessed him, for he hesitated to touch her body. A compulsion like a blow in the back drove him on. He fell against her body. It was warm and firm as the neck of a horse. He began to climb, finding footholds in her wrinkles. He passed Pe-Ellians who lay asleep in crevices and fissures in her body. He observed the tubes as thick as his arm, which came from the queen and snaked through the relaxed flap in the Pe-Ellian bodies.

He came to the place which he knew was his. The smell was musky. A comfortable smell. A smell of home. Of his own body. Of the women he had loved. He crawled back into his niche and it yielded like a bed. A first-class berth, he thought, and lay back.

Above him, below him, and to the side of him was the queen. He felt her abundant life, the sheer vastness of it. He felt the throb and pulse of blood, the contraction and release of a giant muscle. He felt a probing at his side.

Drowsily he was aware that he was entered and possessed.

Thorndyke awoke at home. Harlequin was staring at him. Jet was bending over him and Cook was crouched at the end of his bed. At first he thought it was all a dream and that his visit to the queen was unreal; then he felt a movement as though a cat was resting on his stomach and had stretched in its sleep.

With an effort he raised himself up on to his elbows. He expected the cat to jump off but it just stretched again.

He looked down.

Where there had been a flat belly there was now a hump. As he watched the hump moved slightly, and again he felt the movement deep inside him.

He could not see beyond the hump, but he knew he was unmanned and the knowledge nearly broke his spirit.

He felt the scream before it broke the surface. Observed his hands rise and attempt to strike down at the black hump. Harlequin caught his hands and Jet his feet. Merciful darkness closed over him.

During the next few weeks Thorndyke—no, Menopause-Thorndyke as we must now call him—became accustomed to his new body. He learned how to stand so that he didn't disturb the karitsas lodged inside him too much. He developed a technique of rolling on to his feet and holding his hump-womb in both hands. He spent many hours staring at the alien in the mirror. Now his skin was completely covered in black stars. All his hair was gone, as well as evidence of genitalia. His plumbing had been rearranged but he was not interested in the methods. He was intrigued to find that he still thought as Thorndyke, although it seemed to him that the creature that stared back from the mirror should have had some outlandish Caliban thoughts rather than the gentle memories of Earth and Orchid and of friends.

Days passed and Menopause-Thorndyke became stronger. The pain, however, remained. Harlequin stayed with him and shared the anguish. It was with amusement that he noticed that Harlequin's skin had changed slightly and accommodated a star into its swirling patterns.

He ate one karitsa a day. In the mornings.

He learned to overcome his crawling horror at placing his hands inside his body and withdrawing the flapping shape of a karitsa.

"I am neither man nor woman nor Pe-Ellian nor fish nor fowl nor good red herring," he murmured to himself. He thought of Tomas Mnaba and speculated on how Tomas would react if he could see Professor Thorndyke now.

He decided to write for him.

THORNDYKE'S DIARY: ENTRY 37

This is my diary and I know I have been very remiss. I have let days and weeks slip past without noting things. Life is full of non-sequiturs. But my tale must be told. Our responsibility is always greater than we think. I have realised that my responsibility is not just to Earth and to humankind, but to life itself.

THORNDYKE'S DIARY: ENTRY 38

Harlequin and I frequently converse in thoughts only.

Yesterday I went to the yea-though-I-walk-through-the-valley-of-the-shadow melting pot. It is on a mountainous island. The sea about the island is yellow, but I don't know why and I am too weary to ask. The Pe-Ellians call the melting pot the "eye of the queen" and the translation "melting pot" only describes its function. That is where all Pe-Ellians who have not achieved symmetry come to die. When I travelled there with Harlequin I felt like Dante. I did not know Death had undone so many.

The island is craggy and rocky with few trees and shrubs. Pe-Ellians were there in their hundreds, all picking their way silently over the boulders towards the crater at the centre of the island.

The Pe-Ellians were of all shapes and sizes and had different degrees of skin blemishes. I saw one who was in menopause and had obviously given up hope of perfection. Others looked perfect, but Harlequin showed me how they were flawed, sometimes in the most subtle way.

No-one paid us any attention, though I believe we were the strangest-looking on the mountainside. Me with my belly like a cannonball in a sack and Harlequin looking always out of focus. No matter. I am oblivious to looks anyway.

Helping one another we scrambled over the rocks and up the ravines. We scaled faces and slipped on screes until we were there, on the lip and looking into the "eye of the queen". It is not a beautiful eye. It is rather an orbit—a crater. The depths of the hole are lost in the mist and darkness. This is not an ordinary darkness, though. Normal darkness is merely the absence of light. This darkness is the *denial* of light. As I looked down I felt that even if I carried an incandescent torch it would be dowsed.

Occasionally I thought I detected movements, like the reflection of ripples in the depths of the hole, but this could have been just the movement of mists.

As we stood there we watched hundreds of Pe-Ellians scramble down the slope and into the mist. I cannot say they seemed sad, merely preoccupied.

"Why should they be sad?" Harlequin answered my thought.

"To lose one's life is sad."

"No, to live without hope is sad."

"Do they have hope?"

"They will be reborn in the fullness."

Pause.

"Is this where we shall come?"

"Yes."

"At the same time?"

"Yes."

"What will happen?"

"You will meet the other side of the queen. We will wander underground through old traces. Our only food will be karitsa. Eventually we will come upon her other side."

"What is it like?"

"Exactly like the side you know. You will climb up her. You will find your niche. Everything will be as it was, has been, shall be—"

"Will I. . . ?"

"You will lie down. I shall be close, too. We will bid farewell and I will discover my place. Then will come dreams of love. . . ."

"I have those already."

"These will be better. And the queen will consume you. Your mind and body will enter her, you will become her, part of her in the great flux. You will be disseminated. The same will happen to me. Sometime, karitsas bearing your essence will be delivered to Pe-Ellians."

"Will I retain consciousness?"

"I do not know."

Our conversation ended and we turned back from the lip of the melting pot. The time was not yet. We returned to the cottage in the clearing you know so well.

However, this is my last entry. Herefrom I devote myself to putting the records straight, tidying up my notes and rounding off my studies. There is so much to do and I am running out of time fast, and I have hardly the energy. But I am completely at peace.

Ave atque vale. I shall write one last letter to you before I make the crossing.

Commentary

So end the Thorndyke diaries.

During the two days that Jet and Cook stayed with me I read the diaries many times and asked questions. Sometimes the Pe-Ellians were direct and forthcoming, at other times they were clearly reluctant to speak freely.

As regards the actual circumstances of Thorndyke's death they could tell me nothing. Jet, who seemed to have connections in high places, told me that he had heard from one of the queen's attendants the day after both Thorndyke and Harlequin had entered the melting pot. Apparently everything had gone smoothly. "Seamless" was the word Jet used, as I recall.

My most important questions concerned future relations between Earth and Pe-Ellia, and it was on this subject that the Pe-Ellians were somewhat vague.

The following are the main points which emerged from our discussions. Both Thorndyke and I and our whole contact mission were part of a master plan conceived by some high Mantissa. Jet explained in these words:

"On Pe-Ellia, what is the main subject of concern? You know the answer. Ourselves. Our history. Our growth. That is the subject of all our thought and all our songs. History is our sole science.

"Sure, as a people we have a function in the galaxy. All life which achieves consciousness and is not Balacas has a function. We are some kind of caretaker, but you must excuse my being uncertain and unclear. See, only the high Mantissae see, and we must trust them. I am not a Mantissa and so can only guess.

"But I am a Historian and I will make some guesses for you. Ever since life on our planet moved out and encountered other life we have been involved in a great debate. Now Pe-Ellia is a cross-ways. No longer can the debate remain a nice matter for mental exercise.

"What is this debate? You have two very good words on Earth 'synthesis' and 'isolation'. There in a capsule is the Pe-Ellian dilemma.

"Those in favour of synthesis want Pe-Ellia to meet with, and, more importantly, be influenced by other cultures. They believe that Pe-Ellia is become incestuous, that it is permanently breeding off itself, and that we as a species have reached the end of the line once again. One of our Singers ended his song saying that we are a race travelling towards the point of a cone. That caused ructions, I can tell you. No-one had ever said it so clearly before. The synthesis believers look for the kind of influence that will break open Pe-Ellia. Outriggers are even now at the limits of our space . . . perhaps they overlooked what was already on our doorstep.

"Those in the other camp, the isolationists, believe that Pe-Ellia need only persist in her present course. They believe that Pe-Ellia is gradually working through its destiny and someday there will be no more Pe-Ellians such as Cook and me, but only Mantissae. The isolationists believe that our purity depends on our being uncontaminated and that the Pe-Ellians as a race contain the potential of all thought. You see why Earth is a danger.

"As for me, I don't know where I stand. I'm a fence straddler, as you say.

"But this you must believe: neither Winter Wind nor Harlequin knew the true game in which they were involved. Only me, the watcher, saw how matters were evolving, and guessed that you and Thorndyke, Winter Wind and Harlequin were all part of a Mantissa song.

"It is my guess that it was one of the high Mantissae—perhaps the oldest of all, who has been urging synthesis—who conceived the idea of using Thorndyke to contaminate the thought environment of Pe-Ellia. Remember that thought is living and a thought such as that, once borne by one so high, becomes fate. Thorndyke met him in the North."

I asked next what would happen to Pe-Ellia now that it had been infected with Thorndyke. Again Jet replied:

"This is hard. We must wait, perhaps many generations. Even as we speak, that which was Thorndyke is being teased apart, polarised, skeined and recombined. If he is passed then he will add a certain flavour to the karitsas. The queen must decide whether Thorndyke is finally in the best interests of Pe-Ellia and herself. She was certainly enthusiastic about him. If she decides that Thorndyke will enrich Pe-Ellia, then relations between our two worlds will open up and flower. But we will not know for many changes. Perhaps a thousand of your years. In the meantime there is an Outrigger Mantissa again in your environment. He oversees your movements and retains you within limits. It pains me to have to say this.

"Over the years Thorndyke will enter us and the changes made by him will be evaluated. As a species we will become stronger. Perhaps one day we will be strong enough to face the raw power of Earth without our complicated filters and shields."

"What will happen if the queen rejects Thorndyke finally?" I asked.

"Let us not think of that."

"But what if . . . ?"

"Ah, I am within your psychosphere. Speculation is harmless here. You have already given birth to the thought. If our queen rejects Thorndyke, then it will go bad for Earth. Let us face the facts. The isolationist thinkers will have their tails in the air and they will hunt out the Earth and spoil it. That is an end. I will say no more. It will not happen in your lifetime."

It was late on the second day of their visit that this conversation took place. Jet was visibly tired. Cook had remained silent most of the time. He was moving towards his own nemesis. I knew the time for their departure had arrived.

"Farewell, Tomas Mnaba," said Cook. "We will not meet again. I have a memento for you." He handed me a small package.

"When we knew we were coming to see you, I begged Diver-Thorndyke to let me compose a something for you and record it. These are float-harp foolings by me. They are harmless but they may lift depression and they may, I hope they may, make Earth think kindly on Pe-Ellia. Thorndyke heard them and said you would be pleased."

Inside the package were encoder spools.

I thanked him with my mind and voice. I begged him to stay on with us on Camellia. I said that his entry into the melting pot would be a loss for both our worlds.

I had hoped to surprise Cook with my own present—a selection of cheeses. He smiled and accepted and, stooping, moved out into the dark garden. Under the trees a Pe-Ellian space sphere was already waiting.

Jet gave me glow-globes and I gave him a first edition of the *Seliica* signed by Thorndyke. We parted as close friends. At 01.00 they entered the Pe-Ellian ship and with a final wave were gone.

Since that date there has been no further contact. I do not know whether there will be contact in the future.

We of Earth must face and live within our limits. Thorndyke was right when he suggested that the futures of Earth and Pe-Ellia were linked. Through Pe-Ellia, Earth may enter the wider family of space.

Seconds before he departed Jet leaned out of his pale green ship and gripped my arm.

"Remember us, Tomas Mnaba," he said. "Think of us. Get everyone to think of us. Those thoughts will get through. In its own way Earth also controls Pe-Ellia. You may have the key to our future. Perhaps we are your handmaidens. In our linked destiny perhaps *we* were born to further *you*. Think of that."